PRIVATE
INVESTIGATIONS

Quintin Jardine

PRIVATE INVESTIGATIONS

headline

Copyright © 2016 Portador Ltd

The right of Quintin Jardine to be identified as the Author of
the Work has been asserted by him in accordance with the
Copyright, Designs and Patents Act 1988.

First published in 2016 by
HEADLINE PUBLISHING GROUP

1

Cataloguing in Publication Data is available from the British Library

978 1 4722 0566 7 (Hardback)
978 1 4722 0567 4 (Trade paperback)

Typeset in Electra by Avon DataSet Ltd, Bidford-on-Avon, Warwickshire

Printed in the Great Britain by CPI Group (UK) Ltd, Croydon, CR0 4YY

Headline's policy is to use papers that are natural, renewable
and recyclable products and made from wood grown in well-managed
forests and other controlled sources. The logging and manufacturing
processes are expected to conform to the environmental regulations
of the country of origin.

HEADLINE PUBLISHING GROUP
An Hachette UK Company
Carmelite House
50 Victoria Embankment
London EC4Y 0DZ

www.headline.co.uk
www.hachette.co.uk

This book is dedicated to Mr David Lewis, consultant vascular surgeon, Royal Infirmary of Edinburgh, and his dedicated team. He'll know why.

One

I've never felt more positive than I did when I left home that day for the start of my working week; I was the new Bob Skinner, new career, new attitude, new life; I'd turned a corner.

A couple of months before, I'd been in a proper mess, in such a confused state of mind that I'd taken myself off to Spain to sort myself out, and to try to shape a new life plan.

One exciting road trip with a friend was all it had taken. A different environment, a new challenge, and a satisfactory solution to a seemingly insoluble problem, and I felt that I was back in shape. When our journey was over, I had made a clear decision to walk away from the police service, for good. I even had a new job, part-time, one that was ideally suited to a man of my talents and experience.

Best of all, for the first time in years I had a secure and happy home life. I was reunited with my ex-wife Sarah, the mother of two of my five kids. Although she still had her own house in Edinburgh, we were spending more and more time *en famille* in Gullane.

Okay, my oldest son was a few months into a prison sentence, and his mother was about to marry a gangster, but isn't it true that perfection can lead too easily to complacency?

1

I had set out that morning to spend some time in my office. The new employment? I am a director of a Spanish company, InterMedia, of which my friend Xavi Aislado is chief executive. It owns the *Saltire* newspaper in Edinburgh, but that's only a small piece of its portfolio of online and printed newspaper titles, plus radio and TV stations, across Spain and Italy. It's a real job; I have independent oversight of all group investigative activity, and I instruct young journalists on developing relationships with police that do not rely on brown envelopes changing hands.

Contractually it's on a one day a week basis, but in practice I contribute more than that. I have a base in the *Saltire* building in Fountainbridge, and I share a secretary with June Crampsey, the managing editor.

That's where I was headed on the Monday it all kicked off. I planned to spend the morning finalising a training manual I'd written, preparing it for translation into Spanish, Catalan and Italian, before moving on to a working lunch with an old acquaintance.

He had contacted me a couple of weeks earlier, asking for my help with what he had described only as 'a certain situation'. It had taken that long for him to find time to meet me, so I assumed that whatever it was, it couldn't be too pressing.

Before she left for work that morning, Sarah asked me to do her a favour. 'Honey, I have a sudden, uncontrollable craving,' she confessed, 'for Marks and Spencer lemon drizzle cake. I woke up with it this morning; it must be the effect of reading Mary Clark's book. I don't have time to pick one up on the way in, and I'm not sure when I'll be finished, so . . . would you be a love and call in there on the way to the office?'

What Sarah wants Sarah gets . . . it wasn't always that way, I confess . . . although I was still wondering about 'uncontrollable

2

cravings' as I cruised into the Fort Kinnaird shopping mall, and parked as close as I could to M&S.

Its food store is always busy, even at nine fifteen on a Monday morning: when I reached in and grabbed the last lemon drizzle cake from the rack, I beat a blue-rinse matron to the punch by less than a second. She glared at me, as if she expected me to hand it over. I smiled and shook my head.

'Sorry,' I said, 'but my future happiness may depend on this.'

She sniffed, and gave me another long look. It told me wordlessly that if I died in utter misery she wouldn't give a damn, and allowed me to go to the quick checkout without a single fragment of guilt.

I paid and went back to my car, laying the precious confection, in its five-penny bag, on the front passenger seat. Before starting the engine, I called Sarah via Bluetooth.

'Got it,' I told her, 'although I had to fight for it.'

'I'll bet,' she chuckled. 'Those cakes go like crazy.'

'So, this craving of yours . . .' I ventured. 'Should I read anything into that?'

'No, you should not,' she replied, still with a smile in her voice. 'As if . . .'

'Why not?' I said. 'We have an extra room in Gullane.'

'Which we could need this year,' she countered, 'when Ignacio comes out of the young offenders place.'

She had a point. Ignacio is the teenage son I never knew about until we met last year in Spain, by which time his reckless mother, Mia, had allowed his life to become seriously fucked up; he was going to need a secure roof over his head, and I did not want it to be hers. She was about to marry a man named Cameron 'Grandpa' McCullough, a millionaire Dundee businessman, whose legitimate enterprises had been built with cash laundered from serious organised crime. Better coppers than I had tried to put Grandpa in jail, but none had ever succeeded.

Initially, I had decided not to visit Ignacio in prison; my reasoning was that he'd be endangered if he was revealed as the offspring of a very senior cop. However, a few months into his sentence, I realised that we could waste no more time bonding, and a cooperative governor had allowed us private meetings, away from the open hall where routine visits took place.

'He and I will discuss that next week,' I told Sarah, 'but you have a point. See you tonight.'

I ended the call, and turned on the engine, letting it warm up for a few seconds. With my foot on the brake, I slipped the lever from P for Park, into R for Reverse, then checked my mirrors, all three of them, and the screen that shows the view from my car's reversing camera.

Satisfied that all was clear I began to reverse out of my space, slowly. I had travelled no more than a yard when, on the edge of my vision, I saw it coming, a red car travelling towards me at a speed that was way too high for a shopping mall park.

I braked, instantly, but it was too late; the idiot, a man in a hoodie, I registered, caught the nearside corner of my rear bumper, bounced off it sideways, into the middle of the narrow carriageway and stopped, just in time to avoid hitting a Grand Cherokee that was coming in the other direction.

The law is imperfect; whatever the constitution may declare, there are occasions where there is indeed an assumption of guilt, and that situation was one of them. I'd driven with due care and attention, yet I was well aware that insurance companies, and all too often the courts, take the view that the reversing driver is in the wrong, automatically. When I was a chief constable, I instructed my traffic officers that every incident should be approached with an open mind, but those damn insurers paid no attention.

My car, a nice silver Mercedes, was less than six weeks old, yet there it was with damage to its rear end, thanks to some clown who didn't know the difference between a shopping centre car park and Brands fucking Hatch . . . and chances were, the bloody insurers were going to pin the blame on me!

Worst of all, the bag on the passenger seat had hit the gear lever, bursting it open and smashing Sarah's precious lemon drizzle cake. That lit my fuse; I'd been a happy family man, joking with the love of my life, only to become, in the space of a few seconds, an explosion waiting to happen.

I popped my seat belt and stepped out, ready to do battle with the stock car driver in the red car; it was a BMW, I noticed, with a few years on the clock. I was ready for whatever story the bloke came up with, ready for a confrontation, ready to blow him out.

I waited for him to climb out and face me. To my surprise, he didn't; instead he began to move forward, blasting his horn at the Grand Cherokee that was blocking the roadway, as if the sound could push it backwards. The big jeep didn't move. Its lady owner sat behind her steering wheel, looking bewildered and a little frightened.

Giving her a wave and a sign that I hoped she would read as 'Stay where you are', I moved towards the Beamer. Its driver, seeing no way forward, started to reverse, but got no further than a couple of yards before slamming hard into a Mini that had come to a halt behind him. He was trapped; no escape route.

We made eye contact as I advanced on him. I saw a thin, sharp, youngish Caucasian face within the hood, eyes narrowed.

I guess he saw a tall, angry, grey-haired bloke in a dark suit, white shirt and blue tie.

My view of him lasted for only a couple of seconds, for as long as it took a cloud that had obscured the low winter sun to pass by, and for a ray of light to hit the red car's windscreen, reflecting into my eyes and blinding me momentarily.

I took a couple of steps to my left to escape it; by the time my vision had cleared the man was out of his car and legging it across the park. I gave a moment's thought to chasing him, but abandoned the idea, for he was moving like a bat out of hell. I still go out running along the coastline in front of my house, but I never was a sprinter. I knew that he had too big a start, plus he had at least twenty-five years on me.

Instead I walked round to the Mini. Its bonnet had been crunched, and its engine had stopped, probably stalled on impact. The driver was also a lady, but older than the Grand Cherokee's pilot. She was white haired and in her seventies, I guessed.

She was shocked. She stared straight ahead, heavily veined hands grasping her wheel, so tightly that her knuckles showed bony white.

'What the hell was that all about?' a voice demanded. Grand Cherokee woman, a striking redhead in her thirties who could have been modelling her M&S clothes, had overcome her initial scare and stood behind me.

'You know as much as I do,' I replied. 'This thing,' I nodded towards the BMW, 'hit me, and the driver legged it.'

'Why would he do that?' she asked.

'My best guess,' I told her, 'is that this is stolen, probably from this car park. Look, do me a favour,' I added. 'Will you take care of the old lady? She's had a hell of a fright and might need medical assistance. If you do that I'll call for help and alert site security.'

She nodded and stepped up to the Mini's driver door, while I dug out my phone. I have the police communications centre number stored. I retrieved it and pressed the onscreen button.

'This is Bob Skinner, formerly chief constable,' I told the civilian operator who answered. 'I'm in the Fort Kinnaird car park, close to T K Maxx and M&S. There's been a traffic incident involving my car and two others. The driver of one of them, registration,' I glanced at the plate, 'Charlie Oscar Sierra One Echo, has fled the scene on foot. White male, twenties, slim, medium height, wearing a grey hoodie and blue jeans. I suspect vehicle theft; either that or he's uninsured, and just panicked. I need police attendance, and paramedics for a third driver, an elderly lady who looks to be in shock, after the so-and-so drove into her vehicle.'

'Officers and an ambulance will be with you as soon as possible, Mr Skinner,' the man replied. 'You'll need to remain at the scene yourself.'

'I know that, pal,' I snapped: my temper was still on a hair trigger. In fact, I couldn't have gone anywhere even if I'd wanted to, for our little section of roadway was blocked at either end by the redhead's off-roader and the old dear's damaged car.

Pocketing my phone, I turned to the BMW once again. The driver's door was open and the engine was still running. I walked round, leaned inside and turned it off, using a handkerchief to twist the key and touching nothing else. As I did so I could see my own car through the windscreen. As I had expected there was a dent in the corner, but it looked drivable.

Backing out, I took a longer look at the red saloon. The personalised number gave no clue to its age, but from the dullness of its paintwork and its boxy lines, I judged that it had to be at least ten years old. For sure, 'COSIE', its personalised plate, was worth more than the car itself.

'So why steal it?' I murmured to nobody in particular. 'Not just for the number surely . . . unless the guy's a total idiot, for that only has value to the registered owner.'

I moved slowly around the vehicle, inspecting its damage. The collision impact on the front nearside wing was less than that on my Merc: old steel versus modern plastic, I imagined. There was a scratch along the side, the kind a vandal might leave with a key or a nail, but it was the rear end that had been most affected by the shunt. A light cluster was smashed, and the boot was distorted, its catch shaken loose.

I took out my handkerchief again, wrapping it round my fingers before giving the metal a firm push. But the lock didn't take; instead the lid swung slowly upwards, opening fully and revealing what was inside.

In the moment that I saw it, I jumped backwards, my reactive scream muffling itself in my throat.

A child stared up at me, a little girl. She looked to be around the same age as my younger daughter, Seonaid. Her eyes were wide, and her mouth was open too, as if she was as startled by me as I was by the sight of her. She was dressed in a tartan skirt and a blue quilted jacket. Beneath, she wore a sweatshirt with a cartoon penguin on the front, the type of garment that has taken the place of a blazer in many schools.

I reached into her place of containment and touched her cheek, as gently as I touch Seonaid's sometimes, when she's asleep, but I didn't need to feel the coldness against my fingertips to know that the poor little innocent was dead.

I couldn't put a number to the crime scenes I've visited over a thirty-year police career, or to the number of victims of violence I've stood over.

Latterly, I was involved in a couple of really bad ones; they got to me in a way that others hadn't, and made me vow to walk away, to leave the bloody aftermath to others while I could still feel some compassion for the dead, before I became as dehumanised as they were.

I never quite managed that as a serving officer, not even as a chief constable, but as a civilian, that day in that car park, I did something I'd never done before. I buried my face in my hands, so that nobody could see my tears.

That's how I was standing when the cops arrived.

Two

I suppose that an objective observer looking at my career might say I did all right for myself, but I see it differently. I was okay until a few years ago, and then it all went south.

My problem was that I found myself in a job for which I was totally unprepared, and temperamentally unsuited. Most of my police service, from detective sergeant up, was spent in major criminal investigation. I was a specialist, not an all-rounder.

In my final years I was in a position to take myself out of that; as chief constable of my force, and before that as deputy chief, I could have positioned myself well away from CID.

Sir James Proud, my predecessor in the top office in Edinburgh, was a career administrator. I could have followed in his footsteps and played it his way; if I'd been any good at the job, I would have done that very thing.

But I'm not Jimmy, nor could I ever have been like him. I had no background in the things that he did well, nor any aptitude for them, and that was a problem, for those were the skills that had made him such an outstanding chief police officer.

In my heart, I'd known this. I had resisted, until the very last minute, the pressure that was put upon me to follow in Sir

James's footsteps, pressure applied subtly by the man himself, more overtly by friends and colleagues, and most forcefully of all by she who was my wife at the time.

They meant well, all but one of them. I didn't know it then, but out of all my boosters only one person had her own interests at heart, rather than mine. That's one of a few reasons why Aileen de Marco and I aren't married any more.

My ego won over my common sense; in truth that was never a contest. When Jimmy announced his impending retirement, I put my name forward and I was anointed, as Chief Constable Robert Morgan Skinner, QPM.

So there I was, sat in the big chair, I had all that silvery braid on the uniform that I'd always hated wearing, and I had all the power in my hands, with a few thousand people, cops and civilians, under my command. And most of it bored me bloody rigid.

I was lousy at the job. Nobody said so then, and nobody's said so since, but I know it. As soon as I was properly away from it and could look back objectively I could see that I'd got almost everything wrong.

I made appointments on instinct, without proper consideration, decisions that my head of human resources would have advised me against had I bothered to consult her, as Jimmy Proud always did.

I allowed myself to get sucked into a battle with the politicians, my wife among them, over the creation of a single Scottish police service. It was a proposal by government that I was dead against, and the argument was public and divisive. Inevitably, with little or no political support I lost the fight and, with it, my marriage . . . not that the latter was worth saving.

My old mentor, Sir James, was as opposed to a single force as me, but he would never have tackled it as I did. He would have played its proponents quietly, identifying any divisions in their approach and exploiting them until they fell into line with his thinking without ever realising that they'd been steered in that direction.

But all that said, it wasn't really the battle for the future of the service that derailed me as a chief constable. I'm a pragmatist; let others create the framework and I can work within it. No, my biggest problem was that when it came to the parts of the job that I loved, I could not delegate to save my life; I could not look at a major criminal investigation and stand aloof from it.

Don't get me wrong when I say this, for Jimmy Proud, an Edinburgh toff by upbringing, made a point of getting to know every square yard of his territory, down to the very roughest, but he was always content to leave the messiest part of the job to those of us who were good at it. He had no CID background and he would only ever appear at the scene of a homicide if one of our own had fallen.

Me? I couldn't keep away. When I became chief I had the best head of CID in the country and some of its best detectives, and yet I was all over them, looking over their shoulder in everything they did. I was rarely called to the scene of a major incident and yet I hardly missed one, not even the open-and-shut domestic homicide cases.

I should have known that my constant presence was undermining the people who were supposed to be in charge, but it didn't occur to me. I'm sure they felt it, but they were my friends, not mere subordinates. If they found the situation difficult, they'd have been reluctant to say so.

All the same it might have come to that, if a sudden act of violence hadn't catapulted me from Edinburgh to the place I'd said I'd never go, Glasgow, and into the chief constable's office in the massive Strathclyde force. Unification was on the way, but Scotland's largest constabulary needed a chief to see it out of existence. Sure, I could have turned that job down too, but the Skinner ego really was out of control by then.

It all came to an end when I found out about Ignacio, the Spanish-born teenage son I never knew I had. He's the product of a one-night stand back in the nineties, with a woman named Mia Watson, who had a very shady family background. She had to leave Scotland in a hurry shortly after our encounter, and she didn't come back until she was in even more trouble than she'd run away from. Unfortunately she landed Ignacio right in the middle of it, and that's why he's in prison now.

Ironically, his predicament was my salvation. I decided that it made my position as a chief constable untenable, and so I withdrew my name from candidacy for the leadership of the unified Scottish Police Service. I'd opposed its creation, but career-wise, it was the only show in town, and I wasn't ready at that point to chuck it.

But for Ignacio I'd have gone through with my application and I'd have been appointed. I would have taken the post and been a disaster. It would have finished me.

There has been darkness in me from my earliest days, since my childhood, when I was abused and terrorised by my beast of an older brother. I survived that, and when I was ready I overcame him, but he left his mark upon me.

Myra, my first love, shone some light into my life and gave me my precious daughter Alexis, but she had her own demons. Even if she had not been killed at the wheel of her speeding car, I doubt that our marriage would have endured.

Raising my child alone gave me no time to dwell on my past;

when the job was done Sarah came into my life and, with her, what I call my second family.

I might have put those earlier years behind me, and become a normal human being, but that's not how it worked out. I was stabbed, and almost died; in recovery I unearthed some secrets that would have been better left untouched. Subsequently I was involved in some very serious work incidents, and they took their cumulative toll.

Sarah had her troubles too, and we were heading for the rocks, when Michael, the brother I thought I'd put away forever, came back into my life through his death, reminding me of all my childhood horrors.

I was never the same after that. My humanity started to erode, I grew harder, became less kind, and behaved in all the wrong ways. I cast Sarah aside for a woman who was always wrong for me. I became difficult to work with, testing the loyalty of my colleagues. Even worse, I found it more and more difficult to live with myself, and I found myself hating the man I'd become, yet I was driven onwards by my obsession with the work that had supplanted even my children as the focus of my existence.

Then Sarah came back, and almost simultaneously I learned that I had a teenage son who'd been kept from me all of his life, and who needed me very badly at that time.

Between them, the two events forced me to look at myself, and to own up to my failures, my imperfections, my selfishness. Most of all they made me realise that I had been drowning in a well of loneliness. The greatest blessings this life can give are the people who love us, warts and all, yet for years I'd been keeping them at a distance, and in Sarah's case, I'd been pushing her away from me.

And so I put it all behind me, I set a different course, and through that I felt reborn.

It was a different Bob Skinner who stood in that car park, that morning, shocked and weeping over a dead child.

I didn't hear the officers arrive. I wasn't aware of them at all until someone grabbed my right arm and tried to put me in a restraining hold.

Shaken back into the moment, I reacted instinctively, without thinking, wrenching myself free and planting a hand in my assailant's chest, then shoving violently, sending him sprawling backwards across the roadway. It was only when I turned to face him that I saw he was a cop, a youngster, one of the new breed, probably fresh from college, and from one of those stop-and-search courses that they say don't exist.

He was scrambling to his feet and reaching for his extendable baton when a voice called out, 'Jules, hold up! Do ye no' ken who that is?'

I looked beyond him, and saw a sergeant whom I recognised from past encounters. He was called Jack Lemmon, which used to be worth a few laughs, until his old actor namesake died.

'But Sarge,' the PC protested, 'do you know what's in that car?' The boy was rattled; I doubted that he'd ever been near a body in his brief service.

'I didn't put her there, son,' I told him quietly, then turned to Sergeant Lemmon, who was standing beside me by that time, looking into the boot of the BMW. 'No fuss, Jack,' I murmured, 'but you need to report a suspicious death, and ask for urgent CID attendance. There are paramedics on their way here, but they'll be no use for this. Skip the medical examiner and ask for a pathologist, pronto. Also, you'll need a full crime scene team. More uniforms as well to secure this area.'

I was telling him stuff he knew already, but I couldn't help it. I was back in my old world, in full senior investigating officer mode.

He tore his eyes away from the chid. 'Yes, sir,' he said, then looked at his sidekick. 'PC Hoare, get something to cover the poor wee lass up.'

I countermanded him. 'Sorry, Jack. He can't do that. Nothing can be touched here till the CSIs say so. You know that.'

'Ah suppose,' Lemmon conceded, then began to speak into his radio, doing as I had told him.

'Will you stand back from the scene too, sir, please.' PC Hoare felt the need to show a little personal authority.

'No,' I replied, abruptly. 'I've already contaminated it.' I turned and looked into the Mini. The redhead stared out at me, her eyes full of questions. The elderly driver looked even more shaken than before, if that was possible; I began to worry about her well-being, and wonder where the paramedics were.

They arrived a few seconds later. 'Tell them to attend to the old lady there,' I instructed the constable. I felt sorry for him; I was in his boots once, thirty-something years ago, a first-timer at a death scene.

He frowned at me. 'But what about the wee girl? Should they not look at her first?'

'The child is dead, son,' I said, in little more than a whisper. He flinched, and a look of distress crossed his face. *A good sign,* I thought. *It isn't second nature to him yet, and hopefully it never will be.*

I stood guard over what was in effect an open coffin, my back to it because I wasn't brave enough to face the accusation in the little lass's eyes.

You let me down, they were saying. *You were supposed to protect me, all of you, not lead me here.*

I may not have been looking at her, but nonetheless I could hear those words in my head, and the voice that spoke them was that of my Seonaid.

A few passers-by stopped, curiosity getting the better of them, gazing at me and at the two paramedics as they took the old lady from her battered car and eased her into a wheelchair. One of the pair, a large woman with dark hair and heavy-framed spectacles, spoke to Jack Lemmon, and her message carried to me.

'We're taking her to A and E,' she announced. 'She's not responding to our questions, and she's not moving properly. It might just be shock, but there's a possibility of a wee stroke. Her keys are in the car if you need to shift it.'

As the sergeant nodded assent, I caught a movement out of the corner of my eye, a couple of youngsters, teenage boys who looked as if they had taken a break from a busy morning's shoplifting, were approaching.

'What's up, mister?' one of them called to me. 'Did you bash her motor?'

'Move on, lads,' I said.

'Free country, pal,' the other, a hulking, dull-eyed youth, retorted.

'Whatever gave you that idea?' I growled. 'On your way, now.'

'Fuck you,' the kid sneered. 'What's in the boot? Gaun, let's see.'

Too stupid to read the warning in my glare, the pair closed in on me, one from either side. I was ready to restrain them, bigger one first as always, but it didn't come to that, for PC Jules Hoare manned up and stepped between us.

17

'Do what you're told, or I'll arrest you both.' His uniform had more effect than my suit. The kids stopped, backing off a little.

'Ye cannae,' one of them protested. 'We're only fifteen.'

'That's all the more reason why I should,' PC Jules countered. 'You ought to be in school. Beat it, or I'll take you there myself, in handcuffs. The girls will love that, I'll bet.'

The pair chose the path of wisdom, muttering as they wandered off, leaving me to dwell upon how naked I had felt without a warrant card in my pocket.

As they left, two others arrived, emerging from a grey Ford Mondeo in need of a wash. Familiar faces, at last.

'Detective Inspector Pye; Detective Sergeant Haddock,' I exclaimed. 'Glad to see you.'

'Chief Inspector now,' the young DS told me, nodding sideways at his gaffer.

My eyebrows rose; I really was out of touch, it seemed. 'Indeed? I hadn't heard. Congratulations, Sammy.'

I stepped aside, to allow them a clear view into the boot. 'In other circumstances, I'd say I was pleased to see you, but this . . .'

DCI Pye's face paled a little. He's a father too; Ruth, his wife, used to be my secretary. 'Oh my,' he whispered.

Beside him, Harold 'Sauce' Haddock's eyes blazed with anger. 'Bastard!' he growled. 'We were told that the driver of this thing ran off. Is that right, sir?'

He looked at me, sideways, with a hint of an accusation in his eyes.

'That's right, Sauce,' I agreed, 'and no, I didn't give chase. But I hadn't seen the child then; at that point I thought he was a joyrider, caught at it.'

'I suppose, boss,' he conceded. 'Can you give us a description?'

'Not a very good one, 'cos I only saw him full-face for a

second, through a car windscreen, but I'll be amazed if you don't pick him up on one of the CCTV cameras they have in this place. Twenty-something, white, thin faced, grey hoodie, jeans, trainers. Slim built,' I added, 'and hell of a quick on his feet.'

'Did you do a trace for the owner of the vehicle?' Pye asked.

I sighed. 'Sammy, I'm not a cop any more,' I reminded him.

'But still . . .' He looked at me as his junior had, as if I'd betrayed him in some way. Then he nodded. 'You're not, are you,' he conceded. He turned to Haddock, 'Sauce . . .' stopping short as he saw that the lad was on the phone already to the comms centre.

We waited for no more than a minute for him to finish the call. 'It's registered to Callum Oliver Sullivan,' he announced when he had its results, 'of nine St Anthony's Place, North Berwick. Age thirty-seven.'

'So he wasn't the driver, then,' I said. 'I couldn't be that wrong in my age estimate. Find out what you can about Mr Sullivan; occupation, employer, whether he's on any criminal intelligence database, marital status and most important of all whether he has a daughter aged five or six.'

'And you said you're not a cop any more,' Pye murmured.

He had me there. 'Sorry, Sammy,' I conceded. 'That was me at my worst. I never needed to teach you guys your job, but I never could stop myself. My excuse this time is, I discovered this poor wee lass. Because of that I see it as my bounden duty to find the bastard who did this to her and to put him down, whether I'm a serving police officer or not.'

'Understood, Chief,' Haddock said.

I shook my head. 'Don't call me that any more, Sauce, please. Sir Andrew Martin; he's your chief constable now. My name's just plain Bob.' I paused.

'Now,' I continued, 'the media will be arriving soon, for sure, and it would not be good for me to be seen here when they arrive. God knows what they'd read into that. Any statement you need for the investigation, I can give you somewhere else. In the meantime, you should ask that redhead over there with Jack Lemmon to move her jeep, so that I can get the fuck out of here. I'll be at the *Saltire* office for a while, if you need me. After that, well, you have my mobile number, I think.'

'Yes, we do,' Pye concurred. 'And you're right about getting out of here. I'll have her shift the thing right now. Will she be a useful witness, do you think?'

I shrugged. 'She might give you a more detailed description of the bloke in the hoodie, but that's all.'

'If he's left his DNA in there, and he's a known car thief,' Sauce pointed out, 'that'll give us the best description of all. You didn't touch anything inside did . . .' He blushed slightly, as he saw my raised eyebrow. 'No, of course you didn't,' he added.

'I switched off the engine,' I admitted, 'but no, son, I didn't leave any prints to confuse the CSIs.'

I looked across at the Grand Cherokee and saw its driver climbing up behind the wheel. As I dug my key out of my pocket and headed for my own car, Sammy Pye called after me.

'We'll keep you in the loop, sir. Promise.'

I nodded. 'Thanks.'

'We still need you, gaffer,' he added. 'It's not like the old times. Things have changed, and not for the better.'

Three

'Should you have sounded off to Mr Skinner like that?' Sauce Haddock ventured, as he watched a silver Mercedes cruise carefully out of the shopping centre car park.

Sammy Pye shrugged. 'Why the hell not? The whole world knows he's dead against the unified police service.'

'The vast majority of serving cops were too, but we've got it now. He's got to live with it like the rest of us. Then there's the small matter of our new chief constable being his best pal . . . and practically his son-in-law as well.'

'You're behind the times, chum,' the detective chief inspector said. 'Andy Martin and Alex Skinner have split up, and for good this time, from what I hear. As for Andy and him being close, not as much as before. The story is, the First Minister pretty much offered big Bob any job he liked to persuade him to stay on; he even told him he could define it himself, but he was turned down flat.'

'You and I both know there's another reason for him chucking it,' Haddock countered, 'and he's in jail. Anyway,' the detective sergeant continued, 'we shouldn't even be thinking about that, not here. This is awful, Sammy. It's the first child homicide I've ever attended. It makes me wish I'd pulled a sickie. Honest to

21

Christ, who could have done that to the poor wee lass?'

'We will find out,' the senior officer growled. 'Be sure of that. We've got two starting points: Sullivan, the owner of the vehicle, and the hoodie guy that the gaffer described.'

Pye was known for two things, his undisguised ambition and his even temper, but the latter was nearing breaking point as he waited for the scene of crime team to arrive. 'Where the hell are these people?' he snapped.

'They'll be here,' Haddock reassured him. 'We can't secure this area anyway, until all the parked cars around us are moved.'

'And that could take all day, unless we do something about it.' He moved towards the shopping centre manager, who had been summoned to the scene, and was standing a few yards away, with a sergeant in uniform.

'Mr Hall,' he said, 'I need your help. I want you to instruct every shopping unit in this part of the mall to make an in-store announcement asking all customers to return to their vehicles and move them, as directed by my officers; staff too. I need this whole area cleared. Nothing should be within two hundred yards of that red car.'

The manager frowned. 'That'll be difficult. Some people might have parked here then walked to the other side of the centre.'

'Then make the announcement in every store,' the DCI told him. 'The alternative is that we close the whole damn place.'

'Hey, steady on,' the manager protested. 'What's this all about anyway? Sergeant Lemmon called me here, but he hasn't told me what's happened.'

'You don't need to know the detail. All I'll tell you is that the BMW is at the centre of a major criminal investigation.'

'Drugs?'

Pye shrugged his shoulders. *Let him think that*, he decided. 'Okay, I'll do it now.'

'Good, fast as you can.'

He rejoined Haddock, who had his mobile phone to his ear. 'Got that,' the DS said. 'Thanks. Give us the rest as soon as you get it.' He ended the call. 'The registered owner of our vehicle, Callum Oliver Sullivan, is a dealer in classic cars. Half an hour ago he reported the theft of this red BMW, registration Charlie Sierra Oscar One Echo, from his depot in a village called Kingston, in East Lothian.

'The electoral roll shows two other people registered to vote at his address. One is Mary Jean Harris, the other is Maxwell White Harris, who becomes a voter next month, on the fifteenth of March.'

'Which makes him seventeen at the moment,' Pye observed. 'And we know that Sullivan is?'

'Thirty-seven.'

'What else do we have?'

'Detective Constable Wright's established that Sullivan's not known to the police; no convictions, not even motoring offences. She's looking into his marital status now.'

'I suppose Mary Jean Harris could be Mrs Sullivan,' the DCI suggested. 'It's the in thing for women to keep their own name after marriage. Or they could just be cohabiting.'

'If Maxwell Harris is his son, that would mean they had him when he was twenty. Young, but why not? Jackie's search will tell us one way or another, and it'll tell us whether there are any other kids.'

'Only if they were born in Scotland.'

'True,' Haddock agreed, 'but if the need arises, before we get into a broader search, Jackie will call round the primary schools in North Berwick, to check on infant class girl pupils, named either Sullivan or Harris.'

'We're guessing that she's five or six; she could have been four and big for her age.' Pye said. 'She should check the nursery schools too.'

'If necessary, she will, and she won't need telling; she's smart, is our DC.' He glanced across the car park, at a blue van that was approaching. 'Hey, here comes the crew.'

'About bloody time,' Pye muttered. 'Get them moving, Sauce. I want a tent over the BMW right away. The pathologist won't want to work in public. Do we know who's coming?'

'I asked for Professor Hutchinson, old Master Yoda. I figured that with Dr Grace having a wee girl herself, of the victim's age, it might be better if he attends. You saw how cut up Mr Skinner was after finding the body. I think he'd actually been crying.'

'I'm sure he had,' the DCI agreed. He paused, then asked, 'Otherwise, how did you think he looked?'

'Leaving aside his distress,' Haddock replied, 'I'd say he looks fitter than he has for a while, and more relaxed. Towards the end of his time in the job, he struck me as being wound up real tight.'

'Me too. I wish he was still with us, though. I always liked it when he turned up at a scene. It felt safer with him around, somehow. Right now, carrying the CID ball for the whole of the city, I will tell you, Sauce, I feel exposed.'

'Then report this up the line; spread the load.'

'I have to do that. The new protocol says I have to call our area commander, the chief super. But that's no great help. Mary Chambers is uniform now. I'm senior CID officer in the city. The buck stays mine.'

'I know that, Sammy, but I was thinking higher than that. Why don't you ring the DCC?'

Pye frowned. 'I don't want it to look as if I'm crying for help.'

'It won't. What do you think Mario McGuire would prefer? To read in the *Evening* bloody *News* about a child murder three miles from where he lives, or to hear it from you direct?'

The DCI sighed. 'You're right, of course. Thanks. You get on with setting up the scene. Have the uniforms establish a two-hundred-yard perimeter, and manage the flow of cars out of the area. You do that, and I'll call him.'

Four

'Somebody's stolen my boat, Bob.'

Eden Higgins gazed from the window of his office on the Mound, surveying Princes Street, across the gardens. His head moved very slightly, as if he was following the progress of one of Edinburgh's sleek new trams as it headed westwards on yet another expensive journey.

I was so badly shaken by the incident in the car park that I had come very close to calling off my lunch date. I was full of anger at what I had seen, and hugely frustrated also that I wouldn't be involved in the search for the person who had killed that lovely, helpless child. No, never mind 'involved'; I wanted to be in command of the whole damn show.

One of the jobs that I'd been offered by Clive Graham, Scotland's First Minister, in an attempt to keep me in the service, was as head of a Major Incident Agency, a body that would operate not as part of but alongside the national police force. The idea was that I would form a team of elite detective officers that would provide an added investigative resource in the most serious crimes.

I'd turned it down, because it was a recipe for conflict with Andy Martin from day one, but right at that moment, I wished that I'd accepted.

More than anything else, as I left that shopping mall I wanted to drive back to Gullane, go into the primary school and give my daughter a hug, but that would have raised too many eyebrows, Seonaid's among them.

Instead I went to my office in Fountainbridge, and turned on the journalistic instincts that I'd developed since I'd taken the InterMedia job. I went to see June Crampsey, and I told her what had happened and how the child's body had come to be found, without saying that I was the one who'd done the finding.

The other details I omitted were the car's registration number and its owner's name and address. That was privileged information; plus I didn't want her crime reporter getting in the way of the crucial early stages of a murder inquiry.

That done, I sat behind my desk for an hour, doing my best to pass the time usefully, until I was ready to take a taxi to my lunch date with Higgins, a blast from my past, to use his own words.

'Your boat?' I echoed, feeling an involuntary frown knot my eyebrows, and a sudden flash of anxiety grip my stomach.

He started to turn, as if to face me, then seemed to think better of it. Resuming his inspection of the grey February morning, he nodded. 'Yes. It was taken from its mooring in the Gareloch.'

'Run that past me again,' I said. 'We've just come through the worst spell of winter weather since God was a boy. Who in their right mind would steal a yacht in all that? Are you sure it didn't just sink?'

'No, no; it's been missing for a while, since early last October. The police have been looking for it ever since, but now it seems they've given it up as a bad job. I had a visit from a senior bod a couple of weeks ago. She gave me the pro forma chat about

27

priorities, budgets and all that crap,' he snapped, his tone full of anger, 'then she told me that they've closed the active investigation.'

'That's too bad,' I responded. I understood his frustration and did my best to sound sympathetic, although it was a judgement call that I'd probably have backed, if it had been referred to me . . . as it might have been, for I was in my last few days as Strathclyde chief constable.

'What about your insurers?' I asked.

Finally he did step away from the window, limping over to a tub chair at the coffee table where I was seated, and slumping into it. 'My bloody insurers?' he moaned. 'Given the value of the vessel, I'd have expected them to employ their own investigators, but no, they said that there is no recognised independent expert in pursuing this type of theft, so they elected to leave it in the hands of the police.

'However, they did appoint a maritime lawyer to look into the circumstances of the theft. He looked at the boathouse, interviewed me and then reported back to the insurance company.

'On the basis of what he said, they've now offered me a fraction of its value in settlement, only one million against the insured value of five million sterling. They're claiming negligence on my part, saying that the alarm system wasn't adequate. I could fight them, of course, and my legal advice is that I'd get some sort of a result, but that's not the point! I want the damn thing back!'

'Look,' I began, then paused, trying to work out how best to explain to him that if the investigation had been thorough and the combined police and marine services, nationally and possibly internationally as well, hadn't been able to find his missing

28

vessel, then he'd better get ready to sue that insurance company.

I was about to tell him as much, when a memory broke in and overrode everything.

'Hold on!' I exclaimed. 'I've seen it. I know where it was taken!'

Five

Yes, there is indeed history between Eden Higgins and me. It stretches back twenty years or so, to the days when I was the newly promoted Detective Superintendent Skinner, heading up Edinburgh's Serious Crimes Unit, to the years when I was a single parent, widowed and doing my best to raise my adolescent daughter Alexis on my own.

That said, I wasn't always alone: between Myra's death and my meeting Sarah, my second wife, there were a few ladies in my life, and of those the most serious was Alison Higgins. She was a cop like me, a detective sergeant, then detective inspector, and she matched me in most ways, not least in ambition.

We were a natural couple; we liked each other, we were good together, vertically and horizontally, and our tastes were similar. Alex approved of her too; that was a prerequisite of any relationship, and Alison passed that test from the start. Although we never formally lived together, she was the only woman who had clothes hanging in my wardrobe, and whose toothbrush stood alongside mine in the mug, until Sarah came into my life.

She didn't talk about her family much, not at the beginning. Looking back, I recognise that may have been because in those days, I never talked about mine. I was still hurting too much over Myra, and my childhood was an absolute no-go area. Thus, it was a complete surprise when she invited Alex and me to go sailing with her one weekend, on her brother's yacht.

Anyone who watched commercial television in those days had to be aware of Dene Furnishing; it was one of the nation's biggest retailers, with a huge turnover and an advertising budget to match. When Myra and I set up house as a very young couple, most of our furniture came from its Bathgate store; indeed, I still have some of it.

I knew all about Dene, but I had no idea that it was owned and had been built, from the ground up, by Eden Higgins, Alison's older brother. She'd mentioned him to me, but only vaguely. On the other hand, he knew all about me. Once we met, on board his schooner, it didn't take me long to realise that he'd had me checked out.

I didn't hold that against him. He was a very wealthy man, and if he was on his guard against fortune hunters, it was understandable. Indeed, I felt the same way: Alex was my fortune and I knew that in a few years' time I'd be vetting her potential suitors. (Not very effectively, as it transpired.)

That sailing weekend was a landmark event in my life, but it was never repeated. The offer of another trip was made, more than once, but conflicting diaries, or weather, contrived to ensure that I never returned to the *Palacio de Ginebra*, Eden's casually named *Gin Palace*.

The vessel didn't live up, or maybe down, to its name; it was a sleek, speedy, no-frills racing yacht, and when we berthed in the Inverkip marina, after our cruise to Campbeltown, I had a couple of blisters to prove that I wasn't as hard handed as I'd believed.

31

Eden and I met up again at a few social events over the next couple of years, until Alison decided that being with me was a hindrance to her career. Jimmy Proud, our chief constable, knew of our relationship; he had always kept us apart profession-ally, and Alison came to believe that had ruled her out of the running for a couple of jobs she'd fancied. She may have been right . . . honestly, I do not know, and there's no point in asking Jimmy now . . . but in any event, the truth was that our thing had run out of steam by then.

The split was easy and amicable, not least because we'd never moved in together. Afterwards, when she did come into my police orbit, we kept it formal . . . at her insistence, not mine, for I was never precious about rank. At work I was 'Sir' to her, and she was 'Inspector' to me, then 'Chief Inspector' and finally 'Superintendent'.

She might have become 'Ma'am', if she'd lived, if she hadn't been killed by a car bomb that was meant for someone else.

The last time I'd seen Eden, before our reunion on the Mound, had been at Alison's funeral. We shook hands at the door of the church after the service. All I could say was, 'So sorry, mate.' He nodded briefly, but that was all; his silence may have been because Sarah was with me, or quite simply because he was so choked up that he couldn't speak.

We didn't stay in touch after that, but that didn't prevent me from shopping in Dene Furnishings, or from noticing when Eden sold the business for many millions, to focus on the venture capital involvement that had been a sideline for a few years.

His career was very easy to follow from then on; if he ever put a foot wrong in business, it never made the press, but every success, and there were plenty of them, made headlines.

My progression was high profile too, but boy, how I wish my judgement had been as good as his.

'How can you know that?' he asked me, after I'd had my revelation.

'I saw it, a few months ago: I was in L'Escala, in Spain, where I have a house.'

He nodded. 'I remember. You took my sister there.'

Eden was right; his memory was better than mine, for I'd filed that fact at the back of the mental drawer. I don't believe that I ever loved Alison, or that she loved me, but as I've said, I liked her, more than any woman I've ever been with, apart from Sarah, and her death hurt me more deeply than I let anyone see at the time.

'Yeah,' I murmured, as another recollection came to me. 'She didn't like it in the summer. She said it was too hot for her. But she, Alex and I spent a Christmas there; she enjoyed that.'

'I know,' he said. 'She told me so. Then less than a year later, she told me she'd decided it was you or her career, and her career won.'

'What she told me,' I replied, 'was that she'd make a better chief constable than a wife, and that since she didn't believe she could be both, we'd better pack it in.'

'Did you try to talk her round?' he asked.

'No, I didn't,' I admitted, 'because I felt exactly the same way about myself. I was a lousy husband while I was a cop, Eden. A couple of ladies would tell you that. Now I'm out of it, I find that I'm enjoying domesticity more than I ever have before.'

He paused. 'In that case, am I wrong to be bringing this situation to you?'

'Not at all,' I insisted. 'You're a friend. Also, the chances are that anything I can do will be advisory, no more. Now, back to the matter in hand. Last autumn, in L'Escala, I was in the marina, and I saw the *Palacio de Ginebra* in a mooring there. I didn't believe it at first, thought my mind was going, but I went back and checked and, for sure, it was your boat. So, it looks like we have a starting point.'

He thwarted my triumph with a few words. 'No, Bob, I'm afraid we don't. I sold the schooner years ago, to a pop star looking for a hobby. It had too much of Alison about it. The truth is that she was always a more enthusiastic sailor than I was. Rachel, my wife, has her own sports; she skis and she was an international bi-athlete in her youth, but unfortunately she gets seasick in the bath. As for our boy, Rory decided that go-karting was his sport of choice.

'So I got rid of the working boat, and bought something more suited to a gentleman of means.' He grinned. 'It's a seventy-five-foot motor yacht, and I named her the *Princess Alison*. I use it more for business entertainment than for my own pleasure.' His smile vanished. 'Or I did, until it was taken.'

He was interrupted, by a rap on the door. It opened, and Eden's secretary, a tall late-thirties brunette, who had introduced herself as Luisa McCracken when I arrived, advised us that lunch was ready.

My host led me through to his dining room. The table was large enough to hold a dozen, but there were only four places set. One of them was occupied by a young man; I recognised him from times past. He'd been a child, but even then he'd had his father's high forehead, and his aunt's sky-blue eyes.

His mother sat opposite him. I'd seen Rachel Higgins before, at a couple of those social events, but Alison had never introduced us. She'd never been close to her sister-in-law, and she'd made a point of keeping us apart.

Rory stood as we entered, extending a hand. 'Mr Skinner,' he exclaimed. 'It's good to see you again.'

Higgins Junior was as tall as me, and had a firm handshake. 'And you,' I replied. 'You work with your dad now?' I asked.

'He's my eyes and ears,' Eden said. 'I have a majority share-holding in more than twenty companies in several business sectors: retail, information technology, housing and light engineering, principally. I'm on the board of every one of them, and chairman of eight, but I don't get involved on a hands-on basis if I can avoid it. Rory's a chartered accountant by profession; he's employed by the holding company as a sort of travelling auditor. Each subsidiary's management accounts come to him. If he sees something that needs attention, he points it out to the CEO of the company in question. If he felt that it really,' he underlined the word, 'needed attention he would bring it to me. But that's never happened.'

He smiled. 'Mind you,' he added, 'he's learning the hard way. I can't have him seen as the boss's son throwing his weight around. He isn't on any of the boards, subsidiary or parent company, he has no executive authority, and he's paid the going rate for the job, reflecting his responsibility and experience.'

'Nevertheless, that's a pretty responsible job,' I commented. 'I hope it pays for your karting, Rory.'

He laughed. 'It wouldn't, but that's a thing of the past. When I started I saw myself as a Formula One driver, but that dream died young, when I kept on growing past five feet nine, and my weight went past seventy-five kilos. Now I play tennis and golf.'

'Where did you complete your CA qualification?' I asked.

He replied with a set of initials that I recognised as one of the big three firms. 'I got my practising certificate when I was twenty-three,' he said, 'and worked there for three years, until I joined

Dad two years ago. Higgins Holdings isn't the most glamorous name for a company, but it's a challenging job.'

His answer told me that I'd been right in my calculation of his age. He'd been ten when we'd all gone sailing. Alex was there too; she was into her teens, and so she'd barely noticed him. *She would now*, I thought. He'd turned into a good-looking guy.

'Rachel,' Eden exclaimed, breaking into my thoughts, 'finally, this is the man you always said you wanted to meet. I don't know why it never happened, back in the old days.'

She smiled up at me. 'I do,' she murmured. 'Your sister was afraid I might be competition.'

Pretty brazen, I thought, *to say that to her husband.* I grinned back at her, hoping that she couldn't read the truth in my eyes.

And that was, I wouldn't have fancied her in a hundred years, not because she was physically unattractive . . . which she wasn't . . . but because she had an unfortunate habit of looking at people as if she was appraising them, and making an instant assessment of their worth. I really hate that, and so did Alison. That was the real reason for her keeping a distance between Rachel and me.

However I was her husband's guest that lunchtime, so I shook her hand, doing my best to avoid a large emerald and diamond ring, gave her the full Skinner smile, and replied, 'The only competition Alison ever saw was the job, and ultimately she was right.'

Eden had hired caterers. A little extravagant, I thought, when we could have walked a couple of hundred yards to Ondine, or the Witchery, but if that's what really rich folk do, then who was I to object?

We talked our way through lunch, mostly about our careers and how they had developed. 'I never thought you'd chuck it,'

Eden said, brow wrinkled with the effort of cracking a lobster claw.

'Three years ago, I'd have agreed with that,' I conceded, 'before all this unification crap came above the horizon. Now I look at my life, and every day I thank the First Minister for not giving in to my insistence that he was a crazy man in pushing ahead with the venture that the politicians, probably on the advice of their PR people, have decided to rename ScotServe.'

'You thank him?' Rachel repeated. 'So you agree with the single force now?'

'Hell no!' I retorted. 'It gave me the impetus to get out, that's what I'm saying.'

'There must be some good about it, surely,' she protested.

'Okay,' I conceded, 'there is some good, but not a hell of a lot. The new one-zero-one phone number for non-urgent reports and inquiries, that's okay, but it's general.

'As for the rest,' I continued, 'the detachment of much of the force from its senior management, the problem of the distant communities being policed by a man who's never set foot in those places, that's a disaster waiting to happen, Rachel. Andy Martin knows little or nothing about places like Dingwall. I know little or nothing about Dingwall. Only the locals know all the twists and nuances of their community. If you have a serious crime there, the people who fly in to deal with it, they'll be looked on as an invading army. The same is true of any of the islands and much of the northern mainland.'

'How about morale?' Eden asked. 'I have to say the woman who came to tell me that they've given up on my boat . . .'

He'd started me thinking about team spirit, and Sammy Pye's last words to me as I'd left Fort Kinnaird. When he mentioned 'woman' I held up a hand. 'Name?'

'Chief Superintendent Chambers,' Rory volunteered. 'A big bluff woman.'

I smiled, for I couldn't quarrel with that description.

'How can I put this?' Eden continued. 'She didn't seem one hundred per cent committed to the message she was delivering. That's all she was of course, a delivery person. The investigation into the theft started off as a Strathclyde matter, when you were chief. Now ScotServe's kicked it into touch. It was quite clear that Ms Chambers wasn't a party to the decision, yet she was the one who had to communicate it. Would that have happened under the old system, Bob?'

'No,' I admitted. 'Don't blame Mary, for she's a good cop. If I was still in post and I'd known about it, I'd have told you myself. But it would have been out of friendship, that's all.'

His eyebrows rose. 'And you'd have given me the same message, that the *Princess Alison* was gone for good?'

I smiled. 'I might have put it more subtly than that, but essentially it would have been the same, if that's how the investigation's turned out. If the police and other services haven't found a vessel that size within a month of it going missing, they aren't going to. What's its range?' I asked.

'On a full tank? Maybe around fifteen hundred miles at cruise speed,' Rory volunteered.

'How much fuel was on board when it was taken?' I continued.

'Dunno.' He turned to Eden. 'Dad?'

'Hodgson reckoned about a quarter tank, maybe a bit more,' his father replied.

'Enough to get it to the south of England, for example,' I suggested.

Eden nodded. 'Or the Irish Republic: that's what the police assumed at first. They contacted their opposite numbers over there, but without success. There was no trace of it having docked anywhere to take on fuel.'

'Okay,' I said, 'there was no trace of the *Princess Alison*, but what's the first thing you'd do if you stole a large and very conspicuous luxury yacht?'

'I'd change the name,' Rory retorted. 'And I'd disguise as much of the superstructure as I could.'

'Minimum,' I agreed. 'Eden, anyone who can make a seventy-five-foot power yacht disappear has either taken her a short distance and sunk her out of malice, or they had a very sophisticated plan, possibly with inside help. Does the vessel have a permanent crew?'

'No,' he replied, 'not exactly. It takes only two to run it, captain and engineer.'

'Captain?' I interjected. 'What does that make you?'

Eden laughed. 'It makes me the bloody admiral, I suppose. The captain's name is Walter Hurrell, he's ex-navy, and when he's not driving my boat he's driving my car, and doing other things for me. He's on the holding company payroll as my personal assistant. The engineer is another ex-naval bloke, Jock Hodgson; he's retired. When we need him we hire him by the day. If you're suggesting they might have been involved, either one of them, I'd disagree with you. I'd vouch for both of them.'

I nodded. 'Okay, I'm going to assume that both of them were checked out by the investigating officers and came up clean.'

'Better than that,' he said, 'they were checked out by me, before I hired either of them. They're sound, both of them.'

'Did the police interview them?' I asked.

'I have no idea,' Eden admitted. 'I'm not privy to the extent of their inquiries, only the few details that they've volunteered.'

It seemed that I was being asked for my opinion of little or nothing, but I pressed on. 'Where was the vessel moored? Inverkip?'

'No,' he replied. 'We have a small estate just north of Rhu. It has a purpose-built deep-water mooring with a jetty and a boathouse. The *Princess Alison* was actually in secure premises when she was stolen.'

'It must be a hell of a size of a boathouse,' I observed, 'to hold a seventy-five-foot yacht.'

'It is,' Rory confirmed. 'It's like a bloody aircraft hangar. It has an alarm, linked to a central monitoring station, but it goes through a telephone landline. They cut that as they broke in.'

So what? I thought. 'Didn't that very act trigger the alarm?'

'No,' he said. 'When the phone line goes down, the system switches to a back-up mobile phone. It takes a few seconds; by that time they'd cut the padlock, got in, and had disabled the sensor above the door.'

'Now,' Eden exclaimed, 'the damned insurers are trying to say that the system wasn't effective. Even though they specified it! Would you believe that?'

I had to smile. 'When it comes to insurers, my friend, I'll believe anything. However, you should have asked the police to check it out and look for weaknesses.'

He frowned. 'What damn weaknesses?'

'For a start,' I told him, 'the sensor should have been as far away from the door as possible. I'm guessing,' I continued, 'that there was a big gate at the end of the boathouse.'

Rory nodded. 'Yes, that's right. The boathouse is really a U-shaped dock. The gate goes down to just below the water level. It's powered, of course, and operated by a remote control that's kept on the navigation deck. The thieves closed it after they left. If they hadn't done that the gardeners might have seen that it was open, and we could have found out about the theft a lot sooner. It was discovered on the tenth of October, but we know from the alarm company that it happened six days earlier, at three a.m.'

I took a deep breath, taking time to ensure that what I said next wouldn't be too blunt, then ventured, 'Guys, are you absolutely sure about your two crewmen?'

Eden stiffened in his chair, 'Yes,' he snapped, 'absolutely. Walter's our right-hand man, and as for Jock . . . when you meet him, you'll realise there isn't a dishonest bone in his body.'

'When I what?' I asked, quietly.

He flushed a little. 'I'm hoping that you'll meet the guys, and that you'll take a look at the boathouse. Bob, the truth is that while the insurers are refusing to pay out full value on the vessel on the basis of the police report, they have said they'll go halfers on the cost of an independent review of investigation. If it's successful, and the *Princess Alison* is recovered, they'll pay all of it, plus a premium of ten per cent of the insured value. Will you take it on?'

Would I take it on? That was a hell of a big question. Would I step into an investigation that the police had been running for four months without getting anywhere? Would I waste my time looking for a rich man's corporate toy, one that had quite possibly been repainted, renamed, altered cosmetically and sold on for a couple of million?

Yes, I would, for the original Alison's sake. And of course a success bonus of half a million pounds was an added incentive.

'Very well,' I agreed, 'I'll look at it, but before I do I have to tell you that this was not an opportunistic theft. It's been planned and executed by people who knew what they were doing, and almost certainly by someone who'd seen the interior of the boathouse, because of the way the alarm was neutralised.

'Whoever stole the *Princess* had some sort of insider knowledge; that's a racing certainty, and it should have been the basis of the police inquiry. Tell me, were you ever asked for a list of all the people who've been on board her, going back at least a couple of years?'

'No,' Rory replied. 'We never were. We'd be able to provide it, but only up to a point. Some of our hospitality invitations were general; key execs of some of our customers and client companies regularly joined us for a day's sailing, with partners. We don't have the names of all of those partners, and we can hardly go back and ask them, especially not the customers. "Excuse me, but can you tell me your other half's name so she can be eliminated from police inquiries?" No, I don't think so.'

'No,' I conceded, 'but if I'd been involved in this I'd have wanted that list. Who was the senior investigating officer?'

'His name was Detective Inspector McGarry,' Eden volunteered. 'First name Randolph, I think. He was based in Dumbarton.'

'Did you meet anyone else?'

He shook his head. 'No. Not until Chief Superintendent Chambers came to see me. McGarry was my only contact throughout. I met him on the estate, at the scene of the crime, so to speak. He visited me a couple of times after that, to update me, but nobody else came near me, no more senior officer.'

I was incredulous. I was still in command of the Strathclyde force when the *Princess Alison* was stolen, a five-million-pound heist that nobody had seen fit to report to the chief constable. A major rural crime, dropped into the hands of a detective inspector, whose caseload would be entirely urban and who would have no specialist marine knowledge. If I had known of it at the time, arses would have been kicked. As it was I was going to make a fuss. 'You never thought to take it up the line?' I asked.

Eden stared back at me. 'To whom? I didn't know anyone else.'

'You know me,' I retorted. 'I was in Pitt Street when it happened, getting ready to hand over to my successor in ScotServe. I'd have raised merry hell if I'd known that a DI had been assigned as the investigating officer. I'm not saying that the outcome would have been different, but there would have been a hell of a lot more resources committed, that is for sure.'

'What can you do after the event?' Rory asked. 'Do we have a realistic chance of getting the *Princess* back?' I sensed his accountant's mind at work.

'I don't know,' I told him, candidly. 'I promise you this: as soon as I see it's hopeless, I'll tell you. I won't waste my time or yours.'

'Fair enough,' his father said. 'How will you begin?'

'By seeing how much influence I still have,' I replied. 'I need to get my hands on the police report.'

Six

'As a deputy chief,' Mario McGuire said, 'I'm not going to be crawling over every crime scene like Bob Skinner did, but this one . . .' He shuddered. 'I've attended very few child deaths in my career, but every one's burned into my brain.'

'I've never seen anything like this,' DCI Pye confessed. He looked up at his senior colleague. 'To be honest I didn't expect you to come here, sir. I thought you'd want to know, that's all.'

'You did the right thing, Sammy,' the DCC reassured him. 'And you're not alone. In the last couple of weeks I've had half a dozen calls from crime scenes, from your opposite numbers in Aberdeen, Fort William, Dumfries, Inverness, Falkirk and Motherwell. Strictly speaking none of you should have called me, but we're all still bedding into this new structure, at all levels, and until we all feel comfortable, I'm quite happy with over-reporting.'

'You don't look very comfortable in that uniform, sir,' Sauce Haddock chipped in.

McGuire grinned. 'Don't let it fool you, lad,' he joked. 'This isn't your ordinary woolly tunic, this is Hugo Boss.' In truth he did feel awkward in the clumsy garment. He had spent most of

44

his career in plain clothes, and had never dressed casually for work; on his first day as an acting detective constable, he had worn a pale-blue mohair tailor-made suit. When he recalled that time, he could still hear Bob Skinner's gentle admonition: 'This is CID. We do unobtrusive here.'

As the first chief constable of ScotServe, Sir Andrew Martin had taken a different position. His deputies and ACCs, and all divisional commanders, were required to wear uniform on duty. He had considered extending that to CID, and had backed down only in the face of the united opposition of Maggie Steele, his designated deputy, and McGuire himself.

'When you called me, Sammy,' he continued, 'I was heading for Hawick, to visit CID down there. If I hadn't been in the vicinity I wouldn't have come here, but I was, and when you told me there was a kid involved, I felt that I should.' He looked at Haddock. 'Have the SOCOs got a paper suit to fit me?'

The DS nodded and handed him a package, containing a sterile overall with a hood. He put it on, then added paper bootees and latex gloves. Prepared, he followed his similarly clad colleagues into a large tent that stood in the centre of the cleared area of the Fort Kinnaird car park.

A floodlight had been set up beside the red saloon, focusing on the boot. The child lay as Pye and Haddock had found her, tiny, helpless, her dead eyes shaming them all for allowing what had happened to her.

There was one other person in the tent, a very small man. He wore a face mask in addition to his tunic, removing it as he turned towards them.

'Professor Hutchinson,' McGuire exclaimed. 'I thought you had . . .'

'Not yet, Mario,' the pathologist replied. 'I've got a few weeks till I retire. Even then, I imagine I'll probably help out on a part-time basis, if I'm needed.'

'I'm glad to hear it. You're too good to lose completely. Have you any initial thoughts about this? Can you give us a time of death?'

'No more than three hours ago. I'm certain of that.'

'And the cause? How about that?'

The professor frowned. 'I can't say yet,' he replied, 'and I'm not even going to hazard a guess. All I can tell you is that I see no sign of trauma. There's no bruising to the neck, nothing to suggest strangulation.'

'Asphyxiation?' Haddock suggested.

'That's a possibility, Sauce,' Hutchinson conceded, 'but how? No, I won't speculate; you'll all have to wait until I've done the post-mortem.'

'Soonest, yes?' Pye murmured.

'This afternoon,' he promised. 'I have one observation, though. If you take a look inside the boot, you'll see that it's been lined, with thick foam rubber; it's even been fixed under the boot lid. Why? The only thing I can suggest is that it was done to protect the wee lass from being bumped around too much while the car was moving. That leads me to suppose that poor wee Zena was still alive when she was put in here.'

'Zena?' Pye repeated. 'Why do you call her that? We haven't identified her yet.'

'There's a name tag in the neck of her jacket, beside the maker's label. I believe that's what you detectives call "a clue".'

'Is there a surname?'

He looked up at the DCI, with an eyebrow raised. 'No, but I don't imagine there was another "Zena" in her school class, so it wouldn't be necessary. I'm finished here,' he continued, briskly.

'The poor child can be removed to the mortuary. I'll schedule the post-mortem for four o'clock.' He pulled up the arm of his tunic to check his watch. 'That gives you just over four hours to find out who she is and let her parents have a chance to see her before I proceed.'

The three officers left the tent; as he stripped off his crime scene outfit, Pye glanced across at an area of the perimeter where three television crews and other media were being marshalled by PC Jules Hoare.

'Do you want to talk to them, sir?' he asked McGuire.

'No,' the DCC replied, 'but you should give them a statement. The midday bulletins will be coming on air very soon. Better all round if it's based on the few facts we have rather than rampant speculation.'

'Should I tell them that Bob Skinner was the one who found the child's body?'

McGuire stared at the DCI. 'Are you fucking crazy? Tell them that and it's all they'll report; on top of that they'll hound him for quotes. If it was Joe Soap that had found her you wouldn't have given a thought to naming him. Bob's a private citizen now, and has as much right to that privacy as anyone else.'

'Mmm,' Pye murmured. 'I'll take that as a no.'

The DCC grinned. 'You were winding me up, weren't you? You do that, Sammy,' he said. 'What's your plan of action?'

'We find and interview the owner of the car. We search for the driver who ran off; the site manager says they have some CCTV footage of someone who might be him. We complete the identification of the girl.'

'And there's no chance the owner was driving?'

'No. The boss . . . Mr Skinner, that is . . . was quite certain that the driver was in his twenties.'

47

'Okay. You talk to the media. I'm off to Hawick.' McGuire took a few paces towards his car, then stopped. 'One more thing: no doubt Bob asked you to keep him informed of your progress. Be sure you do, otherwise he'll bend my fucking ear, and I don't want that.'

Pye smiled. 'He did, and I will.'

As the DCC left, he signalled to the duty press officer, and headed in the direction of the corralled media. By the time he reached them, red lights were showing on the three TV cameras, and a clutch of portable recorders were thrust out towards him.

'Morning,' he began. 'I'm Detective Chief Inspector Samuel Pye. I'm the lead CID officer for the City of Edinburgh, and senior investigating officer here. I'm sorry to tell you that two hours ago, the body of a little girl was discovered in a vehicle, a red BMW, that had been involved in a minor collision in this car park. The driver ran off after the incident, before the child's body was discovered. Obviously, finding him is very important to us. We're looking for a thin-faced white man in his twenties, last seen wearing a grey hoodie and jeans. Any help the public can give us will be appreciated.'

He looked at the TV cameras. 'I'm asking anyone who saw a person matching that description in this area at any time this morning to get in touch with us. Even if you can't help us identify him, if we're able to plot his movements that will be a help.'

'Has the girl been identified?' a female voice asked. Pye knew its owner, Lennox Webster, crime reporter of the *Saltire*.

'No. That's our top priority; somewhere there are parents who are facing some tragic news. We need to find them, and break it as gently as we can.'

'So you don't know her age.'

48

'We're guessing four or five; we're asking schools and nurseries whether there have been any unexplained absences this morning. We've already established that no children of that age have been reported to the police as missing in the last few days.'

'Do you know how she died?' an STV reporter asked, breathlessly.

'I'm sorry, we don't. The pathologist's initial examination found no signs of physical assault. That's all I can tell you at this stage.'

'But you are treating her death as murder, yes?'

'We can't, not yet. As of this moment we are investigating a suspicious death; that's all I can say. That may change after the autopsy. In the meantime, I'm as impatient as you are to learn how this little girl died. Thank you.'

Pye forestalled any further questions by turning and walking away, heading back towards Haddock, who stood waiting beside the tent.

'We've located the owner,' the DS announced. 'Callum Sullivan. There was no reply at his address when uniform called earlier on, but half an hour ago he walked into the North Berwick police office to see whether we'd found his missing car. The duty sergeant asked him, very politely, to wait there for us.'

'Excellent,' the DCI said. 'And Zena? Did that name get any reaction anywhere?'

'Not yet, other than this: we know that neither Sullivan nor his housemate Harris has a child of that name. However, he does have a daughter from a previous marriage. She's called Kayleigh and she's five years old.'

'Let's go and talk to him.'

Haddock nodded. 'Oh yes, we should, for there's more.'

Seven

'How the hell do you get parked in this place?' Sauce Haddock exclaimed. 'It's Monday, it's winter and yet there isn't a space to be seen.'

'That's the way it is here on most days,' Pye replied. 'I was stationed in East Lothian for a while, in uniform, so I was here quite often. Most towns this size wouldn't have a manned police station any more, but all through the summer, and on most weekends, North Berwick is bulging with people. It's a resort. There are a couple of caravan sites, there's still property for holiday rent and on top of that there are loads of casual visitors, golfers and day trippers from Edinburgh. Because of that, parking's always murder.'

He smiled. 'Fortunately,' he continued, making a right turn into an opening that came into view as they approached a pub, 'there are a couple of spaces for police cars behind the local nick, and there's usually at least one free during the day.'

In fact, both slots were vacant. Pye parked in the first and led the way to the back door of the station. As they approached, Haddock noticed that all of the windows were barred. 'How many cells do they have here?' he asked.

The DCI laughed as he pressed the door buzzer. 'One of

those is the toilet,' he said. 'There was a celebrated incident in this nick, about thirty-five years ago. They were holding a prisoner here on suspicion of murder. They let him go for a piss and he climbed out the window. Hence the bars.'

They were admitted by a young female constable, a woman with a strong Glasgow accent who made a show of inspecting their warrant cards.

'Mr Sullivan's in the interview room, wi' Sergeant Tweedie,' she told them. 'It's at the end of the corridor. The Sarge said just to go in when you arrived.'

'That was our plan,' Haddock murmured.

Sergeant Tweedie was a woman also. 'Lucy, isn't it?' Pye asked her, after she had introduced them to Callum Sullivan, who was seated at the interview table.

'That's right, sir,' she confirmed. 'I remember you from Haddington. You were a DC then and I was very new. Are you still pally with Karen Neville, that used to work there too?'

'I see her now and again. She reports to me, but not for much longer. She's moving through to the west, on promotion.'

'Did she not marry . . .' Lucy Tweedie began.

Pye cut her off with a nod. 'Our new chief constable, yes: then she divorced him.' He turned to the third man in the room. Heavily built and round faced, he was looking at the two newcomers with curiosity in his eyes. He had a takeaway coffee in a plastic cup clasped in his hands, holding it as if for warmth.

'Would you like one?' the sergeant asked. 'I can send Margie out to Gregg's, no problem.'

'That would be good.' Pye glanced at Haddock. 'Sauce, it's your round.'

The DS sighed. He took a ten-pound note from his wallet,

and handed it over, then seated himself at the table. 'Afternoon, Mr Sullivan,' he said, cheerfully.

'Finally,' the man muttered, his bulky shoulders hunched in a tweed jacket.

'Sorry about that,' Pye retorted, briskly, 'but you might be pleased to hear that we've found your car.'

Sullivan's eyes widened. 'You have? That's good news.' His accent was Scottish, Edinburgh rather than East Lothian. 'Is it in one piece?'

'It is, but it's been damaged, I'm afraid.'

'Have you caught the sod that stole it?'

'No, I'm afraid not. Your vehicle was involved in an accident and the man who was driving it ran off. We're still looking for him.'

'Well, you got the Beamer back,' the owner conceded, 'that's the main thing. Not that it was worth a hell of a lot. I'm a car dealer; I specialise in classic vehicles. That one's a long way short of being classic, it's only a runabout, but I've just sold on the Daimler that I've been driving for a couple of years, and I switched my personalised plate to it until I find something that I like. When can I pick it up?' he asked.

'As soon as we're finished with it,' Haddock replied.

Sullivan frowned. 'What does that mean?' He paused, as if for thought. 'Wait a minute,' he murmured, 'a chief inspector and a detective sergeant, on a car theft; that's a bit heavy-duty, is it not? Has it been involved in a robbery or something?'

'We'll get to that,' Pye said, tersely. 'When did you discover the theft, Mr Sullivan?'

'This morning, when I went to my garage in Kingston: I keep some of my lesser stock there, and I do some refurbishment there too. The rest,' he continued in explanation, 'my best cars, are in a showroom on the way into Haddington, off the dual carriageway.'

'How did the thief get in?'

'Through a side door.'

'When was the last time you saw the car?'

'Saturday. I had a guy interested in a Bristol; it was in Kingston being prepared for the showroom. It's not street legal at the moment, so I took him there to view it. The Beamer was still there when I locked up.'

'What time would that have been?'

'About half four.'

'Did you make the sale?'

Haddock's question drew a scowl. 'No. Nowhere near. The man was a time-waster. He told me he'd phone me back on Sunday with a decision, but he didn't. Nor will he; I could tell at the time he was a chancer. You always know, don't you?'

The DS nodded. 'Yes, we find that too, in our line of work. What was the man's name, the time-waster?'

'King; that's all he told me. No first name.'

'Can you describe him?'

Sullivan frowned. 'He's about my age, give or take a year or two. I'm thirty-seven,' he added. 'He had a beard, glasses with dark frames and he was wearing a Barbour. That's the best I can do. Why are you interested in him anyway? Do you think he came back and stole the BMW? If he did, he's got no bloody taste. I've got better cars than that in the Kingston garage. If you're going to suggest he was looking for a getaway vehicle, that was one of the slowest in the place.'

'We're looking at all possibilities,' Pye said. He broke off as the PC came into the room, carrying two coffees in takeaway beakers. She placed them on the table, laying a five-pound note and a few coins beside them. As she left, the DCI continued. 'Did Mr King give you a contact number?'

'No.'

'How did he get in touch with you?'

'He rang my mobile: he said he'd seen my ad for the Bristol in the *East Lothian Courier*; the number's on that.'

'Do you have your phone with you?'

'I do,' Sullivan told him, 'but if you're thinking you might find his number on it, you're out of luck, lads. I deleted all my recent calls last night.'

'Is that a regular practice?' Haddock asked.

'Pardon?'

Pye sighed. 'Do you do that frequently?'

'Every so often. Like I said, I'm sorry. I'd love to help you but it's just bad luck.'

The DCI nodded. 'As you say. That's life; some you win, some you lose.'

'Good. We're agreed on something. Now, can I leave here?' Sullivan asked. 'I've got a business to run.'

'Not yet,' Pye said. 'We're not finished. When you called this morning to report the theft of the BMW, which phone did you use?'

'The mobile.'

'Where were you when you made the call?'

Sullivan stared at him. 'What do you mean? I was in bloody Kingston. I was looking at the empty space where my motor had been.'

Haddock cut in. 'Do you have a landline in your garage?'

'Yes.'

'Why didn't you use that?'

'I just didn't, okay?'

'No it's not. Can you prove you were at Kingston when you made the call? Does anyone else work there? Do you have a mechanic?'

The dealer shook his head. 'No, I don't need one full-time. When I have to, I use a guy at Fenton Barns. So no, there was nobody else in the garage, only me.'

'Therefore,' Haddock continued, 'as far as we're concerned, you could have been anywhere when you reported the theft.'

'I suppose.'

'You could even have been standing beside the car.'

Sullivan's eyes widened. 'Why the hell would I want to do that?' He paused as a possible answer presented itself. 'Are you thinking this was an insurance scam?'

'No,' Pye replied. 'One, if that was the game you'd have totalled the car. Two, any insurance claim would arise out of the subsequent collision, and you weren't driving when that happened. There is a third scenario where you'd give the car to someone else to take away and write off, but we don't believe that one either.'

'Good for me,' the dealer drawled.

'Maybe not. Do you know, or know of, a child, a wee girl, aged around five, by the name of Zena?'

He frowned. He stared at the two detectives, from one to the other. 'No, I don't. Means nothing to me. What's a five-year-old lassie got to do with my car?' He laughed, a short, barking sound. 'Do you think she stole it? Is that what you're getting at?'

'No,' Haddock said quietly. 'When the boot of your car was opened, after the collision in the Fort Kinnaird car park, and after the driver had absconded, Zena's body was found inside.'

Sullivan gasped and sat upright in his chair, his hand knocking over his coffee beaker and spilling what was left of its contents across the table. His eyes were wide, and suddenly very frightened. 'You're kidding me,' he exclaimed. 'You're making this up. It's ridiculous.'

'Oh, but it's not,' the DS retorted. He took a small iPad tablet from his jacket and switched it on. 'Take a look. There's a photograph to prove it. That's Zena, or so says a label in the jacket she's wearing, and she's dead. In: your: car.' He ground out the last three words.

'Can I get a better look at her face?' the other man croaked.

Haddock scrolled through the photographs in the tablet until he found a close-up.

'Oh my!' Sullivan was close to tears. 'It's not . . . I've got a daughter myself. Kayleigh; she's five and she lives with her mum. Sorry, I just had to be sure.'

Pye nodded. 'I understand,' he said. 'So you see now,' he continued, 'why we need, for the purpose of our inquiry into her death, to establish your whereabouts. Okay, you say you called us from the garage. I'm inclined to believe that, but I need to corroborate it. Who was the last person you saw before you found the theft of the car?'

The car dealer gazed at the table, as if he was looking for the answer in the small streak of cold coffee, 'My neighbour,' he replied at last. 'Her name's Beth McGregor. I left the house just after nine. Mary had gone to work by then. My car was in the drive, and as I went to get in I saw her through her kitchen window. I waved to her and she waved back.'

'Thanks, that's a help. We'll confirm it with her for the record. Now, let's move on. What sort of work do you do in your garage?'

'Like I said, repairs and renewals mainly: if a vehicle needs engine work and it's drivable, I take it down to Fenton Barns. If not, the mechanic comes to me. The other main thing would be upholstery. With a classic car you'll find that the leather lasts forever but the seats degrade. I've got another bloke that comes in to renew them when I need him.'

'I won't ask you to look at the photos again,' the DCI said, 'but the boot of your BMW was lined, with thick black foam rubber. Do you keep that at Kingston?'

'Yes, I do. But there was none in it the last time I looked, I'll swear. What does that tell you?'

'It suggests to us,' Haddock replied, 'that the person who stole your car did so with the intention of using it to abduct Zena. Also, it suggests that whoever took it might have known about the rubber being there in your garage, so it makes us think we're looking for somebody who's been there before.'

'The guy that was driving,' Sullivan ventured. 'What was he like?'

'Thin-faced white man in his twenties, wearing a hoodie and quick on his feet.'

'In his twenties, you say?'

'Yes.'

'Sorry.' He gazed at the table once more. 'That doesn't suggest anyone in particular to me. I know a few people who look like that.'

'Still,' Pye said, 'we might ask you to look at an artist's impression when we can get one prepared.' He looked Sullivan in the eye. 'What can you tell me about your relationship with Mary Jean Harris?'

'Eh? Mary? She's my sister.'

'She lives with you, yes?'

The other man nodded. 'Yes. She has done since just after my wife and I split up, a couple of years back. She lived through in Cumbernauld and she'd had a rough time, so I offered her a change of scene and a roof over her head.'

'A rough time? How rough?'

'Her husband had walked out on her,' he replied, 'and she was struggling financially.'

'So it had nothing to do with your nephew, Maxwell?'

'No,' Sullivan retorted. 'Nothing at all.'

'Is Maxwell still at school?' Haddock asked.

'No. He left at the end of last year.'

'Does he have a job?'

'He helps me out, from time to time. He got enough Higher passes last summer to tie up a university place next autumn, so he's calling this his gap year.'

'How does he help you out?'

'Driving mostly. If I'm delivering a car to a buyer, he'll come behind me to bring me back. If I'm taking one to the mechanic, same thing.'

The DS paused. He looked sideways at Pye, who nodded, a signal to carry on.

'Tell me more about your sister's problems in Cumbernauld,' he continued.

Sullivan drew a breath, exhaling through his nose. 'It just wasn't a happy place for her. She didn't like the town, and she didn't like her job.'

'What did she do?' Haddock asked.

'She's a teacher. Mary was educated at Watson's and did her degree at Moray House. She taught in Royal High at the start of her career, a good school. Then she married Stewart Harris, and it all started to go wrong. They lived in Bathgate at first. She could commute from there, but he was posted to Paisley, and that was the end of that. Then he was promoted and transferred to Cumbernauld. The only jobs she could find in either place were in rough, low-end schools. She just wasn't cut out for them, but she needed to work.'

'What did her husband do?'

'He was one of your lot. He was a PC in Airdrie when they married. He left her two years ago, when Maxwell was fifteen. He was a sergeant by then, but going no higher.'

'What happened?'

'The usual,' Sullivan sighed. 'Another woman, Mary told me. And as can happen in these cases, she was victimised twice. She had to increase her mortgage to give him his share of the house, and it just broke her. She'd been pretty low anyway, and that was the last straw. Coming to live with me worked out well for her,' he added. 'There's plenty of room in the house and she has a job at North Berwick High. Maxwell sat his Highers there.'

'You haven't had much luck in the marriage stakes, you and your sister,' Pye observed.

'You could say that.'

'What happened to yours?'

'Nothing dramatic. We just weren't suited.'

'Did you buy her half of the house?' Haddock asked.

'No, it wasn't like that. I'd sold my main business . . . it made compressors for central heating units . . . so I gave Janine a generous settlement. It included our house in Polwarth. I moved out to North Berwick, and started to do what I'd fancied doing for a while, dealing in specialist cars.' He smiled, for the first time. 'Every man's dream, pursuing his hobby full time.'

'Mine would be golf,' the DS confessed. 'Some day, maybe I'll play the senior tour.'

He straightened in his chair, then leaned a little closer, his hands on the table.

'So,' he murmured, 'your sister's move; you say it had nothing to do with Maxwell?'

'No, why should it?'

'It had nothing to do with his appearance before the panel?'

Sullivan's eyes narrowed; he too leaned towards his interrogator. 'What fucking panel?'

'Three years ago, when he was fourteen, Maxwell appeared before a Children's Hearing in North Lanarkshire. He was accused of exposing himself to a group of three-year-old girls in a park in Cumbernauld. The panel placed him under the supervision of a social worker for a year. Both his parents were at the hearing.'

'I never knew about this! The dirty little bastard. Are you telling me he's on the sex offenders' register?'

'No, he isn't,' Pye said, intervening. 'There was no conviction recorded; the Children's Hearing isn't a court.'

'Still, he's a pervert!'

'Mr Sullivan, we're not rushing to judgement here, but the lad's past does flag him up for attention. Does he have access to your garage?'

The uncle nodded. 'Yes, he knows where the keys are.'

'You've indicated that he has a driving licence. Does he have a car of his own?'

'Not as such, but I've got a general insurance policy on all my vehicles and I let him use one when he wants.'

'When was the last time you saw him?'

'Last night, but . . . Fuck me, my house isn't far from the primary school.' He whistled. 'No wonder Mary was having a hard time in Cumbernauld. There are no secrets in a place like that.'

'You didn't see him this morning?'

'No, nor did I hear him, and I probably would have if he'd been in. He's always got music going in his room.'

'Does he often go out early?' Haddock asked.

'Not often, but it's not unknown. As well as helping me, he works part-time down at the Seabird Centre. It opens at ten, but if there's been an evening event, sometimes they ask him to go in early to clear up.' Sullivan's hands were shaking. 'Christ, you've got me worried. He is a quiet lad, Maxwell, but I've never read anything into that. Now, I feel as if I don't know the boy at all.'

'Can you describe him for us?'

'He's tall, and he's thin . . .' He looked the sergeant in the eye. 'Are you saying it might have been him that was driving the Beamer?'

'No,' Pye replied. 'The description we have is of an older man, and our witness is . . . reliable, let's say. But we do need to speak to Maxwell, if only to eliminate him. As a matter of interest, does he wear a hoodie?'

'He's got one.' The reply was a whisper.

'Thanks . . . but listen,' the DCI added, 'who doesn't these days? It seems to be unofficial uniform for youngsters.'

Haddock nodded. 'I have one myself,' he volunteered. 'So has my girlfriend.'

'How do you want to handle this?' Sullivan asked. 'Do you want me to bring him here?'

'No,' Pye replied, at once. 'If he is at the Seabird Centre, will he go home for lunch?'

'Yes, Mary too. I usually make it for all of us. ' He looked at his watch. 'I should be getting back there. Can I go now?'

'You're not being detained,' the DCI told him, 'but we'd appreciate your cooperation. To be frank, we need to see the boy before you do, and we don't want you to call him before then. Trust us, it'll be in his best interests.'

'Will it? Suppose he's . . .' He stopped. 'No, suppose he can't give a good account of himself?'

'Either way, I promise you, we will be discreet. If the kid has nothing to do with this, we don't want to mess up his life . . . or yours, for that matter.'

Eight

Mario McGuire slid his car into an empty space. It was marked 'Reserved', but there was nobody within half a day's drive who would outrank him, and so he took it without a moment's hesitation. He knew Hawick, from a brief stint in Borders CID a few years before. He had been based in Galashiels back then, much closer to Edinburgh, but the wool town had kept him busy enough.

He switched off his engine and stepped out. There was a dampness in the air, although the clouds were high and rain did not seem imminent. He looked across the car park at the building to which he was headed, a squat, three-storey structure that stood in stark contrast in its ugliness with the elegant houses on the other side of the street, but which redeemed itself by making the area a burglar-free zone.

They would be waiting for him, around the conference table, the area commander and senior staff, and the CID team that he had come to visit, as part of a tour that would take him all around Scotland, in line with Andy Martin's decree that his senior officers should fend off accusations of centralisation by showing their faces in each local policing area as often as possible. The sandwiches would be curling up at the corners; he had been

63

delayed by a lorry accident that had given him too much time to dwell on the awful gut-wrenching sight in the Fort Kinnaird mall.

He had wanted to stay there, to take command and drive the investigation to a swift successful conclusion. He understood the frustration that Bob Skinner must have felt, the impotence of being just another bystander. But the days of action were gone for them both. He was part desk jockey, part tourist and his one-time mentor was a civilian.

'For how long, I wonder,' he murmured, thinking of a night a few years earlier, when he and Skinner were celebrating the arrest of a fugitive killer in a hotel in Monaco.

'You know, Mario,' the chief had said, after a few drinks. 'The traffic has to flow safely, people must be protected against yobbery and anti-social behaviour in general, and our towns and cities must be peaceful places. Ensuring all of that is part of my job; I do it as best I can. But there's one part that drives me on and always has done. We dress it up in fancy terms but when it comes down to it, mate, we are in the retribution business. We are the fucking equalisers, make no mistake. When we nail someone like the bastard we've just locked up, so help me God, I love it.'

Could the man exist without that purpose in his life? McGuire was far from certain.

He was halfway to the police station entrance when his phone sounded. He took it out and smiled as he looked at the caller ID. 'Hello, Bob,' he said as he answered. 'Has Sammy not been back to you with an update?'

'No, but I wouldn't expect him to, not yet, not unless he's got lucky and wrapped it up within an hour or two. This is something else.'

'Oh yes?' The DCC was intrigued by the urgency in Skinner's voice.

'I've just had lunch with Alison Higgins' brother, Eden. I don't think you ever met him, but you know who he is and what he does.'

'I know very well, he's a very successful man, the furniture king, turned business angel and general entrepreneur; a couple of years ago, he made an offer for a controlling interest in our family business. My lovely Paula turned him down politely, but he kept at it, wouldn't take no for an answer, until finally she stopped being polite and he got the message.'

'That's the man. He's got a problem, and he's asked for my help. Just over four months ago, his boat was stolen from the Gareloch: five million quid's worth of boat. My old force handled the inquiry and got nowhere. It was run out of Dumbarton by a DI called McGarry. I knew nothing about it or I'd have given it a hell of a lot more clout than that.

'Now, after all that wasted time, Eden's been told that the inquiry's been wound down. He's not happy, nor are his insurers. Together they've asked me to review the investigation, and I've agreed. I'd like a copy of the police report, so that I can see what's been done and what should have been done but hasn't.'

McGuire had stopped, outside the Hawick station entrance. 'You want to review a police investigation, as a civilian?' he asked.

'That's what I've been hired to do. I could start from scratch, but that might be pointless. The chances are that all I'll be able to tell Eden is that McGarry did a competent job and that his boat's history. If I give the security of his mooring a clean bill of health as well, the insurers will probably pay full value and that'll be the end of the matter.'

'Fine,' McGuire murmured, 'but if you're not satisfied that the thing was handled properly, what will you do?'

'I'll go proactive. I'll make my own inquiries, fill in the blanks in the report and see where it takes me.'

The DCC made a decision. 'I'll need to clear it with Andy, but in principle, yes. If you do find any holes in what's been done, we might want to take the investigation back, but we'll cross that bridge if we reach it. One thing,' he added. 'McGarry's not a DI any longer. He's back in uniform, in Glasgow. His clear-up rates were crap, so he got culled. Okay, Bob, if the chief approves, I'll give you the file. Hell, I might even have a look at it myself.'

McGuire heard him chuckle. 'Do you want me to cut you in on my fee, Mario?' Skinner joked.

'They're paying you?' he exclaimed.

'Two hundred and fifty an hour, plus expenses, plus success bonus.'

'Bloody hell! Is the private sector that lucrative?'

'It's the going rate for the job these people want done. I make a lot more than that working for InterMedia. And you know what? I don't give a shit. It's only money. If I could choose between getting a result for my new client and coming face to face with whoever put that little girl in that car, she'd win every time.'

Nine

'Maxwell?' the Seabird Centre manager repeated. 'Yes, he's here. He's downstairs in the exhibition area. I can ask him to come up, but it's only ten minutes to his lunch break. If you can wait that long, it would be easier all round.'

'Yes, I can do that,' Haddock said.

'You can wait in the cafe if you like,' the woman suggested. 'The coffee's good.'

The detective smiled. 'Is there anywhere in North Berwick that doesn't sell coffee?' he asked.

'Not too many places, that's true. It used to be that this town had more charity shops than anything else, but now the baristas have taken over.' She looked across the counter. 'Why do you want to see Maxwell?' There was the faintest hint of suspicion in her voice.

The DS plucked his reply out of thin air. 'I've been talking to his uncle about a car.' He and Pye had agreed that they would intercept the boy as quietly as possible; the DCI was waiting in the car, parked on the adjacent harbour, out of sight of the centre.

'Oh yes,' the manager said. 'Mr Sullivan's a dealer, isn't he?'

'That's right. I had a question, and he told me that Maxwell

67

would know more about it than he does. He said I'd find him here.'

Haddock moved across to a display of souvenirs. Cheeky, his partner, was a sucker for soft toys; his eye fell on a fluffy white seal cub, and he picked it up.

He had just finished paying for it when a door opened behind the counter and a young man stepped out. He was tall, slim and wore a grey hooded top.

'Maxwell,' the manager called out. 'This chap wants a word, about one of your uncle's cars.'

The boy turned towards him, with a small frown born of curiosity. 'What would I know about . . .' he began, as the sergeant closed the gap between them, displaying his warrant card with as much discretion as he could achieve.

'I'm a police officer,' he murmured. 'I do want to talk to you about one of Mr Sullivan's cars, one that's been stolen, but not here.'

'What?' Maxwell murmured. He seemed hesitant, not sure whether to believe what he was being told.

'I'll explain outside. It's all right; your boss doesn't know I'm a cop. Play along with it and she never will.'

The boy shrugged. 'Okay,' he said. 'This is a wee bit hush-hush, isn't it?'

Haddock let him lead the way outside, then directed him to the waiting car.

'This is my boss,' he told Maxwell, as he ushered him into the back seat, behind Pye.

'Nice tae meet you,' the teenager said, turning to face Haddock as he slid in and closed the door. 'This has got fuck all to do with one of my uncle's cars, has it?'

'Oh it has, really.'

'Bollocks, you're pulling in the usual suspects, aren't you?'

'Is that how you see yourself, son?' Pye asked him.

'No, but you guys do. You were always after me in Cumbernauld, after . . .'

'After your wee bit of bother?'

'Aye!' He hunched up in the car as if he was trying to make himself as small as possible. 'They never left me alone. But when I got beat up in the school, and I did often enough, they never wanted tae know.'

'You should have kept your cock in your pants, son, shouldn't you?' the DCI retorted.

'It was a stitch-up,' Maxwell protested.

'You weren't flashing? It was somebody else's? Is that what you're saying?'

'No, but . . . Look, I was caught short in the park, and the toilets were locked. I was burstin' so I had a slash against the wall of the bogs. It turned out there were three wee girls behind me, with their mothers. I never saw them, and they never saw me, until the two cops yelled at me. I turned around; I still had my thing in my hand. The two mothers started laughin', but the polis didn't. They arrested me, and they told the women they had to make a complaint. They said I'd done it before and that I needed to be stopped.'

'Come on, lad,' Haddock said, patiently. 'You were fourteen and you did something stupid. That doesn't make you a bad person for life, and we're not here to dig it all up, unless you give us cause. Why would two cops fit you up, and for exposure of all things?'

'Because my dad was their sergeant,' the boy exclaimed, his voice rising, 'and they fuckin' hated him. With the women's statements, there was nothing he could do. I went before the

Children's Panel, I got put on a social work report, and my dad got transferred to the other side of Glasgow, which was what those two shitebags wanted all along.'

He was on the verge of tears. 'With him gone I got picked on big time at the school. Then my mum and dad fell out. She said he never stood up for me, and she chucked him out. She told Uncle Callum that he'd gone off wi' a bird, but he never did. She never told my uncle the truth; she never told him what had happened, and she made me promise I never would either.'

'Shit,' Pye murmured. 'I'm sorry, kid, but he knows now.'

The boy buried his face in his hands. 'Thanks a fuckin' million,' he mumbled.

'We'd no choice,' the DCI said.

'Help us with something,' Haddock asked. 'What time this morning did you get to the Seabird Centre?'

Maxwell sniffed and wiped his eyes with the back of his hand. 'Quarter to nine,' he replied. 'There was a film show in the theatre last night, and it always needs sweepin' out after one of them. That's my job. Why? How does that help you?'

'It tells us that you weren't the guy in the hoodie who ran away from your uncle's stolen BMW after it was involved in an accident in Edinburgh this morning.'

He stared, bleary eyed, at the DS. 'You weren't kiddin' about the stolen car?'

'No.'

'Somebody stole Cosie?'

'We're afraid so,' Haddock replied.

'That's a bugger; I like driving that car. Is it smashed up?'

'Not too badly. Do you spend much time at Kingston, Maxwell?'

'Uh-huh. Quite a lot. I like it there. I keep the place tidy, I clean it up after the upholstery man and when a car's ready to go to the main showroom, I'll give it a polish first.'

'Do you ever take friends along to help?'

The boy's face darkened. 'I don't have many friends. I was an incomer at North Berwick High, and I don't play rugby, so nobody really wanted to know me. There's Hazel and Dino, that's all; they've been down at Kingston. Why are you asking anyway?'

'We're considering the possibility that the break-in might have been done by somebody who knew the place.'

'No way!' The protest was instant and loud. 'They wouldn't do that.'

'How long have you known them?' Pye asked.

'I met Hazel at North Berwick High when I went there. She moved out here from Edinburgh last April. She was at a fee-payin' school there but her dad's business went bust and she had to leave.'

'Is she your girlfriend?'

He shrugged. 'I suppose.' He looked sideways at Haddock, anxious. 'Will she have tae find out about what happened in Cumbernauld?'

'You haven't told her?'

'No chance. What would she think of me?'

'If she really likes you, she'd believe the story you told us.'

'Do you believe it?'

'I'll tell you how much I do,' the sergeant replied. 'We're all one force in Scotland now, and you're no longer a minor. If you want to file a complaint with us against the officers who arrested you, on the basis that they coerced the two women into making statements accusing you of . . . what you were

71

charged with . . . we'll see that it's investigated.' He looked at the DCI. 'Agreed, boss?'

'Absolutely,' Pye said. 'Now,' he continued, 'what about Dino?'

'He's local; he's twenty-three. I met him at the centre. He's about the harbour a lot. His dad's a lobster fisherman and Dino works with him. His name isn't really Dino; it's Dean.'

'Surnames?'

'Hazel's is Mackail, Dino's is Francey. You're not goin' to talk to them, are you?'

'Have either of them ever been inside the stolen BMW, Cosie?' the DCI asked.

Maxwell nodded. 'Both of them. There was a gig in the Corn Exchange in Haddington a couple of weeks ago, and four of us went: me, Haze, Dino and his girlfriend, Singer. Uncle Callum let me take the car.'

'Then I'm afraid we will need to speak to them. We'll need their fingerprints, and yours.'

'We never took it!' the boy protested.

'We're not saying you did,' Haddock reassured him, 'but you'll have left traces. Our crime scene people will need to be able to eliminate yours.'

'Do you do this with every car theft?'

'No, we don't, but this one's different. Your vehicle is connected to a crime, a serious crime.'

His eyes widened. 'A bank robbery? Was it a getaway car?'

The DS shook his head. 'No, not a robbery. You don't need to know the details.'

'He'll find out as soon as he sees the news on telly, Sauce,' Pye pointed out. 'It's a suspicious death, Maxwell. The body of a wee girl was found in the boot.'

The boy cringed; his hand went to his mouth. 'You're kidding,' he gasped.

'I wish I was.'

In a flash, a hard, accusatory look came into his eyes. 'And you thought I might have . . . Usual fucking suspects right enough.' He reached for the door handle. 'Let me out of here!'

Haddock caught his arm. 'Son, we've got a tough job. We're accountable, to our bosses, to the public, but most of all to that dead kid. We have to follow up everything; we can't make exceptions. Everybody who's been in that car has to be traced and eliminated until we're left with only one person, the man who took wee Zena.'

'Was that her name?' Maxwell asked; he was calm once more.

The DS nodded. 'I won't lie to you. Your history did come up and it did interest us. We'd have been negligent if we hadn't followed it up, but as soon as we established your whereabouts this morning, you were in the clear. The same goes for your uncle.'

'Okay, fair enough. Where do you want to take my prints?'

'We'll do it in the local police station. We'll use the back door, so you're not seen going in and out. Mr Sullivan's been printed already.'

Pye started the car's engine. 'We'll need addresses for Hazel and Dean, Maxwell. Can you help with that?'

'Sure. Hazel's is . . .' He stopped in mid-sentence. 'That's Dino there,' he said, pointing across the harbour at a tall, lean figure, wearing navy blue denims and a grey hoodie, who was walking past the Seabird Centre, shoulders hunched.

'That's handy,' Haddock chuckled. 'We've got room for one more in here.'

He stepped out of the car. 'Mr Francey,' he called out. 'Dean Francey.'

The young man stopped in mid-stride and spun round. He stared at the DS for a second, and another, then broke into a run. His trainers pounding the tarmac, he slid round a corner, then leapt on to a bicycle that had been parked in a rack, and pedalled off, along the beachfront road, then into a side street.

Pye had begun a three-point turn even before the DS jumped into the front passenger seat. 'Seat belt on, Maxwell,' he called out. 'I think we're going to need more than your pal's fingerprints.'

Ten

'Is this a precedent we want to be setting?' Sir Andrew Martin asked, the computer screen showing his concerned frown.

'Who says it's a precedent at all?' Mario McGuire replied, looking directly into the camera. He was alone in the room that he had commandeered in the Hawick CID office suite.

'I see it as a one-off situation,' the DCC continued. 'A rich man's five-million-pound toy went missing, and the Strathclyde force began an investigation that took months to get precisely nowhere. Our only role since replacing them has been to send a chief super in uniform to tell the complainant that he's not getting his boat back. He's not happy. Would you be?'

The chief constable raised a questioning eyebrow. 'Were you party to that decision?'

'No, I bloody wasn't, and somebody is going to find out how much I dislike being embarrassed by it. That aside, the situation is that Eden Higgins feels that he's been poorly served by the police. He could have come to you or to me and asked that the inquiry be re-opened, but he didn't. Instead he's asked our former colleague to look into it.'

'I haven't spoken to Bob in a while,' Martin remarked, 'but last I heard he didn't have an investigator's licence.'

'Then you're out of touch. He does now.'

'Even so, handing over a complete police report to a civilian . . . if we do it for him, where does it stop?'

'It stops the minute the file lands on his desk, as far as I'm concerned.' McGuire paused. 'What's the alternative?' he challenged. 'Clearly, Mr Higgins is unhappy. If we withhold access to the file and he or his lawyer comes to you or me, we won't be able to ignore him. The very least we'd have to do would be to order a detailed review of the so-called investigation and appoint someone, a detective superintendent or higher, to do it. Would that officer, whoever he or she might be, do a better job than Bob Skinner? No, not in a light year.'

'You make it sound like he's doing us a favour,' the chief grumbled. 'He'll be getting big bucks for this, right?'

'Right. So what? We're not paying him.'

'No.' Martin frowned, and ran his fingers through his thick blond hair. 'Still . . .' he murmured.

'What's your problem?' his deputy asked.

'Ach, it's Bob himself,' he admitted, finally. 'I come into this bloody office every day and every day I have a sense of him being here, like some spectral bloody presence. I want to cut myself free from him, Mario, not give him a toehold.'

'You tried hard enough to keep him,' McGuire pointed out. 'The First Minister offered him more than a toehold, more like a complete bloody ladder, and he wouldn't have done that without your agreement. Why do that and freeze him out now? I don't get it.'

Martin leaned back in his chair and smiled. 'I went along with that idea for a reason. Look, I won't mince words; in every job I've ever had, even when I was deputy chief up in Dundee, I've felt that I was in Bob Skinner's shadow.'

'Come on, Andy,' the DCC protested, 'the man made us both. You and I started working for him on the same day, in Serious Crimes, and neither of us has looked back since. We weren't in his shadow, ever; he lit the way for us to progress in the job.'

'That may be true, I'll grant you. But it's history, and now we're our own men. When I agreed to him being offered a role in the new service, I did it because I wanted it to stay that way. I wanted to tie him down, to limit him.

'Mario, I have this dream; no kidding I do, and some nights it even wakens me up.

'Next month, the chair of the Scottish Police Authority, the body whose statutory role is to hold us to account, comes to the end of his term of office. There are only two people being talked about as his potential successor. One is Sir James Proud, and the other's Bob Skinner.

'You know how bloody hands-on Bob was as a chief constable. Do you think anything'll change if he becomes chair of the SPA? I was keen to keep him on the inside to take him out of the running, and that's the truth of it. That's why I went along with the First Minister's offer. But Bob turned it down, and now I'm left with my bad bloody dream.'

He stopped, looking at the camera, waiting for a response. When it came it was a soft, rumbling chuckle.

'Bob Skinner,' McGuire exclaimed, 'as chair of a committee? Never. The big man doesn't oversee things, he runs them.'

'Exactly! He'd run the SPA too, and then he'd be trying to run us.'

'That's bollocks . . . sir. It won't happen, not least because . . . That post is salaried, yes?'

'Of course.'

'What's the screw?'

'Sixty thousand a year, part-time.'

'For what? Maybe a hundred and twenty days a year, that's five hundred quid a day. Eden Higgins and his insurers are paying him four times that, and his job with the owners of the *Saltire* brings in even more. The SPA can't fucking afford him.'

'My good God,' Martin gasped, 'I never knew that.'

'Well, you do now. We don't want to oppose him in this thing, man.' McGuire's chuckle became a booming laugh. 'We should encourage him, so that when we retire he remembers and puts some of that our way.

'But leaving that aside,' he went on, 'if we give him the report, he becomes an additional resource. He'll either decide that ex-DI McGarry did a competent job, or he'll kick-start the thing and run it properly. Who knows, he might even find the bloody boat.'

Martin capitulated. 'Okay,' he said. 'Let him have it, and tell McGarry to cooperate with him and answer any questions he comes up with. Bloody Skinner,' he sighed, 'he's a magnet for crime.'

'You don't know the half of it,' the DCC said. 'This very morning . . .'

Eleven

'Mr Francey,' Pye murmured, bracing himself against the guard rail of his boat as it rocked in its mooring, 'I've been a police officer for fifteen years. In that time, more than a few people have run away from me. I can't recall a single one of them who "Hadnae done anything", as you put it.'

'Well, he hadnae,' Chic Francey repeated. 'Dean's a good lad.'

'So why did he turn into Bradley Wiggins when he saw us?' Haddock asked. 'We followed him into the car park at the end of the High Street but he left us for dead. And by the way,' he added, looking the man straight in the eye, 'he's done something now. He stole the bike he rode off on, four hundred quid's worth, according to the careless owner who went into the Seabird Centre without chaining it to the rack.'

'You guys would make onybody nervous.'

'Only the guilty.'

'Fuck off.'

'Here's the truth,' Pye told him. 'When your son was sixteen years old, he appeared in the Sheriff Court in Haddington, where he pleaded guilty to seventeen counts of theft from cars, and fourteen counts of malicious damage. He was put on

79

probation for two years. When he was eighteen he was found guilty of taking away a vehicle from the car park in St Andrews Street, North Berwick. He was fined five hundred pounds, and put on probation again. There's no getting round that, Mr Francey; next time he's in court, he's going to prison.'

'You lot would just love that,' the father retorted.

'Get real,' the DCI said. 'I've never met Dean. I don't know him, so I had no preconceptions . . . until he took off. Now . . . I'm investigating a car theft with serious consequences, and he's put himself right at the top of the list of suspects. So please, for his sake, help us.'

'Tae do what? Tae put him in jail?'

'Can we get off this fucking boat?' Pye snapped. He was no sailor; the gentle swell of the harbour at full tide and the combined odours of fish, seaweed and oil were beginning to affect him.

Francey looked at him, a sneer in his eyes, then turned and climbed the few rungs of the steel ladder that was bolted into the quayside. The two detectives followed suit.

On solid ground once more, Haddock took over from his boss. 'Mr Francey, Dean's doing a bloody good job of putting himself in jail without your help, but the longer this goes on, the tougher it could be for him. I'm not going into detail, but a car that he knows and had been in was stolen from its garage over the weekend. It turned up this morning in Edinburgh, and the driver ran off. The description we have fits your son.'

The father shook his head. 'Naw, he was here all morning,' he protested.

'Do me the courtesy of looking at me when you lie to me,' the DS said. He turned and nodded towards the old granary behind him. 'There are upwards of half a dozen flats in that building, overlooking your boat. If he was here, he'll have been seen by at least óne of the residents, for sure. And anyway, what were you doing here, the pair of you? The tide would have been out.'

He gave the man time to consider, then went on. 'I understand you wanting to protect your son; my dad would do the same for me, if he had to. Now tell us, when did he turn up here, honestly?'

Francey's shoulders slumped. 'Just after twelve,' he murmured. 'We were supposed to go out at half ten, tae check the pots. Ah wasnae best pleased when he never turned up, for missin' the tide costs me money. Ah could hae done it maself, but thought he was comin' so Ah waited.'

'Does Dean live with you?'

'Naw. He's got a one-bedroom flat in a buildin' on the main street.'

'We'll check that,' Pye said, his equilibrium recovered, 'but I don't expect he'll be there waiting for us. Do you know of anywhere else he'd go in a crisis?'

'He might go tae Donna's, his sister's, Ah suppose.'

'Where does Donna live?'

'Musselburgh, near the station.'

'Alone?'

'Naw. She's married tae a fireman. Ah can phone her if ye like, tae see if he's there.'

'I think we'd rather ask her that. Give me her address and we'll pay her a call.'

'She'll no' be in. She works at the university. Levon, her man, he might be. He works shifts. Ah could phone him.'

'If you want to phone anyone,' the DCI suggested, 'you could try calling Dean himself, and tell him to go to the nearest police office.' Behind him he heard Haddock speaking on his mobile. He waited for him to finish.

'That was Lucy Tweedie,' the DS announced. 'Her troops have found what they think is the stolen bike, abandoned at the station. If he caught the train they think he might be on, it'll be due in Edinburgh in two minutes. She's asked the transport police to meet it and she's given them a description.'

'If he's thinking straight,' Pye countered, 'he'll have got off earlier, at Musselburgh if he's going to his sister's. Call him please, Mr Francey, then give me your phone.'

The fisherman dug out a scratched and battered mobile from his overalls, peered at it and poked it a few times, before holding it to his ear for a second then handing it over.

The DCI listened to it ring seven times, then change tone as it was answered. 'This is Dino. Cannae talk the noo', so leave us a message or call us later.'

'And this is the police, Dino, one of the officers you pedalled away from. When you pick this up I want you to do one thing and one thing only. Go to your nearest police office and tell them that you're wanted for questioning by Detective Chief Inspector Pye and Detective Sergeant Haddock, stationed at Fettes. Do it, and this morning might not go too badly for you. Ignore this message, and it will.'

He made a note of the number showing on the small screen, then ended the call and handed the phone back to Francey. 'I want your address,' he told him, 'Dean's address and your daughter's address, plus any other places where he might go. If he calls you, tell him to hand himself in. Do not, repeat not, give him any assistance. If you do, we'll know, for we'll be monitoring your mobile. We'll see you again, no doubt.'

He turned on his heel and walked away, leaving Haddock to

note the addresses. It was only when they were both inside their car that the sergeant turned to him and said, 'What were you on about there? We can't monitor his mobile.'

The DCI smiled. 'I know that, and you know that; but he doesn't know it, and neither does his son. Come on, let's pick up Maxwell from the police station, and have him introduce us to his girlfriend. We still need to get her fingerprints for the scene of crime people.'

'Should we involve her parents?'

'According to the boy, she's eighteen so we don't need to. Let's print her and have Lucy Tweedie explain to them after the event.'

'Maybe there's one other thing we should do, Sammy. Dean Francey's photo will be on file because of his convictions. I know Mr Skinner said he didn't get a good look at the BMW driver this morning, but if we run it past him, maybe it'll trigger something.'

Pye nodded. 'We'll do that; and something else too. We've both had a good look at young Mr Francey. The Fort Kinnaird security people said they've got some video of the driver hightailing it through the centre. Let's access it and see if their running styles are similar.'

Twelve

'I can't be one hundred per cent certain,' Bob Skinner began, 'not as in under oath, but there is a very good chance that Francey's our man . . . sorry, your man.'

'Thanks, gaffer,' Sauce Haddock said, over the landline in the North Berwick police office. 'We've just looked at video footage we had sent to us from the car park and we're agreeing with that. We had a better look at him than you did, and we're one hundred per cent certain.'

'What did I tell you about calling me "gaffer"?' Skinner chuckled. 'Those days are over.'

'You'll always be the gaffer to us, sir. You'd better learn to live with it.'

Replacing the handset on its cradle he turned to Pye. 'He . . .' he began, stopping when he saw that the DCI was on his mobile, and looking grim faced.

'Indeed,' he heard him murmur. 'Yes, I've got that. Call me back when you hear more from the hospital. Thanks.' He ended the call.

'That was Jackie,' he said. 'She's in the mobile HQ at Fort Kinnaird. She thinks we've identified Zena.'

'She thinks?' the DS repeated.

'Provisional, but it looks likely. Just after nine o'clock this morning a woman was found by a cyclist at the roadside just outside a village called Garvald, out beyond Haddington on the other side of the A1 from here. She was unconscious with obvious head injuries. The bloke called the three nines, and she was rushed to Accident and Emergency. We attended too; the assumption was that she was a hit-and-run victim . . .'

'Fucking assumptions,' Haddock growled.

'I know, but that's how it appeared to the cops who attended. It was only when the ambulance got to the hospital that the woman was identified, through a debit card she had in her purse. It took a while for the bank to come up with her details but eventually they did. Her name is Grete Regal, and the address they had for her was Shell Cottage, Garvald. The electoral roll has her living there with her partner; his name is David Gates. She went back to the bank and asked about him. All they could tell her is that he's in the Royal Navy, 'cos that's where his salary comes from.

'The cottage isn't in the village itself; it's a few hundred yards along a country road. As soon as the victim had been identified and located, the traffic guys went back to Garvald, to her address. It was locked, but they'd taken some keys that were found on Grete.

'It was obvious that a child lived there; the biggest clue of all was a sign on a door that read "Zena's room". By that time the two of them knew about our investigation, and that we were trying to identify a female child. They were smart enough to take photographs and sent them to Jackie, in the mobile command unit; this is one. It's a framed poster above a child's bed.' He held up an image on his phone. 'It's an entry in a thing called *The Urban Dictionary*.'

'"A Zena,"' Haddock read, peering at the little screen, '"is a beautiful, funny, nice and caring person. Great in all aspects of life. Will kick ass if you mess with her friends! Usually very skinny and has brown eyes. Awesome tastes in music and literature. Zenas are always right." Could the label on her jacket have been a nickname? Aw Jesus, and she was a skinny wee thing with brown eyes.'

'Exactly,' Pye exclaimed. 'At that point, Jackie's check had turned up no reports of missing children as such, but there were the usual absences, and she was thorough enough to note those for follow-up, if it was necessary. As soon as she saw that poster she went back to the note she had on Garvald Primary School. A five-year-old child, called Olivia Regal Gates, was marked absent this morning, without a notifying call from the parents.'

'Is there a photo of her?'

'Jackie called the head teacher. She has pics of all the kids; she's going to scan Olivia's and email it to her. But . . . she said that everyone at school calls her Zena. She was only asked for the names of absent children, and she gave them off the register, without thinking.'

'Did Jackie ask if she has any siblings?'

'Yes, and she doesn't; she's an only child.'

'How about the mother?' the DS asked. 'How's she doing?'

'She's still in surgery; she has a fractured skull and brain swelling. However . . . Jackie spoke to the doctor who saw her in Accident and Emergency. She asked whether there were any other injuries, anything to indicate that she was hit by a car. There were none. So forget the hit-and-run theory. I'm sending the scientists out to the scene to see what they can find.'

Haddock whistled. 'This was well planned, Sammy.'

'It was, mate. Dean Francey knew exactly what he was doing; he, or someone else, must have studied Grete's routine, and worked out when she and her child would be alone and at their most vulnerable.'

'Surely there's no "or someone else" about it, boss. There must be another person involved. Dino doesn't strike me as a planner. And what would he do with a five year old anyway? Ransom her? Nah.'

'Sell her?' Pye suggested, quietly.

'To a paedo ring? No, surely not.'

'Like you said earlier, Sauce, no fucking assumptions. We rule nothing out. For now, everything is focused on finding Dean Francey.'

Thirteen

I have two sounding boards in my life these days, and they're both women.

There's Sarah, who's my therapist almost as much as she's my life partner. That's true, literally. When she came back to Scotland from her spell in the US, and saw how screwed up I was, professionally as well as personally, she gave me a frank assessment, over the dinner table in Mark Greenaway's discreet Edinburgh restaurant.

'I'm not a fully trained psychologist,' she said, 'but I did study it as part of my medical degree. On top of that, any doctor who's ever done any level of general practice has to possess a feeling for a patient's state of mind as well as for his physical condition. Looking at you, and knowing you as well as I do, if I was asked to make a diagnosis, I would describe you as clinically depressed.'

'You're kidding!' I protested. 'I might be a grumpy sod from time to time, but depressed, no, I don't buy that. What makes you say it?'

'You have no barriers,' she replied. 'You have a job in which you see some terrible things and have tough decisions to make, some of them literally life and death. There was a time when you could put all that stuff into perspective and stow it away when you came home. When I left, you weren't able to do that any more, you carried your whole burden everywhere, and I don't see that you've gotten any better in the time I was away.'

I frowned. 'No?'

'No,' she repeated. 'Trust me, you haven't. Bob, when your people experience extreme stress, they're offered counselling. These days it's automatic. Now tell me something. Have you ever had a formal counselling session?'

'Come on,' I chuckled. 'You know the answer to that one. I'm not having strangers rummage about inside my head.'

'And what a goddamn state your head's in as a result,' she countered.

'What about you?' I challenged. 'I'm not the only one with a stressful job. You're a bloody pathologist . . . the perfect choice of adjective, by the way. You spend your day rummaging through dead people's once-vital organs, for fuck's sake.'

'I know,' she admitted, 'and that has got to me too, in the past. That's one reason why I gave it up and went back to America to practise real medicine.' She tossed her head back, clearing her thick glossy hair from her eyeline, then she smiled. 'How was I to know that there are more horrors in the living than the dead?'

'I've known that all my career,' I retorted, casually. 'Bad people are a damn sight easier to manage when they're dead.' I tapped my forehead with my middle finger. 'One round there and they go all floppy.'

'Yes,' she murmured, 'and your predecessor as Chief of Strathclyde Police had three, right through the back of her head. I'll bet that when you stood in that concert hall in Glasgow looking down at her, you weren't flippant then.'

She had me there. 'So what do you want me to do about it?' I asked.

'Not just you: us. We should talk to each other, just us, at least once a week, about our work and the parts of it that have upset us. We should be our own counsellors. There's nobody knows me better than you.'

'Nor than you know me,' I conceded. 'Okay, if you're really serious, let's give it a try.'

We did, and we still do. Since I chucked the job I've had less to contribute, but on the day of Fort Kinnaird I had plenty, and so, once I was back in my *Saltire* office, and after I'd rung Mario McGuire to blag a copy of the report on the theft of the *Princess Alison*, I called Sarah.

'You got a couple of minutes?' I asked. 'Or are you up to your elbows in mid-rummage?'

'I'm prepping for a lecture,' she told me, 'but I've got a few minutes. What's up? Something is, I can tell.'

'I want to tell you how your lemon drizzle cake got smashed.' As I spoke, the scene rushed back into my mind, and all I could see was that wee girl. My eyes moistened once more, and I had to take a moment before I could continue. Since Sarah and I started our mutual support sessions, I find that I'm much more emotional. For example, Michael Clarke's eulogy at the Phillip Hughes funeral just tore me apart.

When I could, I talked her through the story.

'She was just like our daughter, Sarah,' I whispered as I finished. 'Apart from the brown eyes, it could have been Seonaid.'

'But it wasn't,' she countered. 'It was somebody else's baby, not ours, and although we can feel for them in their grief, if we're honest, we have to admit to relief.' I heard a small, stifled gasp. 'Of course,' she murmured.

'What?' I said.

She replied with a question of her own. 'Who attended the scene from CID?'

'The Menu,' I answered. 'Pye and Haddock. That's their nickname,' I explained. 'Someone told them they sounded like a fish and chip shop menu, and it stuck. They hate it.'

'I can imagine,' she chuckled. 'I've been wondering why I wasn't called out myself. The thing is, Joe Hutchinson and I had agreed that he would drop out of CID work. He's close to retirement, and when he does quit he wants a gap, where he isn't liable to be called in from his hideaway in Portugal as an expert witness in a High Court trial.'

'Not by the Crown, that's for sure,' I remarked. 'There's much more money in consulting for the defence.'

'Don't be so cynical.' she scolded. 'As I said, we had that deal, but when the call came in this morning, he told me the police wanted him, specifically.' She paused. 'Were you behind that, Bob?'

'No,' I assured her. 'That's the truth, I wasn't. It was Sammy Pye's call, but I'm sure he was thinking of you when he made it, and I approve, too. I hear what you say about being able to separate professional and private, but sometimes that's difficult, even for you. Has Joe done the autopsy yet?'

'No,' she replied. 'He's holding off for as long as he can in the hope the girl can be identified.'

I was surprised. 'They haven't done that yet? A child that age, I'd expected her absence to be noted pretty quickly.'

'You're itching to be part of this, aren't you?' Sarah observed.

'Yes,' I admitted, 'but I'm trying not to scratch it. But I am standing here wishing I'd chased the guy; if I'd got lucky and caught him it might all have been wrapped up now.'

'Maybe yes, maybe no,' she said. 'A couple of minutes ago you said he might have been an opportunistic car thief who didn't know what was in the boot. And anyway, could you have caught him?'

'Probably not,' I admitted, 'but I'm kicking myself for not trying.'

'Suppose you had,' she asked, 'and run him down, then found the little girl. How would you have reacted?'

That was a good question. 'I can't say for sure,' I conceded, 'but it might not have been pretty.'

'Then it's as well you didn't,' she declared. 'The Menu . . . I like that; it's funny . . . will get him, soon enough. Leave it to them, my love, and do your best to put it out of your mind. I'll see you this evening.'

Talking to Sarah made me feel better, no doubt about it; she always does. With time on my hands, I decided to build on my positivity, by calling on my other sounding board.

A guy in my golf club told me a while back that you really start to feel old when your kids turn forty. I disagree: when Alex, my oldest, passed the thirty mark a wee while ago, it hit me harder than it did her.

She marked the event by doing something completely unexpected, by walking away from a successful and lucrative career as a leading corporate partner in Curle Anthony and Jarvis, Scotland's biggest legal firm, to set up in practice as a criminal defence lawyer and qualify as a solicitor advocate . . . in other words, 'The Opposition', as she put it when I was a cop.

She'd picked up quite a bit of work in the second tier Sheriff Court, while studying for full rights of audience in the Supreme Court. A week before, she'd passed the Law Society exams, at the first time of asking.

I didn't have to go far to talk to her. There is office space for rent in the *Saltire* building, and I'd managed to fix her up with a suite, two floors above mine. The new sign on her door made me swell up with pride as I read it: 'Alexis Skinner, LLB, Solicitor Advocate'.

I was smiling as I stepped inside. 'She in?' I asked Constance, her secretary. The woman barely looked up from the papers she was studying, nodding and waving me on.

'She's busy,' I remarked as I closed my daughter's door behind me.

'In the best possible way,' Alex replied. 'She's doing fee notes.'

'Very good,' I said. 'Plenty of them?'

She responded with a smile. 'Oh yes. Business is good. I'm glad I took that extra room. I may need to fill it soon. I've just been hired for the defence in a corporate fraud case, involving one of my old clients from CAJ. I'm being formally introduced in the Court of Session on Wednesday morning, so I'll be able to appear at the first High Court hearing.'

'Are you going to lead?' I asked.

'Hell no,' she exclaimed. 'This is a complicated, high-stakes trial; I don't have anywhere near enough experience. I can do a lot of the preparation but I've instructed Easson Middleton to lead, with me as his junior.'

My pride indicator went up by at least five points. Easson Middleton is the top QC on the criminal bar, and for Alex even to be sat beside him in court would be a strong marker. 'How long will it last?'

'Potentially weeks,' she replied. 'That's why I may need to pass on some Sheriff Court work to an associate. But it'll all depend on pre-trial negotiations.'

I grinned. 'Plea bargaining?'

'Come on, Pops,' she scolded, 'you know we don't call it that. There's a whole raft of charges in the case; if we can persuade the Crown to drop some in exchange for guilty pleas in others, it will cut down trial time.'

'Will the trial judge agree?' I wondered.

'I expect so,' she said. 'There would be no jail time involved in any of the charges we're looking at. If Lady Broughton gives us the nod that she'll deal with them with modest fines, it'll be sorted. And she will. She doesn't want to be stuck there for three months when it could all be over in one.'

'Good luck.' I paused. 'Hey,' I chuckled, 'will you need an investigator?'

She angled her head back and looked at me. 'Are you kidding? We couldn't afford you.'

'Well, somebody can,' I countered. 'I've just been engaged by a man with a problem. And you'll never guess who it is.'

'That's probably true,' she agreed, 'but clearly you're bursting to tell me, so go ahead.'

'Eden Higgins,' I announced, no doubt with a smirk on my face.

'Alison's brother?' Alex exclaimed. 'The man with the boat that you fell in love with . . . after you fell in love with his sister?'

I nodded. 'The same. You're right about the boat,' I added, 'but wrong about her. I never did that.'

'Hmph,' she snorted. 'You could have fooled me at the time. What problem could Eden possibly have?' she asked. 'He's so rich he could make any trouble go away.'

'Not this one,' I told her; then I filled her in on my lunch date, and on the commission I'd accepted. 'I've asked Mario to give me the police report,' I added.

She frowned. 'Will Andy let him do that?'

I shrugged. 'I hope so. I'm not taking anything for granted, but . . .'

'As well you don't,' she said. 'From what I've been hearing, Chief Constable Sir Andrew Martin isn't the man that you and I have known for all these years.'

'Oh yes?' I murmured. 'And who's been telling you that?'

'Various cops,' Alex replied. 'People I've encountered in my new line of work, who knew him before. They all say the same; he's become distant, remote, aloof.'

'Remember,' I reminded her, 'we're talking about someone who broke up with you not once, but twice. It may be that he never was the man we thought we knew.'

She turned away from me, looking out of her office's smoked glass wall. 'Second time around,' she murmured, 'I persuaded myself that we had found each other, just as you and Sarah have, at last. Then you pulled out of the running for the top job in the new force, Andy got it instead . . . and he changed, almost overnight. My police friends didn't have to tell me that, because I knew already; I'd seen it for myself, close up.'

She faced me once more, looking up at me as I leaned against the door. 'Do you know what I think?' she continued. 'I believe he's trying to distance himself from you as much as he can. He knows that people used to call him Bob Skinner's gopher behind his back. He's always known that, and he's always hated it. Now he's made it to the top, he's determined to kill that image, and if he can do it by publicly opposing you, he will.'

'I see.' I thought for a few seconds about what she was saying to me. 'Are you trying to say that's why he split from you?'

She shook her head, vigorously. 'No!' she insisted. 'The truth is that I split from him. He was taking me for granted, Pops, in every way. He tried to treat me like a subservient little wife; he as good as told me that it was my role to follow wherever he led. When we were together, Andy talked non-stop about his work, but wasn't interested in mine. He wasn't even too interested in the stuff a girl doesn't talk to her dad about. The plain truth is he'd become a fucking bore and a boring fuck, so I binned him.'

I laughed. 'As you suggested, too much information, daughter.'

She grinned back. 'Probably.' Then she was serious again. 'Pops, how do you stand legally with this thing you're doing for Eden? Isn't private investigation regulated these days?'

'Not completely, although it's on the way,' I told her. 'But I'm covered. I've got one of the new investigator's licences, although,' I added, 'I don't plan to use it much.'

I left Alex to her new career and headed back down the stairs to my own office. I was passing June Crampsey's room when she caught sight of me through the glass wall and waved to me to join her.

'Have you heard any more about the child murder?' she asked. I closed the door and stepped inside.

'No,' I said, warily. 'But suppose I had, I might not be able to share it with you. If my ex-colleagues tell me something, it will be out of courtesy and nothing else. I'd have to respect their confidence, unless it was about to become general knowledge. I'll help the *Saltire* whenever I can, but I'm not one of your reporters, June.'

'I understand that,' she replied, quickly. 'I wasn't looking for specifics, rather for general information: what lines of inquiry they might be following, stuff like that. DCI Pye isn't saying anything at the moment.'

'If that's so,' I assured her, 'it's because there isn't anything he can say. Who's covering the story for you? Lennox Webster, your crime specialist, I assume.'

'Yes, she's on it,' June confirmed.

I paused, thinking about practicalities and ethics. 'Okay, pretend you're her,' I suggested, 'and ask me some non-specific questions as an expert source.'

She smiled. 'Such as?'

'What are the priorities of the investigation likely to be?' I began. 'Answer: there are likely to be three. Number one, identify the child, if that hasn't been done already. Two, identify the driver of the car in which the body was found. Three, establish cause of death. Practically, of those the third is the most immediately important. Until you do that you don't know what you're dealing with. Suppose you get lucky and catch the driver straight away, you need to know what the offence is.'

'Abduction and murder, surely,' June exclaimed.

'No,' I contradicted her firmly. 'Nothing is sure until you have all the facts. The only assumption I'd be making is that the child didn't climb into the car on her own and pull the boot lid shut.'

She looked up. 'She was in the boot? You didn't mention that earlier and Pye didn't tell us either.'

'In that case, you never heard me,' I retorted.

'You sound as if you actually saw the child, Bob.' Her blue eyes were piercing. 'It was you who found her, wasn't it?'

I nodded. 'The guy drove into my car,' I admitted. 'But you must not print that.'

'Bob,' she protested. 'That makes the story even bigger.'

I like June, and I respect her as a journalist, but I glared at her. 'Rubbish,' I snapped. 'The story can't get any bigger. It's a dead child; nothing tops that.'

At once, I regretted my anger. 'June, one day I'll have to stand in the witness box in the High Court and tell a jury what I saw, but until then I do not want to be a public player in the story. Look, I'm not trying to order you here; I'm asking you as a friend. If my involvement does leak, from within the police force or anywhere else, you'll have exclusive rights to anything I can say without breaking sub judice rules, but until then, sit on it, please.'

She sighed, then smiled. 'You know,' she murmured, 'I had this same conversation with my dad once.' June's father is Tommy Partridge, a retired detective superintendent. 'The circumstances weren't quite the same but the principle was. He said much the same as you did; I ignored him and ran the story. It drove a wedge between us for a couple of years. So this time,' she paused for a couple of seconds, 'I'll do what you ask, as a way of making up to him.'

I remembered the incident. I was head of CID when it happened and I was hard on Tommy. I made a mental note to call him, tell him what had happened, and apologise for my lack of understanding.

'Pye said there were no signs of physical assault,' June continued.

'There weren't,' I confirmed, 'none that I could see. That's another reason why I'm advising you to back off from labelling it murder. You might have to recant on it.'

'Who's doing the post-mortem?' she asked.

'Joe,' I replied. 'And I'm glad. It's going to be tough enough across the dinner table in our house tonight without Sarah having been involved.'

I left her to it and went back to my own office, quietly pleased that I hadn't known any more about the investigation. I felt a loyalty to my new employer, and didn't like the potential for conflicts of interest with my old one.

That situation was not improved when my mobile rang. It was Sauce Haddock, and he was in a hurry.

'Sir, we need your help,' he began. 'We're in North Berwick. We've pretty much eliminated the owner of the BMW as a suspect, but we've come across someone else who might be a possibility. He has a record, and I've established that we have a recent image on file.'

I didn't need him to go any further. 'Email it to me right away, and I'll take a look. I'm in my Edinburgh office so I'll be able to view it on a decent size screen. Make sure they send it maximum resolution. I only had a glimpse of the guy, so my eyes will need all the help they can get.'

I switched on my computer, opened my email programme and waited, but not for long. Within five minutes a small window in a corner of the monitor told me that I had mail. I clicked to open the message and then again for the attachment.

The man had been photographed against the usual dirty white background. I'd seen that sullen expression a few thousand times, and read the same bored resignation that showed in his eyes. There was a booking number on the image, and a name, 'Dean Francey'. It meant nothing to me, but the face did.

I had seen him before. I looked at the mugshot closely, then closed my eyes, and tried to imagine the face that I had seen, briefly, behind the wheel of the BMW before the reflected sun blinded me, and then again for a fraction of a second as he jumped out of the vehicle and took to his heels.

It was him, I told myself, and yet . . . could I put my hand on a bible, take an oath and then declare that to a jury?

The truth was, I wasn't sure. My gut said 'Yes', but my

professional caution said 'Wait a minute'.

Haddock had called me from North Berwick; the town is three or four miles from where I live and I go there regularly, alone, with friends, and with the kids, when they want to swim in the town pool. Assuming that Francey had a local connection, it was possible that I might have seen him casually in a completely different context.

However I judged it probable that he was the driver, so I called Sauce back and told him as much. By that time, he and Pye had viewed video footage from the shopping centre and were prepared to go firm on the identification.

I thought about going back to June's office and sharing, but only for a couple of seconds before deciding that would be a breach of trust.

As it happened I didn't have time to dwell on it, for my phone rang again, almost immediately. I stared at it. 'If ever I want a quiet life,' I told the empty room, 'all I need to do is drop this fucker into a bucket of water.'

But I'm not in that place yet, so I slid the indicator across the screen to answer, knowing from the readout that the caller was Mario McGuire.

'Yes or no?' I asked him, passing on the preliminaries.

'Yes, of course,' he replied. 'You're not surprised, are you?'

'Maybe just a little,' I admitted. 'I thought Andy might take a position of principle.'

I couldn't see Mario, but I could sense his smile. 'That did cross his mind, but fortunately it didn't dig itself in. I assured him this would be a one-off, and that satisfied him.'

I felt a flash of annoyance. 'Gracious of him.'

'Come on, Bob,' the big guy said. 'You know he wouldn't have done it for anyone else.'

'Do I?' I countered. 'Do you think he'd have turned down Jimmy Proud, or Graham Morton, his old boss in Tayside? I don't, not for a second. With me, it has to be seen that he's doing me a big favour.'

'He is,' Mario suggested, 'but that's not how this played out. Look, as far as he's concerned you're like Banquo's ghost, only potentially worse, 'cos you're very much alive.'

'How about you?' I asked. 'Do you feel the same about me?'

'Hell no!' he protested. 'Not for a second; nor does Maggie, or anyone else. But Andy's the chief now, and he needs to feel secure in his chair.'

'Jesus,' I exclaimed, 'are you saying he thinks I'd try to undermine him?'

My one-time colleague let his silence speak for itself.

'Then it's time he grew up,' I said. 'I will support him in any way he wants, short of coming back into the service. You tell him that from me.' I paused. 'Tell him something else too; I know about the Scottish Police Authority chair coming up next year, and I know what the gossip's saying. For the record, there's no way I'd take that job, ever. I spent the latter part of my career doing my best to ignore people like that, and there is no sodding way that I will ever become one of them.'

'I will tell him that,' Mario replied, 'word for word. And I'm sure it'll be a big weight off his mind. '

'Good,' I declared. 'Now, when am I getting the *Princess Alison* investigation file?'

'I'm having it retrieved and couriered through to you in Gullane,' he told me. 'It'll be with you this evening. Have fun.' I expected him to end the call, but he carried on. 'Just one thing, and this comes from me, not Andy. You might be working for

Eden Higgins, but he's a civilian. These papers are for your eyes only. He doesn't get to see them.'

In the early days of my professional relationship with big Mario McGuire, when he was just a brash kid, it didn't occur to me for one second that he was a deputy chief constable in waiting. I smiled as I thought of the man he'd become. 'As you wish, sir,' I murmured. 'As you wish.'

Fourteen

For all that she tried to present a confident front to her seniors, Detective Constable Jackie Wright felt that she had yet to find her feet in CID. She saw her main strength in sourcing information, and she was pleased that she had been able to help in identifying the child who had been found dead in Edinburgh that morning, but at the same time she recognised that a civilian clerk with computer skills and a contact list could have done the same job.

To compound her doubts about her own value, there were some occasions when she found herself frustrated, all options exhausted, and with nothing else to do but to go to Sauce Haddock, and admit failure.

'I'm sorry, Sarge,' she said. 'I've got as far as I can. The Ministry of Defence are not coming close to being cooperative. All they've done is to confirm that David Gates is a naval lieutenant, and that he's currently on service, an officer in the submarine section. They won't put me in touch with him and they won't even promise to pass a message to him.

'The man I spoke to was unbelievable. I told him that it was essential that we speak to Lieutenant Gates, but it cut no ice. He wouldn't guarantee to get any information to him, or give me a contact number for him. I don't know what to do next.'

'You've done it, Jackie,' the DS told her. 'You've told the man's employer that we need to speak to him, and now you've reported it up the line to me. I couldn't have done any more and I doubt the DCI could either.'

'But the way they behaved, Sauce,' Wright protested. 'It's ridiculous.'

'There'll be operational reasons for it,' Haddock told her. 'The man is a submariner; you've established that. These people go on cruises for months and for a lot of that time they're submerged. If that's where he is, let him stay there.'

'But he needs to know!'

'Does he? If he is on sensitive active service, what would it do to him to get news like that?' The young sergeant paused to consider his own question, then continued with another. 'Who was your contact in the MoD?'

'His name's Blackett; he's in the naval personnel department.'

'Then go back to him,' Haddock instructed. 'Get him to guarantee that as soon as Lieutenant Gates is in a position to be contacted we'll be advised and given facilities to interview him. If he gives you any trouble, remind him that the number two ranking minister in his department is an MP for a Scottish constituency, then ask him whether he fancies being named in a phone call from our boss to one of his bosses. If he brushes you off after that, let me know. I saw the look in DCC McGuire's eyes at the crime scene this morning. If we asked him, he'd make the call in a second.'

'Okay, Sarge,' Wright replied. 'I suppose it isn't important that we speak to Gates right away,' she conceded.

'What makes you say that?' the DS countered, sharply. 'If not right away, we need to interview him as soon as possible, make no mistake.'

'But he can't be a suspect if he's a few thousand miles away.'

'Suspect, no, but regardless of his location, he's a victim. And, regardless of his location, he's a potential witness. Do he or Grete have any enemies? Does either of them have a bunny-boiler ex-partner out there? Until she recovers consciousness, if she ever does, only he can tell us. How sensitive is his naval job? Could the attack and the abduction be connected with that? As for him being a suspect, stranger things have happened . . . and if he is party to a conspiracy, what better alibi than to be sitting under a polar icecap or somewhere similar at the time of the crime?'

'Okay, Sarge. I'll call Blackett back, right away.' The young DC sighed. 'I'll never be any good at this job, will I?'

'Hey, don't be like that,' Haddock chuckled. 'You are good at it.' He turned to Pye who was in the driver's seat as they headed along the A1, towards Edinburgh. 'Isn't she, boss?'

'You're doing fine, Jackie,' the DCI said into the car's Bluetooth microphone. 'I've had to deal with these MoD people. They can redefine difficult if they're that way inclined. If you really want, I'll phone Blackett myself, but I'd rather you had the pleasure of telling him what DS Haddock said will happen if he doesn't loosen up.'

'Thanks, sir,' she replied, her self-confidence shored up. 'I'll do that.'

'Straight away,' Pye added. 'You're doing a great job behind that desk, but you should have some fresh air. I'm going to have to attend poor wee Zena's autopsy, so DS Haddock will need a sidekick when he goes in search of our prime suspect. We'll be with you in ten minutes.'

Fifteen

'What's that building over there? I've always wondered.'

Sauce Haddock glanced to his right, following DC Jackie Wright's pointing finger. 'Queen Margaret University,' he replied. 'How long is "always" in your book? It's only been there for a few years.'

'Has it? Seems like forever.'

'In two hundred yards turn right.' The mellifluous female voice of the navigation system interrupted their conversation.

'Can't you have a male voice on those things?' Wright grumbled.

'I believe you can,' the DS chuckled as he eased into the turn, 'but everybody picks the bird. You don't get as confrontational with her. Cuts down on the road rage.'

'In one hundred yards you will have reached your destination,' Satnav woman announced.

'What number?' the young DC asked.

Haddock drew to a halt. 'Twenty-four. She's as good as her word. That's it, and from the car in the driveway it looks as if there's somebody in.'

He climbed out of their unmarked police vehicle and walked round to join his colleague. The modern, brick-built semi-detached villa had a small garden in front, laid out mostly in yellow slabs interspersed with squares where shrubs were set in gravel. 'That's my style,' he observed. 'Minimum maintenance.'

The front door of the house was opened, just as they reached it, by a large black man who seemed to fill its frame.

'Mr Rattray?' the DS began. 'Levon Rattray?'

The householder nodded, frowning as he looked at the warrant cards that both officers displayed.

'DS Haddock, DC Wright. Is your wife at home?'

'No, she's at work.' The accent was English, metropolitan, Liverpool or Birmingham; the two had always confused Haddock.

'Then maybe we can have a few words with you. Inside?'

'Sure.' Rattray stepped back to allow them entrance to his home, then ushered them through the hallway and into a spacious dining kitchen at the rear of the house. 'I'm making the dinner,' he explained. 'Donna's due back at five and I'm on night shift at six, so that hour's all we have together. Do you mind if I carry on while we talk?' he asked.

'Of course not,' Wright replied 'What do the pair of you do?' she asked.

'Donna works at QMU, just up the road. I'm in Fire and Rescue; my station's five minutes away in the car. There's no commute for either of us; we're all right that way.' He picked up a knife from the work surface and began to slice carrots. 'Now: what do want to talk about? What's the bastard done this time?'

Haddock smiled. 'Which bastard would that be?'

'Take your choice,' the fireman replied. 'Thank God Donna takes after her mother. Her father and her brother are a couple of useless wasters.'

'You have father-in-law problems?'

'I would have, but I keep him at arm's length.'

'What does he get up to?'

'Stupid stuff mostly. The nonsense with the fish was the last straw.'

'What nonsense?' Wright asked, intrigued.

'Ahh,' Rattray exclaimed, then shook his head. 'Chic's a lobster fisherman, right?'

'So we understand,' Haddock agreed.

'Well, that's not all he does. He supplies restaurants in Edinburgh with fish that he says is fresh caught . . . only it isn't. He buys it off trawlers that are over their quota and he freezes it. The trouble is he uses our freezer when his is full up, without a by-your-leave. That's to say he used to use ours. About a year ago, I found some packs of frozen vegetables in the bin, dumped. When I looked in the freezer, a big chest thing in the garage, I found it was full of salmon, whole bleedin' salmon. He bought it from a Norwegian crew who'd brought surplus frozen farmed salmon across to flog in Britain. The things had been dead for a year, but Chic's plan was to thaw them out and sell them as fresh wild fish to his contacts.'

'What did you do?' the DS chuckled.

'Donna and I put it all in boxes. She gave some to her friends in the university, and I spread the rest around fire stations in Edinburgh. The old fart went ape-shit when he found out, until I told him that if he ever tried something like that again he'd be in the freezer himself.' His broad black face split into a grin. 'We haven't spoken much since then.'

'That's probably just as well,' Haddock agreed. 'But it's not Chic that we came to ask you about; it's his son, Dean Francey. We're looking for him. Has he been in touch with you recently?'

'How recently?'

'Like today.'

'No. I can't speak for Donna, but I haven't heard from him for a month or more.'

Wright looked him in the eye, as he took some washed green beans from a colander and picked up his knife once again. 'You are sure of that?'

'Of course I'm sure,' he retorted. 'The little toerag's Donna's weak spot, not mine. Any contact I have with him, it's through her. What's he done?'

'We can't say,' the DS told him, 'but it's a quantum step up from his previous. We need to question him about a very serious crime.'

Rattray's eyes narrowed. 'How serious?' he murmured.

'As serious as it gets. If he should get in contact with you, we need you to urge him to hand himself in at the nearest police office.'

'I'll do more than urge him,' the man replied. 'If he comes here, and Donna isn't around, I'll sit on him until you get here. If she is . . .' he hesitated, 'it won't be so easy. She's four months pregnant, and like I said, Dino's her weak spot. Does she need to know about this at all?'

'Keeping it from her won't be possible, I'm afraid,' Haddock replied. 'We need to speak to her too, and she'll have to know why.'

'Little bastard,' Rattray growled. 'I always knew he was trouble. I hope he does come here; I'll wipe the floor with him for bringing this to our door, whatever the hell it is.'

'Please don't do that,' the DS urged. 'I'll go with a citizen's arrest, Levon, but I don't want a mark on him when he's booked in.' He paused. 'All that said, I know you think Dino's an idiot, but he must have enough brain cells to guess that this is the first place we'd go looking for him. Can you help us by suggesting other people he might go to for help?'

'Friends, you mean?'

'Yes. Has he ever mentioned any mates to you?'

'Sure. He's even brought some here. We'd a big party for Donna's twenty-fifth and he turned up with a crew. Three of them, all with daft nicknames. There was a guy he called Jagger, on account of his big floppy lips, then there was another they called Drizzle; they said it was 'cos he was thick, wet and got on your tits after a while.'

'Very good,' Wright said, 'but did these characters have real names?'

Rattray nodded. 'The Jagger fella was called Michael, Mick, I guess, and I think his second name was Smith. Drizzle, his name was Ian Harbison. I asked Dino how he knew them; he said they had the same probation officer, but I don't know if he was serious.'

'What about the third one?' Haddock asked. 'What was his nickname?'

'Her,' he was corrected. 'The third one was called Singer; she was his girlfriend, and still is as far as I know. Her name's Anna Harmony, hence the nickname.'

'Is she a probation pal too?'

'It wouldn't surprise me, although she did seem like a nice kid. If I was you, I'd be looking at these three to track down my useless, feckless brother-in-law. I'm sorry I can't give you addresses for them, but Donna mentioned something about the girl living in a student flat somewhere.'

'That makes her hard to trace,' the DS said. 'There'll be no problem finding the other two, though, through the probation service. We'll get on to them. Just one more question, and then we're off. Do you believe that Dean Francey has violence in him?'

Rattray scratched his chin as he considered the question. 'I'm not the guy to ask,' he said, eventually. 'I was a cage fighter when I was younger, so he's always been careful around me. But he has a temper on him and I could imagine it boiling over if a fella crossed him.'

'What about a female?'

'I couldn't rule that out,' he admitted. 'I reckon Dino would do most things if the price was right and there was no risk to himself.'

Sixteen

'Are you glad to be retiring, Prof?'

The little pathologist peered up at Sammy Pye, through round-framed spectacles. His eyes were the only visible part of his body, the rest being encased in a surgical gown, cap and mask.

'Would it shock you if I said that I'm not?' Joe Hutchinson replied.

'Probably not,' the DCI admitted.

'Don't get me wrong,' the professor continued. 'I know my time is up; I'm seventy years old as of last week. At the end of next month my contract with the Crown Office expires and I assume emeritus status at the university. Sarah Grace, my successor, was chosen personally by me, so I'm happy with that. My wife and I have travel plans that will involve ticking off our entire, extensive bucket list, beginning with a long, leisurely drive down to Monaco, for the Grand Prix.'

He peeled off his face mask and stepped away from the examination table, and the subject that lay on it. 'Restore the child's dignity please, Roshan,' he said to his assistant as he approached Pye, who had been standing as far away from the action as the examination room allowed.

'I'm looking forward to all of that, and to being a full-time husband, more or less. And yet,' he murmured, 'I'll feel strange, to put it mildly. It'll be like cutting myself off from a family, of sorts. I've never been a dispassionate pathologist, Sammy. I've always bonded with my subjects, and done my best to fulfil my duty towards them. Every deceased person who has come before me for examination has been a victim of something or other, be it disease, misfortune or violence, some premeditated, some not, and it's been my task to speak on their behalf, to their families, to the courts and sometimes just to God.'

'You believe in Him?' the detective asked, surprised.

'Absolutely,' Hutchinson declared. 'I believe in the existence of the incorporeal human spirit, and for me that's the same thing. I'm not talking about the old fella with the white beard, though,' he cautioned. 'I believe that the spirit is a collective of which we become part when we die.'

'Have you ever seen it?'

The little man laughed. 'Seen the soul leave the body? Of course not, Sammy: if I claimed that I'd be eternally screwed as an expert witness, would I not? No, but I have felt it. Every time I perform an autopsy I feel that I am accompanied, and that I am the guardian of the trust of the former occupant of my subject. When I get it right, my unseen companion leaves me. But when I make a mistake, as I've done half a dozen times in my career, or when I'm unable to come to a definite conclusion, as has happened much more often, then I feel reproach, for some time afterwards, and let me tell you that is not comfortable.'

'How do you feel now?' Pye asked as the two stepped into the anteroom.

'Satisfied,' Hutchinson replied. 'I won't be followed home tonight, Chief Inspector. I can tell you categorically that poor little Olivia Gates, Zena as you called her, died from asphyxiation. She suffocated.'

'She ran out of oxygen in the boot?'

'No. That wasn't airtight; I satisfied myself of that at the scene. The makeshift lining did its job too. She had no bumps, no bruises, no abrasions; she must have been placed carefully into her container.'

Pye nodded. 'I'd worked that out. The intention was to abduct her, not to kill her.'

'Exactly.'

'So what went wrong?'

'The child was asthmatic. I found dust from the foam rubber in her airways. Undoubtedly that triggered a severe attack from which she died.'

'Alone in the dark,' the DCI whispered.

'Alone in the dark,' the professor repeated. 'I'd very much like to meet the chap who put her in there,' he remarked, in a matter-of-fact tone. 'Preferably on the table in the next room.'

'I wish I could arrange that,' Pye said, 'but the best we'll be able to do is lock him up. When we do, I can't guarantee that the custody staff won't gob in his coffee, but that's as far as we can go. Thanks, Prof. I'll need to do some thinking about this.'

'Surely it'll be straightforward when you find him?'

'Not necessarily. We know where the child was abducted, but we still have to place our suspect at the scene. We know that he was driving the car when Zena was found, but we need to prove to a jury that he put her in there.'

'In that case, we have something that might help you. When Roshan undressed the child, he found inside her jacket a doll, a soft toy of Makka Pakka, a character from a TV series called

In the Night Garden. I know this,' he added, 'because my granddaughter watched it when she was a toddler.'

'So? It could have been her favourite. She might have taken it to school with her.'

'My granddaughter had outgrown the *Night Garden* by the time she was three years old,' the professor observed. 'Maybe Olivia hadn't, but my immediate assumption was that her abductor had given it to her in an attempt to keep her quiet. The doll is new, Sammy, brand new, so new that Makka Pakka has a price sticker on his bum, from Poundstretcher.'

Pye's eyes gleamed as he peeled off his sterile paper cap. 'And there's one of those in North Berwick,' he exclaimed. 'Dino, we may have pinned you down.'

Seventeen

To an extent, Mario McGuire's day had recovered from its appalling beginning. The distractions of the job had kept her at bay, but whenever he allowed his mind to drift, the awful vision of the little girl's reproving dead eyes crept back in.

The visit to Hawick had been a success. The district commander and his staff had been on the ball, and the CID unit had shown him that they were well suited to the needs of their rural community, which were very different from those of the city in which he had spent most of his career.

Bob Skinner's unusual request had been dealt with successfully, although he was concerned by the hostility of the new chief constable towards the man who had made them both. As he took a long bend, heading north on the narrow Borders road, he smiled as he thought of his last conversation with his former boss and of the way he had seemed able to read Andy Martin's slightly paranoid thoughts. He would enjoy conveying Skinner's trenchant opinion of the Scottish Police Authority, and his derision at the notion that he might ever be persuaded to chair it.

And then the road straightened out, the country music track on his iPod faded, to be replaced by the haunting title music from the TV series *The Bridge*, and in an instant the little girl was back.

'Call DCI Pye,' he said in a loud, steady tone, and his car's voice-activated phone system obeyed. The dialling tone rang out five times before the call was answered.

'Sir, what can I do for you?'

'The wee lass,' McGuire replied. 'Progress?'

'She's been identified as Olivia Regal Gates,' Pye replied, 'known as Zena. Abducted from a quiet road just outside Garvald, on her way to school with her mother, Grete Regal. She was attacked at the scene, and rushed to Accident and Emergency with massive head injuries. We have a prime suspect; all we need to do now is find him.'

The DCI paused. 'When we do, we'll need advice from the Crown Office on the charge. I've just left the autopsy. The child died from an asthmatic attack. Joe Hutchinson says we'll be struggling to sustain even a culpable homicide prosecution, let alone murder.'

'But if the mother doesn't make it,' McGuire countered. 'Even if she does, we've got him for attempted murder surely.'

'Not necessarily: we can prove he had the child when he crashed the car in Edinburgh, but there's work to be done to link him to the attack on Ms Regal.'

'What about the father?'

'That's another complication,' the DCI said. 'He's . . .'

'Bugger!' Mario McGuire barked, cutting him off in mid-sentence. 'You're not going to believe this, Sammy, but I'm just coming into Selkirk and I'm about to be pulled over by one of our patrol cars parked up ahead. It looks as if somebody's decided to do some random breath testing. I'll need to come back to you.'

The DCC pushed a button on his steering wheel to end the call, fading the music as it cut back in, then slowed, pulling into the lay-by where the traffic car was parked, its blue light flashing, and coming to a halt behind a white Range Rover. Its driver was being questioned by a uniformed constable; as he watched, he saw him hand a breath test machine back to the officer who studied it, smiled and nodded.

A second constable approached his own car, a youngster, one of the new breed, the DCC could tell, so full of zeal and enthusiasm that he barely reacted as McGuire lowered his window to reveal his uniform and the silver badges of rank on his shoulder.

'Routine document check, sir,' he announced.

'Bollocks,' the DCC replied, amiably. 'The number recognition system will tell you that this vehicle is taxed and insured. There's no such thing as a routine check of a private vehicle any more. It's a cover for something else.'

The young cop stiffened. 'Can I see your driving licence, sir?'

'No.'

'I require you to show it, to prove that you're licensed to drive this vehicle.'

McGuire maintained a steady smile, but his eyes were flashing danger signs that a wiser man would have read.

'And I choose not to,' he said, 'because my private address is on it. That's not something I'm prepared to share. However,' he paused, 'I will show you this. Read it carefully.' He handed over his warrant card.

The second constable, a woman, joined her younger partner. 'Is there a problem here?' she began, then saw the DCC and realised that there was. 'I'm sorry, sir,' she began.

'Too late for that,' McGuire snapped. 'Were you instructed to do this by a senior officer or are you just filling in time? Don't even think about bullshitting me,' he warned, as he took his ID back from the other cop, 'for I will check.'

'It's our own initiative,' the female PC admitted.

'How many arrests have you made?'

She reddened. 'None.'

'Then it's about time for you to resume more productive duties, don't you think?'

'Yes, sir.' She nudged her colleague. 'Come on, Chris.'

'No,' the DCC said, 'we're not quite done here. Gimme your breathalyser.'

He took the machine from the constable named Chris, blew into it, looked at the reading and handed it back. 'Another innocent motorist hassled,' he growled, his eyes never leaving the young officer. 'You've got a decision to make, son. Either you make a radical attitude adjustment in dealing with members of the public, or you look for another line of work. My memory's long and so's my reach; I'll be watching you.'

McGuire turned on his engine and pulled out into the traffic, cruising slowly through Selkirk, heading north towards Edinburgh, and wondering whether he would have been less hard on that young cop if their paths had crossed on another day.

He had travelled for a few miles and was back in open country before he remembered his unfinished conversation with Sammy Pye. He opened his mouth to issue a voice command, but in that same instant his phone announced an incoming call.

He frowned, but pressed the receive button, answering with a curt, 'Yes?'

'Is that Deputy Chief Constable McGuire?' The voice was smooth, English and ever so slightly annoying.

'It is,' he confirmed. 'And who are you, sir?'

'My name is Rafe Blackett, Captain, Royal Navy, currently on assignment to the Ministry of Defence in Whitehall.'

'Then please tell me, Captain Blackett,' the DCC asked, 'how did you get this number?'

'It was given me by your chief constable's office.'

Cheers, Andy, he thought. 'I see. So tell me, Captain, how can the Scottish Police Service help the Ministry of Defence?'

'You can give me an update,' Blackett replied, 'on a situation that may affect one of our serving officers; his name is Lieutenant David Gates.'

'Never heard of . . .' McGuire began, stopping as the surname flipped a switch in his memory. Simultaneously, he guessed correctly what Sammy Pye's problem had been. 'Wait a minute, Gates, you said?'

'That's correct.'

'Do you have a home address for Lieutenant Gates?'

'I see from his file that he lives in a place called Garvald, in East Lothian, Scotland, when he's not on service.'

'What else does that file tell you?'

'That his next of kin is his partner, a Ms Regal, and that they have one child, aged five.' The man gave a short impatient snort. 'Thing is, Mr McGuire, earlier today a young lady from your outfit, Detective Constable Wright, managed to get herself put through to me, not once but twice. On each occasion she more or less demanded that she be put in contact with Gates. She even hinted that she would go to one of our ministers, a Scots MP, if necessary.'

'Are you calling me to complain that she was rude?' the DCC exclaimed.

'No, no. The young lady was perfectly civil, but she was

insistent that she had to speak to him at once. I'm afraid that I was equally insistent that she couldn't, as he's operational. I asked her what it was about, but she declined to tell me. We left it that Gates would be asked to contact her as soon as that is practically possible.'

'I see.' McGuire saw that he was approaching a lay-by on the single carriageway; he pulled into it, off the highway. 'I can understand DC Wright's reticence, Captain,' he continued. 'She was following protocol, that was all. Equally, I can understand that you have your operating procedures too.'

'I thought you might,' Blackett murmured. 'Thing is,' he went on, 'this has been preying on me. I feel I need to know anything that affects Gates.'

'Which led you to jump the command chain and go straight to the chief, and through him to me?'

'Yes.'

'But you're not going to tell me why?'

'I don't believe I'm allowed to, sir.'

'In that case, I'll do some guessing. I'll speculate that you can't let us speak to Gates because you can't speak to him yourself. That suggests to me that he's either an intelligence officer, in the field, or that he's in an operational situation that prevents communications. Force me to choose between those and I'll guess that he's on a nuclear sub, since their locations are just about the biggest military secret we have.' He chuckled. 'If you like you can cough once for yes, twice for no.'

The car was silent for a few seconds. Then the sound of a single forced cough came through the speakers.

'In that case,' McGuire said, 'I'll share something with you. The news we have for Lieutenant Gates is very bad. This morning his partner and daughter were attacked on a lonely road on their way to the local primary school. When our people arrived they found only Ms Regal; their assumption was that it was a hit-and-run. Not long afterwards the child's body was found in the boot of a stolen car that was involved in an accident, twenty miles away.'

'My God,' the captain gasped. 'What are you saying to me?'

'Nothing definite, only an assumption: that the abduction of the child was the purpose of the attack. I've just heard the autopsy findings: she died from an acute asthmatic attack. She wasn't harmed in any other way.'

'Have you arrested anyone?'

'Not yet, but my officers tell me they have a prime suspect.'

'What was the motive for the attack?' Blackett asked. 'Ransom?'

'We're not there yet,' McGuire told him. 'We have to catch our suspect first and see what he can tell us. You'll understand that I'm not connected with the investigation at ground level. I don't have all the detail.'

'I appreciate that. Sir . . .' The captain stopped, as if he was taking time to choose his words. 'Might I suggest that you consider another motive, that this awful crime might be aimed at Lieutenant Gates because of what he does?'

'I'm considering that already, chum. But it's not at the top of my list. If Gates's job is so bloody secret that you can't tell him his kid is dead until he's, he's . . . non-operational, how is anybody likely to know about it to target him?'

'These people have their sources.'

'From the little I've heard of the suspect, he doesn't fit the "these people" category. I'll take what we've discussed on board in our investigation . . .'

Blackett cut in. 'Discreetly, Mr McGuire, yes? After all, I haven't really told you anything.'

'I said that I would take it on board, not "we". If I need to brief the senior investigating officer on Gates's status, I will, but it'll be for his ears only . . . although frankly my officers are intelligent and will have guessed what the score is.

'Make no mistake, we do need to speak to Gates as soon as you can make it happen, even though he does have the best alibi I've come across in my entire police career.'

'I'll take that to the admiral,' the captain promised. 'There are channels.' He paused. 'The mother,' he ventured. 'You didn't say how she is.'

'The last I heard,' McGuire replied, 'we may be able to speak to Gates before we can talk to her . . . if we ever can.'

Eighteen

'It's a bonus, Sarge, isn't it?' Jackie Wright said. 'Jagger and Drizzle working in the same place?'

'That's assuming that they haven't been taking the piss out of their probation officer,' Haddock replied. 'He didn't seem too familiar with them when I spoke to him.'

'What were they done for? Did he tell you?'

'They've both got records of petty theft, but most recently it was shoplifting in Primark, Debenhams and Topman. Apparently they were pretty good at it; they were never caught in the act in the stores, only identified on CCTV after the event.'

The DC frowned. 'If they got out of the shops with the stuff,' she wondered aloud, 'how were they caught?'

'The silly buggers decided to sell it on a market stall in Dalkeith. Strangers stick out like the proverbial in places like that and attract the attention of Trading Standards. They were nicked on day two. They tried to say they'd bought the gear in good faith themselves, but that's where the in-store cameras came into play.'

'They were lucky they got off so lightly.'

The DS nodded. 'They were, since they were on probation already for previous offences, but they must have had a good lawyer. He persuaded the sheriff that they were saveable and that a mix of fine, community service and extended probation would be a better deal for society than housing and feeding them for six months.'

'They're probably nicking burgers now,' Wright chuckled, as they walked into the fast food outlet in St John's Road.

Haddock stopped just inside the doorway, and looked around. The takeaway menu was displayed above the service counter, and its varied aromas pervaded the premises.

There were two people in the process of being served, but only one attendant, a tall young man in a striped uniform bearing the chain logo, and a peaked brown cap from which a few strands of hair protruded. There was a wide hatch behind him, through which the two detectives could see other people working.

'That's a double cheeseburger with Mexican salsa,' he announced to the first customer, handing over a square polystyrene box. He looked across at the two newcomers, his wide, slightly sensuous mouth open in a smile. 'Hey, they're stormin' the place now,' he called out. 'Corstorphine must be starvin'. And you, Alicia, you're the hauf-pound venison wi' piccalilli, and fries on the side, aye?'

A squat, dyed young blonde in a parka nodded. 'What is venison onyway?'

'Bambi; ye're eating fuckin' Bambi.'

She wrinkled her nose. 'That's gross; poor wee soul. Comes tae us all, though. And a cannae Coke, Jagger,' she added. 'Dinna forget the Coke.'

'How could Ah, hen? It's the same order every day: speciality burger and a cannae Coke. Dae ye no fancy a wee bit of variety in yer life?'

125

'Such as?'

'Ah dinna ken.' He winked. 'How about a hot sausage roll?'

'In yer dreams, ya cheeky bastard,' the girl chuckled, as she took her order. 'See ye ramorra.'

'In ma fuckin' nightmares,' the attendant murmured as she left. 'Now, folks,' he exclaimed, as he turned to face the two detectives. 'Which of our delights would youse like? How can I help youse?'

'By finding somewhere quiet where we can talk?' Haddock replied, showing his warrant card. 'That's who I am, Mr Smith, and this is DC Wright. We need to ask you about a friend of yours, Dean Francey.'

'How dae ye ken my name?' the man asked, perplexed.

'Let's just say you fit the description we were given, Jagger. How about your pal Drizzle? We need him too.'

'Aye, he's here,' Jagger confirmed. 'But we're workin'. We cannae just leave.'

An unnoticed door in the brightly coloured wall behind the counter opened and a second man appeared. 'What's up here?' he demanded. 'I'm Bert Stewart, the manager.'

'CID,' the DS told him. 'We need a word with Messrs Smith and Harbison.'

'What? Now, like? Can it no' wait till they finish their shifts?'

'No.'

'Are they in bother?'

'Not as far as I know,' Haddock said, amiably. 'We hope they might be able to help us with our inquiries. Fifteen minutes max, and they'll be back on duty . . .' he smiled, 'unless they've confessed, of course.'

'All right,' the manager conceded. 'Use my office. It's the wee room in the corridor behind the kitchen; the one on the left, the other's the lav. Take him through, Michael, and collect your mate on the way. Tell Coleen I'll man the counter.'

Jagger lifted a flap in the counter to allow the two officers access, then led them into the kitchen, where two young people stood, one male, one female, each wearing a grease-spattered apron. 'Drizzle,' he said to the man, 'these police want tae talk tae us about Dino.'

'That's very interesting, Jagger,' Jackie Wright began, as soon as the office door had closed behind them. 'When we mentioned Francey outside, your first question was how we knew your name. I'd been expecting you to ask what Dino was supposed to have done. Does that mean you know?'

Michael Smith nodded. 'Aye. It's that fuckin' fish, right?'

'And what fuckin' fish would that be?' she asked.

'The dozen monster halibut that he's got in ma granny's freezer, waiting to be thawed out and flogged on tae a Chinese restaurant in Broxburn. Buggrit, Ah kent they werenae kosher.'

'Halibut are kosher, as I recall,' Haddock remarked. 'I visited a Jewish restaurant in Glasgow last year and I'm sure there was halibut on the menu.'

Jagger stared at him. 'Eh?'

'Never mind,' the DS said. 'As it happens, we're not interested in your granny's freezer. If I were you I'd advise her to donate them to the Edinburgh food bank.'

'Then what is this about?' Calm eyes stared at the detectives from beneath knitted eyebrows and a furrowed forehead. It was the first indication that Ian 'Drizzle' Harbison could speak.

Haddock ignored the question. 'When did you last see Dino, either of you?'

'Saturday night,' Jagger answered. 'We met them . . . him and Singer . . . in Lacey's, at the top o' Leith Walk. They'd been tae the Omni tae see that Hobbit film, and we saw them there after.'

'Lacey's!' Wright exclaimed. 'Are you telling me that Dean Francey took his girlfriend to a lap-dancing club?'

The loose lips beamed. 'She fuckin' works there,' he laughed. 'We get staff rate on the cocktails. We gie her the money and she gets them in for us. The boss disnae mind; she's his best dancer.'

'Was she working that night?' the DS asked.

'Naw. Night aff.'

'How did Dino seem?'

'Same as usual. Edgy fucker, looking for bother.'

'In what way?'

'Singer.' Drizzle's one-word answer was emphatic.

Haddock stared at him. 'What do you mean?'

'He means that when she's about, it's always dodgy,' Jagger explained. 'She's a looker, right? So she's gonnae get looked at. And if Dino disnae fancy the way anybody looks at her . . . Well, it's "Here we fuckin' go", is it no'. Of course, Singer, she kens she's a looker and she's maybe no' beyond givin' the eye tae some geezer when Dino's got his back tae her.'

'I get the picture,' the DS said. 'Yet Dino has no convictions for assault.'

Jagger smiled. 'Naw, 'cos nothin's gonnae happen when Drizzle's aboot. In't that right, Driz?'

'Are you his bodyguard?' Wright asked.

'No,' Drizzle rumbled. 'I'm his mate.'

'Trust me,' Jagger told her, 'where we go, naebody's goin' tae try it on wi Drizzle. That's no tae say,' he added, 'that Dino cannae handle himsel', 'cos he can. But Drizzle? Different.'

'Where were you this morning?' Haddock asked Harbison, abruptly.

'He wis here,' his friend replied. 'Fryin' fuckin' bacon, fae seven thirty till nine thirty. This place dis a good breakfast trade, then we knock aff till lunchtime. Why dae ye want tae know?'

'No special reason. When do you expect to see Dean Francey again?'

'The morra. He's supposed tae be comin' here at twelve tae collect a couple o' thae halibut. Ah've tae take them oot o' ma granny's freezer the night, ken, so they'll be thawed for the customer and he'll think they're fresh.'

'I'd leave them where they are if I were you.'

'Why's that?'

Haddock looked him in the eye. 'If we haven't caught up with him by then, we'll be waiting here for him. Although,' he added, 'the chances of him turning up are about the same as Dunfermline winning the Premier League.'

'Is he in real trouble?' Jagger asked, his cockiness abating for the first time.

'Oh yes.'

'Is it that kid? The one in the car?'

Three heads turned to look at Ian Harbison.

'Why should it be?' the DS murmured.

'I saw the lunchtime news on the kitchen TV,' he said. 'There was a report from Fort Kinnaird, and the cop on the scene gave a description that could have been Dino.'

'You're supposed to be thick,' Wright observed.

'No, miss,' Drizzle replied. 'But I don't mind people believing that. It's good to be underestimated. You want Dino for the dead kid, don't you?'

'Yes, we do,' Haddock admitted.

'In that case, I'll help you find him.'

'Hold on here, Driz,' his friend intervened. 'This is the polis.'

'Yes, and they're looking for our pal because he had the body of a child in the boot of his car. Leaving aside the fact that it would be a jail time offence to help him, it's time you showed just a trace of personal morality. We're thieves, Jagger, that's all; so don't go quoting some stupid Mafia code of silence at me.'

He turned to Haddock. 'If Dino's in trouble, Singer's the only one he'll go to. I don't know where she lives, because he never said, but she's due to be working at Lacey's tonight. That's all I can tell you, but you're welcome.'

He stopped for a few seconds then added, 'No, one more thing. Dino didn't kill a child; he's a fool, he's a thug and he's a coward, but he wouldn't do that.'

Nineteen

'Thanks, Sauce,' Pye said. 'Do you fancy a trip to Lacey's this evening? You and me,' he added. 'Young Jackie would be a wee bit out of place there.'

'What's that?' the DS retorted. 'Denying her overtime on gender grounds? You'll have the discrimination police after you, Sammy.'

'Maybe so, but I wouldn't take a rabbit to a greyhound track either. As for the overtime bit, that's an issue these days. We've all got budgets, every CID area, and we can't exceed them. I'll meet you there at seven. My apologies to Cheeky if she had other plans for you.'

'She hasn't, but if I tell her where we're going she might want to come. There's a pole-dancing exercise class down in Leith; she's been talking about signing up. It's all the rage, apparently; you should tell Ruth about it.'

'With the cost of child care these days,' the DCI murmured, 'that might come in handy. I hear these girls make a lot of money in tips.'

Haddock laughed. 'It's as well for you that you do my job appraisal, gaffer, or I might be tempted to tell her that.'

'Yield not to temptation, for yielding is sin. And as you say, it's

131

bad for your job prospects. What did you make of Jagger and Drizzle?'

'They're a contradiction. Levon Rattray told us that Harbison was a thicko, but it's the other way around. Jagger's the idiot, not him. The probation officer told us that Drizzle is a very good thief, but I didn't understand that till I met him. He has the gift of invisibility. He could be standing on his own in a big room and nobody would notice him. The market stall was Jagger's idea, apparently. Drizzle didn't know about it; he only got drawn in when the investigating officers looked at the CCTV footage.'

'Is he worth keeping an eye on,' Pye asked, 'given that we don't see Dino as a mastermind?'

'Let's not ignore him, but he gave up his mate in a heartbeat when he realised why we wanted him.'

'Fair enough. What about Donna Rattray? Have you spoken to her yet?'

'We're at the university now,' Haddock replied. 'We're waiting for her to finish. Where are you?'

'I'm at the Western General. Grete Regal was transferred there from the Royal because that's where the neurosurgeons are. She's just out of the theatre and I'm waiting to speak to the woman who operated on her. You speak to Dino's sister, then go back to the mobile HQ unit at Fort Kinnaird. I'll meet you there, and we can head for Lacey's together.'

Pye ended the call, then switched off his phone to comply with a warning in the hallway of the building where the surgical wards were located. He followed a series of signs that led him towards the intensive care unit, to which he had been directed.

The entrance was secure, with a video camera and intercom. 'DCI Pye,' he announced to the microphone, 'here to see Miss Sonia Iqbal.'

'Come in when you hear the buzzer,' a voice instructed. 'Then it's the first door on the right.'

He obeyed the instructions and found himself in a room with eight others, some smiling, others intense, but all clearly under stress; patients' relatives, he assumed, wondering if any of them were connected to Grete Regal but not ready to ask.

Five minutes passed, each one observed impatiently on his watch, before the door opened and a soft voice said, 'Mr Pye, please.' He followed the summons and stepped out into the corridor.

Sonia Iqbal was a tall woman, with smooth brown skin and eyes to match. She was wrapped in a long colourful robe and her shiny black hair was pulled behind her head in a bun.

'Can we talk here, Chief Inspector?' she asked, in a thick accent that he found impossible to place, but a small Egyptian flag badge pinned to her dress gave a large clue to her nationality. 'This is as private as I can manage.'

'It'll do,' Pye replied. 'What can you tell me about Ms Regal? How is she?'

'She is very seriously ill, I am afraid, she was hit very hard, several times, by a large stone.'

'You're sure about that?'

'I found fragments embedded in her cranium. Does that knowledge assist you?'

'I have a forensic team at the scene of the attack. It'll help them to have something specific to look for. What's Ms Regal's prognosis? Will I be able to speak to her soon?'

'Mr Pye, you may never be able to speak to her. She has suffered bleeding in her brain, and it has swollen. To relieve the pressure this has caused I have had to remove a large section of her skull, and insert it in her abdomen. We do this to keep the bone nourished so that it can be replaced at a later date.' She grimaced. 'However, she will have to recover for that to happen, and I can give you no guarantee that she will. We will keep her chemically comatose for as long as is necessary, but beyond that she will only come round in her own time. She may die, and if she survives she may have a degree of neurological damage.'

'I see,' Pye murmured. 'Poor lass. It may be she's better off unconscious; that way she doesn't have to deal with the fact that her child's dead.'

'Her child?' the surgeon gasped. 'She was attacked too?'

'Abducted. She died from natural causes. You weren't to know; you must have been operating on her for most of today. Do you know if any of her relatives have turned up?' he asked. 'Her partner's away, and we're making contact with him. I've been busy with the investigation, but I've had officers calling the contacts on her phone to locate other family members. I haven't had time to check on their progress.'

Ms Iqbal nodded. 'There is an aunt, Mrs Rainey. She wants to see Ms Regal as soon as she's out of recovery and installed in the ICU. She is in the room; if you wait here I will fetch her.'

'Sure.' As the surgeon had said, the corridor seemed to be the most private place in the intensive care unit; beyond, green-clad staff seemed to be in one continuous bustle. The detective knew why they were so busy. A few years before, his mother had spent a couple of days in a similar unit in another hospital, after life-saving surgery; he understood from that time how intensive the unit's care was.

'Are you the policeman?' The voice that spoke the question was authoritative, and although its foreign accent was not as strong as that of the surgeon, it was there nonetheless.

He turned to face its owner, to find that she was almost as tall as he. She had been seated on her own in the waiting room, by the window, as if she was trying to position herself as far from anyone else as possible. 'That's right, DCI Pye, ScotServe; Edinburgh Division CID. Mrs Rainey, yes?'

'Indeed, Ingrid Rainey; Grete is my niece. What has happened to her? And what of our little Zena? Where is she?'

Suddenly, Pye felt exposed in the open corridor. He looked at the surgeon, who was standing behind the woman. 'Ms Iqbal,' he asked, 'is there somewhere we can go?'

Understanding the situation, she frowned and nodded. 'There is a staff room,' she said. 'I will take you there, and make sure you are not disturbed.'

She led them into the unit, turning right at the end of the corridor, into another, which ended in a green door with a keypad entry, marked 'Staff only'. She punched in a code. 'There you are; you can lock it from the inside. I'll tell the senior nurse that you are here, and you can advise him when you go.'

'What have you been told, Mrs Rainey?' Pye asked, as soon as he and the aunt were alone and seated.

'The person who called said that Grete had been involved in an incident, that was how she put it, and that she had been taken to the emergency unit in Edinburgh Royal Infirmary. I went there at once, but they sent me here. The surgeon tells me Grete's life is in great danger. What has happened, sir? And where is our Zena? Is she safe? For her daddy is away.'

The DCI took a deep breath. Slowly and carefully, he took her through the events of the day, stage by stage, pausing at times to allow the woman to absorb the story she was being told. Twice he asked her if she wanted him to pause, but she refused, her expression grim as she held herself together. He finished with a summary of the pathologist's findings.

'And the monster who did this?' Ingrid Rainey asked icily when he had finished; her mouth quivered and her eyes were moist, but her voice was strong and controlled. 'Have you caught him?'

'No,' Pye admitted, 'but we believe we've identified at least one person involved. We've alerted ports and airports as a matter of course, and if we don't arrest him by the end of this day we'll issue a public appeal, name, photograph, everything.'

'Be sure you do arrest him,' she hissed. 'My poor girls.'

He nodded. 'Guys like me,' he murmured, 'we're trained not to become emotionally involved in our investigations. But I'm a father, my boss is a father and the man who found Zena, he is as well, so trust me, none of us will rest until this man is convicted. We have to be painstaking in everything we do, and we have to be very cautious in our public statements so as not to infringe the suspect's legal rights, but trust me, we are breathing down his neck.'

'As far as I am concerned,' the aunt snapped, 'this person has no rights.'

'But the law says he does. Mrs Rainey,' he went on, 'this is a terrible thing for you to have to cope with. Are you all right? Is there someone who can be with you?'

'No,' she replied, 'there is not. My husband and I are no longer together; he is in London with another woman, and welcome to her as long as he keeps paying me what he promised in our settlement. My sister Tora, my twin, Grete's mother, she died seven years ago.

'We are Norwegian; Tora and I came to Edinburgh as engineering students, over thirty years ago. We never returned. I married Innes, my husband, and gave up my career. Tora, she worked for an Edinburgh company, until she had Grete. She took time out, but went back when the child was old enough to be left.'

'And Grete's father?' Pye inquired.

Ingrid Rainey pursed her lips. 'He was never a major part of her life. Tora married John Regal when she became pregnant, but soon came to regret it. She threw him out when Grete was five. The man was involved in criminality of some sort, but I never knew what.'

Pye leaned forward on his chair. 'But he's still alive, yes?'

'I have not heard that he is dead.'

'Then where is he? She's still his daughter and Olivia . . . Zena . . . was his granddaughter.'

'I do not know,' she admitted. 'Grete never mentions him; I do not believe he has ever seen Zena.'

'What can you tell me about Lieutenant Gates?'

'David is an engineer, as I was. He is a naval officer, as you know, but I have never been encouraged to ask about his work.'

'He's a specialist?' the DCI murmured. 'I didn't know that. Does he have family? Apart from John Regal, does Zena have grandparents?'

Mrs Rainey nodded. 'Yes, she does . . . or rather she did, the poor little darling. Their names are Richard and Julia, and they live in Dirleton.'

'Are they retired, or do they still work?'

'They are not so old, but they do not work any longer. They had a business, a company that made skylight windows, but they sold it a few years ago. They have another home in Portugal and they spend a lot of time there, so they do not see as much of Zena as I do.'

'Thanks. They may have been contacted already, in the same way that you were. If they're away we'll try to get in touch with them in Portugal. I'll check once we're finished here. Where do you live, Mrs Rainey?' he continued.

'A little closer to Grete, in Haddington; in the Nungate, by the river.' Her chin trembled, the first sign of loss of control. 'Little Zena spent a lot of time with me and she loved to play there. We had to watch her, to stop her falling in. You know how adventurous little ones can be.' Then her face froze again and her eyes hardened.

'Grete looked after her so well,' she said. 'We both did. And now this terrible senseless thing has happened.' She stared at Pye. 'This man, this creature. Why would he want to hurt Grete so badly and to take our precious child?'

'At this moment we can only form theories about that,' he replied, 'but the main line of our thinking is that he didn't act alone, that he had an accomplice, and that he was paid to abduct Zena. When we find him, we'll know more.'

'Be sure you do.'

'We will, however long it takes us.' He shifted in his chair. 'Is Grete a full-time mum,' he asked, 'or does she have a job?'

'She is a graphic designer. She is self-employed and has a little studio beside the cottage. She is quite successful; also it gives her something to do, with David being away at sea for so long.'

'Is she on good terms with all her customers, or has she had any business difficulties that you know of?'

Mrs Rainey frowned. 'There is one client she is having trouble with,' she replied. 'It was a business in Edinburgh; she did a lot of corporate identity work for them. She redesigned their logo and all their stationery. They approved her proposal and she spent a lot of time on it. She produced a manual for them and commissioned the print work on their behalf. She paid for it herself, assuming that she would be reimbursed. But when she submitted her final account . . . it was a lot of money . . . they were slow to pay.'

'What did she do?'

'Grete is not a confrontational person, Chief Inspector; also she has no commercial sense. Effectively I manage her company. After a couple of months I called the people. They promised payment but nothing happened. After another few weeks I wrote to them, and had a letter back saying that the matter was in hand. Those very words.'

'What happened next?'

'Next it all got really nasty. Still there was no money, so I sent a second letter, this time from a solicitor. This time the reply came from someone else, accountants. It said that the client's company had been bought by another business, after it had been closed, wound up, liquidated. There was no money to pay Grete.

'Naturally I went back to the lawyer. He advised that I had to pursue her customer personally for the debt, and so I did. I went to court on Grete's behalf and I won. The money was still not paid. Now, the lawyer has taken charge and is seeking another order to recover the debt, by selling the customer's assets if necessary.'

'How much are we talking about?' Pye asked. 'Do you know?'

'I believe it is just over fifty thousand pounds,' Mrs Rainey said. 'Grete will not get it all, I was told, for there is not enough money there, but there will be some once the assets are realised. I am unhappy about it. And so is Grete, for another reason.'

'I'm not surprised.'

'Ah, but I do not think you understand. It is not losing money that makes Grete sad. There will be enough to pay for the printing costs that she incurred on the client's behalf. It will only be her own time that she loses. No, she is upset because the people involved will lose their home, their car, everything.'

'It's a hard old world,' the DCI remarked. 'I know because I work in it. If people have broken the criminal law they have to face the consequences, and it's the same in civil matters. If a court finds that a company has behaved improperly, its directors can't just fold it up and walk away. There is nothing that your niece should feel guilty about. If you'd come to me instead of going to the civil court I might have ended up charging the client with fraud.'

'But Grete is kind. She never did a single thing in her life to deserve how that company treated her, nor to deserve what has happened to her today.' Finally tears tracked down Ingrid Rainey's stolid face. 'You know I am not sure that I want her to live. That may be terrible, but it is true. I cannot bear for her to wake up to find that she has lost her baby.'

'Yeah,' Pye whispered. 'I don't know how I'd feel in those shoes.'

He paused as the woman dabbed at her eyes.

'The client,' he began when she was composed. 'Can you recall the name, of the company or of the owner?'

'They are the same. It is Mackail.'

It was Pye's turn to frown. *I know that name*, he thought.

Twenty

'I have as little to do with my father as I possibly can,' Donna Rattray confessed. 'He's a . . .' Exasperation showed clearly in her expression. 'A chancer: that's what he is. There's never been any certainty with him, none at all. He's driven my mother crazy over the years. She works, she's a cleaner, but she only ever earned enough to clothe Dean and me when we were young, and herself. Dad's never had a proper steady income as such; she's never known where the next penny was coming from, never been able to plan anything, never had a holiday. Any time she suggests that, he always says the same thing. "What do we need a holiday for? We live in North Berwick." That's my dad. He's interested in nobody but himself.'

She, Haddock and Wright were standing in the reception hall at Queen Margaret University, the meeting place they had chosen when she and the detective constable had spoken by telephone. Haddock had chosen to begin the discussion obliquely, not to reveal at once the real reason for their visit.

'And yet,' he said, 'the pennies do keep coming in, don't they?'

'I'll give him that,' Donna conceded. 'They do. Somehow or other Mum still has a roof over her head, and the fridge is never empty. He goes out in that silly boat of his with his silly pots

141

and always seems to catch enough lobsters and crabs to keep the family afloat.'

'Is that all he does?' Wright asked. 'Doesn't he have any sidelines?'

The woman's face flushed; it was only a slight change of shade, but enough to be noticed. 'He buys and sells stuff,' she admitted, 'on the side, but I know very little about it.'

'You mean the fish?' Haddock murmured.

'Yes, but . . . Look, he might be all the things I've just told you, but he's my father, so don't expect me to shop him.'

'It's all right,' the DS told her. 'We know all about the fish, but it's not our concern.'

Her complexion went from pink to red. 'I'll bloody kill Levon!' she exclaimed.

'That's not the sort of thing you should be saying to two police officers,' Haddock chuckled. 'But it wasn't only him. We were told about it as well by a friend of your brother, Michael Smith.'

'Who's he?'

'You might know him as Jagger.'

A look of disgust flashed across Donna's attractive face. 'Him! Dean knows what I think about him. Has he got my brother involved in that silly business again?'

'We're under the impression it was the other way around,' the DS said. 'Dean supplying the fish and Jagger storing it . . . or Jagger's granny, to be completely accurate.'

She threw her head back, gazing at the ceiling. 'I'm under no illusions about my brother,' she admitted, 'but I keep on trying to convince myself that it's all Dad's fault for the way he was brought up. It isn't. Dad might be a chancer, and a bit of a con man, but he isn't a thief.' She looked at Haddock once again. 'Is Dean in trouble?'

'Yes. Have you heard from him today?'

'There was a missed call on my mobile,' she replied. 'It was from Dean, timed just after ten. But that was all; just that one.'

'Do you walk to work?' Jackie Wright asked. 'We saw a car in your driveway.'

'We have one each. I've got a wee Toyota. Most days I drive here, even though it's not far.'

'And park here?'

'Of course.'

'Is your car still there?'

Donna Rattray stared at the DC. 'Why shouldn't it be?'

'Just wondering. Can you see it from here?'

'Yes.' Donna raised a hand, pointing across the car park in the open area outside. 'There it . . .' She stopped. 'It's not,' she exclaimed. 'It's gone! Are you bloody psychic?'

'Sometimes,' Wright said. 'Does Dean ever drive it?'

'Yes, quite often. He can't insure one himself, with his record.'

'Does he have a key?'

'Yes. Are you saying that he . . .'

'That's exactly what we're saying,' Haddock replied. 'Colour?'

'White. It's the Aygo model. The little . . .' she hissed.

The DS handed her a card and a pen. 'Write the number down there.' She obeyed; he handed it to the DC. 'Call it in, Jackie.'

'This is more serious than fish, isn't it?' Donna said quietly.

'Yes it is,' the DS told her. 'I'm afraid we've got some bad news for you, about your kid brother.'

Twenty-One

'How did she take it?' Sammy Pye asked, just before he bit into his burger.

'Utter denial,' Haddock told him. 'What big Levon said was right. Dean is Donna's weak spot.'

'There is no chance, I suppose, that he could just have stolen Cosie from Fort Kinnaird, after someone else had left it?' The DS stared back at him, both eyebrows raised theatrically. 'No, there isn't,' the DCI chuckled. 'Forget I said that.'

'Remember the Makka Pakka doll that was found on the wee girl?'

'Yes, of course.'

'Control had a message from Lucy Tweedie in North Berwick; it's just been passed to me. She went along to Poundstretcher herself. The boy on the till remembered selling one to Dino yesterday. He remembered because he knows him, and he laughed when he bought it. He even asked him who it was for. Francey claimed it was for his niece. The lad asked him when Donna had a kid, and Dino changed his story. It became his girlfriend's niece.'

'Has anyone come up with an address for this Anna Harmony yet?'

'Not a sniff; she's a mystery. There's nobody of that name holding a National Insurance number anywhere in Britain, or a passport, or a driving licence.'

'The story was, she lived in a student flat,' Pye reminded his sergeant. 'Have the team checked the universities and colleges?'

'Yes. No trace of a student with that name.' He paused, to drink from a large mug of tea. 'However, we asked Donna Rattray about her and she said she has an east European accent. I'm wondering whether Harmony might not be her real name.'

'We may find out at Lacey's. Let's go.'

The two detectives finished their snacks and left the mobile command unit, heading for Pye's car, which was parked close by. The shopping mall was still busy; most of the units were closed, but the newly opened multiscreen cinema was doing good business.

'How long will we keep the HQ van here?' Haddock asked.

'Another twenty-four hours, max,' his boss replied. 'The BMW's gone to the lab for examination, and I doubt if any more witnesses are going to turn up. We might not need any more, truth be told.' He paused to press his unlock key.

'There have been developments that you don't know about,' he continued as he slid in behind the steering wheel.

'I thought you were looking pleased with yourself,' the DS chuckled, fastening his seat belt.

'On two fronts; I had a report from the forensic team at the scene of the attack and the abduction at Garvald. They've recovered the rock that Grete was hit with. It had been tossed into some bushes, but there was plenty of blood and hair still on it.'

'Do they think they'll find the attacker's DNA on it?'

'Unless he was wearing gloves, they're hopeful. Dean Francey

145

wasn't, on the CCTV we've seen, and none were found inside the car.'

'That's assuming Francey was the attacker,' Haddock pointed out.

'Granted, but my money's on him because there's another link. We have the three friends, Maxwell, Hazel and Dean. Maxwell's the link to the car. Dean's the driver, found with the child's body in the boot. And then there's Hazel.'

'What about her?'

'Grete Regal had a legal problem in her design business. A client defaulted on her, leaving her stuck with supplier costs that she'd met herself in the expectation of payment. She won a court judgement against that client, on a personal basis, a short time ago. Her aunt said that she's been pressing Grete to execute it to recover the debt. That would involve seizing his assets, and the only thing he has of sufficient value is his equity in his mortgaged home. The client's name is Hector Mackail: Hazel's dad.'

'Wow!' Haddock murmured, reading the DCI's thoughts as he started his engine and moved off. 'Are you thinking that Hazel put friend Dino up to kidnapping Grete's child as a means of making her lay off her dad, using friend Maxwell's uncle's car to do it?'

'It's a line of inquiry. A kid that age, I doubt it, but could it be her father did? Still, we have a way to go before we get there,' Pye added. 'We need to catch Dino and have him point the finger.'

The journey into the city centre passed mostly in silence. They were passing Meadowbank Stadium before the detective sergeant spoke.

'How are you doing?' he murmured.

'Okay,' Pye replied.

'I don't think so. Sammy, you're not long back from witnessing the post-mortem examination of a five-year-old child. If I was in your shoes, if I was the DCI and you were the DS, you'd still have been there, because I'd have fucking delegated it, as sure as God made wee green apples. That's what makes you a better gaffer than I'll ever be, by the way. But you don't go through something like that and come out of it feeling okay.'

'Maybe not. I'll concede that. But it's not something you share with anyone.'

'Did you see the mother too?'

Pye shook his head. 'No, I bottled that. Anyway there was no need, and no point. Grete's unconscious and will be for some time; it's possible she'll never wake up. If she does, she won't have a crowd of relatives at her bedside, just her formidable aunt. Mother's dead, and father's estranged. We need to find him, if we can; whereabouts unknown at the moment. That'll be another job for our Jackie tomorrow.'

As he spoke, he swung his car round into Royal Terrace, then pulled into a parking space he had spotted. 'We'll walk from here,' he said. 'It's just round the corner, in Elm Row.'

'Do you know the place?' Haddock asked.

'I've been to Lacey's once,' he admitted, 'at a stag night.'

'Rough?'

'Not that bad.'

'I'd never heard of it until it came up today. I thought all the pole-dancing activity went on up at the pubic triangle, in the West Port.'

'No, not all; just most of it. You used to live there, didn't you?'

'Yup.'

'What was it like?'

'Interesting.'

There was a burly doorman on duty outside their destination. 'Good evening, gentlemen,' he said. 'You look like newcomers to Lacey's. The house rules are very simple: look all you like, but touching is not allowed. You want a private dance, in a booth, you negotiate with the ladies.'

'Thanks for that,' Haddock growled, showing his warrant card. 'We'll bear it in mind.'

'Ahh,' the bouncer murmured as he opened the door for them. 'See the boss about a discount.'

Lacey's was dimly lit apart from four poles arranged around an oval-shaped bar. Two were in use, by dark-haired, pale-skinned, long-legged women, each wearing a G-string and black platform shoes with six-inch heels, but very little else, and gyrating vigorously to disco music with a heavy, thumping bass.

They were being watched by no more than half a dozen men, three at the bar, the others in a group at a table. Along the walls were a series of booths; two of those had curtains drawn across them with light showing behind.

Pye whistled the opening bars of Tina Turner's 'Private Dancer' as he walked up to the bar. 'Who's the manager here?' he asked a fully clothed blond woman, who was in the act of pouring a pint of golden Peroni that the DCI recalled from his earlier visit as being horrendously expensive.

'That would be me, officer,' she said. 'Mary O'Herlihy.'

'Word gets around pretty fast in this place,' Haddock observed.

'There's an intercom at the door,' she replied, as she handed the pint to its purchaser and took the money. 'Big Shane tells me whenever he lets somebody in he thinks might be a wee bit dodgy.'

'I think we'll take that as a compliment, Mary,' Pye said. 'We need a word, about one of your girls.'

'Who's that?'

'Anna Harmony. We were told she's working tonight.'

'That's what I thought too,' the manager replied, checking her watch. 'Want a drink? On the house,' she added.

'Thanks, but we'll pass on that. When was she due here?'

'Fifteen minutes ago. But it's a quiet night. If she's just late, like she's missed her bus, no problem. If she's stood me up, though, that'll be a different story.'

'What's her nationality?' the DS asked. 'We've been told she might be east European.'

'She's Polish.' Mary O'Herlihy chuckled. 'Appropriate, eh, for a Pole to be working in here. Maybe it's their national sport; could be, because she's bloody good at it.'

'What's her real name? For sure it's not Harmony.'

'No, it's Hojnowski, Anna Hojnowski. That's how she introduced herself to me when she did her audition, and that's the name on her payslip. The other one, though, Harmony, that's what she uses.'

'How old is she?'

'Twenty-three; at least that's what she told me. I don't ask to see birth certificates.'

'Maybe you should,' Pye observed. 'What can you tell us about her?'

'Not a lot,' O'Herlihy said. 'She's a nice girl, she's clean, she never lets the punters get out of hand, not even in the private booths, and she never gives me any bother. Also she gets more in tips than any of the other girls. Apart from that, I know nothing about her.'

'Do you know where she lives?' the DCI asked.

149

'No.'

'How about a phone number?'

Her attention was commandeered by one of the trio from the table, who came up to the bar with a drink order. 'Gimme a minute,' she told the detectives as she moved to serve him.

'Fucking music's doing my head in,' Pye complained as they waited.

'You're showing your age, gaffer,' Haddock laughed, 'by that and by the fact that you haven't shot the two birds on the poles a single glance, not one.'

'It's been said many times by many people, but I've seen better at home.'

'Is that right? Funny, I've been to your house but I've never noticed a pole. Do you keep it in the garage?'

'Phone number,' O'Herlihy resumed, as she returned. 'That I do have; two, in fact. One's a mobile, the other's a landline. They're in the office. I'll dig them out when Kyle, the barman, gets back. Cigarette break,' she explained.

'Do you know Dean Francey, Anna's boyfriend?'

Her face darkened. 'Him!' she snorted. 'I know about young Dino all right. He's not welcome here. The laddie is nothing but trouble. I've told Anna she should do herself a favour and get shot of him, but the lass is in love. God knows why, because he's nothing but a lanky lump of malice.'

'You don't like him then,' Haddock said, drily.

'Not a bit.'

'What did he do to get barred . . . or is being in your black books cause enough around here?'

'It can be,' she admitted, 'but in this case the offence was starting a fight. The first time he came in here when Anna was working I didn't like the way he was looking at punters. The second time it got worse, and I warned him. The third time, Anna went into a booth with a punter . . . by the way, the girls aren't supposed to touch the guys, but what happens in there, that's their business . . . when they came out, Dino squared up to the bloke. The man didn't back down and a fight started. Kyle jumped the bar to break it up and Dino started on him. I called Shane in from the door, because Kyle was getting battered, and the idiot stuck one on him as well. That was when I hit him with the baton we keep behind the bar.'

'Technically that was probably assault,' Pye pointed out.

'I regarded it as damage control. Big Shane would have hospitalised him.' She paused. 'So that's why he was barred.'

'When all that was happening, what did Anna do?'

'She screamed at him to stop, but he took no notice. The red mist was down. The laddie will do someone some serious damage one day.'

'We think he may have done that already,' Haddock confessed. 'That's why we need to find Anna.'

'In that case I'm not waiting for Kyle,' the manager said. 'I'll get you those numbers now. If anyone wants serving, tell them I won't be a minute.'

She left the oval bar through an opening on the other side, and disappeared from their sight. One of the patrons at the bar disengaged his eyes from the gyrating form above him and stared into an almost empty pint tumbler, just as Kyle, the barman, returned to his post.

'Do you still think Cheeky would want you to bring her here?' Pye asked.

'Once maybe,' his colleague replied, 'but not twice, that's for sure. It's depressing, isn't it? I feel sorry for these women, doing this for money. Did you actually enjoy the stag do you came to?'

'To be honest,' the DCI chuckled, 'I don't remember much about it. It was mine; but I didn't choose the venue, my best man did that. He told me afterwards that I wound up dancing on a pole in my Y-fronts. He was lying though; I know that 'cos I wear boxers.'

'Is there photographic evidence of this event?'

'No, a couple of the guests vetoed that.'

'Bloody killjoys!' Haddock snorted. 'Why would they do that?'

'Neither Bob Skinner nor Andy Martin fancied being in any of the pictures. Neil McIlhenney wasn't too keen either.'

'What about McGuire?'

'He was on the other pole.'

'Right, gentlemen,' the returning Mary O'Herlihy declared, 'there you are.' She handed a sheet of paper to Pye. 'Those are the numbers. I called the mobile while I was away; got no reply.'

The DCI frowned. 'You didn't call the landline, did you?'

'No.'

'Good. We'll run a reverse check on it and find where it's located. We don't want to give Anna advance notice of our interest.'

'What if she shows up here?'

'Say nothing to her about our visit, but call me on that number.' He took a card from his pocket and handed it over. 'We'll come back.'

'What if the boyfriend's with her?'

'Little chance of that,' Haddock answered, 'but if he is, call us and have big Shane keep him company till we get here. I'm sure he'd enjoy that.'

Twenty-Two

'Is there anything in this part of Edinburgh that isn't a student flat?' Sammy Pye wondered, as he and his sergeant walked along Davie Street, searching for number seventy-seven.

'Not much,' Haddock replied. 'I lived here myself for a while when I was one of the rarely washed. My mum was terrified; she thought the place was a fire trap. She was probably right, but it looks as if it's been refurbished since then.'

'What was the number again?'

'Seventy-seven, F two A. That's it, look.' He pointed to a backlit panel beside a blue-painted entrance door, then pressed a button.

'Hi, who's that?' a bright young female voice asked.

'Detective Sergeant Harold Haddock, Edinburgh CID, with Detective Chief Inspector Pye. We're looking for Anna Hojnowski, also known as Anna Harmony.'

'Singer? She's out. I suppose she's down at Lacey's, dancing on her pole.' The speaker fell silent. The DS pressed the button again.

'What?' The girl had a low annoyance threshold.

'We need a word,' Haddock said.

'Sure you do,' she drawled, sarcastically. 'This is a raid, isn't it? I've heard you lot have been cracking down on students lately, since the national shock troops replaced our so-called friendly local bobbies.'

'So young and yet so cynical,' the DS chuckled. 'If this was a drugs bust, it would be two detective constables ringing your doorbell, and at least one would be female . . . in case of a strip search,' he added. 'We don't give a bugger what you've been inhaling, miss. We need to talk to you about Singer, okay? You can come down here if you want but it's fucking Baltic.'

The young woman gave in. 'All right, all right. Come on up, if you insist.' A buzzing sound came from the doorframe; the DS pushed and it swung open.

'Nice touch about the female DC,' Pye murmured as they jogged up the two flights of stairs.

The door of 2A was open as they stepped on to the second-floor landing; a tall blond girl in black leggings and a sweatshirt with Prince Harry's face emblazoned on it stood, waiting. 'I'm Celia Brown,' she announced, in a polished accent that came from somewhere well south of Edinburgh. 'Can I see your ID?'

'We insist that you do,' the DCI said as they produced their warrant cards and held them up for inspection.

When Celia was satisfied, she stood aside and let them in; the atmosphere was a cocktail of odours, a mix of cosmetics and fried food. 'The living room is straight ahead.'

They stepped through the door she indicated. Inside, another blonde, who was lounging on a sofa, frowned at them over her shoulder. 'Corrie's on,' she complained. 'Take them into the kitchen, Celia.'

Haddock smiled; he picked up a remote from the arm of the couch and pressed a button. The screen froze. 'I've got the same Freeview box,' he explained. 'You can watch the rest when we're done.'

'Bugger!'

'And you are, miss?' Pye asked.

'Ilse Brogan.'

'You're a student too?'

'Of course, we all are. Celia and I are doing math and economics, Singer's doing business studies.'

'Anna's a student?'

'Of course. Just because she pays her way by gyrating round a pole for sweaty middle-aged losers, don't assume that she's dumb.'

'That's right,' Celia chipped in. 'She makes more cash on that bloody pole than she will when she graduates and gets a proper job.'

'The tips are that good?'

'They are in the private booths, where special services can be offered.'

'Are you saying Singer's a hooker?' Haddock exclaimed.

'Not really, but if a punter wants a hand job, it's fifty quid. She's a nice girl, but she's not a posh bird like us, with a well-heeled daddy behind her, so it's hard for her to turn down easy money.'

'Is that why her boyfriend caused a ruck in there one night?'

'Dino could start a ruck in an empty house,' Ilse volunteered. 'He's a creep. I don't know why she's so smitten by him.'

Celia smiled. 'There is a certain rough charm about him.'

'He's as charming as a rabid dog,' her flatmate declared. 'I think that Celia puts up with him,' she told the detectives, 'because she has a crush on his friend.'

'I don't see Jagger as being in Celia's league,' the DCI observed.

Both young women laughed. 'God, not him!' Ilse hooted. 'I mean the other one, Ian, the brooding guy that Dino's going to call Drizzle once too often.'

'How did they meet, Singer and Dean?'

Celia frowned. 'I'm not sure. He just seemed to materialise, like some nasty weather.'

'Does he ever stay over here?'

'No, that's not allowed; it's a house rule. We don't have the space here, plus the walls are like paper.'

'So where do they go for . . . privacy?'

'Dino's place, I suppose. It's out at the seaside somewhere, I believe. If she's not on her pole . . .'

'She isn't,' Haddock said.

'Then that's where I'd go looking for her.'

'If they were there we'd have been told by now.'

'I know how they met.'

Three heads turned towards Ilse Brogan.

'Enlighten us, please,' Pye invited her.

'Singer's a couple of years older than we are, yet she's a year behind us at uni. She came to Scotland with Polish entrance qualifications, and had to get them upgraded before she could start a degree course. She had a job while she was studying for her Highers. She worked in a factory, and sometimes she babysat for the guy who owned it. Between us, I think she might have had a small fling with him, but if she did, it wasn't serious.'

'I've never heard this before,' Celia murmured.

'No, but you only moved in here last autumn. This story goes back before that.'

Haddock nodded. 'Go on.'

'Some time early last year, in the spring maybe, Singer told me that her old boss had been in touch and invited her to a party in his new house. His marriage had broken up and he was celebrating, he told her. She went along. I don't know if the chap had any ideas, but if he did, they didn't work out, for that was the night when Anna met Dino Francey. One of the people at the party was drunk and he made a pass at her. Dino saw him off, and that was the start of it all.'

'Interesting,' the DS said. 'Can you remember where this party happened?'

'Sure, and I can even tell you the name of the host. It was in North Berwick, and his name was Callum Sullivan. He introduced the two of them, Singer and Dino.'

The two detectives stared at each other. 'Are you sure about that?' Pye asked.

'Of course. Singer had a Christmas card from him.' Ilse frowned. 'What's this about anyway? Are you going to tell us? So far you've done nothing but ask questions.'

'No, we're not going to tell you,' Pye replied. 'All I will say is that it's Dean Francey we need to locate, not Singer, but as far as we can see, she's our best route to him. So when she shows up, tell her to get in touch with us. I repeat, tell her, don't ask her.'

He caught a look in Celia's eye, an anxious look. 'Ian's not involved in whatever it is, is he?'

He smiled. 'No. As far as we can tell he's on the side of the good guys.'

They left the two students to return to *Coronation Street*, and made their way back outside. 'I'll drop you at the office,' the DCI told Haddock, 'so you can pick up your car.'

'I'd expect no less,' Haddock replied cheerfully. 'What's tomorrow's priority?' he asked.

'Assuming Dino hasn't turned up, we visit the man Mackail.

In fact, we might ask him to visit us, just to sweat him up a little. After that, another chat with Callum Sullivan would seem in order.'

'Sounds like a plan,' the DS agreed.

He was just about to slide into Pye's car when his phone sounded. 'That's probably Cheeky, telling me my salad's in the oven,' he said as he took it from his pocket. 'No it's not,' he murmured as he checked the screen. 'It's Jackie.'

'Sarge,' she exclaimed as soon as he answered, 'I've just had a call from the control room.' Her tone told him, unequivocally, that their working day was not complete.

'A patrol car just answered a call to a location on the road to the Glencorse Reservoir, just past the Flotterstone Inn. They found a Toyota car abandoned and burned out. The number matches Donna Rattray's Aygo.' Her voice quivered with tension.

'There are two bodies inside,' she added.

Twenty-Three

They saw the blue light from a mile away, absorbed and amplified by the low cloud ceiling. The patrol car was waiting at the entrance road to the Flotterstone Inn, a place that Pye knew well. It was one of his wife's favourite haunts, although their visits had been less frequent since the birth of their child two years earlier.

A sergeant in a Day-Glo jacket stood beside his vehicle.

'Where is it?' the DCI asked.

'Go straight on up the Glen road, sir. You'll see the signs. Carry on for the best part of a mile. There's a fire appliance at the scene, although the blaze was out by the time we got there.'

'Who reported it?'

'There's a house a wee bit beyond, beside the reservoir. The householder went out to get some logs and saw the light in the sky. He ran down there and called Fire and Rescue.'

'When?'

'Must be two hours ago now. The fire guys didn't call us in till they had the blaze under control, and could see what's inside the car. By the way, sir, the team leader's going frantic; I don't know what the fuck's wrong with him.'

'What does he look like?' Haddock asked.

'Big bloke,' the officer replied. 'You canna miss him. He's got a couple of stripes on his jacket. I'm not certain but I think he's black.'

The two detectives exchanged glances. 'Thanks,' the DCI said. 'We'll get on up there.'

'Mind the road, sir,' the constable volunteered. 'It's no the best.'

'Fuck!' Pye murmured as he drove on. 'This is not good.'

As they had been warned, the road was rough and narrow, limiting their speed; it took them a couple of minutes to reach the clearing where the fire appliance stood, with its spotlights trained on what was left of the white Toyota.

They saw Levon Rattray at once; two of his crew were beside him as if they were holding him back, but when he saw Pye's car he shook them off, and ran towards it.

'Have they told you?' he yelled, grabbing Haddock by the arm as he stepped out. 'He's in there, Dino and somebody else.'

The DS took hold of his wrist and squeezed it, hard enough to make the man release him, saying as he did, 'Calm down, Levon. We've been told that there may be bodies in the vehicle, but we're making no assumptions. We know that the car is your wife's, and we know that she isn't in it, but those are the only two absolute facts we have.'

'It's Dino, I know it.'

'Then let us take a look,' Pye told him. 'But you, please stay back. You've done your job; now let us do ours. Go and sit in your cab. We'll talk to you when we're ready.'

'I want to come with you,' the fireman insisted.

'If we need you we'll call you,' the DCI said, firmly. 'Now, do as I ask, please.' He turned to Haddock. 'Sauce, get us a couple of . . .'

The sergeant had anticipated the instruction and was in the act of taking two paper crime scene suits from a box in the boot of the car. They slipped them on and walked towards the wreck, Haddock carrying a large halogen torch.

The Aygo was sodden, water was coursing from the roof, and dripping from the empty window frames. They guessed that the glass had blown out from the heat of the fire.

The occupants were soaked also, two black twisted figures that could have been carved from any carbonous material, obscene impressionist sculptures that once might have been part of the woodland that surrounded the site . . . had it not been for the teeth that gleamed in the beam of the detective sergeant's flashlight when he fixed it on the occupant of the driver's seat.

'Dental records or a DNA match, I think.' A soft female voice came from behind them. They turned, as one.

'Professor,' Pye exclaimed. 'Don't you have a junior you could send to a job like this?'

'Yes,' Sarah Grace replied, 'but two dead bodies in a burned-out car is very rarely a job for a postgraduate assistant. How much do we know, Sammy?'

'The car was taken from the park at Queen Margaret University this afternoon. The suspected thief is the owner's brother, who's wanted in connection with the abduction and death of the child the gaffer found at Fort Kinnaird this morning.'

'How sure are you?'

'Percentage scale? About ninety-five.'

'And the other occupant? I'm not even prepared to take a guess at the gender at this stage.'

161

'Look at the feet, boss,' Sauce Haddock said to Pye, training the beam on to the passenger. 'Those things, those shoes, or what's left of them. We've seen something like those tonight, somewhere else. Long heels, platform soles.'

Pye nodded. 'The standard footwear in Lacey's, it looks like . . .' He looked back towards the pathologist. 'We think she's Anna Hojnowski, also known as Anna Harmony, or by her nickname, Singer. She was the driver's girlfriend. Everybody told her he was no use, but she wouldn't listen.'

'It's not a mistake she's going to get over,' Sarah murmured.

'No, but she's left us a few questions. First and foremost, what were she and Dino doing here?'

'Maybe they were having one for the road,' Haddock suggested, bluntly.

The DCI snorted. 'That would have been an odd sense of priorities for someone on the run from a potential double murder charge. And second question, why were they at this spot? It's pretty far off the road. We need to clear the whole area, Sauce, to let the CSI team look for evidence of a second vehicle here around the same time.'

'Which leads us to the most obvious question,' Sarah said. 'Why didn't they get out of the car after it caught fire? Sauce, can I borrow your light?'

She leaned into the car, focusing the beam of the lamp on the blackened head of the thing in the passenger seat. She studied it for almost a minute, then dug into a pocket of her tunic and produced a magnifying glass, which she used to examine a small area above what had been an eye socket. After a few minutes she straightened up and faced her companions.

'She . . . assuming you guys are right . . . appears to have been shot through the head. If so, it's a safe bet that he was as well. They were executed, both of them.'

'Will they be able to recover the bullets?' Pye asked.

'A small calibre soft-nosed bullet might still be in there. But if I can't find it at the autopsy, you should be able to. It'll be embedded in something, either in the fabric of the vehicle or the ground around it.'

'How soon can you do the post-mortems?'

'How soon can you let me have the bodies?' she countered.

'The crime scene team are on their way here. As soon as they've been photographed and filmed in situ, we'll get them to you.'

'For identification I'm going to need DNA samples,' she said.

'That shouldn't be a problem, as far as the driver's concerned. We think that overwrought fireman by the appliance is his brother-in-law, so we can arrange to take a sample from his wife. As for Anna, we know where she lives; with a bit of luck there will be something in her room that'll give us what we need, hairbrush, leg shaver, whatever.'

She nodded. 'All good. In that case I'll head for the city mortuary and wait for the bodies to arrive. I'll call in my assistant, we'll do both autopsies tonight and get the DNA matching under way.' She handed the flashlight back to Haddock and headed for her car. She had gone only a few steps before stopping and looking back at them.

'Given that Bob has a loose interest in this,' she called out, 'can I discuss it with him?'

'Of course,' Pye replied. 'If he wants to know anything else, tell him to call me.'

The detectives watched her leave. 'A change from Joe Hutchinson,' Haddock observed.

'She's just as good,' his boss said. 'She's always been better tuned into our wavelength than Master Yoda, given her police connection through big Bob. She's right about this being an execution. It was a bloody efficient one too. Neither of them even made it out of the car.'

'Do we assume the shooter was the person who planned the abduction?'

'That's the only logical conclusion we can come to. There's no obvious indication that Dean Francey had a personal motive for attacking Grete and abducting wee Zena. He must have been hired to do the job. And when he bungled it, he became a danger to whoever is behind it. Let's go on the assumption that he was lured to a meeting here, for example by the promise of cash for a getaway, and was eliminated.'

'Fair enough,' the DS agreed, 'but why was Anna Harmony here as well? That's assuming it is her.'

'She must have been going away with him. Ilse did say she was "smitten by him", to use her phrase. Maybe she was part of it, maybe she knew nothing of what he had done; either way we've no way of knowing, or of finding out. For now, Sauce, we're left with only one line of inquiry, and that's Grete Regal's business problem.'

'Agreed. Let's pull Mackail in now, tonight.'

'No, we can't do that,' Pye exclaimed. 'He's a person of interest, but no more than that, so far. Plus we'll be tied up here for a while. I don't know about you, but I'm shagged out, and I'd rather tackle the man when I'm fresh. Tomorrow morning, we can draw up a workable strategy for him.'

'If you say so, Sammy. I must admit, I've had enough for today too. Wee Zena was bad, and now this. I need some domestic therapy from Cheeky.'

'Then let's get ready to brief the CSIs,' Pye declared, 'if the buggers ever get here. Meanwhile, I'd better follow bloody protocol, and advise the city commander of a major incident.'

'And phone the DCC?'

'Too right; this is something else he won't want to find out about via the TV news.'

Twenty-Four

I have to confess that I was at something of a loss when I arrived home from Edinburgh. I had passed a couple of gainful hours in my office, but my heart wasn't in it, so I signed myself out. All I could think about was the wee girl in the car; she just wouldn't leave me alone.

Seonaid and the boys were home from school when I got back to Gullane. I granted them some Playstation time, then took my daughter's hand. 'What would you like to do till Mum gets home?' I asked her.

'Story,' she replied, without hesitation.

Trish, the children's live-in carer, had a date to meet a friend at Ocean Terminal; I persuaded her to leave early so that it was just the two of us. I was very glad of that; I needed very badly to spend time with my youngest child.

We settled on *How the Grinch Stole Christmas* and went into the garden room, where she squeezed herself into an armchair beside me, her little face serious as I eased her into the classic yarn. She listened without a murmur, from start to finish, then looked up at me.

'Have you ever seen a Grinch, Daddy?' she asked me.

'I've seen a few grumps,' I told her, 'and a few groaners, and even some people who looked pretty green, but no, I've never actually seen a Grinch.'

'That's because he's not real, silly,' she laughed.

For a moment my mind was overwhelmed by an image of another child, not too many miles from where Seonaid and I were sitting, probably playing out the same scene with her mother less than twenty-four hours earlier.

To fight it off, I picked up another book, A. A. Milne's *Now We Are Six*. My daughter isn't, but as soon as she turned five, she declared herself too old for the companion volume, *When We Were Very Young*.

'Let me read you a story about someone who was real,' I said, and launched into *King John's Christmas*. It took me a little while, for I had to stop to explain what 'supercilious' means, and to explain why he might have signed his name 'Johannes R', but settled for 'Jack', and what India rubber was, and why Seonaid couldn't have a pocketknife that really cuts.

'Was King John really a bad man, Daddy?' she asked when the poem was over.

'That depends on who's telling his story,' I replied. 'I doubt if any king was completely good in those days. But I suspect,' I added, conspiratorially, 'that he was a reasonably good man with bad PR.'

To deflect further discussion on the nature of public relations, I fast-forwarded to the tale of *The Knight Whose Armour Didn't Squeak*, forgetting that it was about a medieval mugging. She laughed out loud at the tale. I'd only just finished convincing her that the cowardly knight Sir Thomas Tom really wasn't a good man when Sarah arrived home and gave me the hug that I needed and the one that Seonaid took as her absolute right, which, of course, it is.

'Bad day, uh?' she murmured, as she held me close.

'Bad start,' I agreed, as we broke the clinch. 'I thought I was done with things like that. I think I'm magnetic, love. Of all the cars that fu . . .' Realising that our daughter was still within earshot I stopped myself short. 'He chose mine; he had to choose mine. I think I must be a magnet for grief.'

'Nonsense,' she insisted. 'To our daughter and me you're a love machine. You were just unlucky, that's all.'

'Not as unlucky as that wee lass.'

Sarah glanced at Seonaid and put a finger to her lips, ending the discussion just as James Andrew exploded into the room with all the energy of a small tsunami. I guessed from his exuberance that he had beaten his brother yet again at whatever game they had played.

'Where's Mark?' I asked.

'Doing his homework,' Jazz replied.

I gave him a look that was meant to be somewhere between curious and severe, but probably didn't make it past amused. 'Don't you have any?'

'Some,' he admitted.

'Then wouldn't it be a good idea to do it before you're too tired to do it than when you are but I still make you?'

He wrinkled his nose. 'I suppose.'

If we were negotiating, it didn't last long. Sarah pointed at the door. 'Go do it while dinner's being cooked,' she ordered. 'Now. And take your sister with you,' she added. 'I want to talk to Dad.'

'What's for dinner?' my son, in the act of leaving, asked me. Since his mother and I got back together, more or less full-time, we take turns in the kitchen. It's another part of my new life that I enjoy.

'Tuna steaks on the Foreman grill, potato wedges in the dry

fryer, beans and fried onions,' I told him. 'A special request by Mark,' I explained to Sarah. 'He's trying to bulk himself up, and reckons that fish is the way to go.'

She grinned. 'Poor kid. For girls or boys, puberty's a bastard, isn't it?'

'Yeah,' I agreed. 'For lads, it brings a whole new set of personal targets. I still haven't hit all of mine yet.'

We headed for the kitchen. For some reason Sarah likes to watch me cook; when I'm in my apron she calls me 'Masterchef'. The wedges were waiting in the dry fryer. I set it for forty minutes and began to slice the onions.

'What about Seonaid?' she asked.

'I've got a smaller steak for her. Not that much smaller, though; I think she's in a growing phase.'

She smiled, and fetched me a Corona from the fridge. I looked at her as she handed it to me. 'You not having one?'

'No thanks. I'm on call, and anyway, I don't fancy beer just now,' she replied.

'Wine?'

She shook her head. 'No. I've . . .' she paused. 'What's that Scots saying? I've taken a schooner to alcohol.'

I laughed out loud. 'That would be "scunner", my darling. And most unlike you.' A thought came to me. 'Hey, what is this? This morning you had an uncontrollable desire for lemon drizzle cake. Tonight you have a booze intolerance. Are you sure there's nothing you want to tell me?'

'Absolutely,' she replied, but I wasn't letting it go. I snapped into interrogation mode, looking her in the eye.

'Okay, there's nothing you want,' I stressed the word, 'to tell me. But is there something that you should?'

'Fucking cops,' she murmured, then took the kitchen knife

169

from my hand and laid it on the work surface. She slid an arm round my waist. 'I'm late,' she said.

It didn't exactly hit me like a ton of bricks. Sarah's mum made a prize-winning lemon drizzle cake, and since her death she'd never mentioned the damn confection, not once, until that morning.

'How late?' I asked, not even trying to suppress my grin.

'Only a week. Too early to be taking it as fact, but you know I'm pretty regular; always have been.'

'Have you done a test?'

'No, not yet.'

'Aw Jesus,' I chuckled. 'Even I know it isn't too early for that. Buy a kit, pee on the stick and that's it.'

'Maybe I don't want to know.'

I paused the fryer. 'Let's say you are pregnant. How did we get to this?'

'When we got back together,' she said, 'I was off the pill. I went back on it sharpish, and that was okay, but my body didn't take to it like before. So I switched to what they call the mini-pill; it has only one hormone, progesterone. The problem may be that I didn't read the advice, that for the first couple of days, you should use a back-up method.'

'Johnnies?'

She nodded. 'We could also have abstained, of course.'

I threw her a mock frown. 'Sure we could.'

She allowed me a hint of a smile. 'But we didn't, and so there may have been a very small window of opportunity.'

'Wow! As marksmanship goes . . .'

'Yeah, we may have shot the arrow right through it.'

'Do the test tomorrow. Otherwise you'll fret for another week.'

'Okay,' she conceded. 'I will.'

'Good,' I said, restarting the fryer. 'Now let me get on with feeding the kids that we have already.'

She fell silent, watching me as I loaded the grill, set the beans to heat, then went to work on the onions in a big frying pan. They were turning a satisfactory golden colour when she spoke again.

'Bob,' she ventured, 'if the test is positive, as I'm sure it will be, how will you feel?'

I glanced across at her. 'Once I get over being gobsmacked, I'll be delighted . . . as long as you are too. How do you feel about it?'

'Honestly? I can't get my head round it. Apart from anything else, the timing's terrible; Joe's about to retire, and I'm about to assume the chair of forensic pathology. I'll have a department to run, undergraduates and postgrads to mentor, people's careers in my hands. It's a huge responsibility, but it's something I've looked forward to as a challenge. And what do I do? As soon as that moment arrives, I go off on maternity leave? That doesn't sit comfortably with me.'

I'd known from the outset she'd feel that way, but I needed her to articulate it.

'Understood. But it's not your fault, accidents happen. You of all people must know that; you've built a career out of examining their consequences.'

'In this case,' she countered, 'there is clear contributory negligence. Mine, not yours,' she added.

I worked the onions even harder, throwing in some Worcester sauce as they started to brown. 'You could have a termination,' I murmured, without looking at her.

'How would you feel about that?'

'I will support whatever decision you make.'

'That's not an answer.'

'It's the best you're going to get,' I told her. 'I love you, and your happiness is paramount.'

'Even if it means killing your child?'

She had me there. Instantly, I was back in Fort Kinnaird; but I steeled myself and answered as best I could. 'It would be as if this discussion never happened, and we'd never mention it again.'

She stepped beside me and hugged me, awkwardly. 'You're a doll. But that's not what we do, you and I, is it?'

'No,' I agreed, 'it's not.' Then I laughed again. 'Hell, we could have Ignacio back here around that time. What's another kid? We'll give Trish a pay rise for the extra workload. We'll make the house bigger, if we have to. Now, you go on and fetch the bears; this masterpiece is just about ready for them.'

We ate round the kitchen table, all five of us. Twelve months before, I could not have imagined that ever happening again, but it has. As I reflected on my own good fortune it brought me back to the ill luck of others, and made me sombre once more. To hide my feelings from the kids I went back to work as soon as I had finished the last of my perfectly grilled tuna, chopping a pineapple and a honeydew melon into cubes, then sharing them out in bowls, each one topped with a scoop of butterscotch ice cream.

We had barely finished dessert when the doorbell rang. I have a discreet security camera that's a holdover from my former career and that I've kept. It lets me see who's calling, just in case whoever it is might have an axe to grind, or might be carrying one. I checked the monitor and saw a uniformed cop, a motorcycle officer, with his helmet in one hand and a package in the other.

'Evening, sir,' he said, as I opened the door. I recognised him from many encounters.

'Craig,' I greeted him. 'This is a blast from the recent past.'

'A welcome one nonetheless, sir. It's good to see you looking so well.'

Fuck, I thought, *did I look so bad before?*

'You have something for me?'

He held out the package. 'This was sent through from Glasgow, sir, by DCC McGuire, with your name on it, marked "urgent". Fettes reckoned that meant tonight.'

'Tomorrow would have done,' I told him, 'but I appreciate it. Will you come in for a mug of something?'

Craig, PC Charlton, to give him his proper handle, shook his head. 'Thanks, Mr Skinner, but I'd better get straight back. I heard some chatter in my ear about a major incident, so it might be all hands to the pumps.'

I wished him well, and took the bundle from him. I'd expected it to be much bulkier than it was. That simple fact told me why Mario had a down on the former Detective Inspector McGarry. I took the file into the garden room, tossed it on to the couch, then went back to the kitchen, but it was deserted. I guessed that Sarah had taken Seonaid off to supervise her night-time ablutions and that the boys had vanished to fight over what to watch in their last hour of permitted television.

I fetched myself another beer, and returned to the parcel. I opened it and removed its contents, and found myself looking at a familiar Strathclyde Police folder, just like the hundreds that had clogged my in tray during my few months as its last chief constable. I was about to open it when Sarah returned.

'What's that?' she asked. 'I thought we'd seen the last of biker cops dropping off parcels.'

'Yes, me too,' I agreed.

'So what is it? An old investigation you were involved in?'

'Half right. Old investigation, yes; one of mine, not really. This came completely out of the blue. Remember I told you I was having lunch today with Eden Higgins?'

'How could I forget?' she said. 'Your late ex-girlfriend's tycoon brother; the man who wrote to you about his "situation". What was it?'

I told her about the theft of the *Princess Alison*, and the abortive police investigation that I had been retained to review.

She frowned, as she sat beside me. 'Should you be doing that?'

'I asked myself that question before I accepted,' I admitted, 'and I couldn't think of a single reason why not. Neither could Andy or Mario; that's why I've got this folder.'

'Won't it be embarrassing for them if you find that the investigation was flawed?'

I laughed. 'It'll be far more embarrassing for me. When this thing kicked off I was chief constable. By any standards this was a major theft, and yet I never heard about it. I should be doing this for free.'

'Then why aren't you, my dear?' she countered, reasonably. I'd been asking myself that question.

'I will, if I find very quickly that the CID investigation was competent and covered all lines of inquiry. I will if I wind up making my own inquiries but don't trace the *Princess Alison*. If she is recovered, and the insurance company cough up as promised, I might take a fee but tell them to give the bonus money to charities of Andy Martin's choice.'

'Won't that rub Andy's nose in it?'

'Not completely. The investigation was closed on Andy's

watch, but like I said, it began on mine. Both our noses will be up for rubbing.'

'Okay,' she said. 'Let's say you do investigate actively. What powers will you have?'

'Those of a private investigator, no more . . . and in effect they're zero. I'll have no powers of arrest beyond those of any citizen, and no powers to access documents, bank accounts, or anything like that.'

'Won't that constrain you?'

'Of course it will,' I agreed. 'But I'll have a very large organisation behind me; if I do need to go somewhere that's closed to me, I'll go to Mario McGuire. This whole thing is very flexible, love; there are all sorts of questions that I won't be able to answer until I've read this file.'

She pointed at the folder. 'So what are you waiting for? Go to it.'

'I can't be arsed,' I admitted. 'I've had enough for today.'

'Of course you have,' she sighed. 'Your day had the worst possible start, didn't it. Have you heard anything from Sammy Pye, or Sauce?'

'They're pretty sure they know who was driving the car,' I replied. 'They sent me a mugshot of the suspect, a lad from North Berwick, name of Francey. I couldn't be a hundred per cent sure he's the guy, but they seem to be. I've heard nothing more than that, but I don't think he'll be at liberty for too long.'

'Good,' she said, her tone harsh. 'I saw Joe when he got back from the autopsy. He told me as much as he knew. The poor child died of an asthma attack. I just . . .' Her face twisted, eyes screwed up in a mix of frustration and anger. 'Here I stop being a pathologist and start being a parent; words fail me, Bob. What sort of an animal would do that to a child? To let her die, alone and terrified in the dark. It's horrible. And she must have seen what happened to her mother.'

'What did happen to her mother?' I asked. 'I know nothing of this.'

'They've identified the child. She's from Garvald. She was snatched on the way to school this morning. According to Joe, her mother was in surgery with severe head injuries.'

'Eh?' I gasped. 'That's weird. He attacks mum, kidnaps the child . . . What was her name? Do you know?'

'Olivia Gates, known to her family as Zena. That delayed the identification by a couple of hours.'

'Why the nickname?'

'From what Sammy told Joe, Mum's a fan of *The Urban Dictionary*.'

'What about dad, Mr Gates?'

'Naval officer is all I know.'

I winced. 'Poor bastard to have to deal with this.' I held up my beer. 'You sure you wouldn't like a drink, to help lighten the mood?'

She smiled and squeezed my hand. 'On call, I told you. And then there's the other thing,' she added. She dug an elbow into my side, gently. 'How has today made you feel?' she asked.

It was a good question, one I had asked myself. 'Alienated,' I replied. 'It's the first time I've felt the faintest flash of regret over leaving the service. I wanted to take command this morning and to stay hands-on until the guy was caught. When Eden told me about his problem, I wanted to pick up the phone and yell at someone. But I couldn't do either of those things, so yes, I felt excluded . . . maybe even a wee bit emasculated.'

'In that case your balls were too big for the job,' she countered. 'Too much testosterone isn't a good quality in any commander.'

That could have been the beginning of a long and interesting debate, if Sarah's mobile hadn't rung before I could respond to the challenge. She snatched it from the breast pocket of the casual shirt she'd put on while she was upstairs and took the call.

Her face darkened as I watched. 'Yes,' she murmured. 'Yes, I know the location. It's not far off the bypass so I'll be there inside half an hour.'

She put the phone away, and pushed herself up from the couch. 'That was Mary Chambers,' she said. 'It's a double fatality; two people found in a burned-out car just off the Biggar Road.'

'That must have been the major incident that Craig was talking about,' I guessed, aloud. 'Will you be okay? I'd come with you, if Trish was here.'

'And I wouldn't let you, suppose she was,' Sarah retorted. 'It isn't your job any more, lover, and I don't need a chauffeur. You stay here with our kids and your file.'

Twenty-Five

I did as I'd been told, not only because there wasn't an option, but also because Sarah was right: it wasn't my job any more. Instead I read Seonaid one last A. A. Milne poem before switching out her light (sleeping without a nightlight is a matter of honour with her) then checked that the boys were obeying standard bedtime operating procedures.

As I did so, all the time I found myself thinking about Sarah's potential bombshell, and considering its practical consequences. Our family home had been built with five bedrooms and a self-contained flat for Trish above the garages. We had one spare en-suite room that Alex used whenever she decided to stay. Ignacio had taken no decision about where he would live when he was released, but I was determined that it would not be with his mother, who was, is and always will be bad news in my book. I'd made it clear that I hoped he'd move in with us and get to know the family he'd been denied for twenty years, and he hadn't rejected the idea. With him and a new baby, space would be tight, even in our big villa.

In my younger days, in the job, when we were in the mire and things looked black, I was fond of telling my people, 'There are no problems, only challenges and opportunities.' My tongue was in my cheek then, but as I wished Mark goodnight and closed his bedroom door, I knew that my rapidly expanding family was giving me an accommodation challenge, big time.

In an attempt to drive it from my mind, I collected the *Princess Alison* file and took it into what I call my office these days, although Sarah still calls it 'the panic room', a sanctuary in those times when either of us really needs privacy.

Leaving the door ajar just in case of sounds from upstairs, I cued up some quiet music on the streaming system and settled down to read. The simple act of opening the file put me back mentally in my old office in Pitt Street, in Glasgow, a room that I'd never grown to love in the way that I'd cherished my accommodation in the command suite in the Edinburgh police HQ. I shoved that image to one side and concentrated on what was before me.

The first pages were a detailed description of the property that had been stolen and, in police-speak, of the way the crime had been committed. It was followed by a series of photographs; the first six were of the empty boathouse, with its massive door raised, then lowered.

A group of four followed; three showed the exterior and the channel of buoys that led into the Gareloch, while the fourth was a satellite image showing the location of Eden's place, two-thirds along the road from Helensburgh and its suburb, Rhu, to the Faslane naval base.

Third and last was a series of images of the *Princess Alison* herself, external and internal. Eden had promised to email some to me, but I hadn't opened my mailbox since then, and so the file gave me my first sight of the lost cruiser. She was a serious piece of kit; a billionaire's toy and no mistake. I looked for anything in her lines that might remind me of the woman after whom she'd been named, but saw nothing. Alison Higgins was a robust, earthy, lusty woman; her image might have belonged on the bowsprit of a pirate ship, but never on a luxury cruiser.

One of the photographs showed a party in progress: men and women in light-coloured clothes, most of them brandishing champagne flutes. I extracted that from the file and studied it closely. As far as I was concerned at that stage, every person who had set foot on the missing *Princess* was a suspect, until they weren't.

'Innocent until proven guilty' is a very fine principle, and it's the foundation of our justice system, but any investigator worth his corn has to begin with the opposite viewpoint.

The rest of the folder was crap.

As I read on, I saw that the first thing DI McGarry had done was to report the theft to the Marine and Coastguard Agency, which doesn't actually have a criminal investigation division. The second was to circulate a description of the missing vessel to all police forces with a coastline south of the Firth of Clyde, including the Police Service of Northern Ireland, and the Garda Siochana, the Irish force. The third was to secure the posting of a description and photograph on a website called stolenboats.org that appeared to be fed with information by the marine insurance industry and the police but to be independent of either.

There were a few notes in response, but all of them were negative, saying that there had been no reports of a boat matching the description of the *Princess Alison*. The conclusion of McGarry's trawl was that she had simply vanished.

The man had done the basics at the site of the theft, but no more: a crime scene team had gone over all the accessible points in the boathouse, and had found nothing out of place, no unidentified fingerprints. The padlock on the sliding double doors through which the thieves had entered had been cut through its arch, then put back in place, helping to delay the discovery of the raid.

Their report solved one riddle that had been niggling me since Eden and Rory had told me the story. If the phone line that serviced the alarm system had been cut, why hadn't the gardeners noticed it? The answer was that the cable was underground, terminating in a box on the wall of the boathouse, beside the door. The cover had been removed and then replaced.

Nothing else that McGarry had done showed a scrap of real initiative. He had taken a statement from Eden, and had interviewed the part-time crew of the *Princess*, Hurrell and Hodgson. At least he'd shown the nous to ask those two for their whereabouts at the time of the theft, 3 a.m. on 4 October. Hurrell had been driving Eden and Rachel home to Edinburgh after a dinner at Gleneagles Hotel, and Hodgson had been visiting his niece, in Rochdale.

Beyond that the file was bare. There were notes of visits to marinas in the Firth of Clyde, and of telephone calls to those in its islands, and more remote mainland areas. There had been a discussion with Eden's insurer, but that amounted to nothing more than a lack of progress report.

The investigation had been founded on a very basic assumption, that the vessel had been stolen by persons unknown with the motive being simple profit. My problem was that it had never occurred to McGarry to look anywhere else. I'd told Eden and Rory, without even having seen the boathouse, that there had to have been inside knowledge in the planning of the operation, and yet that hadn't dawned on an officer who'd reached detective inspector rank.

Unless . . .

I picked up my phone and called Mario McGuire, mobile to mobile. He must have been home, for in the background I could hear wee Eamon yelling for sustenance.

'Hi, Bob,' he said. 'Got the report?'

'Yeah,' I replied. 'Have I ever.'

'Is it okay?'

'Hah,' I chuckled. 'Obviously you haven't looked at it yourself.'

'No, I wasn't in Glasgow today. I had it sent straight to you once it had been pulled from the archive. Is it dodgy?'

I gave him a brief rundown of the contents. As I finished I could hear him gasp. 'And that's it?'

'Yup. That's as far as it goes. It says several things to me. But the most immediate concern is that McGarry is either stupid, bone idle, or corrupt. In your shoes, I'd be having him invest-igated, very quietly, to rule out the latter. More than that, I'd be doing what I'd have done in Strathclyde if I'd known about this. I'd be rooting out his entire reporting chain, and looking over every closed investigation that division ever undertook.'

'Bloody right!' he snorted. 'First thing tomorrow, that gets done.' He paused. 'Listen, you know the people through in the west better than I do. Short of bringing somebody in from another area, which would be noticed, is there anyone you can suggest to do the job discreetly?'

'What's Sandra Bulloch doing now?' I asked. 'She was my exec, but I don't suppose that Andy kept her on in that role.'

'She's been promoted DCI, on major crimes,' he replied. 'I interviewed her and I can see why you rated her. I'll put her on it. Will you want to talk to McGarry yourself?'

'That would be pointless,' I told him. 'All that would happen would be me losing my rag. There's nothing he could tell me that isn't in his file, unless Sandra comes up with a link between him and anyone connected to the *Princess*. If she does, it would be good to know, but that's all.'

'Will do,' Mario said, 'although my money's very much on stupidity or laziness.' Then he paused. 'How are you feeling after what we both saw this morning?' he murmured.

'It won't go away,' I admitted, 'and believe me, I'm trying to block it out.'

'Have you heard from the Menu lately?'

'Not since this afternoon,' I replied, 'when they asked me if I could ID their prime suspect as the driver of the BMW. I did the best I could. They seemed pretty certain, though; I had the feeling I was just being asked out of politeness.'

'They know for sure now,' he growled, grimly.

Something in his tone made a piece of the day's jigsaw click into place.

'Are you going to tell me,' I ventured, 'that the double fatality that Sarah's just been called to attend is . . .'

'That I am. I've just had Pye on the phone. They've been sure from early on that Francey didn't plan this thing all on his own. It seems that they were right and that he's picked up the tab for failure, and his girlfriend alongside him. They'll need dental or DNA identification, though. They were both burned to cinders. Don't expect Sarah home in a hurry. She's going to do both autopsies tonight.'

'Oh God,' I sighed, then shuddered. 'What a job she's gone to. Now I'm wishing she hadn't had that tuna steak.'

Twenty-Six

Sarah called me from the scene of the call-out, fifteen minutes after my conversation with Mario, to confirm what he had told me, that she was heading to the mortuary from the crime scene.

'I've just called Roshan,' she said, 'and he's on the way there too. I have no idea how long it'll take us to do both examinations, but you can set the alarm before you go to bed, because I won't be home. I'll get some sleep at my place when I'm done and go in to work from there tomorrow.'

'They're sure it's the lad Francey?' I asked.

'It's subject to DNA confirmation, but they seem to be. The number plates on the car are still recognisable. It's bizarre, Bob; the fire crew leader says it's his wife's, and that the dead man's his brother-in-law. As for the girl, if Sammy and Sauce are right about her identity, they know where she lives, so proving it won't be difficult.'

'Doesn't sound like it,' I agreed. 'Mario says that the lads are treating the deaths as linked to the attack and abduction, but I suppose that's a no-brainer.'

'Literally,' she replied, grimly. 'She was shot in the head. It's not so easy to tell by looking at what's left of him but my expectation is that he was too.'

I've seen pathologists at work, Sarah among them, more often than I care to remember. It's horrible, bloody, smelly work, and I knew how she'd look once she was finished. I've seen, on occasion, how long she'd spend in the shower after a particularly nasty one, ridding herself of the last possibility of contamination by her subject. I knew that if she changed her mind and came back to Gullane after dealing with Dean Francey and his girlfriend, even in the middle of the night she'd be reeking of expensive shampoo and Chanel Number Five.

'Go to it, baby,' I told her. 'They couldn't be in better hands.'

I hung up, but some images that I really didn't want in my head lodged themselves there. In a bid to drive them away I went back to the police report and to the gaps that could be filled.

Eden had given me his mobile number, saying I could call him any time. I took him at his word; when he answered I could hear festive sounds.

'It's Rachel's birthday party,' he explained, his voice raised. 'Hold on, while I go somewhere private.'

I waited as the music and chatter faded, then disappeared entirely with the sound of a closing door. 'What can I do for you, Bob?' he asked.

'I've got the police report,' I replied. 'It's not the most thorough I've ever seen,' I added, diplomatically. I should explain that for all his failings, DI Randolph McGarry was nonetheless a serving police officer, and I was not about to excoriate him to a civilian.

'As Mary Chambers told you, the inquiry got nowhere, neither in what used to be the Strathclyde area, nor with any of the other forces who were asked for input.'

'So it's a goner?'

'Probably,' I conceded, 'but there are things I can still look at. For starters I want those lists of guests at your floating reception, and also, details of anyone else who was there in another capacity: caterers and their staff, I'd imagine. I'd like them annotated, with an explanation of who each guest is and why he or she is there.'

'Can do,' he said, crisply. 'I'll put Luisa on it first thing in the morning and have the stuff emailed to you as soon as it's done.'

'Thanks.'

'What are the prospects of success?'

'I have no idea. To be frank, Eden,' I admitted, 'in all my career I've never encountered a theft like this. Sure, things have been stolen from boats, and maybe even the odd dinghy or inflatable's been taken, but in my experience this one's unique.'

'Mmm,' he murmured. 'Are you telling me you haven't a clue where to start, Bob?'

'Hell no,' I exclaimed. 'I'm going to start with the "why". If I can establish a motive, other than the sheer value of the vessel, then the rest might well fall into place.'

I let him go back to his party. Rachel and I crossed paths a few times when I was with Alison, but we'd never really got to know each other until that lunch in Eden's office. From the early times, though, my impression had always been that what she wanted, she got.

My chat with Eden had focused my attention on my lack of expertise in the task I'd undertaken. I wasn't kidding when I told him that I'd never encountered the theft of a boat.

As it happens, there's a guy I know from my Spanish trips who was in marine insurance until he retired. He's called Bob too. On impulse, I gave him a call.

He was surprised but when I explained what I was after,

he got right down to business. From what he told me, it seemed that the insurer had followed standard practice by sending in its own assessor. But, significantly he added that in all his career, he had never come across the theft of such a high-value yacht.

We chatted for a little longer about this and that, and promised to meet up next time our paths crossed in our Spanish town. By the time we had finished, so had my quiet music playlist. I was about to cue up some more when the door opened a little wider. My daughter stood there, her hair ruffled and her eyes bleary from interrupted sleep.

'What's up, love?' I asked.

'I had a funny dream,' she mumbled. 'About King John. Where's Mummy?' she asked.

'Mummy's had to go to work, sweetheart,' I told her. I picked her up and carried her upstairs, back to her room.

'Can I have another story?' she asked, drowsily, as she slid back into bed.

I reached for *Now We Are Six*. 'Okay. Let's find one we haven't had before.'

We may have finished the collection, but I can't be sure; when I woke still sprawled across her bed at two in the morning, from a dream about a burned-out car that wasn't at all funny, the book was still open on Seonaid's pink duvet. She was deep in the sleep of the innocent, but I knew that mine was done for the night.

Twenty-Seven

'Did your Cheeky have much to say when you got home?' Sammy Pye asked his colleague.

'"What's that fucking smell?"' Haddock replied, 'and that's word for word. She went on to ask where the fire had been. It shows you how much of a barrier those paper suits really are. How about Ruth?'

'She said something similar when I crawled in beside her at two o'clock. We should have had a shower after the autopsies, I suppose.'

'I don't think Professor Grace was for sharing.'

'Maybe not.' The DCI looked sideways. 'You didn't have to come, you know. One police witness would have been enough.'

'Yes I did. You'd already done one yesterday. It's you that could have skipped it.'

'Did you sleep much?'

'You are fucking joking, gaffer, aren't you?'

'I suppose,' Pye conceded. 'Me neither; maybe a couple of hours. I had coffee for breakfast; I didn't fancy anything else.'

The DS stared at him. 'No? I was starving. I'd a roll and black pudding.'

'Ohhh! Stop it, you bastard.'

'It's okay, I'm joking. My nostrils still feel like they need to be steam cleaned. Maybe we can grab something a bit later, after we've seen this householder.'

They had retraced their route from the previous evening, past the Flotterstone Inn and past the clearing where the burned-out Aygo still stood, and where crime scene officers continued to work in the cold, crisp winter morning air.

Two hundred yards further along the narrow roadway, Pye slowed, coming almost to a halt as they approached a stone-pillared gate that marked the entrance to a driveway, leading to an impressive white villa. He turned in, parking well short of a double garage that was set to the right of the dwelling.

The crunch of tyres on gravel had announced their arrival. As they walked up to the front door, it opened and a woman stepped into view. She was tall, wearing tan trousers that could have been moleskin, and a check shirt, hanging loose. Her hair was golden brown, with a sheen that Pye reckoned had cost well into three figures at one of the city's top hairdressers.

'You'll be the police, I suppose,' she exclaimed as they approached. 'I'm Nancy Walker. You've missed my husband, I'm afraid. He had to leave for the office.'

Pye was not impressed. 'Even though he's a witness in our investigation, and you were told we were coming to see you first thing this morning?'

'Even so. Roland is a senior civil servant, gentlemen, very senior; he has a meeting with the Secretary of State at ten, and I think you'll find that the Secretary of State outranks you.'

The DCI's eyes narrowed, as he and Haddock held up their warrant cards. 'I think you'll find that in this context, he doesn't, ma'am.'

'Be that as it may,' Mrs Walker drawled, as she inspected the credentials, closely, 'he's gone and the world is still turning, officer. Life goes on.'

'Not for Dean Francey and Anna Hojnowski, it doesn't,' Haddock snapped, his customary calm disturbed.

'And who would they be?'

'They would be, or rather they were, the two people inside the car that your husband reported burning last night.'

For the first time, Nancy Walker's self-assurance was ruffled. 'It was a car?' she exclaimed. 'I saw flames from the kitchen, a short distance away; Roland went to investigate, then he called the fire brigade, but he didn't go close enough to see what it was. We heard no more, indeed we thought no more of it, until one of you chaps called us to say we could expect a visit. People died, you say?'

'I'm afraid so,' Pye confirmed.

'That is unfortunate,' the woman said. She hugged herself and gave a small shiver. 'I suppose you'd better come in; you might not freeze out here in your overcoats, but I shall, pretty soon.'

She stood aside to allow them to enter a spacious wood-panelled hall. 'Come along with me,' she instructed, 'and I'll show you the view I had.'

They followed her along a corridor that led to the back of the house, into a kitchen that was flooded with light by the low winter sun. It was a mix of traditional and modern, with an Aga cooker and a farmhouse table, surrounded by fitted units and black granite work surfaces.

The sink was below the window. 'Take a look,' Mrs Walker said, gesticulating. 'I was rinsing the salad when I saw the flames.'

The detectives stood beside her; from their viewpoint they saw a thick green stand of leylandii, capped at a height of around twenty feet.

'It's for privacy; we can't see through and nobody can see in, but last night the light of a fire was visible even above that. I called to Roland . . . he was pouring the Prosecco at the time. He came rushing through, swore like a trooper when he saw it and rushed off again.'

'Didn't it strike you as weird?' Haddock asked. 'I mean, a fire out here in the middle of winter.'

'This is the countryside, young man,' Nancy Walker replied stiffly. 'People do the silliest things here. They think they can park and have barbecues anywhere, any time, and they are all careless with their fires.'

'In February?'

'That is unusual, I admit. You're telling me that two people managed to set their car on fire, with themselves inside it? Too preoccupied, I imagine, to notice anything until it was too late.'

'Not quite,' Pye said. 'Before you saw the light of the fire, did you hear any noises?'

'What kind of noise?' She sniffed. 'People having sex?'

'No, I wouldn't expect you to hear that from a couple of hundred yards away.' A bizarre image of Nancy and Roland Walker leapt into his mind, and then to his relief it went away again. 'Sounds that might have been gunshots.'

The woman frowned, placing her index finger against her chin. 'Now you mention it,' she murmured, 'yes, I did. I'd just checked the trout that I had baking in the Aga, when I heard a couple of bangs.'

'That didn't alarm you?'

She shook her head, firmly. 'No. Chief Inspector, there are deer in this area, and where there are deer these days, there are poachers. It might surprise you but gunshots are not unusual around here.'

191

'Even at night?'

'Especially at night: that's when poachers work. I met one, a couple of years ago. He had radiator trouble and he came to the house to ask if we could fill his water can. He was quite open about what he was doing. He told me that he used a night sight; assured me that we were quite safe, that it could tell the difference between a person and a deer.' She paused. 'So, are you now telling me that the people in the burning car were shot?'

'I'm afraid we are.'

'That's quite appalling. What is this world coming to?'

'A good question,' Haddock conceded. 'Mrs Walker, have you seen anyone recently who was out of the ordinary?'

'Around here, most people are out of the ordinary. You may think of this as an isolated spot on the edge of a busy city, but it isn't. Further on up the road, the reservoir, and the one beyond, are very popular places. They're stocked with trout; lots of people pass by here on the way to a few hours' fishing. Some stay longer; I believe there is holiday accommodation. The fact is, if we see strangers here, we don't give them a second glance.'

'Don't you feel exposed?'

'No.' For the first time, she allowed them a hint of a smile, although it was condescending. 'We have complete faith in the police, and we have a very good alarm system, with cameras.'

Pye was about to remark that having a double murder a hundred yards from their driveway might make them think about reviewing their security, when he was interrupted by his phone, vibrating in his pocket. 'Excuse me,' he murmured, taking it out.

A warm female voice sounded in his ear. 'Sammy, it's Sarah Grace here.'

'Hello, Prof,' he replied. 'It seems hardly any time since we left your place of work. You have been home, haven't you?'

'Not for long. There was a question from the autopsies that I wanted to answer as soon as I could,' he could sense her smile, 'and now I'm happy to say I have.'

'Good for you. Does it take us any further?'

'It might, although it might also need a bit of legwork on your part. Remember the stomach contents that I wasn't sure about?'

'I'll never forget them.' Pye's own stomach threatened to heave as he recalled the moments of their recovery.

'I've identified them. Dino and Anna had the same last meal, no more than three hours before they died: venison burger, in a bun. She had mustard on hers, he had piccalilli. I hope that helps you.'

The DCI beamed. 'Oh I think it might. Thanks, Sarah.'

He winked at Haddock. 'Our next port of call, after we do the press briefing,' he announced. 'Mrs Walker, thanks for your help. I don't think we'll heed to haul your husband out of his meeting with the Secretary of State. Nor will we need a formal statement from you; if there is anything else, we'll get back to you.'

The DS waited until the front door had closed behind them before giving in to his curiosity. 'So?' he exploded.

'Remember Jagger's speciality burger yesterday?' Pye retorted. 'Well,' he said, not waiting for Haddock's nod, 'after we left, he had two more customers.'

Twenty-Eight

Mario McGuire had ordered that Sammy Pye should be senior investigating officer on both the Zena case and the murders of Dino and Anna, and that he should take a press briefing at the former Edinburgh police HQ.

The DCI was used to being on camera, but he had never been in the hot seat at a formal media conference before such a large audience. He was set to be flanked on the platform by Haddock, for little more than moral support, and by a woman he had never met before. Her name was Isabel Cant, ScotServe's deputy head of communications, and to Pye, she set new standards in abrasiveness.

'There's your statement,' she said, as they waited in a small room behind the conference hall, five minutes before they were due on stage, and as she thrust a sheaf of paper into his hands. 'Your Q and A brief is there too, but I'll field the questions and decide which we can answer.'

'We?' Sauce Haddock murmured, beside him.

'This is a team event, Detective Sergeant,' she snapped.

'Fine,' he chuckled, 'so where's my team sheet?'

'You don't need one. You won't be saying anything. This is a very high-profile situation, and very sensitive in media terms.

I can't run the risk of you coming out with information that can't be revealed at this stage.'

'In that case,' Pye intervened, looking up from the text, 'what's this doing here? We're naming the child?'

'That's been decided at the highest level,' she said. 'The father is incommunicado and could be so for months. In those circumstances, we can waive the "next of kin informed" tradition on this occasion. It's only ever done as a courtesy anyway.'

'The highest level? Does that mean the chief constable, or DCC McGuire?'

Cant's stare reminded him of one of his primary school teachers: he had hated that woman. 'No, it means the director of communications.'

'And is that person,' he began, his voice low and slow, 'aware that the mother is still unconscious in hospital after surgery? Is he aware that the link between her injuries and the child's death hasn't been revealed to anyone outside my team? Is he aware that I don't want her waking up to find a posse of journos outside her room?'

He took out his phone, scrolled through his contact numbers and offered it to her. 'There. That's DCC McGuire's number. Would you like to call him and tell him what we're about to do?'

'I don't need to. This is my department's remit. We're responsible for all media communications.'

Haddock laughed. 'So you're going to swan in here and tell an SIO what he can and can't say about his own investigation?'

'Welcome to the world of ScotServe,' Isabel Cant said.

'Welcome to the world of the Menu,' Sammy Pye retorted. 'It'll still be our arses on the line out there, never yours, so we will make the rules.' He checked the time on his phone and put it back in his pocket. 'We won't be needing you in there.'

'I think you'll find that you do,' she snapped back at him.

'I'll tell you what. Why don't you call your boss while you're waiting here, and find out who's right and who's wrong about that? Meantime we're going to do our job the way we see fit.'

He opened the door and stepped into the conference room, leaving Haddock to close it behind them.

Twenty-Nine

'Are you prepared for the wrath of God to crash around your ears?'

'If necessary, sir,' Pye told the deputy chief constable. 'I made a judgement and acted on it.'

'And personalities had nothing to do with it?'

'I hope not. How can I put this? I'd like to think that Ms Cant and I had different perceptions of our relative roles in a police investigation, and that mine prevailed.'

'Thanks to Haddock slamming a door in the face of a senior civilian colleague?'

'Not true, sir.' The DCI winked at the detective sergeant. 'He closed it very gently.'

'Jesus,' McGuire sighed, the sound amplified by the phone's speaker. 'You do know that the new media structure was signed off personally by Sir Andrew?'

'I didn't, but I hope he'll support his officers when it leads to a conflict of priorities.'

'For fuck's sake, Sammy, cut out the diplomatic language. You were told to release the child's name and you countermanded that instruction.'

'As senior investigating officer, sir,' Pye countered, 'I take my orders from my line managers. As far as I know, Isobel Cant isn't one of them.'

'As far as you know,' the DCC mimicked. 'Man, it doesn't work like that any more. In a force of our size, there has to be a recognised communications structure and the professionals within it must have their own form of authority. If Ms Cant, or Peregrine Allsop, her boss, give you a draft, you have to think of it as coming from Sir Andrew himself. What you don't do is tell her to stick it up her arse.'

'That's not fair, sir,' Haddock protested. 'The gaffer was a damn sight more polite than she was.'

'Butt out, Detective Sergeant,' McGuire growled. 'I'll tell you what's fucking fair, and what's not.'

'Sorry, sir.'

'Accepted; remember it. Now: incredibly fortunately for you two, I agree with you in this instance, and I've managed to calm the chief down. Ms Cant breached the new protocol herself, by not discussing the communications strategy with the SIO and taking his views into account. That's your wiggle room. You are doubly lucky, in that once I explained your view to Sir Andrew he agreed with that too, albeit grudgingly, and asked Allsop to tell Cant to stay out of your hair for the duration of this investigation.'

'Thanks, sir,' Pye said. 'I knew you'd go to bat for us.'

'Yeah, well, don't go taking it for granted,' the DCC mumbled. 'You'll need to make your peace with them both at some point, but for now, do things your way. So,' he continued, 'what did you tell the media?'

'I told them as much as I could. I told them that the results of the autopsy on the dead child led us to continue treating her death as suspicious, rather than murder. There was a lot of grumbling when I said I couldn't name her . . .'

McGuire interrupted. 'How did you explain that?'

'With the truth: that there's a problem contacting the father. They pressed me on why, but they gave up on it when I told them that the prime suspect in the abduction, and his girlfriend, had been found shot dead in a burned-out car.'

'Yes, that would get their attention,' McGuire chuckled. 'Did you name both of them?'

'Yes, I was able to do that. The DNA confirmation came through at nine thirty, and the police in Gdansk, Anna's home town, called us to confirm that they'd spoken to her parents.'

'Photographs?'

'Issued. Francey's we had on file; the university had one of Anna on her admission record. Mind you, I'm sure it won't be long before the red-tops are using the one that's on a poster outside Lacey's.'

'And their killer?' McGuire asked.

'I told them what I told you, sir, that we're still examining the crime scene. What I didn't add was, outside that, there are absolutely no leads.'

'Then you'd better go and get some, lads. In today's news cycle, that'll keep them busy for a couple of hours.'

'Maybe a bit longer,' Pye chuckled, softly. 'One of the Fire and Rescue team must have a pal in the *Daily Record* newsroom. Their reporter collared us afterwards; she said they'd had a tip-off that the fire team leader at the crime scene went bats when he saw the car. I'd no reason to "no comment" her, so I confirmed it, and said that the guy was Francey's brother-in-law. She went off in search of Levon Rattray. As soon as they break that online, the rest'll have to play catch-up. They'll be off our backs, for a wee while at least.'

'Good,' the DCC said, 'use that time well; you have to keep

199

ahead of the media on this one. There's a lot resting on this investigation for you, chum. You're not completely off the hook with the chief. He might have backed what you did this morning, but you still crossed him. The last thing he said to me was that if you don't get a result, he'll think about seconding you to the Communications Department. I don't think he was joking either.'

Thirty

'Do you think he meant it, Sauce?' Sammy Pye murmured, as he parked on a yellow line on St John's Road. He had been quiet throughout the drive from the Fettes building.

'Nah,' the DS replied, dismissively. 'The DCC was winding you up.'

'I'm not so sure. I've known Mario McGuire for a lot longer than you have; I reckon I can tell when he's serious and when he isn't.'

'Then the chief was winding him up.'

'Unlikely. Only two guys ever did that: his mate Neil McIlhenney, who's a commander in the Met these days, and Bob Skinner. You don't know Andy Martin either; you were a wet-eared plod when he left for Tayside. He might be a smooth operator on the outside, but inside he's a hard, ruthless bastard. Look at the way he treated Alex Skinner.'

'How did he treat her?' Haddock asked. 'You're right; I'm new on the block as far as that's concerned.'

'He had it off with her when she was barely out of her teens. Big Bob went ballistic when he found out, but they got engaged, he calmed down, and Andy was flavour of the month again. Then he chucked her . . . nobody ever found out why . . . and went off and married Karen Neville. A couple of kids later, he walked out on Karen, and he was back in with Alex. Karen rejoined the force and moved back down here from Perth. Then the top job came up, Andy got it, and it was all off again with him and Alex. On top of that, Karen's got a DI promotion through in the west, and so Andy can be nearer his kids.'

'And nearer his ex-wife too?'

Pye shook his head. 'No, there's not a prayer of that happening. Karen's a pal from way back; we're close still, so I know that even if the thought crosses his mind, he'll get nowhere. She's done with him.'

'And I suppose the chief knows,' Haddock ventured, 'that you and Karen are close. Do you think . . . ?'

'That he might have it in for me? Fuck, that never occurred to me. I'll tell you one thing, Sauce,' he growled, 'if he does try to second me into some backwater desk job, I'm not having it. I'll be off.'

'You can't. What would you do?'

'I don't know, but I'd find something.' Pye smiled. 'Maybe I'd join Bob Skinner.'

'Join him in what?'

'In whatever he's doing. I don't buy in to all this media stuff, or the Security Industry Authority board job that's just been announced. There's too much cop in him to walk away from it altogether. He's an investigator; it's what he does. It's in his blood.'

'How does he feel about his pal now,' Sauce asked, 'after what he did to Alex?'

'I don't know. The only thing I will say is that if you hurt her, you are in more trouble than you could ever imagine, and I don't care who the fuck you are.'

Pye took the key from the ignition and laid a crested 'Police on duty' card on the dashboard. 'Come on,' he said, 'let's go and lean on these two clowns.'

The detectives stepped out of the car and walked the few yards to the door of the takeaway. There were no customers, but Ian Harbison was behind the service counter. As they entered, he did not react; instead he continued staring at the wall. Radio Forth was playing in the background, a news reader halfway through a football news story.

'Drizzle,' Haddock said quietly, turning the sign on the door from 'Open' to 'Closed'. Harbison jumped, and turned to face them.

'You two,' he murmured. 'What I just heard on the radio: it's true, is it? Dino's dead?'

'Afraid so,' the DS replied. 'And Singer.'

'Yeah? Bloody hell!'

'What time did they leave here yesterday?'

Drizzle stared. 'What are you talking about? They were never here.'

Pye glared at him. 'That's not what the pathologist says. Unless some other takeaway was doing a venison special yesterday, they were here.'

'If they were, I never saw them,' he insisted. 'I told you, if I'd seen Dino, I'd have called you. But . . . I was front of house in the afternoon. Jagger was in the kitchen.'

'Is he there now?'

'Yes. Hold on.' Harbison turned and opened the door behind him. 'Jagger,' he barked. 'Get your fucking arse in here!'

A few seconds later, Michael Smith appeared, in an apron and a white trilby, frowning. 'What the fuck's up wi' . . .' He stopped in mid-sentence as he saw Pye and Haddock. 'Aw no! Gie's a break.'

'Dino's dead,' his friend said, bluntly. 'Him and Singer.'

'What?' he gasped, mouth agape.

'It's just been on the radio. They were found last night, shot dead in a car, up in the Pentlands. Dino didn't have a car that I know of, but I've got a hell of a feeling that there was one parked out the back of this place yesterday afternoon.'

Jagger flared up and took a step forward, his loose lips pouting. 'Aye, well?' he snarled. 'He's ma mate, so . . .' Drizzle met him halfway, with a headbutt that landed above his left eye; he howled and reeled back, his hands going to his face.

'You half-witted twat,' Harbison snapped. 'You knew the guy was wanted for taking that kid. We are on probation, both of us. If you get caught helping him, here, in this place, that lands me in it as well.'

'Did you guys see that?' Jagger wailed, as he straightened up. A trickle of blood came from a cut on his eyebrow.

'No,' Pye told him, 'and if he banjoes you again we won't see that either. So tell us: what time was he here?'

'The back of five,' he confessed. 'Like Drizzle said, he came in the back door, him and Anna. There wis a white motor parked ootside. He was scared, ken; they both were, but Dino was kackin' himself. I asked him if it was right, that he'd kilt that lassie.'

'What did he say?' Haddock asked.

'He said that she was alive when he put her in the motor, and that the boot was padded, wi' an air hole in it. He said that he ran intae some guy in the Fort Kinnaird car park. The fella came for him, big bloke, hard lookin', so he legged it.'

'So why did he come here?'

'For cash,' Jagger said. 'He told me that he'd gone back tae North Berwick, to get his old man's car and pick up dough frae his flat, but that he bumped in tae polis. Wis that youse?'

Pye nodded. 'Take us on from there.'

'He told me he'd got away then caught the train tae Musselburgh. He'd taken his sister's motor frae the uni, where it's parked durin' the day, and then picked up Singer.'

'Why did he do that?' the DCI asked. 'Why did he involve her?'

'Ah don't now. Ah never asked him. Mibbe he didnae want tae leave her behind. He wis daft on her, man.'

'Did you give him money?'

'Aye. A kept a tenner for masel', and gave him the rest o' what Ah had on me, about thirty-five quid. Ah gave him ma bank card too. Ah told him he could have three hundred quid out of that and post it back to me. He said that if Ah wanted, I could take thae fish out ma granny's freezer, deliver them tae the Chinese in Broxburn and keep the money. He gie'd me the address, ken.'

'And you gave him and Anna venison burgers, for the road.'

'Aye. An' a box o' crisps and a case o' Vimto.'

'Did he say where they were going?'

'As far away as they fuckin' could. But he said he had tae meet a bloke. The guy owed him more cash.'

'But he came to you for money as well?' Haddock exclaimed.

'He said they were goin' tae need all the dough he could raise. He said if they could, they were going tae get on a car ferry and head for Holland and then Poland.'

'Did he have a passport?'

'Ah dinnae ken.' Jagger shrugged. 'Like Ah said, he was crappin' himsel', no' thinkin' straight.'

'And Singer, Anna, how was she?'

'Like Ah said, she was feart too, but no' as bad as Dino. She was under control.' His eyes widened. 'Aye, that's right. Ah remember noo; she said she had her passport and that when they got tae the ferry, she was goin' tae hide Jagger in the boot, just like he hid the kid. She reckoned that once they got tae Holland she'd be able tae use her credit card.'

'You're a couple of bastards, you and Dino,' Drizzle growled. 'Anna was a nice kid. What the hell she was doing with you bum holes I'll never know.'

'Ah, fuck you,' Jagger sighed. He looked at Pye. 'So what happens now?' he asked. 'Ah've told yis what Ah know.'

'This is what's going to happen,' the DCI said, smiling. 'This is the bit I like. Do the honours, Sauce.'

'My pleasure, gaffer. Michael Smith, he began 'I am detaining you under Section Fourteen of the Criminal Procedure, Scotland, Act, nineteen ninety-five, because I suspect you of having committed an offence punishable by imprisonment, namely giving assistance to a person or persons you knew to be fugitives to escape from the police.

'The reasons for my suspicions,' he continued, 'are the facts that on your own admission, the suspects were here yesterday afternoon after you knew that one of them was wanted by the police in connection with a serious crime, and were given financial assistance by you.

'You will be detained to enable further investigations to be carried out regarding the offence and as to whether or not you should be reported for prosecution. You will be taken to a police station where you will be informed of your further rights in respect of detention.'

The DS stopped, then added, 'It's a bit of a mouthful, but it means you're lifted, Jagger. When you're sitting in the remand wing in Saughton, I want you to think on this. If you'd done the right thing by the dead child and called us when Dino and Singer turned up here, they'd still be alive, and you wouldn't be locked up. I hope you choke on your porridge, pal.'

Thirty-One

'Is this really a holiday resort?' Haddock asked, as he drove carefully through the narrow, crowded streets of the seaside town.

'Absolutely,' Pye assured him. 'In the old days they called this the "Biarritz of the North". It's still popular. You're thinking like a young single man, Sauce.'

'I'm not single! We're a couple.'

'No, you're a Dinky: as in, Dual Income No Kids. It's the same as being single, in most ways. When you think of a holiday, you think of getting on a plane and getting off somewhere twenty degrees warmer. When you think of a beach it has to be so bloody hot underfoot that you can't walk on it.'

The DS grinned. 'That just about sums it up, I'll admit.'

'Then wait till you're like Ruth and me, with Junior to look after. We did it once, the package holiday thing. Nightmare. Getting him on and off the plane, to the hotel, never taking our eyes off him while he was crawling about near the pool, finding something he could eat without him spitting it out.

'Ever since then we've rented a cottage. Next summer we're going to CenterParcs in the Lake District. If it's warm at the weekends and we fancy the beach, we take him to North Berwick, or over to Fife. Elie's nice, or would be if it had more facilities.'

'We'll bear all that in mind,' Haddock said, 'in five years' time, or maybe in ten. Meanwhile, in this place there isn't even a yellow line we can park on.'

'Go back to the police station,' the DCI suggested. Haddock was about to take his advice when a space opened up for him, as a Volvo estate pulled out. 'See? Patience.'

'Not my strongest suit,' Haddock grumbled. 'Don't we have DCs who could be doing this job?'

'Yes, but it's one for us. I want to see Dino's flat, not hear about it second hand. The boy Jagger can stew in the cells at Fettes until we're ready for him.'

'Are we going to charge him?'

'Too bloody right we are. I've already told the depute fiscal as much. He may have talked to us eventually, but what you told him was spot on. His help and his silence sent them to their deaths.'

'He could say he confessed under duress.'

'The only possible duress was applied by Drizzle's forehead, and that was part of an altercation. Sauce,' he said, 'the Crown Office might decide eventually not to prosecute because he wasn't under caution when he told his story, but he's going to be charged and stuck up in court before anyone's had a chance to think too deeply about it. Apart from anything else, he's media fodder. It'll be reported as a positive development.'

'And get you brownie points with the chief?' Haddock murmured, laughing.

'Us,' Pye countered grimly. 'If this thing winds up in the unsolved column nobody's going to come out with pass marks at the next review . . . apart from Jackie, 'cos I'll make sure she does. Now, where is this place?'

'There it is.' The DS nodded towards a doorway on the other side of the road, where Sergeant Tweedie stood, waiting. 'Did you get the keys?' he asked her as they crossed.

'Yes,' she replied. 'The landlord wanted to come with us, but I told him that wouldn't be appropriate in a criminal investigation. He liked that.' She grinned. 'It'll give him something to tell his pals in the Nether Abbey at the weekend.'

She led them through a door that opened directly from the street into a dimly lit corridor. The detectives counted three flights of stairs, until there were no more to climb.

'You two won't remember DCS Pringle, who used to be head of CID in the old force,' Pye told the sergeants as they reached the top. 'By the end of his career he used to insist on being given a detailed description of a call-out. If there were stairs involved he wouldn't go. Stevie Steele, God rest him, told a story about the last time he did, a visit to a fourth-storey flat. When they got to it, they found the door painted purple. Stevie said Pringle's face was about the same colour.'

He stood back, as Sergeant Tweedie produced the keys. Only the Yale was needed. 'Gentlemen,' she said, moving to one side, then following them into the attic apartment. It was small, but freshly decorated, with a dormer window that allowed a view across the putting green and towards Fife.

'What are we looking for?' she asked, as the trio put on rubber gloves.

'Anything that links to associates of Francey,' the DCI replied. 'Did you get anything out of Chic when you gave him the death message?'

'Nothing useful,' Tweedie told him. 'Like you told me to, I asked him to make a list of his son's associates. The only names he gave me were people he drank with in the County and the

Ship. I know them all, just like I knew Francey. There are a couple of rowdies in there, but nobody who I'd consider for a minute for this sort of thing.'

'Did he mention Callum Sullivan?'

'No; nor his nephew either. I've been asking around and my impression is that he and the boy Maxwell Harris were no more than acquaintances. The kid was struggling for friends when he moved here, and that's why he latched on to Francey.'

'Friendly enough for him to have been in Mr Sullivan's garage and seen the car, though,' Haddock pointed out.

'True,' Tweedie conceded, 'but you know what I think? I think Dino smelled money, so he cultivated the kid, just to see what might come out of it. And at the end of the day, something did.'

'The red BMW.'

'Exactly. I was suspicious as soon as I heard that he helped Maxwell polish the cars. That was far too much like work for Dean Francey. There had to be something in it for him.'

'As there was,' the DS murmured. 'Far more than he could handle.'

'Hey!' Pye's call came from the other side of the room, by the window. He had lifted the television set down from the cabinet on which it stood, then opened the rectangular unit and looked inside. 'I might have something here.'

He reached into the box and took out a passport, and then a brown envelope with an elastic band securing it from the outside. He carried both to a gateleg table that stood against the wall.

He removed the fastening from the envelope then slid out its contents: a wad of cash, secured tightly by another elastic band. Holding the bundle carefully, he rippled through the notes with his thumb.

'Used notes,' he murmured. 'Clydesdale Bank issue, on the outside at least.'

'How much is there?' Haddock asked, as the DCI returned them to the envelope.

'I'm not a bank teller, and I don't want to handle them any more than I have to, not until the scientists have had a chance to print and swab them. But, if they're all tenners, as they seem to be, I'd take an uneducated guess at five grand.'

'Do you think that's payment in full, or a first instalment?'

'The latter surely,' the DCI suggested. 'Didn't Jagger say Dino was going to meet a guy who owed him money?'

'Hold on,' the DS exclaimed. 'If it was half in advance and he was going to collect another five K, why did he need Jagger's thirty quid and his bank card?'

'We know that. He and Singer were going away for good; and maybe also because after the utter bollocks he'd made of the job he was sent out to do, he might have had doubts about whether he would actually get paid the rest.'

'Are you sure the money relates to the abduction?'

Both men turned and stared at Lucy Tweedie as she asked her question.

'This much I am sure of,' Pye said, quietly. 'He didn't make it selling frozen fish as fresh to Chinese restaurants.'

Thirty-Two

I have never been the best sleeper; all through my life there's been plenty to keep me awake, whenever I close my eyes and try not to think of it. Scenes from my childhood, scenes from my early adult past, and scenes from more recent times; they're all there waiting to be replayed. The most recent, and because of that the most vivid, is set in a mountainside lodge in the Pyrenees, but we won't go there.

It's worst when I'm on my own. Mostly my nights are uninterrupted when Sarah's beside me. It marks her out as special to me; none of the others, not even Myra, and certainly not Aileen, ever came close to banishing my nocturnal horrors.

I tried that night, after I'd left my Seonaid to the peace that I hope will last her a lifetime, but as I'd known, it was a no-hoper. What kept me awake? What else but the newest clip in my library, the vision of sad-eyed little asthmatic Zena Gates, revealed, reproachful, after spending her last moments in terrifying darkness, struggling for one last breath that didn't come.

I left her to it, because I didn't have the courage to face her. Instead, at around four thirty, I rose, showered, had what would be, given the time, my first shave of the day and went downstairs.

I made myself coffee, a good strong filter brew of which Sarah would have disapproved. It was a minor act of cheating on her, I suppose, and I did feel guilty, but I needed it.

In the office, I picked up the McGarry file again, and had another look at it. I was no more impressed than I'd been the first time. I'd covered up for the guy when I'd spoken to Eden, but I was still enough cop not to have criticised him to a civilian. I made a mental note to call stolenboats.org, on the crazy off chance that it might have some intelligence on the fate of the *Princess*, then put it aside, turned on the computer and read my online morning newspapers. The dead child case was covered wall-to-wall as I'd expected, with many more questions than answers, but nothing about Dean Francey and his girlfriend had been picked up at that stage. I guessed that even the virtual media must sleep sometimes.

Sounds from the kitchen at seven thirty told me that Trish had come in from her apartment to start getting the kids up and ready for school. She's a godsend, that girl. She's been with the family for years, since not long after she arrived from Barbados, and shows no sign of wanting to leave us. It occurred to me as I listened to her rattling dishes that if Sarah did turn out to be pregnant again it would be good news for her.

I went through to tell her that Sarah was in Edinburgh and that she was in full charge of the brood. Then I went upstairs and dug out my running gear. At least twice a week, all year round, I run in the morning. In the summer I can go where I want, but when the nights are long, and the sun comes up with the eight o'clock news, I have to keep to the village, where there's enough light.

A complete lap of my route is just over four kilometres. I did that easily in under half an hour, concentrating on nothing but the music from my iPod. My choice varies; it's dependent on how fast I want to run. I had stuff to get out of my system, so that morning I chose Status Quo.

When I was done, rather than tackle another lap, I went into the village gym and spent some time on the weights. I've never been one for bulking myself up, but I do have levels that I like to maintain, although it's harder now that I'm past fifty. Fifteen minutes in the sauna and I jogged home for my second shower of the day, feeling more like a human being and much less alone.

I called Sarah from the bedroom. I was taking something of a chance; the two autopsies might have gone on into the early hours and she might have been trying to grab some sleep. But no, she wasn't. In fact, she was in her office.

Pathology is a big subject in university terms; she works entirely on the forensic side, and with Joe Hutchinson's retirement looming, she was about to become head of a five-person unit that is part academic, part NHS, providing services under contract to the Crown Office, not only in and around Edinburgh, but in Fife and across much of the Scottish Central belt .

She could have based herself pretty much anywhere, but she had chosen the Royal Infirmary, the department's administration centre. That's where she was when I reached her.

'Have you been home?' I asked. She still has her own house, a relic from when we were still apart. It had been useful until then, but it was something we had to address.

'Not for long,' she admitted. 'I didn't get cleared up in the mortuary until much before three, but I needed to be around early to take the first lab results.'

'Everything as expected?'

215

'Pretty much. There's something in the tests that might help the guys, but then again, it might not.'

'The guys?'

'Sammy and Sauce. Mario's decreed that the links between these murders and the child are so close that they're a single inquiry.'

'I'd have done the same,' I admitted.

'Yes,' she laughed, 'and when you were chief, if your head of CID had taken a different view you'd have overruled him.'

'That's how bad I was?' I asked.

'From everything I've heard . . . although I wasn't around for much of that time. How were the kids? Good night?'

'Better than I had. That package I got from Mario wasn't exactly full of information. In fact it was bloody annoying; a real shoddy job done by a real shoddy operator. I know I wasn't in Strathclyde long, but honest to God, love,' I grumbled, 'I should have had a better grip on it than that.'

'So think of this as your second chance,' she suggested. 'Got to go now. Have a good day and I'll see you later.'

'With that testing kit?'

'Yes, I promise. I'll call by Boots on the way home.'

Downstairs there was peace and quiet in the kitchen, with all three youngsters having gone off to school in my absence. I made myself a slightly late breakfast, melon, muesli, rye toast and mineral water, then carried it to the office, on a tray, to enjoy it at my leisure.

I had finished, and was taking a second look at the online *Saltire*, paying particular attention to the coverage of Sammy Pye's investigation . . . by that time the Flotterstone deaths were being reported but not labelled as homicide, or linked to the other . . . when my email alert pinged.

I checked my box and saw a message from Luisa McCracken. I opened it and read:

Mr Skinner,
Please find attached a list of all guests and other attendees at events and receptions on board MV *Princess Alison* over the period requested by Mr Higgins. Should you need any more information, please give me a call.

She was either a fast worker or the list wasn't very comprehensive, I surmised. As soon as I opened it I saw that the former was the case. Her boss had been more socially active than he'd led me to believe, for it ran to several pages. I scanned through it, quickly but carefully, looking at every name that had been recorded.

Some of them were known to me, people about town, a few stars of sports and entertainment, other men and women who were there, as the list indicated, for no other reason than friendship with Eden Higgins, and one or two that he might have had reasons for being seen with himself, politicians for example, and a couple of mid-ranking members of the royal family.

The rest were all business contacts: clients of his companies, suppliers to those businesses, and executives and directors of the enterprises themselves. I studied them, looking for anything that might point me in a positive direction, but nothing jumped out at me.

'Why didn't you just sell the *Princess Alison*, Eden,' I found myself wondering aloud, 'and buy the Royal Yacht *Britannia*? That would do the hospitality job and you'd never have to leave Edinburgh.'

I sat down and went to work. I made a copy of the document, then used it to strip out all of those labelled 'Casuals', the footballers, the friends and the freeloaders. When I was finished, everyone who was left had a business reason for being on the *Princess*. That was where I would begin . . . or rather, where somebody else would.

Thirty-Three

I picked up the phone and made two appointments then went back upstairs and changed my clothes, swapping my casual gear for a dark suit and a light blue tie, my new uniform. When I'm on business, I want people to know I'm serious.

Both of my visits were in Edinburgh; I took the train from Drem, since I can't abide driving through the chaos that generations of bad traffic management has brought to the city centre.

The first was to a small office, just off the Royal Mile, not far from the station. The name on the door was 'CMcD Investigations'. Its occupant had been surprised by my call, and I'd made a point of letting her stay curious.

'I need to see you,' I'd told her. 'I have some work for you; it's confidential and nobody should get to know that it's being done. It'll be boring and tedious but it'll need to be done thoroughly. I'll give you the details when I get there.'

Although her office suite had only one room and a toilet, Carrie McDaniels' door had a secure entry system. It was opened with a buzzer, once I'd identified myself through a microphone. This was in obedience to a sign that said, 'Say your name, then state your business.' I glanced up as I spoke and saw a tiny camera focused on me; a sensible precaution, given that she was a female lone trader in a business that isn't without its risks.

'How are you doing, Carrie?' I said as I stepped inside. 'How's the boyfriend?'

'I'm okay, but I can't vouch for him,' she replied. 'We're spending some time apart, so I can work out how I feel about a man who took me for a fool and proved himself right.'

Carrie and I had met a few months before, when she was on a surveillance assignment in which, unfortunately for her, I was the subject. Her route to professional private investigation had been through an insurance company and a few years in the Territorial Army Military Police. It hadn't taught her everything she needed to know, but she had impressed me once I'd sorted out a few things between us.

'I must admit I didn't think I'd be seeing you again,' she confessed.

A reunion hadn't been uppermost in my mind either, but I don't hold grudges. I had a job that needed doing. Time being money, the task was well below my pay grade, and it made sense to contract it out. The only question was, to whom?

I know a couple of people who did brief stints in the police service, then left to set up as private investigators. If they'd impressed me they might still be in the force, but they hadn't so they weren't on my very short list of candidates. On the other hand, Carrie had been a Territorial military cop for several years, and she hadn't backed off when she'd been posted to Afghanistan. That moved her right to the head of the queue.

'I can walk away if you'd rather,' I replied.

'No, no,' she laughed, 'don't do that. I need all the business I can get.'

'Times are tough?'

'They're okay, but you know how it is in this trade. It takes a while to build up a solid customer base; at my stage you grab all the work that comes your way.'

'Hopefully you've learned not to take on work without knowing exactly who your client is?' Her basic naivety had been at the heart of the initial difficulty between us, and later it had come back to bite her.

'Oh yes,' Carrie replied. 'I'm very careful who I work for now.'

'Do you want to work for me?'

'Is it legal?' she asked, with a smile.

I grinned back at her. 'Anything that isn't I'll be handling myself.' I opened my briefcase and took out a folder. 'I need you to run background checks for me on a list of people. I want to know if any of them have a grudge, overt or hidden, against this man.' I took a photo, one that I'd printed myself, from the file. 'Do you know who he is?'

She took it from me and studied it, carefully. 'That's Eden Higgins, isn't it, the businessman?'

'Got him in one. How much do you know about him?'

'Personally, nothing. Although . . .' she hesitated. 'A few months ago, his wife made a claim against the insurance company I worked for, and I checked it out.'

'Much involved?'

'Quite a bit. A suite of her jewellery was nicked, a necklace, matching bracelet and a pair of earrings, Christ knows how many carats of diamonds in the lot. She and her husband were staying in a country house hotel in Argyllshire, attending some sort of international business summit. When she arrived she deposited the jewels in the hotel safe. The following evening, when she wanted them for the main event dinner, they were gone.'

'Did the insurers pay out?'

'They had to,' she said. 'There was some talk of arguing that the swag had been left at the owner's personal risk, but that fell very quickly and they settled for the full insured amount.'

'How much was that?'

'Two hundred and fifty thou. The irony was that we insured both parties, but it'll be the hotel's policy renewal that'll be hammered next time round, for its owners were held at fault.'

'Have the jewels been recovered?' I asked.

'Not a chance. The local Inspector Clouseau was baffled, and the Pink Panther got away with it.'

'Was anything else taken?'

'Nothing. That was remarked on at the time. One of the other guests had a large quantity of bearer bonds on his possession, and they'd been signed into the safe too. They were left untouched, yet they were worth ten times what the jewellery was. The thief couldn't have been as smart as he thought.'

'Or a lot smarter than the police reckoned,' I countered.

'What do you mean?'

'Let's say you're the Pink Panther. You're after jewellery. You find it, and alongside it there's a few million quid in out-dated old-fashioned, but still entirely legal tender, and,' I added, 'entirely untraceable, bearer bonds. What are you going to do?'

'Fill my pockets,' Carrie chuckled.

'Are you really?' I asked.

'Why not?'

'Possibly self-preservation,' I said. 'Look, you're a jewel thief, it's what you do. Mainly, almost invariably, you're actually stealing from insurance companies, not individuals. If you're good enough to evade Clouseau, and you have a safe market for the gear, you're free and clear.

'But,' I continued, 'yield to greed or temptation . . . a hell of a lot of temptation, I'll grant you . . . and trouser the bearer bonds, you are stepping into the unknown. Those things are a risky form of security and, historically, they've been used by some very risky people. Yes, they are untraceable and you could be set up for life, but the chances are you'd spend the rest of that potentially short life looking over your shoulder.'

'I see what you mean,' Carrie admitted. She looked up at me and winked. 'I wouldn't like to steal your bearer bonds.'

I smiled. 'Best not to, I agree.' I paused and then went back on subject. 'I take it you didn't meet Eden Higgins in the course of your work for your company.'

'No. Only his wife and his son, who's quite tasty as I recall.'

'So you have no preconceptions of him?'

'No. He's just another very successful bloke. Why do you ask?'

'Because ultimately,' I told her, 'he's your client. You're working for me, and I'll pay you, but my assignment is from him. By the way, you never told me; which insurance company did you work for?'

'Edinburgh Co-operative.'

That was okay; the *Princess Alison* was insured with another firm, marine specialists.

I handed her the folder. 'Get to work. Remember; confidential and none of the subjects find out that it's being done. I could have gone to the business staff at the *Saltire* with this, but they'd have asked why I needed to know, so don't you take that route either. Don't go asking journalists.'

'Why do you need to know?' she ventured.

I shook my head. 'Just you concentrate on the task, and leave it at that.'

'I'm thirty-five quid an hour,' she said, bluntly. 'Plus exes.'

'That's fine, but don't take the piss. Any extra costs above a hundred, you clear with me first.'

I gave her my card with all my contact numbers on it and left her to get on with the job. I didn't ask what else she had on her plate, but the lack of paper on her desk had made me think that it might not be much.

My second appointment didn't require a taxi trip or even a long walk, only a stroll up a quarter of the Royal Mile to the Higgins Holdings headquarters on the Mound. But it wasn't Eden that I'd arranged to see.

Luisa McCracken greeted me nonetheless; in the absence of her boss and his son, she seemed to be in charge of the small staff of analysts and accountants.

'Was the list satisfactory?' she asked, as soon as she met me in the foyer.

'Entirely,' I replied. 'You're a fast worker. I didn't expect it until the afternoon.'

'When Mr Higgins asks for something,' she explained, 'he never says "As soon as possible", but that's what he means. Have you known him long?'

Her question took me by surprise; I've always assumed that the term 'confidential secretary' is all-embracing, but apparently it wasn't in her case.

'Twenty years,' I said. 'I met him through Alison.'

'Ah, of course,' she murmured. 'His sister was a police officer in Edinburgh, so you and she must have worked together. I should have realised.'

I could have enlightened her further, but I didn't see the need. 'I'd never met Mrs Higgins until yesterday, though,' I volunteered. 'Not properly at any rate.'

'Rachel takes nothing to do with the management of Eden's companies,' the secretary retorted, with a little sharpness in her tone that started me wondering whether she had ever harboured ambitions beyond the workplace.

'Wasn't she involved at the time of the jewel theft?' I asked. 'Didn't that take place at a business event?'

She frowned at me, over her long eyelashes. 'How did you know about that? It was never reported in the press.'

'You said it yourself. I used to be a police officer.'

'But it happened in Argyllshire,' she said. 'You were based in Glasgow, were you not?'

I pinched Carrie's analogy. 'You don't think Inspector Clouseau circulated details of the stolen items to every police force in the country?'

'I suppose he would have,' she conceded. 'As for your question, yes, that was a business event, but sometimes it's necessary, or at least desirable for him to be accompanied. That's as much as Rachel ever has to do with the business . . . apart from owning half of it,' she added.

'She does?'

'Of course. Higgins Holdings has no outside shareholders; Eden and Rachel own the company, fifty fifty.' She looked at me as if she was considering how much she could tell me, then made a judgement. 'It goes back a long way, to the start of Dene Furnishings, the original business. Rachel's father loaned Eden the start-up cash; the deal was that everything that flowed from it would be jointly owned between husband and wife, on the record.'

Funny, I thought, that Eden would tell Luisa all that and yet say nothing about Alison and me. 'You really do have his confidence,' I remarked.

'Oh I do,' she replied, 'but I didn't get all of it from him. The share split's on the record at Companies House; it's public information. Rory told me the background.'

Did he, by God? From speculating about her having a thing with the boss, I moved on to wondering whether she might have moved down a generation.

Either she read my mind or she knew that she'd been too frank, for she gave a quick laugh. 'That sounds awful,' she exclaimed, 'as if I pump him for information. That's not how it was; he and I were going over the company annual report when it arrived from the auditors. The shareholder information's set out there, and he just came out with it. "You know why that is?" he said, and then he volunteered the answer.'

'That must have pleased you, in a way,' I suggested. 'After all, it shows that you have the complete trust of the son as well as the father.'

It occurred to me that it showed also that Rachel had Eden by the balls, suppose Luisa did harbour ambitions there. But I didn't say that; I said nothing, and allowed her to carry on being frank.

'I suppose,' she admitted, 'although Rory really is only learning the business. His father's bringing him in gradually, with a view to retiring in five years or so. As it is, Rachel already lives in Monaco for quite a few months out of every year. It's an easy commute,' she added. 'The company has its own plane.'

All of that set me wondering once again about her and Eden, with the cat being away so much, but I let it lie. I hadn't come to interrogate Luisa; that had been a bonus. She'd started talking; all my experience has taught me that when people do that, if it's news to you, shut up and listen.

'Mr Hurrell,' I said abruptly.

'Yes.' She too snapped back to the reason for my visit. 'He's in his room, waiting for you. He has nothing to do until Eden's return flight gets in from London this evening.'

She led me towards a door, next to her own and two away from Eden's office, rapped quickly on it and opened it. 'Walter,' she called out, 'Mr Skinner's here to see you,' then stood aside to let me past.

If I'd been expecting a little man in a chauffeur's uniform, I couldn't have been further from the reality of Walter Hurrell as he stood up to greet me. He was around the six foot mark, in the same age bracket as Luisa McCracken, late thirties, and was dressed in a grey suit so sharp that if you'd seen Eden and him side by side you'd have assumed that he was the billionaire.

He was lean, and I suspected that the expensive tailoring covered a powerful build; he was clean shaven with a perma-tan, and his thick dark hair was brushed back from his forehead. His only irregular feature was a conspicuously broken nose that reminded me of Inspector Drake in *Ripper Street*. There wasn't a hint of a smile as he looked at me, and his eyes were cool and appraising. We shook hands; I was prepared for a crusher grip but it didn't come. Instead those grey eyes stayed fixed on me. 'Ex-Navy,' Eden had told me, but this was no everyday sailor. The guy's body language was yelling 'Special Forces'.

'SBS?' I asked.

Hurrell relaxed a little and finally I saw a flicker of a smile. 'That obvious?' he answered.

'It was the suit that gave you away,' I joked.

The room was small, and so he didn't have a desk, just a side table and three chairs. I took a seat that faced the window, with its view of Princes Street.

'Were you a commando?'

'No, I was Royal Navy, not Royal Marines.' His accent was English; south of Birmingham, west of Southampton, I guessed. 'I was a petty officer on a minesweeper. It bored the shit out of me, so I applied for Special Boat Service training. It's a less common entry route, but it is possible.'

'So I've heard.'

'You've encountered Special Forces before?'

I nodded. 'Several times. I had a friend who did the whole tour; SAS, Defence Intelligence, you name it.'

'Is he still in the service?'

'Note the past tense. He isn't anywhere any more.'

'Ahh, I'm sorry,' Hurrell murmured. 'Killed in action?'

'Of a kind: I'm sorry to be mysterious,' I added.

He whistled. 'Spooky stuff? I never did any of that.'

I hadn't gone there to talk about my past, and certainly not that chapter in the story.

'Suppose you were going to steal the *Princess Alison*,' I asked, abruptly. 'How would you go about it?'

The grey eyes narrowed, grew colder again. 'Are you hinting at something?'

'Hell no,' I laughed. 'I don't take you for an idiot. It was a straight question.'

'Mmm.' He didn't look one hundred per cent convinced, nor should he have been. I knew nothing about ex-Petty Officer Hurrell, nor did I know how thorough Eden's vetting had been. 'In that case,' he replied, 'all I can say is that I'd have done it the same way they did. Cut the phone line, in fast, blind the sensor, and out of there as soon as the boat was powered up.'

'You agree with the thinking that whoever did it had advance knowledge?'

'Up to a point. They might not, depending on their hacking skills. The detailed plans of the boathouse will be on the local authority website. The schematic of the alarm system, that'll be somewhere too.'

'How would they know how to open the doors?' I asked.

'From the planning application; that detail would be there. Also, there's a manual override of the remote opening system.'

'But the door was closed again after the boat was taken.'

'Maybe that was a bonus,' Hurrell suggested. 'Once you're on the bridge and at the controls, the remote control device is bloody obvious; it's right there beside the wheel, in a holder. But if not, if the operation was planned down to that last detail, the name of the door supplier is right there on the outside and its IT system will be accessible too. As for the layout of the *Princess*, she's a piece of work, but she's not unique. She doesn't have many sisters but there are some.'

'Are you telling me, Walter,' I quizzed him, 'that the police assumption that the theft involved insider knowledge is all wrong?'

'No, I'm saying it's not a safe assumption to make.'

'I get it. Let's move on. Do you have any thoughts on what's happened to her?'

'Thoughts maybe, clues no. I might imagine her cruising around the Black Sea, crowded with dodgy Russians quaffing champagne and Beluga caviar, but I've got no reason to believe that.'

'Could she have been loaded on to a ship?'

'No,' he declared, emphatically. 'First, it would need to be a bloody big ship, and second, it would have to be done in a dock, given the size of crane you'd need to lift the *Princess*.'

'But it's not impossible?'

'It's not,' he admitted, 'but are you going to steal a yacht then show her off in a public place, before loads of witnesses?'

'Understood,' I said. 'Could she be sunk?'

'She could, but why?' Hurrell leaned back, looking at me. 'I know, you're suggesting that that somebody hates the boss, and stole his boat to piss him off, then scuttled her. The problem with your theory is that nobody does hate the man, or has any reason to. He makes people rich, and they love him for it. On top of that, he's a genuinely nice bloke. You of all people must know that. From what I hear you were practically family at one point.'

'I wouldn't put it that strongly,' I snapped.

'Sorry, sir,' Hurrell murmured, quickly. 'But he is, isn't he?'

'Apology accepted, and I won't deny it.'

'She's been sold,' he declared abruptly. 'That's what I really think. The theft was carried out by professionals. and it was about money, pure and simple. The weather was fine that night and the sea conditions were calm. There was enough fuel in the tank for them to get her to the west coast of Ireland. Once they were there, they'd have no problem finding a nice quiet spot to change her appearance as far as they could, and give her a new name. Once that was done, they could take her anywhere they bloody liked, across the Atlantic even, if you chose the right route and carried some extra fuel on board.

'There are many possibilities, but what I said earlier, about her cruising around in the Black Sea: that's as likely a scenario as any.'

I nodded. 'Received and understood,' I said. 'Thanks for that, Walter. I won't take up any more of your time.'

'Not at all, sir,' he replied as we both rose to our feet. 'It's been a pleasure.'

I said my farewell to Luisa McCracken, and left the first-floor office. I was on the stair down to street level when my phone sounded.

'Sorry to bother you, Chief.' Wherever Sauce Haddock was, there was background noise. Unnecessarily, he raised his voice so that it boomed in my ear. 'There's something we need to run past you. One quick question.'

'Shoot,' I said. 'And no need to shout,' I asked.

'Yesterday, at Fort Kinnaird; after the collision between you and the BMW, when Dean Francey got out and ran away, did you follow him, at all?'

'Yes, I did. It was a natural reaction, Sauce; I began to chase him, but only for about twenty yards or so, till I realised I'd never catch him.'

'So you were focused on him?'

'At that moment, yes.'

'Is it possible that while you were distracted, someone else got out of the passenger side and ran off?'

I took a couple of moments to think and replay the scene. 'It might have been,' I conceded. 'But . . . there wouldn't have been time for them to get clear before I turned round and spotted them. Why?'

'We're just trying to complete the picture, sir. We suspect that Anna Harmony was involved in the abduction, but we're not sure how far.'

'Does it matter, since she's as dead as Francey?'

'Probably not, but we've had word from on high there are to be no slip-ups on this one; or else.'

I was intrigued. 'How high?'

'As high as it gets.'

That surprised me. 'Why the "or else"? The job's tough enough without that sort of pressure.'

'A difference of opinion with the Communications Directorate.'

'What?' I laughed. 'That's a service department. Since when did it have a fucking opinion?'

'Don't ask me, sir. I'm just a detective sergeant, dog-shite on the shoes of the high and mighty. And I've probably said too much as it is. Thanks, sir, so long.'

Before I put my phone away I made one more call. 'One down, one to go,' I murmured as I retrieved the number I'd been given for Jock Hodgson, the part-time engineer of the *Princess Alison*, and keyed it in.

My call rang out seven times before the BT answer woman cut in and invited me to leave a message. I did: my name, the fact that I was on Eden's business, my number, and a request that Hodgson call me as soon as possible to arrange a time for us to meet. Before my discussion with Hurrell, I'd intended to speak to the engineer by phone, but I'd changed my mind on that.

My mind was still on new regimes as I left Eden's building and headed along the King George IV Bridge. I had called Alex from the train and arranged to meet her for a sandwich lunch in the Balcony Café of the National Museum.

'Who's stolen your scone?' she asked, as I joined her at the table she'd nabbed. She'd ordered too; a platter of sandwiches and a large bottle of sparkling water awaited my arrival.

'Sorry,' I chuckled, brightening up instantly. 'Was I looking grumpy?'

'Just a bit,' she said. 'Are you still dwelling on yesterday?'

'Just a bit,' I admitted, grinning.

'From what I read into the police statement, the little girl died of natural causes. Is that right?'

'Yes, it is. But the guy who took her, and his girlfriend, that was different.'

'Yes. I caught a piece of the lunchtime TV news on my iPad a couple of minutes ago. Sammy Pye looked very tense, Pops.'

'From what I'm told, he is. I'm beginning to think I've made a big mistake.'

'How?'

'In supporting your ex's application for the chief constable post.'

'What did I say yesterday?'

'But would I, or anyone else, have done any better than he's doing?' I wondered.

'It doesn't matter, Pops,' she declared. 'The ashes of the bridge are long gone down the river and I won't let you rebuild it. So, what have you been up to?'

'I've been working on my commission for Eden Higgins. In fact I've just come from interviewing his personal assistant. His duties included captaining the missing boat.'

'Eden has a personal assistant now, does he?'

'Three of them, if you include Rory. He'll be fronting *The Apprentice* before you know it. This assistant, though, he won't be a contestant; he's a minder, pure and simple.'

'I suppose you need one,' Alex said, 'when you've got as much money as he has. He's as rich as they say, you know. When I was a corporate partner at CAJ, I was involved in a couple of deals that touched on his interests.'

'Even so,' I murmured.

'You have your doubts?'

'About Eden, no, not for a moment. But about his factotum, Hurrell, that's another matter.'

'You weren't impressed?'

233

'It's not that,' I said. 'He's an impressive bloke and well qualified for the job, but . . . As I asked him about the theft, I was left with a nagging suspicion that he was trying just too hard to steer me . . . nice choice of verb in the circumstances . . . in a specific direction.'

'Do you think he's a suspect?' Alex asked.

'No, he's too close. He'd be crazy to be involved. All the same, he's left me with a niggle.'

'Another itch you have to scratch?'

'Yes, and I will.' I picked up a prawn sandwich. 'Sarah says I should lay off these. High cholesterol.' I bit off half of it nonetheless.

'And what else?'

Her question cut in just as I was reaching for my second sandwich. I stared at her. 'What do you mean?' I asked.

'There's something else bothering you. I can tell. Since you walked in here there's been an underlying tension in you, Pops. What's up? Have you and Sarah had a row?'

'No!' I protested. 'Absolutely not. Those days are over forever, I promise you. If there's a tension in me it's because lately I've been thinking just how much I regret every single day that she and I spent apart.'

That was true, and it seemed to satisfy her, but it wasn't the whole truth. The rest was that I couldn't wait to get home to see how the pregnancy test worked out.

Thirty-Four

'What I don't understand, boss,' Haddock confessed, 'is what we're doing back in Edinburgh. I thought we were going to tackle Hector Mackail today.'

'Not quite,' Pye told him. He was perched on the edge of the sergeant's desk in the busy CID room in Fettes. 'He'll keep; he's not going anywhere. I want to brace Sullivan about Anna and that party before we get that far. But before we even do that, I have a theory that I want to chase down.'

'Is that what your mysterious phone call to Jackie Wright was about?'

'Spot on.'

'Fine, but where is she?'

'Where's who, Sarge?' a female voice asked.

He turned to see the DC standing in the doorway. 'Good,' he muttered. 'That's one effing mystery solved.'

'Did you get anything?' Pye asked her.

'I think so.' Wright took a memory stick from her pocket and brandished it. 'This has a section of CCTV footage copied on to it. And it may have what you're after.'

She crossed the room to her computer, fired it up and inserted the stick in a USB port, then opened it with a click. Two more moves and a still image appeared on the screen, showing an area of the Fort Kinnaird car park, and the corner of a building.

'There's a camera on a pole beside the electrical store,' she said. 'It covers the front of Marks and Spencer up to the corner of the T K Maxx building. Check the time; it's the same as when the collision happened between Mr Skinner's car and the BMW. Now look.'

With Pye and Haddock peering over her shoulder, she hit an arrow to start the movie. For a few seconds the scene was undisturbed, save for a blue Nissan reversing out of a parking space. Then a dark-haired woman in a cagoule and a black skirt ran into the frame from the right, moving awkwardly, on high-heeled shoes with a thick sole. The DC waited until she was in mid-screen then froze the image once more.

'I've got a still close-up image as well: at least, as close as the operator could give me. But what do you think of that?'

'Anna Harmony,' Haddock declared. 'Those shoes are a dead giveaway. She must have been waiting for Dino in the car park. She wasn't just his girlfriend, gaffer, she was his accomplice.'

'Looks like it,' Pye agreed, 'but how far was she involved? That doesn't tell us conclusively she was only waiting there for Francey, Sauce. Could she have been in the car as well?' He frowned. 'Could she have bolted out the other door? There's one man can tell us. Have you got Bob Skinner's number on your phone?'

The DS nodded.

'Then call him and ask him.'

Haddock walked to a corner of the noisy room, his phone to his ear. His colleagues waited, watching him for a full minute as he spoke, until he finished and returned to them. 'He says he was concentrating on Francey at first, but he's pretty certain she wasn't in the car with him.'

'So Dino went to Fort Kinnaird to pick her up,' Pye muttered. He looked at the still figure on the computer monitor once again. 'She's carrying bags,' he said, 'two of them.' He leaned close, bending over and peering at them. 'It's not very clear but from the colour, they could be M and S.' He straightened up. 'Come on, Sauce, we have to nail this down. Let's go back to Davie Street.'

'Celia and Ilse might have classes,' Haddock pointed out.

'Then the door gets kicked in and we send a joiner to repair it. The chief constable can pick up the tab.'

Thirty-Five

The door stayed in its frame, for Ilse Brogan was at home when they returned to the student flat. She was pale faced and shocked, with tear bags under her eyes. 'I've just seen you on telly,' she mumbled through a handkerchief as she let the detectives in. 'I can't believe it. There couldn't be a mistake, could there? If there was a fire . . .'

'No,' Pye said, quietly. 'There's no mistake, Ilse. Anna had a locker at Lacey's. There was a brush in it, and we found hair samples for a DNA comparison. It was her, beyond a doubt. Same with Francey; we got a familial match with a sample from his sister.'

'So the bastard got her killed.'

'She got herself killed,' Haddock murmured. 'She didn't have to be there. That was her choice.'

'And Dino took that kid? You're sure of that too?'

'Again, completely. He did more; he put her mother in a coma.'

'Did Singer know?' she asked.

'We think she knew something,' Pye replied. 'What we want to find out is, how much. How far was she implicated and why? We need to look in her room. Once we've done that, we need you to be frank with us.'

The young woman blinked, then whispered, 'Okay. It's this way.' She led them down the hall, past the bathroom to the last door on the left. She stood watching as they put on disposable gloves and began to search.

Pye moved to the built-in units. He opened the wardrobe; a few garments remained, three dresses and a couple of jackets, but most of the hangers were empty. Six pairs of shoes stood on the floor, neatly ordered. He checked the rack of drawers at the end; they had been cleaned out.

'Here,' Haddock called out. The room's single bed was close to the window. He reached across it and picked up a carrier bag, branded with the Marks and Spencer logo, then emptied its contents on to the duvet. They were clothes, a young girl's clothes. He peered at the label on a woollen jumper. 'Five year old. And there's a till receipt.' He picked it up and read. 'Dated yesterday morning, just after nine.'

'Talk to us, Ilse,' Pye said, quietly.

She leaned against the doorframe, still dabbing lightly at her eyes. 'I don't know much,' she began. 'And I've never seen that bag before. All I can tell you is that Singer left early yesterday morning, eight at the latest, and came back a few hours later, I think around two. She went straight to her room and shut the door, hard. I was studying in mine, so I never saw her, but I could hear noises, stuff being pulled about, drawers opening and closing and so on. That went on for about half an hour, then she left again. Celia was in the living room. I heard Singer tell her that she had to split, and that she'd be gone for a long time, maybe for good. Then she said, and she said it really loud, "Whoever comes looking for me, tell them you didn't see me leave and you know nothing." Then I heard Celia ask her what was the matter, and she said something like, "My crazy boyfriend, he screw everything up." Then she swore in Polish, and I heard the door slam.'

'What time did she leave?' the DCI asked.

'It must have been three o'clock.'

'Did you speak to Celia about it after she was gone?'

'Of course. She said Singer had taken her suitcase. She only had the one that she used when she went back to Poland to see her folks, that and her big shoulder bag. And she was still wearing those big "fuck me" shoes that she'd gone out in earlier on.'

'You could have told us this last night,' Haddock said.

Ilse winced and chewed her lip. 'I know, but we thought we were helping her. You see, we thought she was running away from bloody Dino, and that she needed a head start. If we'd known she was going off with the idiot, of course we'd have told you.' She sighed, heavily. 'Are we in trouble?' she whispered.

The detectives exchanged looks. 'We've just locked Jagger up for something similar,' Pye told her, severely. 'But he helped them both, and he kept quiet about it. You thought you were helping Anna for the right reasons, so we won't hold it against you. Besides,' he added with a gentle smile, 'we don't have a spare cell down at Fettes.'

'Thanks. I'm sorry, really.'

'It's okay.'

She frowned. 'So,' she ventured, tentatively, 'the thing with the poor little girl. Are you saying definitely that Singer was involved?'

'It looks that way,' Haddock replied. 'The child wasn't murdered, if that's any consolation to you. She died from natural causes, technically, if being stuck in the boot of a car can be called natural.'

'The mother? Will she live?'

'The last we heard from the hospital, she was still unconscious, but stable. She's got a chance.'

'Fingers crossed.'

'That won't help a fractured skull and swelling on the brain,' Pye said. 'Come on, Sauce. Repack that M and S bag and bring it. Let's go and see if we can piece this thing together.'

Rather than return to Fettes, the two detectives took a break in compensation for a missed lunch, and walked a short distance to a café in Nicolson Street that Haddock knew. As they waited for their lattes and pastrami-filled baps to arrive, the chief inspector broke the silence.

'Are you knackered?' he asked.

'Moderately,' his sergeant admitted. 'But I'd only admit it to you. After that run-in with the communications woman this morning, nothing will stand between me and a result.'

'My view absolutely,' Pye concurred, pausing as a young waiter delivered their order. 'Of course,' he continued as he picked up a bap, 'it could be argued that we've got a result already. We've identified Dean Francey beyond any doubt as the man who put Grete Regal in the Western General, and abducted Zena. And now Dean Francey's dead. Whether we caught him ourselves or not, it's still a tick in the plus column.'

'We'll let Isabel Cant spin that one,' Haddock snorted. 'You know as well as I do, Sammy, the result that matters is finding the person who paid for the job and, we're assuming, put Dino and Anna Harmony away. That's the only one that's going to earn us a pat on the head from Sir Andrew, or from the DCC for that matter.'

His boss nodded. 'I know,' he admitted as he finished chewing. 'I was just trying to make lunch go down better, that's all.'

'Piece together, you said earlier,' the DS continued. 'How do you see Anna's role in this? We know she was in on it.'

'You tell me; I'm busy eating.'

'Okay. This thing was pre-planned; I'm guessing that Dino was smart enough to have nosed around in Garvald, and to have established Grete's school routine with the wee one. He'd have seen that they walked along a pretty much deserted road and that he couldn't have imagined a better spot to snatch the child.' He paused to take a swig of his latte.

'Obviously, killing the kid was not the objective or he'd have done it there and then; he was ordered to take her. He chose Sullivan's Beamer for the purpose, and kitted it out by cushioning the boot.

'If the snatch had worked, but what would he have done then? He couldn't have looked after a captive five year old. He'd have needed help to do that, and if it was female help, so much the better.

'That's where Anna fits in. We'll never know what story he spun her; maybe he told her he was looking after a niece. Whatever, it worked. She was besotted with the scrote, and she fell for it. So he sent her to Marks to buy clothes for the child, and said that he'd meet her there.'

Pye nodded. 'I buy all that. If he hadn't run into big Bob's motor it would have worked.'

'It would have worked,' Haddock pointed out, 'but only until they got wherever they were headed and opened the boot.'

'True. It's worth remembering that when Dino and Anna ran away from the scene of the accident, in different directions, neither of them knew that the child was dead. Sure Dino must have recognised that what he did to Grete left him in big trouble, but he may have thought he could get away with that.'

He nodded, as if to confirm his thinking. 'I imagine that he called Anna, as soon as he was clear. Probably they arranged to meet, then he headed for North Berwick, to pick up his cash, his passport and maybe his dad's van. He nearly managed it, only we got in the way. At some point, he or Anna must have heard that Zena had died. Without that, maybe he hoped she could be kept out of it, but with it . . . even he must have been smart enough to know we'd crawl over everyone who ever knew him, and there was Anna, having bought kids' clothes that very morning, on her credit card.'

Pye stopped for breath and more bap.

'And at that point,' Haddock said, 'Anna headed for home and packed her suitcase.'

'Yes, and Dino phoned his client, paymaster, call him what you like, said he wanted the rest of his cash, and a meeting was arranged. All that we know, pretty much for certain.'

'So what don't we know?' the DS asked.

'Where were they going yesterday morning?' Pye paused. 'How many sets of clothes are in that bag?'

'Three of everything.'

'Which suggests that wherever they were headed they were planning to stay there for a few days, long enough for Zena to be ransomed.'

'If ransom was the motive.'

'What else, Sauce?'

'Pain. Mental torture. Revenge. Which brings me back to the man Mackail. When are we going to front him up, gaffer?'

'When we've answered the question that's still open,' he replied. 'Where were they going to take her?'

Haddock finished his bap, then nursed his coffee, staring at the table while Pye, a slower eater, polished off his. As he did so, his eyes began to narrow. 'Hey,' he whispered, 'what did Nancy Walker say, about Glencorse Reservoir?'

'Remind me.'

'She said there's a lot of activity around it, that it's a bit of a resort for fishermen, hill walkers and the like. And she said there are holiday cottages up there. You don't suppose . . .'

'I don't know,' Pye replied. 'But the fact that they met their killer close by might point in that direction. If that's where they were planning to hole up, might we be lucky enough for the accommodation to have been booked by the person who was paying Dino?'

'Let's find out,' Haddock said, reaching for his phone.

Thirty-Six

'There are seven holiday cottages dotted around Glencorse Reservoir and the Loganlea Reservoir beyond,' Jackie Wright reported, before Sauce Haddock had closed the door of the CID room behind him. 'I've located and spoken to all the owners,' she continued. 'There are four of them in total. Your guess . . .'

'Guess?' Haddock exclaimed, eyebrows raised.

The DC grinned. 'Sorry. Your intuitive speculation was spot on. At this time of year they usually lie empty, but one of them was rented for three weeks, beginning last Saturday.'

'By whom?' Pye asked.

'That's as far as your luck goes, for the tenant was a young woman; she paid the full rent in advance plus deposit, in cash, to the owner's agent, a property firm in Walker Street. The description their guy gave me was a dead ringer for Anna Harmony, so I emailed him her photo. He confirmed it.'

'Bugger,' the DCI grunted. 'A door opens, then some bastard slams it in your face again.'

'So now,' the DS said, 'can we, please, go and tackle this Mackail man?'

'Hold your horses, Sauce. You keep going on about him, but I still want to follow up on Sullivan. He had a link with Dino

245

through the nephew, that was established, but for him to have known Anna as well . . .'

'Come on,' Haddock countered, 'if you're suggesting that Sullivan set up the job, even though he had no apparent reason, would he let Dino use his own car to do it?'

'If he planned to kill them afterwards, why not?' Pye smiled, then turned to another detective constable, the quiet man of the team, who was seated at the next desk to Wright. 'Have you had any joy with that check I asked for this morning, William?'

'Yes, sir,' the thin, lugubrious DC Dickson replied. 'Three weeks ago, Callum Sullivan withdrew twelve thousand pounds from his personal account, in cash. The money was in used notes, at his request.'

'What a surprise,' the DCI laughed. 'And where does he bank?'

'He uses the Clydesdale in Lothian Road; he does all his personal banking there.'

Pye, smiling in triumph, looked at Haddock as if he were peering over imaginary spectacles. 'Well?' he asked.

The DS glowered back at his boss. 'Nobody loves a smartarse,' he muttered. 'Back to North Berwick?'

'No, we've been there enough in the last couple of days. Jackie, I'd like you to call Mr Callum Sullivan and tell him we'd like his help with a couple of aspects of the inquiry, and we'd be grateful if he'd join us here at Fettes tomorrow morning.

'William, while we're talking to Mr Sullivan, I want to know everything there is to know about the man that we didn't find out in the check we ran a couple of days ago: business life, private life, secret life, everything. Start now and don't stop till you've answered all the questions.'

Thirty-Seven

'There's no doubt?' I asked, as I sat beside her on the edge of the bed, staring at the words on the stick that she had handed me.

'None.'

'This says it's certain?'

'It's as certain as it gets.' Sarah snorted. 'We can do it again if you doubt it. You can even come in and watch me pee. But the result will be exactly the same. I'm pregnant, Bob.'

'Jesus.'

'We can call him that if you like,' she said, 'as long as he's a boy.'

To my surprise, I started to giggle. 'We might have to,' I chuckled, a little manically. 'We'll be running out of boys' names soon.'

My mild hysteria passed very quickly. 'Have you thought any more about this?' I asked.

'Pretty much all day.'

'And?'

She shrugged. 'I'm forty but I'm fit. There's no physical reason why I can't deliver a normal healthy child. At my age any consultant will want to do an amniotic fluid test to check against

247

the outside chance of Down's Syndrome and other foetal abnormalities. As for my work, maternity leave is my statutory right, regardless of my job.'

'And?' I repeated.

'No,' she said, firmly. 'You first. How do you feel about another child?'

I drew a deep breath, then exhaled slowly, and all the time I was thinking. I didn't reply until I was truly certain of what I wanted to say.

'I'm fifty-three,' I began, when I was ready, 'and I'm fit. I have my last police medical, eight months ago, as evidence. I have four children by three different women, plus one who's adopted . . . Ray Charles had twelve by ten, so I'm nowhere near a record-breaker. My daughter is thirty, and my older son, the one I've only just learned about, is about to be twenty. The thought of all that should scramble my brain, but it doesn't. I love all my children in different ways, but I love them all equally. Love isn't something you can quantify. It isn't something of which there is a finite supply in every person. It's unlimited.'

I took Sarah's hand and looked her in the eye. 'If you go ahead and have this baby, I will love him or her as I love all the others, no more no less, in the same special, individual way.'

'Is that a yes?' she asked, quietly.

'It's a statement of unqualified support for whatever you decide,' I promised her.

'In that case, it's a yes.'

'You're sure?'

'I've been certain since I saw the message on the tester. I've been doubting myself all day, trying to pin down how I feel, but when I saw that word in the window, it all went away.'

'How pregnant are you?'

'From the date of my last period, five weeks; I'll be due some time in October.'

'Around the time Ignacio's due for release on parole. I'd better call the architect,' I said. 'We will definitely need to crack on with that extension.'

'I'll sell the Edinburgh house; that'll pay for it.'

'I can afford it,' I protested.

'We can afford it,' she corrected me.

'Can we afford a small wedding reception as well?'

She dug me in the ribs, and looked up at me, sideways. 'You sure about that?'

'I have been for a while,' I confessed. 'I've been meaning to broach the subject.'

She winked at me. 'In that case, I accept.'

'Champagne to celebrate?' I suggested.

'Not until the bombshell arrives,' she said. 'We should let Trish provide that,' she laughed. 'This keeps her in certain employment for the foreseeable future.'

In the event we decided to postpone the announcement until the weekend, when Alex had promised to visit. Instead we had a normal family supper, with me wondering whether we'd need a bigger table as well.

Thirty-Eight

Next morning I had trouble refocusing on the job, but once Sarah had gone to work, and the kids to school, with an effort of will I managed it.

I was slightly annoyed that Jock Hodgson hadn't got back in touch, irked enough to call him again, and leave a slightly testier message on his phone. With that out of the way, I decided to pick up on my discussion with Walter Hurrell and on the leads that had come out of it.

Before I got round to that, though, I made one more phone call.

Clyde Houseman and I go back a long way, twenty years in fact, to the time when I was a detective super and he was a teenage gang-banger in the very roughest part of Edinburgh. These days, he credits me with pointing him in the right direction when we had our street encounter. If so that's all I did; the journey and the hard labour it involved were all down to him.

It led him to the Marines, to Special Forces and finally to the Security Service, where he is now, in its secretive Glasgow office. Its number is programmed into my phone, under the label 'Chiropractor'.

He was in when I called. 'Sir,' he said, his voice clipped, without accent. 'How are you?'

'I'm great,' I replied.

'Are you going to be joining us any time soon?' he asked, boldly.

'You never know,' I replied. 'If the director has a need for me, she knows she can call.' In truth, Amanda Dennis, my friend and his boss, and I had talked around the idea, but only in the vaguest of terms.

'But right now you have a need for us. Is that the case?'

'More for you than for the service,' I told him. 'I've come across a man who claims to have been in your old outfit. By that I mean Special Forces, not the Marines. A naval petty officer; he's called Walter Hurrell. I'd like to know about him.'

'There's something familiar about that name,' Clyde said, 'but I can't pin it down. We weren't big on surnames or ranks in the SBS. Let me make inquiries and come back to you. What's the context?'

'I'm doing a private job for a rich acquaintance who's been robbed of a high-value item. Hurrell works for him and there's a vibe coming off him. If he isn't straight, I need to know.'

'Okay. I'll find out,' Clyde promised.

That done, I went back to the notes that I'd made after my session with Hurrell. He'd been adamant that the *Princess Alison* hadn't been spirited away on a larger vessel and I was inclined to agree with him. He was almost as sure that she was still afloat, sold on to wealthy, wide-boy buyers, possibly, even, in the US.

Thinking about her range and about possible routes, I struggled to see why anyone would have chosen the American option. Fuelled up, Iceland would be well within her range. But from there, the closest refuelling point would be Nuuk, in

Greenland, or St John's in Newfoundland. Either would be stretching it, and more; in winter it would be a cold and risky voyage. Why take the chance when you could go south and into the Mediterranean, where there would be potential buyers aplenty? Finally I decided to trust Hurrell and make that my first choice.

Which would mean the part of criminal investigation that I have always hated the most: a desk job; just me, a computer and a phone. To find where the *Princess* had headed, I would have to find her first refuelling station.

'*There was enough fuel in the tank for them to get her to the west coast of Ireland*,' Hurrell had said. How many marine diesel fuel pumps were there within that range? I had no idea, and I didn't have much of an idea of how to find out. It was another job I'd have been happy to delegate to Carrie McDaniels, but she was fully occupied. I could understand why Randolph bloody McGarry couldn't be arsed to do it himself, even if I couldn't excuse him his omission.

I went on to my computer and eventually found a website called Marinas Online that gave me particulars of eighty-nine marinas in the UK. Fortunately they weren't all coastal; once I had filtered out inland waterways I was left with a list of a dozen, dotted along the north-west coast of England and down into Wales. Manageable, I thought, until I moved on to Ireland and found another web page; that trebled the number of potential stopping places.

My next problem was the lack of a specific date. I knew that the boat had been stolen on 4 October, but that was as precise as I could be. The only advantage I had was the sheer size of the beast. There couldn't be too many seventy-five-foot motor cruisers around, surely.

I picked up my list and went to work, haunted by the memory of my very first day as a detective constable, when old Alf Stein, who went on to become my mentor, gave me a desk, a phone and a list of bystander witnesses, made by two PCs who attended a near-fatal stabbing, and told me to get on with interviewing them.

I did too; the fifth person I spoke to told a story that was so much at odds with the first four, who had all painted more or less the same picture, that I stopped what I was doing and dug a little deeper into his background. The 'witness' had professed no knowledge of the victim, and yet a simple check showed me that when he had served six months in Saughton for assault, the two had been cellmates.

I decided to look more deeply at the victim: I pulled his record and called the detective sergeant who was listed as his last arresting officer. He told me to fuck off if I knew what was good for me. I invited him to say that to my face, then went to Alf and told him what I had discovered.

We pulled in the witness and sat him down in a windowless, airless room in Gayfield Square, my least favourite of all the Edinburgh police stations. His name was Thomas McGraw, and he went down in my personal history as my first ever CID collar. Ten minutes of Alf's relentless, unblinking interrogation . . . from then on I modelled my own interview style on his . . . and he coughed the lot.

The victim, one Scott Hancock, a recidivist criminal, had been on the payroll of Ernie Lewis, my detective sergeant acquaintance, as an informant, but that relationship had been tarnished when he confessed to McGraw in an unguarded moment in their cell that much of the information he had provided had come from a man called Dougie Terry, also known as the Comedian, and had been designed to incriminate his enemies while protecting his friends.

McGraw had gone straight to Lewis, with a view to securing the DS's favour, and had been told to prove himself by serving notice on Hancock with the weapon of his choice. It had all gone according to plan, until the two PCs arrived ahead of schedule, having heard the victim's cries. With his escape route blocked, McGraw had mingled among the growing crowd of passers-by at the scene. When asked for his details he had been foolish enough to give his real name.

Hancock survived, McGraw pleaded guilty to an assault charge rather than attempted murder and both men gave evidence against Ernie Lewis. By the time he came out I was a chief inspector. Alf let me charge McGraw, but he kept Lewis for himself, for he didn't think it wise for a rookie DC to have another a cop on his arrest docket.

My trawl of the coastal marinas of Britain and Ireland was nowhere near as successful. In fact it was a total bust, as I had feared from the outset. Most of the places told me they couldn't handle a vessel of that size, and the rest said that if one had turned up, they would have recalled it, but couldn't. For the sake of thoroughness I checked out the fuelling points at Inverkip and Oban, but had no joy at either.

The only credit I could give myself was for doing something that McGarry hadn't, but that was offset by the truth that his slackness had actually saved police time.

For the sake of thoroughness, I called the managers of the stolen boats website, but they had no fresh information, and nothing waiting to be added. The *Princess Alison* was gone, and if Walter Hurrell was right, gone for good.

I was pretty certain that before the week was out I would be reporting back to Eden, recommending that he negotiate the best settlement he could with his insurers, but I still had one place left to go.

Jock Hodgson still hadn't got back to me. I tried him again, with no more success than before, then I called Luisa McCracken.

'Jock does other things as well as crewing the *Princess*,' she told me. 'We have first call on his time, but he does quite a bit of engine maintenance work.'

'Could he be on holiday?' I asked.

'That's unlikely; being single, he hardly ever takes any. When he does he always gives us plenty of notice. Hold on.'

I did, for a couple of minutes.

'I have a folder on him,' Luisa said when she returned. 'There are no notes about holidays, just timesheets.'

'When did you hear from him last?'

'Last October. Walter told him that the boat had been stolen, then I called him to arrange a meeting with the insurance underwriters. There's an understanding that when the boat's recovered or replaced, we'll get in touch with him.'

'Do you have an address?' I asked. 'I won't be ignored; if he won't call me back, I'll go and bang on his door.'

'I thought you'd want that,' she said. 'I have it here; it's Ailsa View, Dunglas Avenue, Wemyss Bay. It's a long drive, mind.'

'Nah, I can do it in a couple of hours.'

It was just after midday; I fixed myself an early lunch, ham slices and coleslaw in a couple of wholemeal pitta breads, then grabbed a Snickers bar and a bottle of water for the journey, and headed off in my still-wounded car, after making a mental note to dump the repair in the hands of my insurers, and let them fight it out with the owner of the BMW, whoever he might be.

Gullane to Wemyss Bay is a coast-to-coast drive, Firth of
Forth to the Firth of Clyde, round Edinburgh and through
Glasgow, motorway for all but the first ten miles and the last
fifteen. I made good time; it was two fifteen and I was on the
outskirts of Greenock, when my phone sounded.

'Mr Skinner?' It was Clyde Houseman.

'Yes,' I replied. 'I'm on the road and I'm alone. You can
speak.'

'Good. I have feedback for you on the man you asked about.
It wasn't easy to get, and I can understand why. I told you that
the name rang a bell with me; it should have been an alarm bell.
Yes, Petty Officer Hurrell was operational in the Special Boat
Service, but not for long. He served in Iraq, in a different zone
from me, up in the north of the country, chasing a cadre of
Saddam's old Revolutionary Guard who were taking revenge on
civilians in and around his home town. He was part of a three-
man team, who caught up with some of them in a house near
Tikrit. By that time they weren't much of a threat; there were
only five of them left and they'd hardly any ammo. Hurrell's unit
was under the command of a Marine sergeant, a lad I knew. He
was under orders to take prisoners back for interrogation, so he
gave them the chance of surrender.

'They took it. They threw their weapons out of the window
and came out in a line, hands on head. One of them twitched;
he scratched his ear, my friend told me. Whatever he did, it
spooked Hurrell. He mowed the fucking lot of them down.'

'Was he court-martialled?' I asked.

'In another unit he might have been, but not in Special
Forces. He was kicked out, unceremoniously. They sent him
back to his minesweeper. Six months later, he left the service
and went to work for your man Higgins. His CO knew nothing

about the Iraq incident, and wrote him an excellent reference. It's still on file.'

'The reference,' I said. 'Does it square with the rest of his service record?'

'It does,' Houseman replied. 'His reports show him to have been an exemplary sailor.'

'Apart from killing five unarmed men in cold blood,' I chuckled.

'We all have our off days, sir.'

I thanked Houseman and drove on, letting my navigation system guide me for the rest of the journey. One big difference between the Firths of Forth and Clyde is that ferries still run in the latter. Wemyss Bay is one of the terminals; a rail service from Glasgow delivers Rothesay-bound passengers all year round. My dad took the family there on holiday when I was six. God bless him, it was his idea of a good time.

Satnav took me straight to Dunglas Avenue, but Hodgson's house wasn't so easy to find. The street was a short cul-de-sac, and none of the dozen bungalows had numbers, only names. I looked at them all, one by one, but couldn't see Ailsa View anywhere. Puzzled, I thought about calling Luisa to recheck the address, but before I could do that, I was hailed by a white-haired lady in a tweed skirt and heavy purple jumper, standing in the doorway of a little dwelling called Barrhead.

'Excuse me,' she called out. 'You look lost. Can I help you?'

'Possibly,' I replied, walking to the end of her short garden path. 'I'm trying to locate a house called Ailsa View and a man named Hodgson. I was told it was in this street, but I can't see any sign of it.'

'Not surprising,' she said. 'It's pretty well hidden. If you go to the end of the street, there's a house called Lindisfarne. It looks as if it has a double driveway, but in fact half of it leads to Ailsa View. It's hidden behind it. Hodgson,' she repeated. 'That's the chap's name, is it? Funny, isn't it, that you can live in a street as short as this one for twenty-five years, and still you don't know all your neighbours. No wonder they call him the Hermit.' She laughed. 'Maybe he should change the name to "The Hermitage". More appropriate than "Ailsa View". You don't get a glimpse of the Ailsa Craig from here.'

I thanked her and followed her direction. She was right; at first glance I'd taken the gravel driveway as leading into Lindisfarne. It was only when I was close to it that I saw the bifurcation and the curve beyond it.

I followed it, the stones crunching beneath my feet, until Hodgson's place came into view, facing at ninety degrees to the one in front. It wasn't much of a house, smaller than any other in the street; it had a garden, or rather a grassy area in front that didn't come close to resembling a proper lawn. I wondered if the owner of Lindisfarne had cashed in on half of his plot, but the place looked as old as any of its neighbours and in a poorer state of repair. Whoever developed the land had jammed it into maximise profit, I decided.

Its name was on a small plaque, wall mounted, to the right of brown wooden double doors that looked in want of a coat of varnish, and above a white plastic bell stud. I pressed it, leaning hard for five or six seconds, then waited: in vain.

I tried the storm doors, but they were locked. I rattled the letter box, in case the bell wasn't sounding indoors. I took out my mobile and called Hodgson's number. From within I could hear it ring out seven times, then go silent as it switched to auto answer.

'Bugger,' I muttered.

There was a square bay window to the left of the entrance and a smaller single pane to the right. I peered in each, but they were screened by Venetian blinds, closed tightly enough to deny me any more than the narrowest glimpse of the rooms inside.

Sure as hell, I hadn't driven all that way to turn around and go home without having a bloody good look around. I walked round to the back of the house, checking the window of each room as I went, but none of them offered any better view than the two in front, other than the kitchen, at the back.

I peered through the dirty glass. There was a milk carton on the work surface and a packet of biscuits, but nothing else in sight other than a few lazy flies.

Jock Hodgson's garage was at the end of the driveway, in the rear left-hand corner of the plot. It had an up-and-over door that was locked, and another to the side that wasn't.

I opened it and stepped inside.

I hadn't seen a Ford Escort in years, not one from the late sixties with what they called the Coke bottle body style, but Jock Hodgson had one, F registration in the old number style. Unlike his house, it was immaculate. The body shell looked as new, and the paint was brilliant white, beneath a coating of dust. The bumpers were shiny without a speck of rust to be seen. I opened the driver's door and leaned inside; even the blue imitation leather seats were pristine. The only thing about it that wasn't original was a Samsung mobile phone lying in the footwell on the driver's side. I knew for sure that if I raised the hood, I'd find that the cylinder head was polished. It was a collector's car, an engineer's car, a show car.

And the key was in the ignition. And the side door to the garage was unlocked.

I don't know much about collectable cars; these days I buy

mine new and trade them in before they're old enough to need an MOT. But looking at that Escort, which was nearly as old as me, I guessed it had to be worth close on ten grand. Clearly, the man Hodgson loved that vehicle, yet anyone could have gone in there, raised the up-and-over from the inside and driven off with it.

That was the point when my instincts told me that something was very wrong. I knew I should have twigged it earlier, that something else should have rung my alarm bell, but I couldn't pin it down. While I thought about it, I turned the key in the ignition . . . and all I heard was the clunk of a stone dead battery. I tried the lights; the dashboard panel barely flickered. I gripped the steering wheel and my hand became enmeshed in a spider's web that I hadn't noticed before.

And that's when I realised what had been out of place: those flies in the kitchen. How many flies do you expect to find in a cold house in the first week in February?

There were three other keys on the ring that fed the ignition. I pulled it out and examined them. One was long and thin, and had to be for the up-and-over, another was a Yale, and I suspected that it matched the lock I'd noticed on the side door.

The third was for a mortice lock. I returned to the back door, looking into the kitchen again as I passed the window. There were quite a few of those damn flies, especially if I counted the dead ones that lay at the foot of the pane. I tried the key; it turned, I opened the door, stepped into the kitchen . . . and that was when the smell hit me.

The geeks who post on lurid online forums say the odour of decomposing human flesh is unique; they're wrong. In my experience, the smell of death is more subtle than that. There's an underlying, cloying sweetness to it, but it varies with the stage of decomposition and with the shape and bulk of the person before life became extinct. The one thing that is universally accepted is that it's horrible and you don't want to be breathing in the molecules that create it.

I've asked Sarah how she copes with it; all she says is 'mental conditioning', and yet the same woman has repeating deodorant sprays in every bathroom in our house.

I grabbed a towel that was hanging from a hook on a cupboard door, held it over my nose and mouth and went in search of the source. All I had to do was follow the flies; the closer I got the thicker they swarmed.

I found him in the living room. Jock Hodgson had been tied to a chair; his wrists and left ankle were secured by some form of restraint that I couldn't see properly because they were so swollen. His face was black, and his head lolled on his left shoulder; his body was distended, and his clothes stretched, by gases. He looked ready to burst; I hoped he would contain himself, literally, until I was gone.

The swelling was most obvious in his feet, for he wore neither shoes nor socks. They had been removed and lay beside him. I could guess the reason.

I backed out of there. I didn't want to contaminate the scene, nor did I want the scene to contaminate me, any more than it had already. In the garden I drew deep breath after deep breath, and blew my nose hard, on the handkerchief from my breast pocket, yet the stink of the dead Hodgson was still with me. My suit wasn't going to the dry cleaner, that I knew; it was bound for the incinerator.

I took my phone from its pocket inside my jacket and thumbed through my directory until I reached 'M'. A few months before I'd probably have stopped at 'Martin', but in the new situation there was no guarantee that my call would be accepted. Instead I carried on to 'McGuire'.

'Bob,' my friend answered on the first ring. 'What's up? Have you decided you need to speak to McGarry?'

'No,' I replied. 'I've got somebody else in mind, two people in fact. My assignment for Eden Higgins has just become very complicated and very smelly. You need to send a CSI team to Dunglas Avenue, in Wemyss Bay; that and the best matched CID pair you've got.' I told him who they were.

'They'll all be on their way inside ten minutes,' Mario promised. 'And I won't be far behind them. I've hung around you too long, chum: I can't stay away from a juicy crime scene either.'

Thirty-Nine

As it happened Mario beat the crime scene team to Wemyss Bay by fifteen minutes, but he trailed behind his detectives by five.

Detective Inspector Charlotte Mann and I didn't have the best of starts to our professional relationship, the first time that we met in Glasgow. A major public figure had just been murdered, she was the senior officer attending from the Strathclyde force, and she thought I was getting in the way. But once the new reality had been explained to her, and we had a chance to watch each other at work, we got along just fine.

If I could go back five years, and was still running CID in Edinburgh, I'd poach her like a shot. For all that she's had a subtlety bypass, she's as good a DI as I've ever met. Lottie is a big woman, all of six feet tall, and she has a presence about her that makes it easy for her to take a command role in what can still be a predominantly male environment.

As for her perennial sidekick, Dan Provan, he's best described as an anachronism. He's a year or so older than me, but he stuck at detective sergeant rank over twenty years ago, principally because he had no ambition to go any higher. I've heard people described as wizened, many times, but I never really understood the term until I met him.

He's deliberately scruffy, with a chameleon-like quality that's been invaluable to him throughout his career. He gave up smoking years ago, I'm told, and yet his badly trimmed moustache still looks as if it's stained by nicotine. Walk into a busy pub and you probably wouldn't notice him, but by God he would notice you. He knows Glasgow like he knows his own features. He carries two football club lapel badges, one Celtic, the other Rangers, and always wears the right one in the right place. For him, no-go areas in the city do not exist.

Not long after Mario McGuire took charge of criminal investigation in ScotServe, he asked me what he should do with him. My advice was, 'Cherish him, but on no account let Andy Martin anywhere near him.'

When they emerged from their car and saw me standing at the start of the Ailsa View driveway, I found myself wishing I'd had my phone ready to snap a photo. It was obvious from the simultaneous widening of their eyes and dropping of their jaws that their DCC hadn't told them the whole story.

'What the . . .' Provan gasped. 'Has all this Polis Scotland stuff just been a bad fuckin' dream?'

'Some would wish that it was,' I replied. 'But no; this is reality and I am here, a private citizen who's happened on a crime scene and done his duty. That said, it's good to see you.'

Lottie Mann was frowning. 'Did you ask for us, sir?'

'That I did. I figured it would be better if the responding officers knew me, rather than having to explain my whole fucking back story to a couple of fast-trackers. Do you have a spare protective suit?' I asked. 'And a face mask. That's important.'

'One o' them, is it?' Provan grunted.

'Ripe.'

I led Mann up the drive and round to the house, leaving the DS to fetch the paper tunics. 'Would you like to tell me what this is about now, sir?' she asked.

'I've been looking into a theft for a friend,' I replied. 'I came here to interview a witness. It seems he isn't in a position to talk to me.'

'I take it we're not talking about a missing garden gnome,' she murmured.

'Leave Provan out of this,' I retorted, drawing a smile. 'No, we're talking about seventy-five feet of motor cruiser, value five million.'

'We didn't find it, then?'

'Do you know a guy called Randolph McGarry? Ex-DI, now back in uniform.'

'I've come across him,' she said. 'He couldn't find his arse with a compass, but he and ACC Gorman had a thing going . . . or so they said.'

'Bloody hell,' I gasped. Bridie Gorman was my acting deputy during my brief spell as chief constable of Strathclyde. I'd never heard as much as a whispered rumour about her private life, far less the suggestion that she was protecting her fancy man's work from proper scrutiny.

'As soon as she left the force after the unification,' Lottie continued, 'Randolph was on borrowed time. Nobody was surprised when DCC McGuire moved him out of CID.'

'What's Bridie doing now?'

'Gardening, from what I hear.'

'And you, Inspector,' I asked, 'what job have you landed in the brave new world?'

'Dan and I are in Serious Crimes. In theory we could

be deployed anywhere; in practice, most of them are in the Glasgow area.'

'Who decides what's serious?'

She grinned. 'That is the million-dollar question.'

Then she frowned, just as Provan arrived with the paper suits. 'I suppose this is a crime, yes?'

'From what I've heard and seen, Jock Hodgson was a skilled engineer, but I doubt that he tied himself up.'

We suited up, and I took them inside. We were still in the kitchen when Provan, for all his experience, started to retch. I paused until he had his heaving stomach under control, then led them to the doorway of the living room, through the fat, buzzing flies.

'Are you sure this is Mr Hodgson?' Lottie asked, a perfectly decent question.

'I'm open to correction,' I admitted, 'but I don't see that it can be anyone else.'

'How long do you think he's been dead?'

'Weeks, I'm guessing.' I went back into the hall and opened a glazed front door. A pile of mail lay beneath the flap in the storm doors. 'The earliest date on those letters should give you a clue, but let's leave it to the CSIs to sort them out.'

'Did ye see any signs of forced entry?' Provan asked.

'No,' I told him. 'There are none.'

'How did you get in?' Mario McGuire's muffled voice came from behind us, announcing his arrival. I turned; he too was wearing a sterile suit, hat and face mask.

'I found a back door key in the garage.'

'It wasn't unlocked?' He was surprised, and I knew why.

'No, and neither was the front door. Which means that whoever killed the guy actually locked up when they left.

They didn't want him to be found in a hurry.'

'Eh?' Mann exclaimed. 'If that's right, wasn't it a bit risky to leave him here?'

'Probably less risky than moving him and chancing being seen,' I suggested. 'This house is a cul-de-sac at the end of a cul-de-sac. Hodgson's neighbours called him the Hermit. The one I spoke to didn't even know his name, and I'll bet she doesn't miss much.'

'They'll know his name from now on,' Mario McGuire observed. 'It'll be all over the press tomorrow.'

'If he's a hermit, sir,' Provan countered, 'how are we going tae get a formal ID that fast?'

'That won't bother our communications department,' the big DCC chuckled. 'They make their own rules these days.' He looked at me, giving me a wordless signal that we should leave.

I followed him into the garden happily, having seen enough of Jock Hodgson for a while. He went straight to the point as he ripped off his paper mask and cap, posing the question that I'd been turning over in my own mind.

'Could this be related to the job you're working on?'

'I have no idea,' I admitted. 'No, let me rephrase that. I have no evidence of that. I didn't come here expecting to find Hodgson dead, or even missing. I marked him down as a bloody nuisance of a man who was lazy about checking his voicemail, or who only returned calls from people he knew.'

Mann and Provan had followed us outside, and heard my reply. 'What do you know about him, sir?' the DI asked.

'Not a hell of a lot. That's what I came here to find out. He was an ex-naval engineer, and in retirement he worked part-time on my client's stolen motor cruiser, and, I'm told, on a variety of other jobs. I know nothing about any of them. I know nothing about the man, period. Did he piss off one of his other clients? Was he in debt to the wrong people? Was he shagging somebody else's wife? You're going to have to do it the hard way, Lottie, and eliminate possibilities until you've only one solution left.'

'That's fine, Bob,' Mario said, 'but leaving aside by-the-book policing and proper procedure, what does your instinct tell you?'

I looked at my old colleague, my old pupil, and I smiled. 'It doesn't tell me anything, but it suggests to me that somebody else wants to know what happened to Eden Higgins' boat.'

'If that's the case,' he pointed out, 'by rights you should hand your inquiry over to us.'

'As far as Hodgson's death is concerned, you're absolutely correct,' I agreed.

'But you're not going to, are you?'

'I will if you insist,' I told him. 'I have too much respect for you all to do otherwise. But if Hodgson's death is linked to the theft, or it looks as if it might be, I'm offering to cooperate with Lottie and Dan, if they want. I've already got someone working on one aspect of it. I can share her findings if they're relevant.'

'Do you want?' the DCC asked Mann.

'Of course,' she replied. 'I was going to ask Mr Skinner for his help anyway.'

'I'll need to tell the chief; I can't authorise this behind his back.'

'I took that as read,' I said. 'You must tell him. If he has a problem with it, you can add that if he vetoes it, I'll work independently. I'll be trying to find the stolen boat, not Hodgson's killer, but if my investigation bumps into yours, tough shit. I have a commission from Eden Higgins and I intend to see it through.'

'Understood and okay. Assuming Sir Andrew approves, how do you want to go forward?'

'On the basis of shared information. As a first step, I'd like to attend the post-mortem.'

Mario whistled. 'Rather you than me!'

Forty

I'd been in the old Glasgow City Mortuary, in the Saltmarket, once or twice but never in the new twenty-first-century model in Govan. As these things go, it was state of the art, everything stainless steel and spotless and, most important of all, the air purification system worked perfectly.

I'd been expecting Mario to call me the evening before to give me a 'Yes' or a 'No' on whether I could attend, but he didn't. Instead it was Andy Martin who called, the Chief Constable of Scotland himself.

'Bob, how are you?' he began, heartily, as soon as I picked up the phone in the office, having been advised by an operator that he was on the line. Even before the last of those four words were out, his tone had sent me a message of irrevocable change. But I was ready, for it cut both ways.

Those who've observed me over the years will have realised by now that I have very few close friends outside the police. Within the service I have half a dozen, and for many years Andy Martin was one of the closest. Back then he wouldn't have needed to ask how I was; he'd have known, because we'd have spoken every other day. That call, that evening, was our first contact since I'd congratulated him on his appointment a few months before.

Since then he'd dumped my daughter, and, it was apparent from the distance in his greeting, that he'd dumped me too.

'I'm fine, Andy,' I assured him, 'and if word hasn't got to you yet, I wouldn't touch the Scottish Police Authority chair with a bargepole.'

'I didn't think for a minute that you would,' he lied. 'Bob, about this suspicious death . . .'

'Suspicious fucking death?' I laughed. 'The guy was tied up and left sitting in his own shit for some poor sod like me to find him. Don't go all PC on me, Andy. The word is murder.'

'Okay, it is,' he conceded. 'And that makes me hesitant about you being involved.'

'Your hesitancy has fuck all to do with it, my friend,' I pointed out. 'Indeed, it isn't relevant, for I am involved. I've undertaken an investigation for a client, and it led me to Jock Hodgson. I'm not backing off just because he happens to be dead. If you think I'll impede the police inquiry, tell me, but if that's what you do think, you're insulting two of your best detective officers, and by the way, you're insulting me.'

'Still . . .' he said.

I'd had enough. 'Sir Andrew,' I growled, 'if you want to deny me access and you refuse to let Lottie Mann share information with me, remember that cuts both ways. And remember also that I'm a director of a bloody newspaper group!'

'Don't threaten me, Bob,' he murmured.

'My only threat to you is in your mind,' I snapped. 'Listen, boy, if I'd wanted your job I'd have had it. I didn't; instead, having mentored you since you were a sprog detective and seen you rise through the ranks, I stepped aside and helped you into the chair you're warming now.'

'So you do regret not going for the post,' he murmured.

'Listen to what I'm saying, for fuck's sake! I don't. But frankly I'm beginning to regret not backing Maggie Steele or Mario rather than you.'

'Ah,' he exclaimed. 'This is about Alex, isn't it?'

'Don't bring my daughter into this,' I warned him. 'That's different, because it's personal. I should have seen you off when you worked your way back into her life after you left Karen. Hurting her once was hard to forgive. Doing it again means you'll have an enemy for as long as I'm breathing.'

'No middle ground then,' he said, sarcastically.

I came close to slamming the phone down, but I didn't. Instead, with an effort, I regained control of my temper.

'Like I said,' I went on, 'that's personal. The Hodgson investigation and my work for Eden Higgins, that's professional. There may be a common interest or there may not. While we find out, do you want me inside the tent pissing out, or would you rather it was the other way round?'

'Oh, go ahead,' he sighed. 'I'll authorise DI Mann to cooperate with you. Mario says she's a good operator.'

'She is; very.'

I thought we were done, but he wanted the last word. 'You're not perfect yourself, you know, when it comes to women.'

'I'm probably even more imperfect than you know, sunshine,' I admitted, 'but that cuts you no slack when it comes to my Alex.'

It crossed my mind that Andy might have shown up at the Hodgson post-mortem, but he didn't. Neither did Mario, who was heading for Inverness to cast a beady eye over Northern Division CID. Lottie Mann was the senior officer present; indeed she was the only officer there, as Dan Provan had used me as an excuse to wriggle his way out of a singularly unpleasant duty.

The lead pathologist was a man I'd seen in court but never met. His name was Graeme Bell and he was the senior man in the Greater Glasgow area, although unlike Sarah he had no university responsibilities. He wasn't the talkative type; he worked in silence while we looked on from a viewing gallery, happy to be screened from the action and the odour.

He worked away for two hours, cutting, measuring, extracting, probing his subject from head to foot. Once he had completed his initial examination and got down to detail, he paid particular attention to the head, and that interested me. Then he switched to the other end and that held my attention even more closely.

It was only when he was done that he acknowledged our presence, telling us that he'd see us in the briefing room once he'd cleaned up.

Sarah uses Chanel after a very messy one; Bell used the gentleman's equivalent, liberally. As he joined us, and poured himself a coffee, suddenly he stared at me.

'You're Mr Skinner, aren't you?' he ventured, as he sat. I nodded. 'I thought you were gone from all this.'

'So did I,' I acknowledged. 'I'm here as a civilian observer, that's all.'

'Mmm. How's Sarah?' he asked.

I smiled. 'Blooming.' Clearly, word of our reunion had made its way through the pathology community.

'What's the verdict, doctor?' Lottie Mann, not being one for small talk, asked abruptly.

'He's dead,' Bell replied, winking as he took a sip from his mug.

'We sensed that when we saw him yesterday,' she sighed. 'It's nice to know we haven't lost our touch.'

'The subject died from a single gunshot wound to the head,'

the pathologist announced. 'It was fired at close range, from the side and slightly downward. I've recovered a nice clean bullet lodged in the zygomatic ridge just in front of the right ear. That's the only way I've been able to give you a cause of death; the body's too decomposed for a straightforward autopsy.' He hesitated. 'How long has he been dead? That's difficult to say for sure, but six weeks, minimum.'

'No worries,' Lottie replied, drily. 'The mail we found behind his front door suggests that he died at the beginning of December.'

'That's probably right. The rate of decomposition isn't an exact science. When I visited the scene I noticed that it was cold.'

She nodded. 'Yes, it was. The central heating was oil-fired, but the tank was empty. We're guessing it ran out after he was killed.'

'I see. Lucky, in one way; in a warmer environment there would have been even more flies.'

'Were there many pre-mortem injuries?' I asked.

Bell nodded. 'The plastic strips that secured his wrists and his left ankle to the chair were pulled so tight that they cut into the flesh. Painful, but by comparison to the other thing, insignificant.' He paused. 'If you were at the scene, you might remember that Mr Hodgson was barefoot. His shoes and socks had been removed.'

'Yes.'

'Well, there's just about enough flesh left for me to be sure that he was tortured by burning. Something like a blowlamp was used on his right foot, extensively. It's for you to determine, Inspector Mann, but I'd say that either this man had seriously upset someone, or whoever went to work on him wanted information, and wanted it very badly indeed.'

Forty-One

'Do you want to come back to Pitt Street for a chat and a bite of lunch?' Lottie Mann asked.

'To the first, definitely not,' I said. I'd seen enough of the former Strathclyde Police headquarters building to last me a couple of lifetimes. 'Lunch is on the agenda, though.'

We settled on the public cafeteria in the massive new general hospital for our post-mortem of the post-mortem, and found a table there. I'd skimped on breakfast with the morning's business in mind, and found my appetite catching up with me. I loaded a plate with corned beef hash from the self-service buffet, trying to contain my amazement as my companion put together the biggest fry-up I'd ever seen.

She caught my glance and read it right. 'I know,' she admitted, 'it's a classic, lethal Weegie all-day breakfast, and I do my best to resist. Usually I succeed, but after this morning, what the hell.'

'How's your wee lad?' I asked her, as we tucked in.

Lottie Mann is a single parent with a son around the same age as my James Andrew. Her marriage collapsed when her ex-cop husband went to jail, along with his still-serving woman on the side, for their peripheral involvement in a high-profile crime.

'Jake's great, thanks,' she replied. 'We've moved house. I bought a three-bed mid-terrace in what was the Commonwealth Games Village. It's not huge but it's big enough for the two of us, and for my mother when she stays over.'

'But not for Scott, when he gets out?' I ventured.

'Not a chance,' she replied. 'The only way I want to see that man again is standing over his open coffin with a wooden stake in one hand and a hammer in the other. There are times when I have an insight into the mentality of a murderer. Thinking of him brings it on. It's not so much what he did to me; it's how it affected Jakey.'

'I've been through two divorces,' I told her. 'The first one was a huge mistake, which I've been lucky enough to have the chance to rectify. The other was very bitter and very public, as you and the whole world know; but I'm over it.' I smiled. 'I even watched a Joey Morrocco movie the other night.'

Joey was the actor with whom the third Mrs Skinner was caught on camera; a household name but not in mine.

'Is he still in Hollywood?' Lottie asked.

I winked at her. 'If he knows what's good for him.'

She raised an eyebrow. 'Are you sure you didn't meet Jock Hodgson before yesterday?'

My laugh was loud enough to draw a sharp look from the next table, reminding me that we were surrounded by people who were under the stress of visiting friends and family in hospital.

'Detective Inspector,' I replied, more quietly, 'I built a career on getting information out of people, without ever laying as much as a finger on them. If I'd wanted Hodgson to tell me something, I'd just have asked him and he'd have told me.'

'Is that what you think? That he was tortured for information, rather than being killed brutally by a sadist?'

'He wasn't killed brutally,' I pointed out. 'Remember what Dr Bell found; he died from a single shot to the head. Death would have been instantaneous, and he'd have been out of his misery in that split second. Of course the killer was after something, and it's a safe assumption that it was information: but information on what? You and Dan, and your team, have to do a complete background check on Hodgson before you can hazard a guess.'

'We will do,' she promised. 'But how does that justify your interest, and your presence here? You must suspect that his death's linked to the job you're doing.'

'I don't suspect anything,' I countered. 'I'm an interested party, that's all. One step at a time, Lottie: we know that the man was murdered, but really, we know eff all else about him, other than what I was told by one of his several employers. You fill in the gaps, and we'll take it from there.'

I left her to add sticky toffee pudding to her cardiac cocktail, and drove back east. I was passing the Harthill motorway service area, driving cautiously through a light snow shower that had sprung up from nowhere, when I decided to call Carrie McDaniels for a progress report.

'Nothing yet,' she said. 'Your meter is still running. I can see why you gave me this job rather than doing it yourself. It's bloody tedious.'

'I know that,' I chuckled, 'but have you got anything positive from it?'

'Not so far,' she admitted. 'Actually you saved me a phone call,' she continued. 'I'd like you to loosen the strings you put on me yesterday.'

'In what way?' I asked.

'There's a hint of something I've picked up in a newspaper report on one of the companies on your list. I'd like to look into it in more detail, but to do that I'll need to speak to someone. It's a guy I know, but the problem is he's a business journalist, and you said no press.'

'How well do you know him?'

'Very well; we were at school together. I used to give him information when I was with the insurance company.'

'Can you talk to him without bringing me or our client into it, and without giving him any clue of what this is about?'

'Mr Skinner, you're forgetting; I don't know what this is about. I'm just running down a list of people and companies you gave me.'

'Maybe so, but can you talk to him without making him too curious?'

'Yes, I can. If he did get difficult,' she added, 'I know who his newest lady friend is, and he knows I know.'

'What's that got to do with anything?'

'She's a television presenter, and she's married.'

'Tread carefully,' I warned her, 'but go ahead.'

The snow disappeared as quickly as it had arrived, and I was able to pick up pace. Since I ceased to be a cop I've always been careful to stick to the speed limits, or at least to stay within the unofficial tolerance zone. Too many tabloids would love to report on a Bob Skinner court appearance. Even at that gentle pace, I had time on my hands so I made a detour to the Mercedes dealership on the edge of Edinburgh to pick up a detailed estimate for the repair of my damaged car.

I was almost home when my phone sounded again. I hadn't expected to hear from Lottie Mann for at least twenty-four hours, and so I was taken by surprise.

'What's up?' I asked. 'Was there something we forgot to cover over lunch?'

'No,' she said breezily. 'I thought I'd give you a heads up on what we've got so far. We've still got a way to go before we have the complete picture, but we know some of it. Hodgson was fifty-four; he graduated in marine engineering from Heriot Watt Uni in Edinburgh and joined the Navy aged twenty-four. He served in the surface fleet, including some time in aircraft carriers during the first Gulf War. He retired, or he was retired, ten years ago and joined the Royal Fleet Auxiliary: that's a civilian support . . .'

'I know what it is; it gets people and things to wherever they're needed by the military.'

'That's right. He turned that in when he was fifty, and moved to Wemyss Bay from the Portsmouth area. He was married from nineteen eighty-nine to twenty zero two. That ended in divorce; no children.'

'Where did you get all this?' I asked.

'Department of Work and Pensions . . . if that's what it's still called,' she chuckled. 'He's been paying self-employed National Insurance contributions for the last four years. We don't yet know who his clients are apart from Mr Higgins, but when we can access his bank details and see where his payments have been coming from, that'll give us a better idea.'

'Where did he bank?'

'We found an ATM card for a Santander account among his effects in the house. He had one of their credit cards as well, and a Barclaycard. Dan's on to the bank now; as usual, they're being difficult.'

'Let DCC McGuire know if it becomes a problem,' I suggested. 'He has a special way with difficult jobsworths, plus he knows the Data Protection Act inside out.'

'Will do, Mr Skinner, thanks,' Lottie said.

'Were there no papers in the house to help you?' I asked.

'Precious little. He had a file with council tax details in it, and another for insurance, but no receipts for utilities, gas, electric, the phone.'

'Me neither,' I confessed. 'Everything in my household is online, and settled automatically by direct debit. But if that was the case with Hodgson,' I pondered aloud, 'it should be on his computer.'

'And it probably is,' she agreed, 'but we don't know where that is. A week or so before his death, he reported a break-in at his house. The missing property listed in the investigating officers' notes was a hundred and fifty quid in cash, an inscribed Omega watch that was a leaving present from his Navy pals, some gold men's jewellery, a valuable ring that he said was his mother's, and a Dell laptop computer.'

'Did the responding officers have the place dusted?'

'Of course they did,' she said, reprovingly. 'And it was clean as a whistle. The ring was insured for five grand and Hodgson had a photograph of it. It's a nice-looking piece. That was circulated to all the likely jewellery buyers, including pawnshops, but nothing's shown up.'

I could see her frown, and her pursed lips, in my mind's eye. 'Go on, Lottie,' I challenged, 'tell me what you've got in mind. See if you're wondering the same as me.'

'If you insist,' she responded, 'although I'll only have your word for what you're thinking. I'm wondering whether all the other items were stolen to disguise the fact that the laptop was the real target.'

'Then take my word for it,' I told her. 'But I'm not even wondering. I'd bet your house on it. A laptop's worth bugger all in sell-on value. The dogs in the bloody street have got laptops these days. You may assume that Hodgson's burglar was after the Dell, and I reckon that you can assume also that either it was password protected and he couldn't crack it or there was nothing on it apart from email files of his phone bills. And so he came back,' I concluded. 'And here's where I leave you behind, DI Mann,' I went on, 'for I might even hazard a guess at who he was.'

'Are you going to share that?' she asked.

'Not yet. Do something else for me first. If the CSIs did their job, they went over the garage and they found a Samsung Galaxy phone lying in his car. If they didn't, it's still there. Either way,' I said, 'you should get hold of it and see what's on it. If I'm right, then I'll share, and as far as Chief Constable Martin's concerned it was your idea all along.'

Forty-Two

'Thank you for joining us, Mr Sullivan,' Sammy Pye began as the visitor took a seat in his small office, facing him across his desk. Haddock made up a threesome, looking on from a chair beside the window, through which the low morning sun shone into Sullivan's face.

'You'll remember us, DCI Pye and DS Haddock.'

'Of course, and thanks for the lift,' the man replied, taking a pair of Ray-Ban Aviator sunglasses from the top pocket of his sports jacket and slipping them on. 'That's better,' he murmured. 'Now I can see you guys properly.'

'Sure,' Pye said. 'Would you like a coffee?'

'No thanks, I'm fine. Anyway, I'm not here for coffee, am I?'

The DCI smiled. 'Not exactly. We want to give you an update on your stolen car. And we have a couple of questions. We're recording this for the purposes of our investigation. Although you're here voluntarily, we'll be happy if you feel you want to have legal representation.'

'To hell with that,' Sullivan retorted. 'I have nothing to worry about, so I don't need a lawyer. As for an update, I've had that from the papers. You're dead certain it was the lad Francey who stole it?'

'One hundred per cent,' Haddock replied.

'I see,' he muttered. 'The other guy I told you about, the man King who came to see the Bristol: did you get anywhere with him?'

'No, but frankly we haven't been looking. He stopped being of interest quite early on.'

'Good, for he turned out not to be a time-waster after all. He phoned me on Monday evening and said he wanted to buy the Bristol, subject to a road test and independent inspection. We've done a deal.'

'Then we're happy for you.'

Sullivan frowned. 'Okay, so you're sure it was Dean Francey that took the Beamer, and used it to kidnap that poor wee girl. Are you working up to telling me you think our Maxwell might have been involved too?'

'No, there's no evidence of that at all,' Pye said, 'and it's never been in our thinking. But that's not to say that Francey acted alone. We believe that Anna Hojnowski was his accomplice.'

'The girl that was in the car with him when he was found?'

'The very same. You probably knew her as Anna Harmony.'

All the colour drained from Sullivan's face, in an instant. 'You what . . .' he gasped.

'Anna Harmony,' Haddock repeated. 'You did know her, didn't you?'

'Well, yes, but . . . I never knew that was her real name.'

'You had a party at your house about a year ago, and she was there, wasn't she?'

He nodded. 'Yes, so what?'

'It wasn't a casual invitation, was it? You knew her before that.'

'Yes,' Sullivan admitted.

283

'She worked for you?' Pye asked.

'In the factory, that's right. But I never knew her real name; I didn't hire her personally, or do the wages. She was always Anna Harmony to me . . . although I did hear people calling her Singer.'

'And she babysat for you?

'Once or twice.'

'And you had a relationship?'

He nodded. 'For a while.'

'Was she the cause of your marriage break-up?'

'Hell no. Janine never knew about her, and anyway there were others. What I told you before, it was true; Janine and I just weren't suited. We both wanted out. It was amicable, and Anna had nothing to do with it. When the divorce went through she and I weren't seeing each other.'

'But you thought you might re-start it?' the DCI suggested. 'Was that why you invited her to your party in North Berwick?'

Sullivan's smile was fleeting, and had a touch of shyness about it. 'Maybe.'

'So you must have been pissed off when she and Dean Francey hit it off.'

'You could say that,' he snorted. 'I didn't even invite him, Maxwell did. I barely knew the guy, and anything I'd heard didn't impress me. As it's turned out, I was right. There was an incident,' he continued. 'One of my Edinburgh guests had a bit too much and got fresh with Anna. She could have handled it herself, but Francey rode in to her rescue like the Lone fucking Ranger. Maxwell and I had to pull him off the bloke. Anna was impressed, of course; so impressed that she left with him. That was that . . . and it got her killed.'

'Eventually,' Haddock agreed. 'But let's get back to wee Zena. Does the name Grete Regal mean anything to you?'

'No. Why? Should it?'

'I don't know, that's why I asked. Thing is, she was Zena's mother, and at the moment she's lying in the Western General, unconscious, having had her skull fractured by Dean Francey.'

'That's very sad, but . . . so?'

'So, Mr Sullivan,' the DS said, 'you knew Francey, and you knew Anna Harmony. He assaulted the mother and kidnapped the child. She was going to help look after her in a rented cottage up in the Pentlands.'

'Does that mean they were going to hold her for ransom?'

'They weren't taking her on her holidays,' Pye snapped. 'She was going to be exchanged for money, or something, that's for sure, but what's equally certain is that those two young people, Dino and Singer, weren't acting on their own initiative.

'They were being paid to do it. We know that beyond doubt. And what we believe is that when Francey screwed up, the person who paid them shot them both, to silence them for good and all.'

'Okay,' Sullivan protested, 'but why the hell are you talking to me?'

'Because we have a problem,' Haddock told him, his 'good cop' tone calming the situation. 'You bank with the Clydesdale in Lothian Road, sir. We know that. It's quite a way from North Berwick, isn't it?'

'Yes I do,' he agreed. 'You want to know why? When I sold my company, I had to stay in there for two years because the price was profit-related, over that period. It's called an earn-out. One of the sale conditions was that its banking had to be integrated with that of the new parent company. So the business accounts moved from HSBC to the Clydesdale. When it happened I was offered sweeteners to shift my personal accounts there as well, so I did. That's what's behind it. However,' he added, 'my car business accounts are still with Bank of Scotland in North Berwick. Satisfied?'

'Not quite,' the DS said. 'In the middle of last month, you withdrew twelve thousand, in untraceable used notes of the bank's own issue, from your Clydesdale account. When we searched Dean Francey's flat on North Berwick Mains Street, we found five thousand, also in untraceable used notes, many of them from the Clydesdale. Given that it's a relatively small bank and there aren't a hell of a lot of those around, you might understand our curiosity.'

Sullivan ran his hand over his chin, muttering a muffled, 'Oh fuck.'

'Does that mean, "Oh fuck, you've got me", sir?' Pye asked.

'I think I want a lawyer,' the other man replied.

'If you feel you need one, we'll suspend this informal discussion and resume it under caution, where everything you say will be on the record.'

Sullivan leaned forward. 'Look, that money you found in Francey's, it didn't come from me. But . . .'

The DCI held up a hand. 'Stop. If you're going to admit to criminal activity, yes, probably you do need a lawyer.'

'I don't know. Tell me something first. How do you guys relate to the taxman?'

'HMRC handles its own investigations,' Pye replied. 'We don't report everything we hear to them.'

'Then don't report this, and switch off the recorder.'

'Okay.' He pressed the 'stop' switch.

'Remember the car I told you about, the Bristol?'

'Yes.'

'The twelve grand was for that. I bought it from a classified ad in the local paper. It was only described as a classic car, no make specified, and it was price on application. The seller wanted fifteen K, but he would only do a deal off the books. He said he needed money but he didn't want his wife to know how much the thing was worth. She'd always thought it was an old junker, so he was going to tell her he got two grand for it and pocket the difference.'

'Husband of the year, but go on.'

'Normally,' Sullivan continued, 'I wouldn't do that sort of deal, but the car was worth twenty-five, with a minimum of touching up. So I beat him down to twelve and we shook on it.'

'As a matter of interest,' Haddock asked, 'what's Mr King paying for it?'

'Twenty-eight.'

'Jeez!' the DS whistled. 'Gaffer, are you sure that's not criminal?'

'Not unless there's misrepresentation,' Pye laughed. 'If someone wants to pay that much for a forty-year-old car, good luck to all parties involved.'

'That's right,' the dealer declared. 'I've had people pay upwards of ten grand for a Mark One Escort, ten times the original costs.'

'Not this fella,' the DCI said, tapping his chest. He frowned at Sullivan. 'You do realise we'll need to confirm your story with the original seller of the car?'

The dealer shrugged. '*Que sera, sera*. His name's Paul Cockburn and he lives in Longniddry. If you can do it when his wife's out you'll be doing him a favour.'

'We'll try. Meantime, if you put that sixteen grand profit through your company accounts you'll be doing yourself a favour. I'm not saying we'd go running to HMRC, but it's never a good idea to give guys like us a club to hit you with.'

Sullivan winced. 'I'll bear that in mind. Can I go now?'

'Yes,' Pye said, 'we're done. We'll arrange a lift back for you.'

'That's okay. I'll hang around town till lunchtime and visit Kayleigh and her mum.' He sighed as he stood. 'It's too bad about Anna; I'm struggling to get my head round that. She was a really nice kid; friendly too. If only I hadn't let Francey come to that party, they'd never have met. She might even have been with me today.'

'My granny used to say,' Haddock murmured, with a wistful smile, '"If wishes were horses, we'd all get a hurl." Maybe she would have been, but I'm not sure how you'd have handled your girlfriend being a pole-dancer, Mr Sullivan.'

The man stared back at him. 'Why would it bother me? I own Lacey's. How do you think Anna got the job?'

Forty-Three

'That's quite correct,' DC William Dickson declared. 'Callum Sullivan bought Lacey's bar nine years ago; it was called the Peregrine then. His ex-wife's owned fifty per cent of the place since the divorce, and she's the licensee of record. It's vested in a limited company called CJ Inns that owns a total of four pubs in the city.

'The fact is,' the DC continued, 'he's a very wealthy man; he sold his company, CS Compressors, for eight million. Since then all he's done is play around with his classic cars, but that's profitable too. His company accounts showed a taxable profit of a hundred and seventeen thousand pounds in his first year's trading. He has no debt, he's a member of the Renaissance and North Berwick golf clubs, and of the New Club in Princes Street.

'He's been single since his divorce, with no particular attachments. Everybody likes the guy, including his former brother-in-law, Sergeant Harris. I spoke to him and he's full of praise for the way that Callum's looking after his son.

'Most important of all, I can find absolutely nothing to connect him with Grete Regal. Nothing, period. That's it, sir, Sarge.'

'Who bought the company?' Haddock asked.

'It's now a subsidiary of Higgins Holdings,' the DC replied. 'That's the holding company for Eden Higgins, the guy who used to be a furniture tycoon and now does even better as a venture capitalist.'

'Never heard of him,' the DS admitted. 'I don't read the business press.'

Pye shifted in his chair. 'Ever heard of Alison Higgins?'

'Yeah. She was a detective super, wasn't she? Killed on the job?'

'That's right; she was also Eden Higgins' sister. And Bob Skinner's . . .' His voice tailed off.

'What?' his colleague asked.

'Never mind. It was fifteen years ago, and more. Ancient history now.'

'Okay, so back to the present,' Haddock declared. 'If we're all agreed that Callum Sullivan's a paragon, now can we have a look at Hector Mackail?'

'Okay,' Pye laughed. 'You win.'

Forty-Four

'You do realise we might as well have interviewed Sullivan at home,' Sauce Haddock grumbled as he stared into his cup. 'Two hours later and here we are in bloody North Berwick . . . again. They should change the name to fucking Punxsutawney.'

'Puncture-what?' Pye laughed.

'Punxsutawney. Have you never seen *Groundhog Day*? It's about a town where the same thing happens over and over again. That's us, Sammy. We're trapped in a fucking time loop.'

'There are worse places to be trapped, mate. This Sea Bird Centre coffee's quite acceptable, and so are the scones. I'll tell you what; there are a couple of holiday parks here, why don't you and Cheeky buy a wee cabin? Then you can nip down for the weekend.'

'Why don't you . . . ' He threw up his hands in exasperation. 'Sir.'

Pye reached down and picked up a document case from the side of his chair, then produced an iPad. 'Okay, let's take a look at Dickson's report on Mackail.' He opened a Pages document and read through it. 'The business was called Mackail Extrusions,' he began.

'What the hell does that mean?' Haddock asked, puzzled.

'It made window frames for the double-glazing industry,' Pye explained. 'It seems to have been a victim of the slump. It suffered three consecutive years of trading losses, until finally its bank pulled the plug. Quite a few suppliers caught a cold in the collapse, Grete Regal Graphics among them, but she was the only one who pursued the directors personally. Actually there was only one director, Hector Mackail. His address is given in the final court decree as Seventy-five Adelaide Avenue, North Berwick, and he's described as unemployed. Dickson checked the electoral register; also listed as voters there are his wife, Gloria, and daughter Hazel.'

'Did William come up with anything else?'

'No. That's it.'

'Does he know we're coming?' Haddock asked.

The DCI shook his head. 'No, I don't want him forearmed.' He drained his coffee and finished the last of his scone. 'Come on, let's give him a pleasant surprise.'

Adelaide Avenue was not the prettiest street in the coastal town, but it looked respectable and its houses were well maintained. The street had begun life as part of a council estate, but most of its homes had been purchased by their tenants in the right-to-buy surge of the nineteen eighties, and so their appearance was less uniform than once it had been, with a variety of window designs and decorative colours and one or two substantial extensions.

'I grew up in a street like this,' Haddock observed.

'Me too, funnily enough,' his colleague said. 'It's ironic, that the Mackail family should wind up here. It's a monument to the double-glazing industry, where he made and lost his money. I'm older than you, so I remember when the C. R. Smith and Everest vans were everywhere.'

Number seventy-five was a semi-detached villa, painted in off-white Snowcem. A privet hedge enclosed the garden, and the drive to the side was laid in brick.

The detectives walked up the path to the front door, and Haddock rang the bell. They had been waiting for no more than a few seconds when a gruff male voice called to them from the pavement. 'They'll be naebody in.'

'Do you know where we could find them?' the DS asked the grey-haired septuagenarian shuffling along with a Co-op bag in each hand.

'Ye'll look far for him, but she'll be doon at the Eddington. She's a nurse.'

'Thanks. What's the Eddington?' the sergeant murmured.

'It's the health centre cum cottage hospital,' Pye replied. 'I know where it is; it's not far from here.'

In fact it was less than half a mile away, along a wide road and beside a church. The car park was full, and Pye was forced to find a space in the street, uncomfortably close to a set of traffic lights.

The reception area was busy as they stepped inside, filled with people with heavy eyes and puffy noses. 'Whatever they've got, I don't want it,' Pye whispered, as they approached the counter.

'We're looking for Mrs Mackail,' he told the receptionist, quietly.

'Sister Mackail,' she corrected him, primly. 'I'll see if she's free. Who will I say is calling?'

In reply, the two officers displayed their warrant cards. 'Oh,' the woman exclaimed. 'You've got somewhere at last, have you? Just wait here.'

She left her post and turned into a corridor behind her.

Within a minute she returned. 'Gloria's available,' she said, pointing behind her. 'Along there, second door on the right.'

They followed her finger, to find the door ajar; they stepped into a square surgery, with a frosted-glass window behind a desk and an examination bench against the wall on the left. Gloria Mackail stood beside it, in uniform, eyeing them with a frown on her face.

'Gentlemen,' she began, 'this is a surprise. I honestly thought the police had given up on me.'

'Oh no, Sister Mackail,' Pye replied. 'We never give up.'

'Does that mean you've caught him?'

The DCI felt his eyebrows rise. 'Pardon?' he exclaimed. 'Caught who?'

'Caught the man who knocked down Hector, of course!' she snapped, then paused. 'Are you telling me you don't know that my husband was the victim of a hit-and-run? That you don't know he's dead?'

I'll fucking kill Dickson, Pye thought.

I'll fucking kill Dickson, Haddock thought.

'I'm sorry, madam,' the senior detective replied, deadpan. 'We're involved in another investigation altogether. I'm the senior CID officer in Edinburgh, not East Lothian, but of course, if you wish, I'll make it my business to find out about the inquiry into your husband's death.'

'I'd be grateful if you would,' she said stiffly. 'Nonetheless, I'd have expected you to know about it before you turned up here.'

'I can only apologise.'

'No matter. What is this other investigation?'

'In the circumstances,' Pye said, waiting for the ground to open beneath him, and half hoping that it would, 'we'll be quite happy to postpone this.'

Gloria Mackail shook her head. 'That won't make it go away. You're here, so out with it.'

'To be honest, I'm not sure whether you can help us. It relates to your husband's former business, and to a claim against it by a woman named Grete Regal, a graphic designer who did some work for the company, then missed out on payment when it went into liquidation. You may not even be aware of it.'

'Oh yes,' the woman declared, bristling in her blue uniform, 'I'm only too well aware of it. Ms Regal was late with her invoice, or rather her bloody aunt was. By the time it was received by the liquidator of the business, he had already closed his list of creditors and they had all agreed a payment schedule, to be met from the sale of the company's assets. They were all going to get around fifteen pence in the pound, that's all.'

She fell silent, sniffed, and for a few moments the detectives thought she might break down. 'It wasn't Hector's fault,' she murmured. 'He was let down too, as badly as everyone else was. Those bloody bankers,' she hissed, bitterly. 'That bloody company. That bloody man.'

Composing herself, she carried on. 'Anyway, Grete Regal didn't take it lying down . . . or rather, her harridan of an aunt didn't.'

'What did the aunt have to do with it?' Haddock asked.

'She manages her business. Grete Regal couldn't run a raffle; she's a brilliant designer, but as a businesswoman she's all over the place. Her work is excellent, her costs aren't excessive and she never missed a deadline for Hector, but if she didn't have the Rainey woman behind her she'd be lost. Grete's a lovely girl; Ingrid Rainey is not. Have you met her?'

Pye nodded. 'Yes, but I can't comment on that.'

'I suppose not. But I will tell you that the woman pursued Hector through the civil courts, on the advice of a lawyer who should be ashamed of himself. The bloody sheriff found in their favour of course, with costs. He found that Hector had acted irresponsibly in commissioning the design work when he should have known that the business wasn't viable any longer. He even banned him from acting as a director. It wasn't fair; he had this idea that rebranding would help him turn the corner. If his biggest customer had paid him, and the bloody bank had given him another few weeks, that would have seen him all right.'

She paused, to dab at her eyes with a tissue. 'It would have meant our house going on the market,' she continued, 'not the one in Gilmerton, that was long gone; no, the house here, although we didn't have nearly enough equity in it to meet the claim. Our car too; Ingrid Rainey would have taken that too. We'd have been beggared, out in the street.'

'That's too bad,' Haddock said, feeling that a show of sympathy was in order.

'Damn right it was!' Mrs Mackail snapped. 'Rainey didn't even stop when Hector was killed. Her lawyer tried to arrest the insurance money, but fortunately, that was tied to the mortgage, so he couldn't. Instead Rainey told him to get a court order against me, personally, for Hector's debt.' She glowered at Pye. 'That's the background. Now, what does it have to do with your visit?'

'Have you seen much of the news this week?' he asked.

'Some, why?'

'Did you see the sad story of a child being found dead in a car in Edinburgh?'

'Yes, I did. Awful.' She frowned. 'And wasn't . . .'

The DS cut across her. 'The child was Grete Regal's daughter. Grete herself is in a coma, in hospital in Edinburgh.'

Gloria Mackail gasped. 'And they're saying that the young man Francey did it?'

'We're saying it, Mrs Mackail. Dean Francey abducted the girl and attacked her mother. That's a given, although he's beyond being called to account for it.' He glanced at Pye, who nodded for him to continue. 'Thing is, Francey was paid to do it. I'm sorry to be blunt about this, but we're looking at anyone who might have had a grudge against Grete. By your own admission you've been in serious dispute with her, and in addition to that, your daughter Hazel knows Dean Francey. So you see, we have to ask the question.'

Silence seemed to engulf the room as the nurse stared at the floor. The tension that was building in her was almost palpable and it communicated itself to the two officers.

'You have to ask the question,' she whispered.

'I'm sorry,' Pye said, 'we do.'

'Then here's the answer. Suppose I was the sort of sadist who'd use an innocent child as a weapon to right a grievance, suppose I was that sort of animal, I'd have had to pay Francey with Monopoly money, because I don't have any of the real stuff! I have just spent my daughter's pitifully small university fund on burying her father, after your colleagues finally deigned to release his body, and I am down to my last seven hundred quid. Having seen one mortgage paid off I'll have to take out another just to keep myself afloat. It's either that,' she shouted, 'or bloody Wonga!'

The DCI reached out and put a hand on her shoulder, as if his touch would draw the anger from her.

'We had to ask the question,' he repeated, gently. 'And now we have, and we believe you.'

She shuddered and then she was calm once more. 'Is Grete going to die?' she asked.

'We hope not. I can't say any more than that. But the word coming out of the Western General is a bit more optimistic today.'

'Then pray God she makes it, poor girl. I say that selfishly for if she doesn't, I'm probably back to square one. Grete and I, and Ingrid Rainey, and Harrison, their damn lawyer, all had a meeting last week. Rainey and the bloodsucker wanted my house, but when Grete realised what I'd been up against, she said no, that enough was enough.

'She said that she would take fifteen per cent of the debt, the same amount that the official creditors got, and she and I agreed a repayment schedule. I'll still have to mortgage to pay off bloody Harrison's costs, but the rest is manageable. She's a decent, generous girl, and to have such a horrible thing happen to her . . . it puts my situation into perspective. Now I'm terrified that if she doesn't make it, her awful aunt will revert to type.'

'If she does survive, Sister Mackail,' Pye said, 'she'll need friends. Maybe you can be around for her. We won't trouble you any longer.'

As he turned to leave, Haddock picked up a pad from the desk. He scribbled on it, ripped off the sheet, and handed it to her.

'That's the number of a very good lawyer, and I have a feeling she'd enjoy eating your Mr Harrison. You might like to call her. If you do, mention my name. Hers is Alex Skinner.'

He followed the chief inspector outside, into the street.

'Should we check out her bank details, for the record?' he asked, a dispassionate cop once more.

'That needs to be done,' Pye agreed, as he started the car. 'But we'll get Dickson to do it . . . or what's left of him when I'm finished chewing him out.'

Haddock nodded. 'I want a bite too,' he growled. 'That was bloody embarrassing. When you're asked to check someone out, the fact that he's dead ought to show up fairly early on.'

They were waiting for the lights to turn green when an incoming call sounded through the Bluetooth speakers. Pye touched a button on the steering wheel.

'Yes?'

'Sir, it's Jackie.'

'I knew that as soon as you opened your mouth,' he replied cheerfully. 'What's the new crisis?'

'No crisis, sir,' the detective constable said. 'The opposite really. Ms Iqbal from the Western General's been in touch. Grete Regal recovered consciousness just after ten this morning. She's stable and you can talk to her.'

'Call her back,' the DCI ordered, 'and tell her we're on our way.'

They were approaching Dirleton Toll, listening to Pablo Milanés, a Cuban singer who was a favourite of Pye's wife, when Haddock cut across his Spanish anthem.

'I'm just thinking, gaffer. I know someone, a girl I was at school with; her name's Macy Robertson and she's a business journalist so she might be able to give us some more background on Hector Mackail.'

'Do we need that?' Pye asked. 'Doesn't being dead cross him off the list of suspects?'

'It didn't get Francey off the hook,' Haddock pointed out. 'He

299

could have set it up before he walked in front of that car. Hazel knew Francey; he was handy for the job.'

'Then it went wrong and he came back from the dead and shot Francey and Anna?'

'Bugger!' the DS moaned.

Pye laughed at his frustration. 'Talk to your friend anyway, Sauce,' he said. 'There's no such thing as too much information.'

Forty-Five

When the chief inspector pressed the intercom at the entrance to the intensive care unit, and was told that Grete Regal was no longer there, his instant reaction was one of panic.

Relief took its place as the tinny voice continued, 'She's been transferred to the general ward; she's still on high dependency nursing, but she's doing fine.'

The two detectives followed the directions they were given; they were uncertain of the layout until Pye spotted Ingrid Rainey, seated in the corridor. 'That's the aunt,' he whispered to Haddock, stepping aside and into the ward office before she saw him.

He showed his card to the senior nurse. 'You're here for Grete?' the man asked. The DCI nodded. 'Ms Iqbal's with her just now; she'll just be a few minutes. Her aunt's waiting outside her room. Why don't you have a wee seat with her?'

'I want to avoid Mrs Rainey,' Pye confessed.

'On brief acquaintance I can understand why,' the nurse murmured.

'Does Grete know about her child?' he asked.

'Yes.' The man pursed his lips. 'The bloody aunt came out with it as soon as she saw her. Ms Iqbal had arranged a counsellor to break the news, and she told Mrs Rainey as much, but the woman insisted it was her duty.'

'How much does she know?'

'The aunt told her that the child was suffocated, that's all.'

'That's not strictly true, but there's no way of softening a blow like that. How has she reacted?'

'Ms Iqbal gave her a sedative, but she's still conscious and responsive. She did say that she wants to talk to you.'

'That's right, Chief Inspector,' Sonia Iqbal said, from the doorway. 'She is very anxious to speak to you.'

'You're okay with that?'

'Yes, or you wouldn't be here. I wish I could keep her family at bay, though. You can go in now, if you like.'

'How is she?' Haddock asked.

'She's remarkably well,' the surgeon replied. 'The brain swelling has lessened and she seems to have all her motor functions back.'

'And her memory?'

'Vivid, as you'll discover. I can't say, though, how much of it is real and how much imagined. Come with me, both, I'll take you along.'

She led the way along the corridor. Ingrid Rainey's chair had been vacated; she was waiting inside her niece's room, standing by her bedside with her back to the door. She was speaking in hushed hospital tones, but both detectives could still hear her well enough.

'This is what happens when you're nice to people, Grete. You feel sorry for them, now look at you; look at poor little Zena. I had to identify her, you know.'

'Fuck's sake!' Haddock whispered.

'Mrs Rainey,' Pye said.

The woman turned. 'Chief Inspector. You are here; you can tell poor Grete what happened to her.'

'We're hoping that Grete can tell us, ma'am, and we'd be grateful if you'd leave us with her.'

'I'm not doing that!' the aunt protested.

'I'm sorry,' Pye murmured, calmly, 'but that wasn't a request.'

'You can't make me leave.'

'There's a maximum of two visitors per patient at any given time,' Sonia Iqbal pointed out. 'You can come back in when the officers have finished.'

'Go on, Ingrid; please.' Grete Regal's voice was half whisper, half croak. Her aunt glared at the two detectives but finally she left the room, with the surgeon following.

'Ten minutes,' Ms Iqbal murmured, 'but at the first sign of distress . . .' She pointed at the monitor beside the bed. 'If her heart rate goes above ninety, you stop. Understood?'

'Understood.' Haddock said, as he closed the door.

'It's true, then?' the prostrate woman whispered.

'I'm sorry, Ms Regal,' Pye replied. 'It is. But what your aunt told you, that Olivia was suffocated, that's not correct.'

'Zena, we always called her Zena,' she corrected. 'Only the school called her by her given name.' Despite her Norwegian parentage her accent was Scottish.

'Of course. Zena was asthmatic, yes?'

'Yes, severely. Is that what happened?'

'I'm afraid so. She was placed in a confined space, and the belief is that it triggered an attack that she didn't survive.'

'Was it quick?'

'Very,' Pye lied.

'If there's any consolation, it's that. What about David,' she asked, 'does he know yet?'

'That's been difficult,' the DCI admitted. 'We've contacted the Ministry of Defence of course, but . . .'

'No,' Grete whispered. 'They will tell him whenever they can, but the Navy will not interrupt a mission for anything. He's the engineering officer on a Trident submarine, and nobody can ever know where they are.'

'They didn't even tell us that much,' Haddock said, 'but we'd worked it out. Now,' he continued, smiling gently, 'for we're on a meter here, how much can you remember of what happened?'

'All of it,' she replied, slowly. 'We were walking to school, as we always did when the weather was dry. Then a red car pulled in in front of us, and a man jumped out. He was wearing a black thingie over his face, a balaclava, so all I could see were his eyes and his mouth.

'He shouted at me. "Get back! Get back!" he yelled, and then he tried to grab Zena. Of course I tried to stop him. I went for him. I hit him about the head and I grabbed a handful of the balaclava and I pulled it, I pulled it half off. I saw his face, a mean, nasty face. I'll know him again, don't you worry; I'll never forget him.'

Pye was on the point of telling her that Dean Francey could never harm her again but she continued.

'That was when he hit me,' she said. 'With his fist at first; that knocked me backwards. Then he picked something up and hit me again really hard. It was like an explosion inside my head. Not sore but very loud, and then everything faded away . . .

'Until this morning, when I began to hear sounds around me, and to be aware, of being touched and moved, and of tubes going into my neck and in other places.

'And then I woke up,' she sighed, with a tearful sadness that the young detective sergeant found hard to bear, 'and now I wish that I hadn't.'

'I know,' he murmured, squeezing her hand.

She smiled, weakly, but only for a second or two. 'There's something that Ingrid said, about Gloria, Gloria Mackail, that she caused this to happen.'

'We don't believe that,' Pye told her. 'Mrs Mackail had nothing to do with it. We know who attacked you, and took Zena. We know also that someone paid him to do it, but he can't tell us, because he's dead.'

Her eyes widened as she stared up at him. 'The man who killed my baby is dead?'

The DCI nodded. 'Yes. He was shot. We believe it was because of what happened to Zena. As I said, we knew who he was, and we'd have caught him before too long. The person who paid him couldn't rely on him to keep his mouth shut, and so he silenced him, permanently.'

'That's the first good news I've had since I wakened,' she said, her voice stronger. 'You didn't have to tell me that Gloria was not involved. Poor woman; to lose her husband in such a stupid way. A drunk driver, the police from Haddington told her; there's no chance of them finding him, not now. Ingrid still wanted me to pursue her for the money he owed me, but I wouldn't do it. Everything's about money with my aunt. I pay her to manage my affairs, and she feels that everything I'm owed is partly hers. But I don't need it from Gloria; with David's salary we're not short.'

She tugged on Haddock's hand. 'Tell Gloria to come and see me, please. I'd like that. I don't know many people, and I don't want to be left alone, with nobody but Ingrid till David gets back. If I am I'll think about what's happened.' A look of concern came into her eyes. 'This couldn't be about David's job, could it?'

'Not a chance,' Pye assured her. 'The Ministry of Defence ruled that out. The people who have anything to gain by exerting pressure on a submarine officer know that it wouldn't work, because they couldn't get to him, under any circumstances, as we discovered when we tried.

'We don't know who was behind this, Grete, and I won't promise that we ever will, but I do promise that we're doing our damnedest to find out.'

He looked at his watch. 'Our time's up,' he said.

She tried to nod, but found it impossible because of the tubes that fed into her neck. 'Tell the surgeon lady, and Ingrid, that I want to sleep. Especially Ingrid,' she croaked. 'I can take no more of her today.'

'We'll do our best,' Haddock chuckled.

She smiled again. 'You're nice, both of you. I'm glad you came; you make me feel safer.'

They were at the door when she called after them, using all her strength. 'Can I see her?' she asked. 'Can I see my baby?'

'As soon as you're well enough,' Pye replied, 'we'll take you to her.'

Forty-Six

'We've got to stop these late finishes or our other halves will get suspicious,' Haddock laughed, leaning against the high back of the booth.

'I thought I was here to stop yours being suspicious,' Pye retorted.

'Not quite, gaffer. Okay, Macy and I did have a wee thing for a while, after we left school . . .'

'Were there any girls in your class that you didn't shag?' the DCI asked, casually.

'Most of them, and only the one while I was still there. Macy was a couple of years later, when we were students.'

'And of course you told Cheeky about her, in the spirit of full disclosure.'

'Of course.'

'And you're worried about her finding out that the two of you have met up.'

'I told her!' Haddock insisted.

'And she said, "Oh yes, Sauce, that's nice."'

'She did. And then she said, "Can I come too, I'd like to meet her," and I said, "No, it's business," and she went a bit quiet. So I said, "It's all right, Sammy's coming too." And here you are.'

'Very convenient,' Pye murmured. 'Now you won't have to worry about getting on the wrong side of her gangster grandpa.'

'I've never worried about that. Did I tell you we've been invited to his wedding?'

'No, you didn't. That's a surprise, isn't it?' Pye exclaimed 'There's a lady as brave as you, to be marrying into the Dundonian criminal family from hell.'

'Yes, and you know her. Remember the woman we nearly locked up last year, in the Cramond Island business?'

The DCI's orange juice stopped halfway to his mouth. 'What? Mia Watson? Bob Skinner's . . .'

'The same; the big man's fling from the nineties, his teenage boy's mother.'

'So that means,' Pye gasped, 'that Grandpa McCullough, the notorious Grandpa McCullough, is going to be Bob's son's stepfather?'

Haddock beamed. 'Exactly: the son who's doing time for culpable homicide. How will he go when he gets out? Will Bob train him as a Jedi, or will the Dark Side of the Force get him?'

'See you guys and your *Star Wars* analogies!' Pye spluttered. 'I'm still looking for whoever it was christened me Luke Skywalker.'

'Don't look too hard,' the DS chuckled. 'Everybody knows it was Mario McGuire. Anyway, you love it, admit it.'

'It gets a laugh, I'll grant you.' He glanced at his watch. 'Where is this girl?'

'She'll be here, worry not.'

Two minutes later she was: the double doors of Bert's Bar swung open and a stocky red-haired woman stepped in from William Street. She was wrapped up against the cold, in a thick woollen coat, a snood and a Cossack hat, and she wore boots that were as black as her long skirt.

'Macy!' the DS called as she looked around. He stood and eased himself out of the confines of the booth. 'What are you having?'

'Gin and tonic, large, ice, no lemon,' she said, her eyes on the other man, who was still seated.

'My boss,' Haddock explained. 'Sammy Pye, Detective Chief Inspector.'

'I know who he is,' Macy Robertson replied. 'I've seen him on TV a couple of times this week. Is that what this is about? The child murder?'

Pye nodded. 'In a way. But it's not a murder. It'll be a suspicious death until the Crown Office makes up its mind what box to fit it into. There's no rush about that, since the perpetrator's dead. So tell me, Ms Robertson, who do you work for?'

'Didn't Harry say?'

'Harry?' the DCI repeated 'The entire Scottish police service and everyone attached to it knows him as Sauce.'

Macy's eyes widened as did her smile. 'Really? That's wonderful. That'll be round all my Facebook friends before the night's out.'

'Have fun with it. Now, who do you work for?' Pye repeated, as his colleague returned with the gin and tonic.

'Bloomberg.'

'What?'

'Bloomberg,' she repeated. 'It's a business-based American TV channel, on satellite and cable. It has an Edinburgh office, although not too many know about it. So, what do you want to pick my brains about,' she paused, and winked, 'Sauce?'

Haddock scowled across the table. 'Thanks, pal,' he muttered.

'The last group of people that still used my proper name, and you've blown it.' He glanced to his right. 'We're looking for background on a company called Mackail Extrusions. Oh aye,' he added, 'and we're looking for it off the record.'

'What if a real story develops?' she asked.

'A head start on it,' Pye promised. 'Does it stir any recollections?'

She smiled, slowly. 'As a matter of fact it does; very vivid ones. I'm glad I came already.' She sipped her G and T. 'You know what the company did, yes?'

'As we understand it, it made UPVC window frames for the double-glazing industry.'

'Spot on,' she confirmed. 'I don't have to tell you that when the recession hit and the housing market, which hadn't seen it coming, died in its sleep, life became very difficult for that sector. Mackail Extrusions was hit as hard as anyone else, but it was a well-managed, family-owned company with a decent cash base, since Hector Mackail didn't overpay himself or stuff his pension fund, as happens in all too many self-managed enterprises.'

She sipped again, and Haddock realised that her glass was almost empty. She raised it, an unspoken suggestion that it might be refilled. 'In a minute,' he said.

'I've got to earn it, have I?' Macy chuckled. 'Okay. The company traded on through the tough times; it pared itself right down, and focused on the home improvement market where there was still a certain amount happening. It lost money, but it wasn't immediately calamitous, for as I said, it had gone into it with a strong balance sheet. It had an underlying weakness, though. No, sorry, two. The first was that it was heavily dependent on a single customer. The second was that its banker was, not to beat about any bushes, a real See You Next Tuesday.'

'You haven't lost your command of the language, Mace,' Haddock remarked.

'No . . . Sauce,' she giggled, 'I've got more subtle with age, that's all. Anyway, this is how the story developed; I got this from Hector Mackail, personally. I can tell you that now he's dead, poor sod. Basically, the customer saw off most of its rivals, by landing a couple of big contracts when central government started to pump money into public sector projects, and by securing work from other companies within its group.'

'What group?' Pye asked.

'I'll get to that,' the journalist replied, 'as soon as you get me another large G and T.'

The DCI muttered something mildly obscene, but headed for the bar.

'So how's it with you and the *chica*, Harry?'

'She's the best thing that's ever happened to me,' Haddock said.

'And the richest, from what I hear. Pity about her mother being in jail.'

'We don't talk about that across the dinner table. But you're out of date,' he added. 'She's on parole.'

'There.' The returning Pye placed a fresh drink before her, and a second pint before his sergeant. 'Get singing.'

'Certainly. The customer was called Destry Glazing Solutions. For the last several years it's been a subsidiary of Higgins Holdings, the umbrella company of Eden Higgins, the squillionare. Although he owns it, he doesn't run it. Day-to-day management is in the hands of the widow of the company's founder. His name was James Stewart, obviously a man with a droll sense of humour.'

'In what way?' Haddock asked.

'I can tell you that,' his boss said, drily. 'In the movie *Destry Rides Again*, guess who played Tom Destry, the hero?'

'Who?'

'Jesus! James bloody Stewart, that's who! Remind me never to have you in my pub quiz team. Go on, Macy.'

'He was never any use on film questions,' she laughed, 'if it involved real actors. Walt Disney was his limit. So, there's Mackail Extrusions, kept going purely by its orders from Destry Glazing, the problem I identified earlier.'

'Except,' Haddock, keen to re-establish some authority, interrupted, 'Destry wasn't a problem as long as it paid its bills on time.'

'You've got it: which Destry didn't. It wasn't that it couldn't, for it was cash positive; no, it was the widow Stewart's policy to keep her suppliers waiting. Eventually that proved fatal for Mackail Extrusions. By that stage the company's viability was on a knife-edge; it was operating on a big overdraft with a usurious interest rate.'

'And the See You Next Tuesday pulled the plug?' Pye asked.

'Precisely. He knew the debt was out there, but he refused to extend further credit. Hector Mackail had run out of cash, even though by that stage he'd re-mortgaged his house to stay afloat. He couldn't pay his own creditors and he couldn't pay his employees' wages. He had no choice but to call in the receiver.'

'He wasn't completely innocent,' Haddock said. 'While his business was effectively down the tubes he ran up a bill with a design company, trying to generate new orders by rebranding it.'

'I didn't know that,' the journalist admitted. 'It doesn't surprise me, though. Mackail wasn't the brightest; he should have gone legal with Destry Glazing at an early stage, but he didn't.'

'Why didn't he?'

'Because it was owned by Eden Higgins, that's why not. Scotland's business angel is not a man people like to cross.'

'I thought he was squeaky clean,' Pye observed.

'He is, but that's because nothing ever sticks to him.'

'There's mud to throw?'

Macy contemplated her second drink. 'I'm starving,' she said, looking at Haddock, who took the hint and went to the bar, returning with a pie on a plate.

'Beef chilli.'

She flashed her eyes at him. 'Darling, you remembered.'

'How could I forget? You used to put those away two at a time.'

'Of course I did, when you were paying. You're lucky I'm on a diet just now.' She took a bite of the pie. 'Tasty,' she murmured. 'Yes, Eden Higgins. Guess what happened to the leavings of Mackail Extrusions?'

'We feed you and we have to play guessing games?' Haddock exclaimed.

'Fair enough. The liquidator put the bite on Destry Glazing. It paid up without a murmur, and then it bought the assets of the failed company for a song, those assets being all its plant and equipment. By the time the bank was paid, and the liquidator himself, of course, the other creditors were left with something like fifteen pence in the pound. Effectively, Destry Glazing Solutions bought itself an in-house extrusion facility for little more than zero, right at the moment when the construction industry's coming out of hibernation.'

'That's a hell of a story, Macy,' Pye remarked. 'I read the business press, so how come I've never seen it anywhere?'

'You don't watch Bloomberg, since you'd never heard of it before tonight.'

'You ran it?'

'I ran a piece about the role of the bank. When I put it together I called Destry Glazing's PR people and asked for a comment. They promised to get back to me, but they never did. Instead I had a call from Eden Higgins' lawyers, threatening me with an action for defamation if his name was even hinted at in my report.'

She renewed her attack on the pie. 'Nobody else in Edinburgh touched it,' she mumbled. 'So I guess that my colleagues in the printed media were all warned off.' She leaned forward. 'Now,' she said, 'how does all that relate to the dead child?'

'It doesn't, not really,' Haddock confessed. 'The designer that Mackail ran up the bill with, she was the mother. She was attacked as well, but that never made the press. We've been looking for a connection, but I don't see one.'

'Oh no?' Macy murmured. 'There's a PS to the story. I heard it a month or two back, from a bloke I know on the *Daily Record* business staff. Yes, it's a red-top but it does have a business reporter. His girlfriend had just chucked him, and, well, I consoled him.' She beamed at Haddock. 'I always was good at consoling, Harry, wasn't I?'

'No comment,' 'Harry' muttered.

'Anyway,' her second drink had disappeared without either detective noticing its demise, 'in the aftermath, when we were wondering what the hell to say to each other, he came out with a story that the ex had told him in confidence.'

'Under similar circumstances no doubt.'

'Probably. Her name's Luisa, and she's Eden Higgins's PA. The tale was that after the liquidator had done his worst, Hector Mackail turned up unannounced at Eden's office up on the Mound. He accused him of being in cahoots with the See You

Next Tuesday at the bank . . . in which Higgins has a substantial stake, did I forget to mention that? . . . and of masterminding the whole thing.

'Eden told him to go away, or words to that effect, and Mackail lost it. He banjoed him and knocked him down a flight of stairs, buggering his ankle in the process. Luisa was going to call your lot, but Eden told her to do no more than chuck Mackail out. He wanted no police involvement, no exposure of the story. He walked about with a cast on his ankle for five weeks and never told anyone why.'

'I can see why he'd want to keep that quiet,' Pye said. 'Did you think about running it?'

'No, and neither did my one-night stand. The fight would have been denied, Luisa would have been fired and nobody would ever have proved any collusion between Eden and See You Next Tuesday.'

Macy finished the pie and stood up, abruptly. 'I hope that was all worthwhile, guys. I've got to go now; Goldman Sachs is having a champagne reception in the Balmoral Hotel. There will be food.'

She leaned over and kissed Haddock on the cheek, leaving a lipstick impression. 'Bye, Sauce, your secret is totally unsafe with me.'

'Fuck me!' Sammy Pye gasped as she left. 'Now I understand why you wanted a minder.'

Forty-Seven

'It's a hell of a story, boys,' Mario McGuire said, 'but how does it relate to your inquiry? Your target is the person who killed Francey and the Polish girl, because it's almost certain that he paid them to kidnap Zena. The other thing, this corporate skulduggery, there's no way that it relates.' The DCC scratched his chin. 'Mind you,' he mused, 'I'm interested, for other reasons, that Eden Higgins is caught up in it.'

Sammy Pye had called him the previous evening, almost as soon as the doors in Bert's Bar had stopped swinging after Macy Robertson's departure, to ask for a review meeting on the investigation. McGuire had been on his way south from Inverness at the time, and had been only too eager to grab an excuse for avoiding the chief constable's routine morning meetings with his deputies and assistants. He would admit it to nobody but his wife, but he was becoming irked by the micromanagement of the new force at the very top level and the spread of that culture downwards.

'Surely Bob Skinner was a classic micromanager?' Paula had argued, when he had voiced his concerns, over dinner.

'Bob was an interfering so-and-so at times,' he had replied, 'on the criminal investigation side, but when he did stick his

316

nose in, it was always to support the people on the ground, never to second-guess them. Andy Martin is trying to keep a grip on everything that's going on, rather than trusting people to do the job he's given them. Today he came down on me like a ton of bricks because Sammy Pye took a decision that he saw as questioning his judgement. I never told Sammy, but he ordered me to take him off the case and replace him with Lowell Payne.'

'Who's Lowell Payne?'

'He was a Strathclyde man, the head of organised crime and counter-terrorism; what we used to call Special Branch. Bob appointed him, and I'd have kept him in post, but Andy told me to move him out and replace him with Renée Simpson from the old Grampian force. So now Payne's a detective superintendent without portfolio.'

'Did you replace Sammy?'

'Like hell I did! I told Andy that I wasn't going to undermine one of my best detectives and that he could replace me if he had a problem with that. He backed down, but the boy Pye's future in CID is hanging by a very thin thread if he doesn't get a result.'

'And you? How are you placed with him?'

'Honestly? I have no idea. I don't know the man any more.'

He was still brooding as he sat with the two Edinburgh detectives in the Fettes canteen, a mug of tea enveloped in his very large right hand. He was focused on one single objective, preserving his own authority as deputy in charge of all criminal policing, and protecting Pye's position was inextricably linked to that.

If the Zena investigation collapsed, and Martin carried out his threat to transfer Pye out of CID, it would be a resignation issue for him . . . and he would not go quietly.

'The man Mackail's death,' he murmured. 'What's your thinking on that?'

'We reckoned . . .' Haddock began, but went no further as he felt the weight of McGuire's heavy black eyebrows.

'Sergeant,' he growled, 'when I put a question, unless I'm actually looking at you, it's for the senior officer at the table to answer me.'

The DS gazed at the tabletop. 'Sorry, sir,' he murmured, icily.

'Sauce and I reckoned,' Pye began, then paused.

McGuire glowered at him; then he grinned, breaking the tension. 'Nice one, Sammy; I appreciate you standing up for your sidekick. So go on, give me the benefit of your combined wisdom.'

'We don't have any,' the DCI confessed. 'We are stuck; we have no positive lines of inquiry left open. Callum Sullivan's bank withdrawal was a red herring, as DCs Wright and Dickson have confirmed, and the banknotes found in Francey's flat are untraceable. The Mackail connection to Grete Regal was all we had, and now that's blown.'

He paused as the DCC drank some of his tea.

'You're right,' he continued when he had his full attention once more, 'that the corporate skulduggery, as you call it, doesn't relate to the main investigation in any way we can see, but the aftermath . . . what about that? Hector Mackail was involved in a physical confrontation with Eden Higgins and a few days later he died in a hit-and-run, on his way home from the pub in North Berwick.'

'Shit happens,' McGuire grunted.

Pye laughed. 'Sir, that's just about the worst piece of devil's advocacy I've ever heard.'

'Maybe, but are you saying that one of Scotland's richest men ran over a guy just because he'd stuck one on him?'

'No, because his foot was in plaster; but he could have paid someone to do it, someone who knew the lie of the land and might even have known that Hector Mackail drank in the Nether Abbey bar with his pals every Friday and then walked home.'

The DCC swirled the dregs of his tea around the bottom of the mug. 'North Berwick's not awash with hit men, is it?' he said.

'No, sir, it's not,' Pye agreed. 'But there is one, or rather there was, that we know of, someone who actually knew Mackail, or knew of him, through his daughter. What if . . .'

McGuire beamed. 'Some of the greatest results in the history of criminal investigation began with those two words,' he observed. 'Go on.'

'What if the money we found in Francey's flat wasn't a down payment for the Zena abduction, but payment in full for knocking over Hector Mackail?'

'What if . . .' The deputy chief paused. 'Okay, you've established that Francey took the child and injured her mother, but nothing in your investigation of the bloke has suggested that he had a reputation for that sort of work.'

'No,' Pye accepted. 'Maybe Mackail was killed by a drunk who panicked and drove off. But if he wasn't, then at the very least, Francey should be investigated as a suspect. And if he was involved, is it likely that two different people, entirely unconnected, would approach him and hire him to commit violent crimes?'

The DCC leaned back and looked at the ceiling. 'But what possible connection is there between one of Scotland's richest men and an obscure graphic designer from Garvald?'

'That's the question, sir,' Sauce Haddock ventured.

'Then don't just sit there,' McGuire boomed. 'Go and fucking answer it!'

Forty-Eight

'Did it not occur to you to advise CID of Mr Mackail's death?' Sammy Pye asked.

Inspector Carmel Laird gazed at him. 'Why should it have?' she replied. 'It was a traffic fatality.'

'It was a hit-and-run,' Sauce Haddock pointed out. 'A man was killed, and the driver left the scene; that's a crime. FYI, the "C" in CID stands for Criminal.'

She kept her eyes on Pye. 'Is your gopher always insubordinate?' she murmured.

'Detective Sergeant Haddock is a law unto himself,' Pye replied quietly. 'I kick his arse occasionally, but never when he's right.'

'Hold on a minute,' Laird protested. 'This is Haddington; we're East Lothian, you're Edinburgh. Suppose I had asked for CID assistance, it wouldn't have been you I'd have gone to.'

'We share information in the department.'

'We share information too. We posted a report of the fatality on the ScotServe website . . . and we appealed for witnesses. Naturally, we also reported the fatality to the procurator fiscal. Those are the laid-down operating procedures, so don't question me, question the senior command if you've got a problem.'

'I question them all the time,' Pye replied. 'In fact I've just come from a meeting with my big boss where I asked him how a man's violent death isn't automatically the subject of a major criminal investigation. He's just gone off to ask your immediate boss the same question, and I don't think he was planning to ask politely. Time to circle your wagons, Inspector, and cooperate.'

'So how can I help?' she asked, stiffly.

'You can begin by taking me through the story. So far the only information I have came from the victim's wife.'

'You could have looked at the website . . .'

'But we didn't,' Haddock said, 'because we're technically inept, and old fashioned enough to believe that there's still room for common sense in the service.'

'See when you're back in uniform,' she hissed, 'and posted out here . . .'

'If that ever happens,' the DCI snapped, 'he'll be an inspector at the very least. You, on the other hand, will be lucky to be a sergeant, if you annoy me any more. Let's forget what you did, and focus on what you should have done. Take us through what happened.'

Laird picked up a folder from her desk and found a document; she began to read through it, commenting as she went.

'Deceased was found in Station Road, just past the fire station.'

'Who found him?' Haddock asked.

'A passing motorist saw him and called 999. Deceased was lying on the pavement, against a stone wall and a traffic sign. Paramedics arrived, followed by a medical examiner. Deceased was removed by ambulance but he was DOA at the hospital.'

'What about the attending officers?'

'Sergeant Chocolate . . . that's Sergeant Brown, and PC Raymond.'

Pye frowned. 'When did they get there?'

'A couple of minutes after the paramedics, and just before the ME.' Inspector Laird seemed to wince, slightly. 'They'd been attending a reported disturbance at a rugby club dinner in Aberlady, and there was no other patrol car available.'

'So they got there more or less as Mackail was being removed.'

'That's right. They followed the ambulance.'

'And he was found lying on the pavement, you said.'

'That's right too. He was still in the position he was found in when my officers arrived.'

The two detectives looked at each other; Pye raised an eyebrow, Haddock nodded.

'So when did they realise it was a hit-and-run?' the DS asked.

The inspector's face flushed. 'Not until he was examined at the hospital,' she replied. 'The admitting doctor suspected crushing injuries, and that was confirmed by a post-mortem.'

'What about the medical examiner who attended?'

'From what the lads told me, the paramedics had everything in hand by that time. The ME took a quick look but he didn't do anything. He waved the ambulance off, more or less, and went back to being on call.'

'At what point did . . . the lads . . . identify the victim?'

'He wasn't identified until the ambulance reached the hospital. By that time he was dead. His driving licence was in his wallet.'

'Did they return to the scene once they realised what had happened?'

'No. I ordered other officers to do a house-to-house first thing next morning.'

'Next morning?' Pye exclaimed, his voice rising. 'Why didn't Brown and Raymond go straight back there?'

'They were called out to another road traffic accident on the A1, from the infirmary,' Laird protested. 'They were tied up with that for hours. That's the resources we've got; that's the real world.'

'Okay, leave that to one side. You canvassed householders at the scene the next morning. Any response?'

'A woman in a house in Old Abbey Road said she thought she heard a squeal of tyres, around eleven forty-five, but that was all.'

'Did you order a forensic examination of the scene?'

'No, I decided that too much time had passed.'

'No you didn't; you decided to keep the whole thing under the carpet. Your guys arrived, saw a man on the ground and assumed he was a heart attack victim or a drunk.' The DCI paused for a second, then flew a kite. 'On Monday morning, when Grete Regal was found in Garvald, who attended that scene?'

Laird reddened. 'Brown and Raymond.'

'No bloody wonder they were so quick to decide that one was a hit-and-run.' Pye sighed. 'So, now we have no way of knowing whether Mackail staggered off the pavement after a few pints and into the path of a vehicle, or whether it mounted the pavement and hit him.'

Inspector Laird sat, silently staring ahead.

'Who told Mrs Mackail?' the DCI murmured.

'I did. Brown called me; although I was off duty, I went to the address he gave me, and informed the widow.'

'What was her reaction?'

'What do you think?' Laird retorted. 'Shock.'

323

'Did she say anything?'

'Yes, she did. She said, "Finally they've taken everything." Then she went into hysterics; her daughter appeared from upstairs, and the whole thing went into meltdown. I sent for a doctor, and waited till he arrived. He sedated both women; I left a WPC from the North Berwick office to stay with them overnight.'

'Who took Mrs Mackail's statement?'

'Nobody. I'd established from her that her husband had been for his usual Friday session in the Nether Abbey. I didn't deem it necessary to trouble her further.'

'Okay,' the DCI said. 'I get the picture. I see why you kept this in-house. This whole thing reeks of sloppiness and even negligence. You were protecting your officers, and as their manager, protecting yourself.'

'Wouldn't you?' she retorted.

'Possibly. But I wouldn't have sat on my hands. I'm taking this situation over, and I'm going to see what I can rescue.'

'Feel free, but please, keep Brown and Raymond out of it.'

'They were hardly ever in it from what I can see.' He turned to Haddock. 'Sauce, get a forensic team out to Station Road. You never know, even at this very late stage we might scrape something up.'

'But suppose you do,' Laird said, 'you won't be able to tie it conclusively to this incident.'

'That depends what we find. And by the way,' he added, 'until we know for sure to the contrary, we're treating this "incident" as a homicide.'

Forty-Nine

'I didn't expect to see you here, Arthur,' Sammy Pye said.

'I fancied a trip to the seaside,' the senior scene of crime technician replied, gruffly. Arthur Dorward was renowned for being no respecter of persons, a reputation he had earned even before he transferred from the police force to the new civilian central service operated by the Scottish Police Authority.

'On your own?'

The former inspector frowned at the serving DCI. 'You call me out to look at a piece of pavement weeks after an incident occurred, and you expect me to come mob handed? Why should I waste another specialist's time as well as my own?'

Pye nodded. 'Fair enough.' He recognised the near impossibility of the mission.

'Where's your sidekick? He called me, so I thought he'd be here.'

'Sauce has gone up to Edinburgh. I sent him in search of a post-mortem report.'

'Tell me what happened. Young Haddock didn't go into detail; he just said it was a fatal RTA, driver left the scene.'

'That sums it up.'

'So why am I a couple of months late in getting here?' Dorward asked, casually.

'SFU,' the DCI replied, tersely. 'Somebody fucked up. I'm not looking for miracles, Arthur.'

'That makes a change for you guys. But suppose you were, then as always you've come to the right man. What am I looking for?'

Pye turned to a uniformed officer who was standing a few yards away, leaning against a patrol car. 'Sergeant Brown,' he called out, 'draw an outline of where Mr Mackail was lying when you arrived at the scene.'

'Sir.' Solemnly he stepped forward and did as he was told, chalking a crude outline of a human form, tight against the high stone wall that ran along the inside of the pavement, with its midsection against a grey pole that held a yellow 'No waiting' sign.

'What were the weather conditions?' Dorward asked.

'Dry. It was a clear night,' Brown replied.

'Was the victim bleeding?'

'He'd a cut on the side of his head and there was blood coming from the corner of his mouth. There was a strong smell of booze and he'd been sick.'

'Conscious?'

'No' really. He was moaning, but he didn't respond to questions. My neighbour and I thought he was a drunk, and that he'd fell over and banged his head. I said as much to the paramedics and the doctor and nobody argued with us.'

'It wasn't their place to argue with you, Sergeant,' Pye pointed out, 'any more than it was yours to jump to conclusions.'

'What was the victim wearing?' Dorward asked.

'A dark coat, it could have been black or navy; we couldn't tell in the light, and they'd taken it off him when we saw him in the hospital. By that time he was dead.'

'Was it a raincoat?'

'No, it was heavier than that. Woollen, I'd say; it looked expensive.'

'What happened to it?'

'I've got no idea. They'd give it to the widow, I guess.'

'Okay,' the crime scene investigator said. 'You've got a supposed drunk who turns out to be a hit-and-run victim. With that knowledge, if you think back to the scene, can you recall anything that might be of interest to me?'

'Nothing,' Brown replied, instantly.

'That took a lot of consideration,' Dorward growled. He turned to Pye. 'This guy's in the wrong business, Sammy; he should be a chocolate fireguard salesman. They're bloody useless as well.'

'Hey,' the sergeant exclaimed, 'you hold on a minute!'

'No,' Dorward barked. 'You hold on. You were at the scene of a fatal hit-and-run accident, but you never even considered that possibility. If you had, we'd have had something to work with, because it's pretty much impossible to kill somebody with a motor car without leaving some sort of a trace. Now we're several weeks down the road and everything is compromised.'

He picked up his equipment case. 'Sammy, you might as well leave me to it. There's nothing you can do here other than get in the way, and listen to me swear. I won't be long here, and if I find anything that might be relevant, I'll let you know soonest. If I don't, well, it's a no-hoper, so you're not going to be disappointed, are you?'

Leaving the investigator to his nearly impossible task, Pye had Sergeant Brown drive him to Edinburgh. He sat in the back of the car and the journey was spent in silence.

When he walked into the squad room in the Fettes building, Haddock followed him into his office.

327

'Did you get it?' the DCI asked, as he hung his coat on a hook behind the door.

'Yes,' his sergeant replied. 'One of the deputies had the case file in his out tray, ready to go to the fiscal with a recommendation that they write it off as an untraced hit-and-run, with no fatal accident inquiry necessary. He seemed a wee bit nonplussed when I told him we were taking an interest in it. The cheeky bastard asked me whether we were having to invent crimes to keep ourselves busy.'

'He sent you the file, though?'

'Oh yeah, once he'd had his wee moan. I've been through it; there's not much to it. Apart from the PM report, there's the two cops' statements, and another from the barman in the Nether Abbey. I'm a bit suspicious about that. He was interviewed by Brown and Raymond, and the way it reads . . .'

'You think they were coaching him?' Pye asked.

'It wouldn't surprise me. One minute he's saying he's not sure how much Mackail had to drink, the next he's saying he was unsteady on his feet when he left.'

'What about his pals? What did they say?'

'They weren't interviewed.'

'You're joking!'

'Do I have my Joker mask on?' Haddock retorted. 'They're not even named on the report. The way I see it, Brown and Raymond preferred the official version to be that Mackail might have been partly culpable himself, so that the fiscal wouldn't look too closely at their performance.'

The DCI nodded. 'You could be right. Brown certainly wasn't in a rush to help Arthur Dorward, and he got quite aggressive when he was challenged. What did the post-mortem say about Mackail's blood alcohol level?'

'A hundred and thirty milligrams per hundred millilitres; not quite three times over the driving limit. In other words, he'd have been a bit pissed but he shouldn't have been falling about.'

'What about the rest of it?'

'He died from massive internal bleeding; his spleen was ruptured, and his liver was torn. Several ribs were fractured and one had pierced his lung. He'd a broken right hip as well.'

'Poor guy,' Pye said. 'CID should have been informed on the night. I'm going to have that pair,' he promised, 'and their inspector too.'

'How long is it since you've been in uniform?' Haddock murmured.

'Come again?' his boss retorted.

'You heard. Brown and Raymond reacted to what they saw, a badly injured man on the pavement. The priority was get him to hospital; that's what happened, but his injuries were unsurvivable. They were in the middle of a hectic night shift, and they followed their instincts.'

'What about Laird?'

'She was off duty at the time,' the DS reminded him. 'When she was advised she probably realised straight away there had been a screw-up, but she hid behind protocol to protect her guys.'

'Nobody's protecting us.'

'Are you sure? Big guy, half Irish, half Italian, wears a DCC's uniform and hates it?'

'Mmm. Maybe.'

'No maybe about it,' Haddock declared. 'Look, Sammy, we were talking about priorities. Pursuing two fellow cops who might have been sloppy under pressure isn't one of ours.'

'Okay,' Pye admitted, 'you've got a point. I feel under pressure myself, and probably I'm lashing out.'

'Well, I'm buggered if I do. Have we done anything wrong in this investigation?' The question was bluntly put.

'No,' the DCI replied. 'I don't believe so.'

'Are we following every possible line of inquiry?'

'Yes.'

'Then where's the pressure? It's not coming from big Mario. It's not coming from Mary Chambers.'

'No, it's coming from the man at the top, because I crossed him over that media briefing. That would . . .'

Haddock laughed. 'I know what you're going to say: that would never have happened in Bob Skinner's time.'

'Well, it wouldn't.'

'Probably not, but that time is over. Now, it is what it is, but one thing remains: all we can do is our best. So, remind me. Why are we looking into Mackail's death, when there's every chance that he was hit by a driver who was even more drunk than he was, and who buggered off into the night when he realised what he'd done?'

Without allowing his boss a moment to reply, he answered his own question. 'The investigation that began in the Fort Kinnaird car park has turned into a hunt for a double murderer. Now we're looking at the outside possibility that he might have been responsible for a third.'

Pye smiled. 'Do you want to swap desks, Sauce? You're enjoying this job a hell of a lot more than I am just now, and you're better at it.'

'Not a prayer. I'm still learning from you. Gaffer, if anyone can catch this bloke it's you and me. If we don't, it won't be your fault, and if our fearless leader tries to follow through on his silly threat to take it out on you personally, I will personally go to Stirling, kick his fucking door in and tell him that he's not fucking on.'

The chief inspector sighed. 'Thanks for that, Sauce. You're right; it's our investigation, not his, so let's focus on it. Have you heard from Lucy Tweedie?' he asked.

'Yes, she called a couple of minutes before you got here. She's recovered the coat; Mrs Mackail still had it, although twenty-four hours later it would have been off to the dry cleaners, then the charity shop.'

'Good. It must be a chunky garment if it's still wearable after what happened to its owner. Maybe forensics will be able to . . .' Pye stopped in mid-sentence as his phone sounded. He snatched it from his pocket and took the call. 'Arthur,' he exclaimed.

'The impossible I do at once,' Dorward said, in his ear. 'Miracles take a little longer and need a bit of imagination. Before I go any further, the caveat to what I'm going to tell you is that everything I've found could relate to a completely different incident, or incidents, but here goes. Is your pencil poised?'

'As it ever will be; go on.'

'Right. First, on the pavement, just beside your man's crude chalk victim, there are traces of rubber, burned into the slabs. It's consistent with marks left by wheelspin, and it could have been there from the time of the incident, fading gradually, but still just about visible.

'Second,' he continued, 'I was able to extract from the stonework of the wall against which the victim lay traces of white paint, consistent with a vehicle having scraped against it. The height of these marks indicates that they weren't made by a saloon, but by a mid-sized van, a Transit or something similar.'

'Well done, Arthur,' Pye exclaimed. He looked up at Haddock.

'Remember Chic Francey's van?' he asked. 'What was it?'

'Vauxhall Vivaro,' the DS responded, immediately. 'Dirty white; it's seen better days.'

'Have I made your day?' Dorward asked.

'Potentially.'

'Well, here's some more.' He paused. 'I don't have to tell you that I've forgotten more about crime scenes than you high-flyers will ever know.'

'Can you hear me touch my forelock, Arthur?' Pye chuckled.

'I wondered what the grovelling sound was,' the scientist retorted, deadpan. 'Anyway, based on a career's worth of experience, I took a look at the broader scene. The fact that two CID bigwigs are involved in this told me that it isn't your standard knock-down, panic, and drive away, like we see most of the time. So I asked myself, if this bloke was hit deliberately, how was it done?'

'We . . .'

'Shush! Don't interrupt. From what young Sauce said I assumed that the driver knew of, or had worked out, the victim's habits, and knew his route on his way home. I reasoned that he was hardly going to follow him all the way, looking for a chance. No, he was more likely to have waited for him, somewhere along the road. Agreed?'

'Agreed.'

'Right. If you remember the location, you'll recall there's a wee street joins Station Road from the left, at an angle. I went and had a look there and I found, in the gutter, three cigarette ends. They'd been there for a while, and been stood on, squashed, rained on and run over, but one of them was still recognisable. If a vehicle was parked there, on the wrong side of the road, and the driver was smoking, that's where he'd have dropped the ends.

The brand is Camel, filter tips. Again they could have been left by any bugger, but . . .'

'Will there still be extractable DNA on them?'

'I'll find that out when I get them back to the lab, but in theory yes.'

'If there is,' the DCI said, 'I want you to compare it against a body found on Monday night just outside Edinburgh, shot and left in a car that was burned out. Male, early twenties, went by the name Dean Francey.'

'Will do. If I do get a match, it'll be as well he's dead, for it would be no use as evidence at any trial, any more than the paint scrapes would be.'

'Don't be so sure. If we can find the van . . .'

'Maybe,' Dorward conceded, 'but who are you going to try if your prime suspect's a cadaver?'

'I'll tell you that when we catch him. Before you leave North Berwick, I want you to call by the police station. The victim's coat's there, waiting to be collected.'

'How do you know it's my size?'

'Fuck off, Arthur,' Pye laughed. 'I'll be back in touch when we have a vehicle for you to examine.'

He ended the call, and turned back to face Haddock. 'Think back to Dino's flat,' he said. 'There was an empty cigarette packet on the coffee table. What brand?'

'Camels,' the sergeant replied. 'Is that what . . .'

He nodded. 'This is beginning to pay off. I want Chic Francey's van impounded for examination, today, and I want Chic, in a room with you and me, tomorrow morning.'

'North Berwick?'

'Hell no, even I've had enough of the place.'

Fifty

The family dinner was a strange affair. Sarah and I had decided that we were going to say nothing to the kids about the potential extra place at the table until the end of the first trimester, but I found it difficult to look at any of the three of them without a smile spreading across my face.

It didn't take Mark long to notice.

'What's up, Dad?' he asked, in his newly broken voice. 'You look like Phil Mickelson.'

Nothing my middle son says will ever surprise me completely, but that came close. 'Come again?' I chuckled.

'You know, the golfer. He's always smiling, like he sees a joke that nobody else gets.'

It wasn't an original quote, but Mark has a brain like blotting paper. If he sees something and it registers above zero on his scale of interest, it's there forever.

'Or like he's very happy,' I suggested, 'which I'm sure he is. He's probably as proud of his family as I am.'

'I like it when you smile,' James Andrew, his younger brother, chipped in. 'You didn't always.'

That almost cut the feet from under me. He'd never said anything like that before.

'Didn't I?' I exclaimed. 'I thought I was always jolly.'

'No. Sometimes you were sad. Before Mum came back from America.'

That wiped the smile off my face. Had my marriage to Aileen been so bad that even my younger kids had noticed?

'I had lots of things to worry me then,' I said, to myself as much as to Jazz. 'Now I'm not a chief constable any more I don't have to look at serious stuff,' the man who had spent his morning at a post-mortem added. 'Now I can concentrate on happy things, like you three.'

'And Alex.' There's something ferocious about James Andrew's love for his older sister. She'll never be without a champion as long as he or I are around.

I nodded. 'And Alex.' I drew Sarah to me and kissed her. 'And Mum.'

'How are we going to keep our secret,' she asked later, 'with you grinning like a Cheshire cat over every meal?'

'Hey,' I pointed out, 'could be it has nothing to do with the baby. I am happy, that's all.'

'A week like you've had and you're happy?'

'I know. Fucking weird, isn't it?'

I was still smiling next morning in my office in the *Saltire* building, when Andy Martin called and changed my mood . . . or to be completely accurate, when his executive officer called and told me that the chief constable was on the line. That's what he said. Not, 'Are you available to speak to the chief constable?' just 'The chief constable is on the line.' As if refusal was not an option.

'Andy,' I said, when we were connected, not attempting to hide my irritation. 'What's up?'

'I didn't like the way we left things yesterday,' he began.

'Neither did I, but it is what it is. Now, what can I do for you?'

'I've just asked Mann for a personal update on Hodgson. She took me through it step by step, and then she said that she needed to speak to you before she could go any further. She actually said that. I just blew up at her, Bob.'

'You're taking your life in your hands,' I told him. 'Lottie once entered a CID boxing night. It was men only but she insisted on fighting. She knocked her opponent out inside a round. The poor guy never had a chance. Now, tell me exactly what she said.'

'She said that you'd suggested she find a phone that you'd seen in Hodgson's car, and take a look at it.'

'Correct.'

'She said she'd done that and I asked her where it took her. That was when she said she'd have to get back to you before she could go any further. And that was when I blew up at her. This can't go on, Bob. I made a mistake when I let you involve yourself; from now on it's handled in-house. '

I came close to blowing up at him, but I managed to restrain myself. 'If you want to be that petty, chum,' I growled, 'that's your privilege. But before I hang up on you, tell me exactly what Lottie said.'

'She told me that she'd found the phone among the effects recovered, and she's looked at it. She said there wasn't a hell of a lot on it. The browsing history was clean and there was no email account attached to it.'

'That's odd for a start,' I remarked.

'Is it? Maybe all that Hodgson did was make phone calls.'

'Was it a pay-as-you go phone,' I asked, 'or did he have an inclusive package?'

'A Vodafone account, Mann said; thirty pounds a month. So what?'

'Oh fuck,' I sighed. 'When did you stop being a detective? For that amount of money he's paying for internet access, and if so, he'll be using it. What else?'

'The only thing she found on it were photographs. They were of various engines and boats, motor yachts mostly. One of them, the most recent in the sequence, she said, was very large. Could that be the boat you've been hired to find?'

'I'd guess that it is. It sounds as if Hodgson photographed the vessels he worked on.'

'Sounds like it,' Andy agreed, grudgingly. 'The only other images that Mann found were of the inside of a building. When I asked her what that was about, she said that she couldn't comment without speaking to you first. And that's when I blew up at her. '

'Bloody hell,' I gasped. 'What she told you was the literal truth. She doesn't know any more than she told you. I didn't know what was on that phone but I'd a bloody good idea what might be. Rather than guess, though, I kept my thoughts to myself until Lottie had recovered it and checked.'

'I see,' he murmured.

'Yes, so do I,' I said. 'I see that you've made an arse of yourself and alienated one of your best detective officers. But,' I sighed, 'it's my fault.'

'How do you work that out?' he asked quietly.

'Because you're making exactly the same mistakes I made as a chief. Andy, in the history of modern warfare there's a reason damn few generals were killed. They had to stand back from the action and see the broad picture, not just the hot spots. It's the same with the police service. A chief constable's a director, not an executive. That's where I got it wrong; now you're doing the same thing on an even bigger scale.'

'You flatter yourself,' he retorted. 'I wasn't checking up on DI Mann, I was checking up on you. So, are you going to tell me what you would have told her, if I hadn't forbidden her to have any more to do with you?'

'No,' I said. 'I'll only speak to Lottie, for it's none of your fucking business really. All you need to do is bask in the glory of the clear-up rate; it isn't your job to create it.'

'Effectively,' he laughed, bitterly, 'you're telling me to apologise to her.'

'Yes I bloody am,' I snapped. 'Don't you think you owe her one?'

'Probably,' he retorted, 'because I shouldn't have created a situation where she felt she had two masters.'

'Over to you, then,' I told him. 'Just one final piece of advice: do it yourself, don't get your exec to make the call.'

Finally, I did hang up on him. I was feeling bad about Lottie Mann, but I was feeling worse about the future of the service to which I'd devoted too much of my life, putting it too often before the people I love.

One of my favourite sayings, one I will repeat at the drop of the smallest hat, is as follows, 'The noblest of all dogs is the hot dog; it feeds the hand that bites it.'

I came upon it when studying the philosophy of a Canadian named Laurence Johnston Peter. The management theory that he defined is globally famous, yet he is not. Millions know of the 'Peter Principle', but most have forgotten the man after whom it was named.

Peter argued that anything that works will be used in progressively more challenging situations, until it fails. In human terms, he argued, the potential of a person for promotion is commonly based on their performance in their current position, leading to their rising to their highest level of competence and ultimately to the one beyond, the level of their own incompetence.

If I had spent more time studying management when it mattered, I would have realised much sooner that as a chief constable I was a classic example. I see it now, and with the benefit of that self-knowledge, I recognised that morning that so was Sir Andrew Martin.

That's when I knew for sure that he'd never cut it as head of ScotServe.

I'd just been listening to a man who was out of his depth, and running out of the energy required to keep himself afloat. It was a matter of time before he drowned, or grabbed a lifebelt and was hauled out of there.

I hadn't expected Lottie to call me, any more than I'd expected Andy to call her, so when she did ring, half an hour later, I reached a logical but erroneous conclusion.

'He saw reason, did he?' I asked.

'Who?' She sounded puzzled or a second. 'You mean the chief?' The pieces slotted together. 'You know I've had a bollocking? He's spoken to you?'

'He's spoken to me. We had a frank exchange of views. I told him he should apologise to you; I'm glad he's taken my advice.'

'He hasn't,' Lottie said. 'My ears are still ringing from his one and only call.'

'Then what the hell are you doing speaking to me?' I exclaimed.

'I'm not.' She hesitated. 'Well, I am, but I dialled a wrong number. These damn phones; it's too easy to auto-redial by mistake. But if I was speaking to you, I might want to ask you . . .'

'Lottie,' I warned her, 'this is career-threatening stuff. You're working for a seriously insecure man.'

'And I've got a seriously unstable murderer to catch. I've had a look at Hodgson's phone, like you suggested.'

'I know. Andy told me what was on it and what wasn't.'

'What do you take from it?' she asked.

'It satisfies me beyond any reasonable doubt that Jock Hodgson was involved in the theft of the *Princess Alison*. I don't even need to see the images of the building that your chief mentioned to know that they show the interior of Eden Higgins' private dock on the Gareloch where the boat was kept.'

'I can send them to you,' she offered.

'No you can't. This might be a misdialled call, but if you email me photos it'll be sackable. I won't put you at that risk. Let me think aloud for a while.'

'Think away,' she laughed.

'Okay.' I paused to get some things in a row, then continued. 'If I was running the Hodgson investigation, I'd be assuming that the dead man sent those images, and maybe gave other assistance, to a third party. The boat was normally crewed by two people. The other is a man called Walter Hurrell. Like Hodgson, he's ex-Navy. However I wouldn't waste time exploring whether he was part of the theft. If it had been a joint operation between the two of them, there would have been no need for the pics.'

'Couldn't the third party still have been involved?'

'No need: three would have been a crowd in the theft. Hurrell wasn't a party to it; trust me on that. But,' I added, 'if I was investigating I would like very much to know whether Mr Hurrell has been to a DIY store lately to purchase a blowlamp.'

'You think . . .'

'The man isn't only ex-Navy, Inspector,' I told her. 'He was Special Forces. My investigation would focus very strongly on him; I'd be looking for his DNA and fingerprints. If they weren't

taken for elimination purposes at the time of the *Princess Alison*
theft, then Bridie Gorman's boyfriend really plumbed the depths
of incompetence in his investigation. I'd be finding them and
looking for them to show up in Hodgson's cottage.'

'Couldn't he have been there anyway, if they were crew
colleagues?' Lottie suggested.

'It's possible,' I conceded, 'but if they were concentrated in
the vicinity of the body, that would be significant.'

'Would you be hauling him in for interview?' she asked.

'First I'd try to establish his whereabouts at the time of
Hodgson's killing, and at the time of the break-in to his house.
In his day job Hurrell is Eden Higgins' minder; if he was off with
the boss and can prove it on either or both of those dates, it's an
abortive line of inquiry. If he wasn't, I might be having a chat
with him, and trying to persuade a sheriff to give me a search
warrant for his house to look for the laptop and other stolen
items.'

'Hold on, sir,' the DI said. 'If he's close to Higgins, could he
be involved?'

'No,' I replied, firmly. 'Eden didn't get to be a billionaire by
being stupid enough to invite me to investigate a theft knowing
that it might, that it would, lead me to other crimes in which he
was involved.'

'So why would Hurrell . . .'

'I don't know, and I'm not saying he did. I'm offering him to
you as a suspect, that's all. You might get lucky and find
Hodgson's ring in his house, but I doubt it. No,' I concluded,
'whoever did it, this is what I think happened. Hodgson was a
suspect, because Hurrell wasn't; that could make Hurrell the
killer, but not necessarily. The first step that was taken was the
theft of Hodgson's laptop. Knowing what we do about his phone

being clean says to me that the laptop didn't give up anything either, so the killer went back and tortured him.'

'Until he talked?' Lottie asked.

'Who can say?' I replied. 'But we haven't found the boat yet, have we?'

'You are sure his death is connected to the *Princess Alison?*'

'Have you and Provan come up with anything else in the man's life,' I challenged her 'that could have led to someone torturing him and then shooting him?'

'No, nothing,' she admitted. 'He was an ordinary man with no bad habits.'

'Other than involvement in a multimillion-pound theft,' I pointed out. 'There's just one thing,' I added. 'My hunch, and please do take my hunches seriously, is that he talked before he died. In my experience, and I've seen a couple, one last year in fact, torture murderers don't stop until they've got what they want, but once they have, then it's goodnight. Hodgson only had one burned foot; that tells me he didn't hold out long.'

'So what can we expect to find, Mr Skinner?'

'That I really don't know.'

'So we might find it and never realise,' she suggested.

'That's possible,' I admitted. 'There's only one other thing I'd do,' I added, 'if I was leading this hypothetical inquiry. I'd go through Hodgson's credit card and bank card activity in the weeks before the theft of the *Princess.*'

'Why?'

'I'd be looking to place him somewhere unusual, somewhere that was away from the norm for him. Put him there and see what shows up in the vicinity.'

'We'll do that, sir. Can I come back to you if I need to?' she asked.

'Not without DCC McGuire's express permission. I've got too much on my conscience already without a broken career adding to it.'

'Not the chief's consent?' She's shrewd, is Lottie.

'The DCC's your line manager. If he's fully in the picture he'll make his own decision. That's how it should be. And by the way,' I added, 'you should protect Provan from any fallout. If that wee guy thought you were being picked on, he'd go for whoever did it, regardless, and he's got far too much pension to lose.'

It wasn't until I'd pocketed my phone that I heard a sound from behind me and turned, to see Alex standing in the doorway, holding a Costa coffee in each hand.

'What the hell are you involved with now?' she asked.

'Nothing if your ex has anything to do with it,' I told her. 'Is one of those for me?' I asked.

'Yes. I saw your car in the park, and I reckoned it was about that time. Who was that on the phone anyway?'

'One of my former foot soldiers from Strathclyde,' I replied, 'Detective Inspector Mann; you'll probably come across her in court one day. She has a formidable arrest record.'

'I'll look out for her.' She handed me a coffee, then frowned. 'I've just had a funny phone call myself,' she said. 'It was from a woman called Mackail; she said that she was calling on Sauce Haddock's recommendation. Her story is that she's in a situation and that she should really have a lawyer on her side. She should too; she's up against a guy called Oliver Harrison, a very nasty piece of work with a whole string of Law Society reprimands to his name. I told her that normally I only handle criminal cases these days, but she sounded really anxious, so I said I'd think about it. Does the name mean anything to you?' she asked.

'No, nothing at all. I haven't heard from Sauce or Sammy since Monday.'

'What's the matter, Pops?' she asked, out of the blue.

'Nothing,' I insisted. 'What makes you think there is?'

'Thirty years' experience,' she laughed. 'You're fidgety. Did you expect the guys to report back to you every step of the way? If so, that's not how . . .'

'I know, I know,' I sighed. 'It's not how it works any more. That has nothing to do with it. If you must know I've had a couple of up and downers with Andy, over the thing I've taken on for Eden Higgins. It's . . . grown legs, you might say. I've identified a prime suspect. The problem is, someone else identified him before I did.'

She pursed her lips. 'Wow. Is that what the call from the DI was about?'

'Yes. I landed her in the shit with her big boss. That's what our most recent barney was about,' I confessed.

'Father,' she said heavily, 'has this fallout anything to do with Andy and me?'

'Of course it has!' I retorted. 'I told him he's made me his enemy for life.'

'Then you're overreacting,' she countered. 'I chucked him, not the other way round.'

'Because of his wholly unacceptable behaviour,' I insisted. 'He put you in that situation.'

She looked at me and then she smiled, in the way she does that melts my heart. 'There's no reasoning with you, is there?'

'No,' I agreed, cheerfully, 'not where you're concerned. Thanks for the coffee; now bugger off and free a couple of victims of police oppression . . . or get stuck into the man Harrison, whatever gives you the most fun.'

She nodded. 'Will do, but there's something else too, underneath the angst with Andy. You're not quite as angry as you insist. Something's pulling you in the other direction.'

'As always,' I said, 'you're right. Sarah's pregnant.' There can be no secrets between Alex and me. 'But not a word about it, and beam with astonishment when she tells you.'

My news achieved the near-impossible. It silenced her for at least half a minute. When she had finished hugging me, and telling me that at our age we should have figured out what caused the condition, finally she went back to work.

So did I, for the benefit of InterMedia, answering a question from the crime editor on the Girona daily. He was concerned about potential obstruction of one of his reporters by the Mossos D'Esquadra, the Catalan police force. I looked at his story, reckoned that he was absolutely right, and made a phone call to an acquaintance of mine who happens to be its director general. Xavi's company pays me well for my experience and my contacts, but like David Ginola with that shampoo, I like to think I'm worth it.

I had just sent off my email telling the editor that his problem was solved, when my phone sent me off in another direction.

'Can we meet?' Carrie McDaniels asked. 'I can't think of an excuse to screw any more money out of you, so I'd better report on what I've done.'

'Fine,' I told her, 'but you come to me. My car's parked and I'm not moving it.'

I gave her directions to the Fountainbridge office, then told the front desk to send her up when she arrived. Like all newspapers, the *Saltire* is pretty choosy about who it lets into its building.

She was with me inside fifteen minutes: I reckoned there

would be a taxi on the expense account when she sent me her invoice. She looked pleased with herself, with an added sparkle in her eye that made me wonder if she and the boyfriend had patched things up.

'What have you got for me?' I asked, when she was settled into the chair that Alex had vacated an hour before.

'A bonus,' she began. 'Remember that hotel robbery I mentioned?'

'Rachel Higgins' jewels? Of course.'

'There's one thing you don't know about me. I still work for the insurance company; it's my biggest client. That's how I was able to set up on my own. As such I still have access to the stuff I've worked on. I thought you might like a copy of the report on the Higgins case, so I pulled it.' She handed me a small black memory stick. 'It's on there.' She smiled, adding, 'It's a freebie, by the way.'

'Thanks very much,' I said, pocketing it. 'Now, to the main business in hand. What have you got for me?'

'As much as there is,' she replied, 'which isn't a hell of a lot, to be honest. I hope you weren't expecting me to close your case for you. All I can tell you is that your client keeps very good company indeed. As a general rule, you have to be the brightest and best to get on his guest lists. You couldn't give me an introduction, could you?'

'If you've got undisclosed marine engineering skills,' I said, 'there might be a chance, otherwise, I don't think so.'

She stared at me for a moment, puzzled, then shrugged and pulled a folder from her case. 'Your client is a very popular man,' she began. 'He has a track record of making money for people, even if he does make even more for himself in the process.'

She took a single sheet from her folder. 'Before I begin I have to tell you that my report's incomplete, because I had no access to some of the people on your list, for example those who had no obvious business connection to Mr Higgins, like the footballers and rock stars, and the catering staff. All that I've been able to do is focus on those where there is a connection, through his business.'

'Fair enough,' I agreed. 'Cut to the chase.'

'This is it. Higgins Holdings is a family investment trust, owned by Eden and his wife, Rachel. One son, Rory, a chartered accountant who has floating oversight of all the companies.'

'That's history to me, Carrie,' I grumbled. 'I've known them as a family for twenty years. Concentrate on the business side.'

'I was going to,' she complained. 'You're a bloody awful client, you know.'

I grinned. 'But I pay my bills promptly.'

'In that case, you're the perfect client and I treasure you,' she declared, cheerfully. 'The trust is a majority shareholder in seventeen companies, in the engineering, light and heavy, property and construction sectors.'

'Not retail?' I asked.

'No, when Eden sold his furniture chain to a Middle East consortium for six hundred and twelve million, he signed a five-year restrictive covenant denying him involvement in that sector. He hasn't missed it; the value of his investments across the board is estimated at one point two billion; in other words . . .'

'He's doubled his money.'

'Precisely,' Carrie said. 'His dividend income is fifty million. God knows what he does with it all, that's to say with the thirty million he's left with after tax. That's one reason he's a media darling,' she added. 'He pays his taxes in the United Kingdom and has never been caught in any form of tax avoidance.'

'It's not about money for Eden,' I told her. 'It's about success. Go on.'

'Okay, the business guests on his hospitality days on the *Princess Alison* were nearly all directors and senior managers of the trust companies. The exceptions were targets, owners of companies that Higgins Holdings wanted to bring into its network, either by direct acquisition or through takeover by subsidiary companies. Almost invariably, when Eden set his acquisitive eyes on a company, the deal was done. I traced them all through to completion. There was only one failure, but that worked out in the end.'

I thought I detected a touch of disapproval in her tone and said as much.

'It's true. It's his one blemish as far as I can see. A company called Mackail Extrusions was . . .'

I held up a hand. 'Stop! Repeat that name, please.'

'Mackail Extrusions. Why?'

'I heard that surname no more than an hour ago, from my daughter,' I told her. 'But there might be no connection. Go on.'

'Mackail Extrusions,' she said, for a third time, 'was a supplier to Destry, the group's oddly named double-glazing company. It was a perfect fit and Eden wanted to bring it into the group, but its owner, a man named Hector Mackail, wouldn't sell. Like the sign says in pubs, a refusal often offends, and in this case, somebody was pissed off. Since none of Eden's managers ever takes a major policy decision without clearance, it was assumed it was him. Mackail's cash flow was suffering badly in the recession and Destry put the squeeze on by delaying payment. Mackail went bust and Destry bought the assets.'

'Did you speak to Mackail?' I asked.

'I'd have needed a medium,' she replied. 'He was killed in a road accident a couple of months ago.'

'Are you sure about all this?' I asked.

She nodded. 'I verified it with a friend of mine, a crazy business journo called Macy. Funny, she said I was the second person to have asked about Mackail this week.'

'Very funny indeed,' I agreed. 'Did she say who the other was?'

'She did. It was one of your old team, an old flame of hers called Haddock. Sounds fishy, if you ask me.'

Fifty-One

'Before we go any further, Mr Francey,' Sammy Pye began, 'I'm sorry for your bereavement.'

'That'll be fuckin' right,' the lobster fisherman whined. 'You said he killed that wee lassie, and you put his picture in the paper. Nae wonder he got kilt.'

'No,' Haddock contradicted him. 'We didn't say that; even though he was driving a car with her body in the boot, we didn't say that. If you want to be accurate, he caused her death, just after he put her mother in a coma and brought her within sight of the Pearly Gates. And for the record,' he added, 'when my boss says he's sorry for your loss, he's speaking for himself. Your son was a cowardly, murderous, psychotic scumbag and I couldn't care less that he's lying frazzled in the city mortuary. What I do care about is the fact that he dragged a girl he was supposed to have cared about into his crimes, and he got her killed in the process.'

He turned to the DCI. 'Sorry, gaffer,' he said, 'but I can't sit here and have this guy suggest that his son's death is in any way our fault.'

'No,' Pye agreed. 'I was only being polite, but my compassion's used up too, all of a sudden.'

He switched on a tape recorder on the table at which they sat, and pressed a remote that activated a video camera set high on a wall in a corner of the room. He identified the three people present, for the record, then continued.

'This is an informal interview, Mr Francey, but it is being taped; thank you for attending. We want to talk to you about a pedestrian fatality that occurred in Station Road, North Berwick, on the twenty-seventh of December last year. Do you recall hearing about it?'

Their guest frowned. 'Was that the bloke that was knocked over on his way home frae the Nethers?'

'That's right. Mr Hector Mackail. Did you know him?'

Francey shook his head, then gazed up at the camera. 'Naw,' he murmured.

'Can you speak up, please,' Haddock said.

'Naw,' the man repeated. 'Ah drink in the Golfer's Rest, mostly.'

'Did Dean ever mention the name?' the DS asked.

'No' that I remember.'

'How about his daughter, Hazel Mackail?'

The dull eyes showed a first faint flicker of interest. 'There was a Hazel,' he conceded. 'She came tae the hoose a couple of times, wi' the boy Maxwell, Mr Sullivan's nephew.'

'Mr Callum Sullivan?'

Francey looked at Pye. 'Aye. Rich bloke; hasnae been in North Berwick a' that long. We supply him wi' lobster, Dean and me; that's why the kids were at the hoose, ken, tae collect them. They were both new tae the toon, Dean said. He said her faither had been a businessman but that he'd lost the lot.' The eyes narrowed. 'And it was him that was kilt like?'

'It was,' the DCI confirmed. 'So Dean knew him?'

'He must have, Ah suppose.' He nodded. 'Aye, probably. One time she and the boy came for the lobster, he gie'd her a crab, a big bugger frae down behind Torness Power Station, for her folks, he said. Free, like.' A nasty, lascivious grin flickered across his face. 'He might have been gettin' something in return, ken. Ah wondered about that.'

'Where were you on the twenty-seventh of December?' Haddock asked, suddenly, sharply.

'Eh?' Francey exclaimed. 'How the fuck wid Ah ken? That's weeks back.'

'It was a Friday night, if that's any help.'

'Friday? Then Ah'd have been in the Golfer's Rest. Darts night,' he added.

'Was Dean there?'

'Dinnae ken. He might hae been; he sometimes drops in, if he's got nothin' else on.'

'How do you get to the pub?'

Francey looked at the sergeant, warily. 'Ah walk, son. Ye'll no' catch me out like that. Ah need ma licence; Ah'm careful.'

'And how about Dean?' Haddock shot back. 'Is he careful too?'

'Too fuckin' right.'

'He didn't have a car of his own, did he?'

'Naw.'

'He drove your van when he needed to?'

'Aye.'

'Did he have his own set of keys?'

'Naw. We've only got the one set.'

'And on December twenty-seven, did he collect them from you at home or in the pub?'

'In the pub.' Francey paused, mouth open. 'Hey, wait a minute!' he exclaimed.

'No,' Pye said. 'We'll settle on that for an answer. Now the really difficult question: did he say why he wanted the keys?'

Staring at the table, the fisherman shook his head.

'For the tape please.'

'Naw.'

'Louder please.'

'Naw!'

'Are you certain?'

'Aye. Ah mind, noo. Ah wis on the oche and he came in. He said, "Ah need the motor." That wis all. Ah never asked why, I just gie'd him the keys and got on wi' the game. Ask the lads,' he suggested. 'They'll mind. Thon Grant Rock, he said to me he hoped the lassie didnae mind the smell o' fish in the back.'

'When did he bring it back?' the DCI asked.

'Dinna ken. It was there next mornin', and the keys were on the kitchen table.'

'So you remember that?'

'Oh aye, Ah mind,' he replied firmly.

'Why so vividly, if it was just another Saturday morning?'

'Dinnae ken.'

Haddock leaned forward. 'Was it because you went outside and saw the dent in the front offside wing?'

Francey looked away. 'What dent?' he muttered.

'Wrong answer, Chic; the correct answer is "Yes, Sergeant". We know that on the evening of December twenty-seventh, your van knocked down and killed Hector Mackail in Station Road. We can match the scrape that you never bothered to have repaired to paint on the wall where he was crushed. We can match fibres that were still embedded in that mark when our scientists examined it to the coat that Mr Mackail was wearing when he was killed. We can place your son at the scene from DNA traces left on cigarette ends found there. We can't place you there, but if you carry on denying knowledge of the damage to your van, we might be inclined to think you knew what it had been used for.'

'Ah never!' Francey protested. 'Aye okay, Ah saw the dent. Who wouldnae? Ah asked Dino how it got there, and he said he skidded on the road intae Aberlady. It's easy done there in the winter, ask anybody.' He paused, and resumed his study of the table, and the scratches left on it by previous visitors. 'Anyway,' he muttered, 'what does it matter? Dino's deid, and the other fella's no' comin' back, so . . .'

'It matters,' Pye told him, 'because it wasn't an accident. Your son used your van to kill Mr Mackail, quite deliberately. We believe he was paid to do so, just as we believe he was paid to abduct the dead child Zena Gates, and keep her for a couple of weeks in a rented cottage. We need to know who paid him.'

'Well, don't look at me! This is all fuckin' news tae me! Why would anybody want tae do all that?'

'We're still working on why. There may be no connection between the two crimes; that's still conceivable. Dean may have had his own reasons for killing Mr Mackail. Did they have any sort of relationship, any contact that you know of?'

'No,' Francey replied. 'Dean didnae even know the man.'

'How can you be so sure?'

'The time the lassie and the boy Maxwell came for the lobster and he gie'd her the crab, he said tae her when she was leaving, "Tell your faither if he wants a part-time job he can come out on the boat wi' us." The lassie just laughed. I asked Dino what that was a' aboot, and he said her faither had been in the Navy. Then

Ah asked him, "Have ye met him, like?" and he said, "Naw never, but Hazel telt me." That's how Ah can be sure, pal.'

'We can check that with Mrs Mackail and her daughter,' Haddock warned.

'Check all yis fuckin' like. It's the truth Ah'm tellin' yis.' He pushed his chair back. 'Can Ah go now? Ah've had enough of this shite.'

'Sure,' the DS replied. 'You can go. You've always been here voluntarily.'

'And can Ah get ma van back?'

'That's different. Your van has a special status; it's a murder weapon in an open investigation, and we'll need to keep it until it's closed.'

'What am Ah going tae do for ma work?' Francey protested.

Pye shrugged. 'The same as you'd do if it broke down: buy or hire another. This interview is over,' he said, switching off the recorder and the video.

'Bastards,' the fisherman muttered.

'That may be,' the DCI retorted, 'but it has nothing to do with us holding on to your van.'

'And ma boy? When dae Ah get him back?'

'I'm afraid that's up to the fiscal's office, not us. But it won't be before we've arrested the person who shot him.'

'Then get a fuckin' move on.' He looked at the DCI, and the faintest of grins touched the corner of his mouth. 'Dae ye think Ah'll get a discount on the cremation?'

Fifty-Two

'What a nice man,' Haddock said, as he and Pye watched Francey walk down the driveway of the police office, from their vantage point in the CID suite.

'A gem,' Pye agreed. 'When all this is over, we must set the Trading Standards people on him. I'm sure they'll be interested in him selling frozen fish as fresh.'

'When all this is over we might be working for Trading Standards. I hate to point this out, boss, but we've just made a rod for our own backs. We were under pressure already to close one major inquiry, and now we've gone and opened another.'

'Do you take pleasure in ruining my day, Sauce? Have we got any positives?' He moved across to Dickson, who was working at his desk. 'What about Dino's stash of cash, Walter? Have forensics come up with anything on that?'

'No, sir,' the DC replied, mournfully. 'As you'd expect from old banknotes, they're a whole database of fingerprints in themselves. They found Dean Francey's prints on the notes on the outside, but nothing else they can match to anybody. There were prints overlaying prints, making it virtually impossible to come up with anything for comparison with the central register.'

'Great,' Pye moaned.

'There was one oddity though,' Dickson continued. 'You got excited by the Clydesdale Bank connection, I know, but when the bundle was opened up, they found that there was only a hundred quid in those notes, together on top. The rest were all Bank of England; a mix of tens and twenties. You were right about the total though; five thousand.'

'Where's the oddity?' Haddock asked.

'This is Scotland, Sarge. If you draw a large amount of currency from a bank here, even if you ask for it in used notes, you're likely to get predominantly Scottish issue. So doesn't that indicate that the bulk of that money came from south of the border?'

The DS nodded. 'Probably it does. But does that take us one step forward, Walter? No, it doesn't.'

'However,' Pye began, then stopped.

His team gazed at him, waiting.

'However what?' Haddock said

'Quiet, I'm thinking.' He walked back towards the window, then turned, retracing his steps, beckoning the sergeant to follow him into his office. 'We live in the age of money-laundering, right?'

'And then some,' his colleague agreed. 'So?'

'So, if you were putting together a pile of cash for illicit purposes, as in to pay a hit man, would you go to the bank for it? And suppose you did, would you ask specifically for old cash?'

'Probably not, gaffer.'

'No, Sauce, certainly not. But here we have the best part of five grand in old notes, almost exclusively with the Queen's head on the front, not Sir Walter Scott or some other figure from Scottish history like we have on our money. That's suggesting two things to me: one, that the cash Dino was paid with wasn't exactly legitimate and two, that as the other Walter suggested, it was obtained in England.'

Haddock walked to each of the four corners of the small room, peering into each with his hand shading his eyes.

'What the hell are you doing?' Pye asked.

'I'm looking for a straw you haven't clutched at yet.'

'Fuck!' the DCI shouted as he slumped into his chair. 'If you weren't my mate, I'd have you on points duty.'

'Sorry, Sammy,' the DS said, 'but that's what it sounded like. The money's not going to take us anywhere, other than in ever-decreasing circles, until we disappear up our own arses.'

'I know,' Pye sighed. 'But what have we got? All I can see is the end of the tunnel, and the only light's an oncoming train.'

'That may well be, but there's still one line of inquiry that we haven't explored, one strand that links our two crimes. We've got two victims, the Gates family and now the Mackails; and in each one the father was, or is, in the Navy. Do they connect, and if so, how?'

The DCI pulled himself up in his chair. 'You're right, of course,' he said. 'I'm tired and I'm under pressure. Thanks, Sauce, I needed that kick up the arse.' He paused, frowning. 'We should check Mackail's Navy background, but let's not get too excited. The two families were connected professionally; if the two men did know each other in the Navy and kept in touch afterwards, yes, I can see where that could have led Grete to work for Hector, but the likelihood is that the link extends no further than that.'

'It still has to be ticked or crossed off,' Haddock insisted.

'Agreed, but that might be easier said than done. Remember, Lieutenant Gates set off all sorts of security alarms last time we asked about him. That might happen again.'

'And it might not. Stay positive, gaffer.'

'I'm trying,' Pye said, 'but I know in here,' he tapped his chest with his middle finger, 'that there's something we're just not getting, a link in this chain of events that we can't see, and my problem is I have no idea where to go looking for it. I tell you this, Sauce, and only you; this new set-up makes me feel completely exposed. Oh how I wish Bob Skinner was here!'

As he spoke, with a huge frustrated sigh, his office door opened, and a familiar voice exclaimed, 'Be careful what you wish for.'

Fifty-Three

I will carry with me to the grave the expression on Sammy Pye's face as I stepped into his office. He turned towards me, in his old swivel chair, eyes wide open, jaw slightly dropped, and he murmured, 'Have the last six months been a dream?'

Even young Haddock was taken aback by my inadvertent timing. He jumped from his perch on the edge of his boss's desk; for a moment I thought he was about to come to attention.

'As you were,' I said.

'How did you get in?' he asked.

I grinned at him. 'Seriously?'

Mind you, I did feel a little weird myself. Twenty years before, that room had been mine, when I ran Serious Crimes as a detective superintendent, surrounded by good cops, among them much younger versions of Andy Martin and Mario McGuire, and with Alison Higgins not very far away.

It hadn't taken me long after Carrie McDaniels came up with the name Mackail to realise that I had to touch base with the guys. I didn't rush into it, though. Instead I paid a visit to Mario, not in his office in Stirling but in his very posh penthouse in Leith, in the evening.

My friend, the deputy chief constable, is probably the most

dedicated cop I know, if only because he doesn't need the money and never has done. On his mother's side he's a member of one of the most successful business families in Edinburgh, and his dad was a building contractor. He could have taken up either option at any time but he never did. Instead he joined the police force in his early twenties after completing a degree in business administration that he never talks about.

Initially, his choice had something to do with a simple desire to prove to his family that he could be a success in his own right, on his own terms. He achieved that years ago; by that time he loved the job so much that he never contemplated leaving.

I arrived at Eamon's dinnertime; he's a little over six months old and looks very like his dad. The sight of him reminded me of what Sarah and I have coming to us later this year.

Mario and I left mother and son to it and went out on to the deck. It was a brilliant, cloudless, starry evening, with a cold edge to it, but an electric space heater made it tolerable.

He understood that I hadn't come to socialise. 'I know about it,' he said, as soon as we were alone. 'I had Sir Andrew in my ear this afternoon, threatening to boot Mann off the Hodgson inquiry, and out of CID altogether. He did the same with Sammy Pye the other day; if he carries out all of his threats we'll have no bloody detectives left.'

'What do you want me to do?' I asked. 'I'm deeply involved in this thing, by accident in the main, but if that's threatening officers' careers, I'll back off, just disappear. I can tell Eden Higgins to get somebody else to find his boat and be no more than a witness, in Edinburgh and in Ayrshire. That's what your boss wants me to do, I'm sure.'

'I'm sure too,' Mario agreed, 'but it's not what I want. Andy's vision is of everyone across the country conforming to strict rules and protocols, yet still being expected to maximise clear-up rates. But it's not mine; in my visits to CID around the country, I'm preaching pragmatism and flexibility.'

I whistled, softly. 'You're ignoring him?'

'That's not how I see it,' he replied. 'My version is that I'm exercising my own authority as DCC Crime. He and I are heading for a bust-up, no question, but I won't be anybody's message boy.' He rolled his massive shoulders inside his heavy jacket. 'It can't go on,' he said quietly, then looked me in the eye. 'Can you help?'

'You mean can I sit him down and talk to him?' I asked. 'No, we're way beyond that. We have no relationship on a personal or professional level, not any more.'

'The service is in crisis,' Mario murmured. 'Can you really sit back and watch it implode?'

'Are you asking,' I countered, 'whether I'll go public and attack Andy's management? If you are, the answer's no.'

'I was thinking more of going private. The First Minister's a friend of yours.'

'I'm not so sure that he is any more,' I said, 'not since I told him he could stick the chairmanship of the Scottish Police Authority where the sun doesn't shine. Look, if it gets to the *Caine Mutiny* scenario, if Andy turns into Captain Queeg and starts counting the strawberries, it'll be up to you, and Maggie Steele, and Brian Mackie and the other deputies and assistants to sort it out. Effectively the command team of ScotServe is a board of management. If you pass a vote of no confidence in your executive chair, and stand behind it strongly enough . . .'

He nodded. 'I get it. I think that Maggie and I are heading towards that conversation. She's his nominated deputy, yet she told me the other day that she doesn't know what her job is.'

'Then let it play out,' I advised. 'In the meantime, in the current situation, what do you want me to do?'

'What is the situation?' he asked.

'The two investigations are overlapping,' I told him. 'By that I mean Zena and the subsequent murders of her abductors on one hand, and the torture and shooting of Jock Hodgson on the other. Their convergence, I know for sure: the link is a man called Hector Mackail. He's emerged as a person of interest in the disappearance of the *Princess Alison*. At the same time, I've discovered that the Menu have been looking at him as well. I know nothing about their inquiry, but if I'm going to carry on, I need to.'

Mario's shoulders relaxed and he settled deeper in his chair. He took a deep breath of the frosty air, then exhaled. 'You must carry on,' he declared. 'If you're willing, I'd be a fool not to use your insight and experience. I want you to coordinate the two investigations, to be the link between the teams, and,' he paused for a second, 'to advise as you see fit. You'll be acting in a private and confidential capacity, but I'll tell Sammy, and I'll tell Lottie Mann . . . you're right, by the way; she is a fucking monster of a detective . . . that any suggestion from you should be seen as a direct order from me.'

I held his gaze. 'You sure?'

'Certain.'

'What about Andy?'

'I am DCC Crime,' he replied, 'until he tells me otherwise. I don't feel the need to report on every operational matter. Now, let's get inside; it's bloody freezing out here.'

As it transpired, next morning I beat Mario to the punch, but only just. Pye and Haddock were still recovering from my surprise, and perfectly timed, arrival when the phone rang. As soon as I heard Sammy say, 'Yes, sir,' I knew that he was being given the message.

'So,' he said, smiling as he hung up, 'just like old times.'

'No,' I countered, 'my role will be advisory, that's all.'

'I know what your role will be, boss,' he laughed. 'That's just been made clear. Where do we begin?"

I took one of the two uncomfortable chairs in the room and motioned Haddock towards the other. 'Bring me up to speed, please, from the time when you asked me to identify Dean Francey.'

I sat back and listened as they related every detail of their investigation in a shared presentation style that they seemed to have developed. It struck me that for a fairly junior DS, young Sauce wasn't slow to offer a view, but it neither surprised nor annoyed me. He's always been that way and he will be all the way up to the top of the tree, where he's headed.

Some of it I knew from the media, but I didn't know of Hector Mackail's naval background. I did my best to stay impassive when Sammy dropped those pieces of information, but I made a mental note to chide Carrie McDaniels for not digging a little deeper into the man.

The fact that he was dead, and the circumstances of his demise, were hugely significant for me, but I sat on that initially. Instead I focused on the journalist Macy's pillow talk gossip about a confrontation between Mackail and my client, Eden Higgins.

'Knocked him down a flight of stairs, she said?'

Haddock nodded. 'And smashed his ankle.'

'That explains why Eden was limping when we met,' I said.

'We've been thinking it might also explain why Mackail wound up squashed against a wall.'

364

'I wouldn't spend too much time on that thought,' I told the youngster. 'I don't believe for one second that Eden Higgins would countenance anything as foolish as that. There was a known connection between them and, besides, the man Mackail was already broken, financially.'

'What about the minder Macy mentioned?' Pye asked. 'Could he have taken it into his own hands?'

'Walter Hurrell is a volatile and potentially dangerous man,' I conceded. 'But he wouldn't act on his own initiative. No, I believe we, sorry, you, should focus on the naval connection, Mackail and Zena's dad, with a third man in the equation.'

'Who's that?'

'His name was Jock Hodgson,' I said. 'He was the inside man on the theft of Eden Higgins' boat and he's just as dead as Mackail. He's also ex-Navy. I want to know whether the two of them and Gates ever served together.'

'We wondered the same about Mackail and Gates,' Sauce volunteered, 'but Gates seems to be a no-go area. The Ministry of Defence won't say a word about him.'

'You can leave that to me,' I told him. 'I'm not going to ask the MoD.'

Sammy Pye rocked slightly in my battered old chair. 'What's your thinking on this, boss?' he ventured.

I didn't bother to correct the 'boss', for at that time, effectively I was. 'I won't go there yet,' I replied. 'I need confirmation on a few things. What I'd like to do now is make a couple of phone calls; then I'm going to take you guys for lunch.'

Fifty-Four

'I need some more information,' I told Clyde Houseman. 'Some of it I could get from the Ministry of Defence, but I don't have time to wrestle with their bureaucracy.'

'Will I have to clear it with my boss?' he asked.

'Part of it, no; but I don't mind if you check with her. I'd phone her myself but I'm sure she's busy enough already.'

'Meaning I'm not.' He chuckled softly.

'Meaning you're not the Director of MI5; one day, maybe, but not yet. I need information on three people, all of them Navy, like Walter Hurrell. The names are Jock Hodgson . . . although I'd guess that might be John in the records . . . Hector Mackail, and David Gates. The first two have left the service, but are recently deceased; the third is still operational. I know that Mackail and Gates connect professionally, but I'd like to know if and how Hodgson relates to either of them.'

'That shouldn't take long,' Clyde remarked. 'Do you want the MoD to know that you're asking?'

'I don't care,' I said, 'not about that part. But the next bit's a little more sensitive. Gates is an engineering officer on a Trident sub; that means he's totally isolated.' I told him about the attack on his wife and the abduction and death of his child.

'Even then, the investigating officers are being denied access.'

'That's very tough,' my young friend agreed, 'but you can understand why, sir, can't you?'

'Sure I can,' I replied. 'And that's why I need you to get involved.'

'I don't know if I can.'

'On your own authority, no, you can't. But this is the part where you will need to involve Amanda Dennis. She does have the clout to ask certain questions, and insist on an answer.'

'Okay,' Clyde said. 'What do you want to know?'

Fifty-Five

There wasn't much conversation on the journey. Even Sauce Haddock stayed silent until we were well clear of Edinburgh, heading west, until his tongue just wouldn't stay at rest any longer. Finally, from the back seat of my slightly damaged car, his voice raised above the Miles Davis playlist that I had on that morning, he asked the question that I'd been expecting for over an hour.

'This man Hodgson, sir: you said he's dead.'

'That's right,' I agreed.

'How did he get that way?'

'Suddenly,' I said. 'Hopefully I'll be able to expand on that over lunch.'

'Where are we going?' I sensed that his curiosity was giving way to impatience.

'Mystery tour,' I chuckled. 'It won't be long now.'

We passed the newish Heartland interchange, then the old, isolated Kirk O'Shotts on the left, heading on until I ended the game by leaving the motorway at junction six. I negotiated two more roundabouts, and we had reached our destination.

Pye looked up at the sign over the entrance. 'The Newhouse,' he murmured as he stepped out of the front passenger seat, reading the sign above the entrance.

368

'Used to be the Newhouse Hotel,' I told him, 'a place of legend. Back in my father's time,' I explained, 'the only way you could get a drink on a Sunday was in a hotel, and even then only if you were what the law called a bona fide traveller. That meant you had to be on a journey of at least three miles. You even had to sign a declaration in a book. In those days, this place was pretty much three miles from everywhere. They used to have bus parties coming here, every Sunday afternoon.'

'That's weird,' Haddock exclaimed. 'My grandad used to talk about that but I always thought he was taking the piss.'

'No,' I assured him, as I led the way inside and through to the dining room. 'It's a genuine relic of our colourful Presbyterian past. Where I live, in Gullane, it's about a three-mile walk to and from Dirleton, the next village. The old-timers say that on Sundays the drinking populations of the villages used to pass each other on the road, there and back. The licensees changed the date on the book every week, to save time.'

'Is this a nostalgia trip for you, boss?' he asked.

'Hell no,' I replied. 'The law changed not long after I was born. I chose this because it's a midpoint. We're being joined here.'

The head waiter recognised me . . . sometimes I hate my media profile . . . and showed us to a table for five, by the window. The quorum was completed a couple of minutes later, when Lottie Mann and Dan Provan came through the door. I stood, and waved them across to join us.

I allowed my former colleagues to size each other up for a few seconds; each of them looked as puzzled as the others but none of them was ready to break the silence.

Finally I did. 'Each of you guys has been under my command at different times and in different places,' I began. 'Now I'm gone, and you're all colleagues; it's time you met.' I made the introductions, and stayed on my feet as east and west shook hands.

Provan looked across at me as he took his seat, his eyes narrowed. 'It's nice of you tae invite us to lunch, big fella . . . I'll be havin' fillet steak, by the way . . . but . . .'

'Dan!' his DI hissed.

'It's all right, Lottie,' I said. 'His irreverence is part of his eccentric charm. You'll be having it well done, I'd imagine, Sergeant.'

He nodded. 'Absolutely. Anything else is too big a challenge for my teeth these days.'

As I mentioned, Provan and I are around the same age, although I like to believe that I look about ten years younger. Possibly that's why he shows me less respect than most people do. Even when I was his chief constable it had taken the little toerag all his time to call me 'Sir'. Clearly there was no chance now I was a civilian. 'You should get a new set,' I suggested. 'The ones you've got look a bit yellowed; age and tobacco, I guess. When are you chucking it, Dan?' I asked.

He nodded to his right, towards Mann. 'When she does,' he replied. 'They cannae kick me out on age grounds now.'

No, I thought, *but 'they' could make your life a misery if 'they' chose.*

'Not if you behave yourself,' I agreed. 'Which could be a problem for you.'

'I know when to touch my forelock,' he assured me.

'You couldn't find your fucking forelock,' I laughed, not only at his malignant leprechaun act, but also at the obvious puzzlement of Pye and Haddock, neither of whom seemed to know what to make of him. By the way, you might wonder about

370

my industrial language with a female officer present, but Lottie is more likely to be offended by its omission than its use.

The arrival of the waiter cut short the banter. Provan kept his word, ordering steak, 'Burnt and covered wi' onions.' The Edinburgh side both ordered fish. I settled for a York ham salad and was more than a little surprised when Mann asked for the same.

'Yesterday was a blip,' she volunteered. 'This is what I eat normally.'

'So,' Provan resumed as soon as the interruption was over, 'since there's been nothin' on our bulletin board about you bein' seconded to do CID team-building, gonnae tell us why we're all here?'

He was right; it was time to get down to business. 'There's nothing about this on any bulletin board,' I shot back, with a glance at Lottie. 'You haven't told him, then?'

She shook her head. 'No,' she replied. 'I thought I'd leave that to you.'

I knew that she'd had the same call from Mario that he'd made to Sammy Pye. It was one of the things we'd discussed when we'd spoken earlier, before I'd left Edinburgh.

'Good shout,' I agreed. 'You'd have had him in your ear all the way here. Did you bring that stuff I asked for?'

She nodded and took two envelope folders from her briefcase, handing one to me and one to Sammy Pye.

'This is a copy of the paperwork in the investigation into the murder of Jock Hodgson,' I told him. 'He's the third link in our naval chain.'

'The dead guy?' Sauce Haddock asked.

I nodded. 'The same. He's dead because somebody shot him.' I looked at Lottie. 'Any joy from forensics?'

She smiled. 'You knew there would be, didn't you?' she said. I smiled back.

She looked across the table at Pye and Haddock. 'The single bullet that killed Hodgson came from the same gun that accounted for your two victims in Edinburgh the other night.'

'Which means,' I declared 'that you four are all investigating the same series of crimes. And they are all linked, to the matter I was hired to review: the theft of Eden Higgins' multimillion-pound boat.'

'How?' Pye asked. 'Why?'

'I believe that the *Princess Alison* was stolen as an act of revenge, by Hector Mackail, who blamed Higgins for the collapse of his company, and his personal bankruptcy.'

'And was Higgins responsible for that?'

'He benefited from it,' I said, 'but that's all I'll say for now. It's the consequence of the theft I want to focus on.' I raised an eyebrow in Mann's direction. 'Did you get anything from Hodgson's card activity?'

It was Dan Provan who replied. 'There's one thing that's unusual. All his shopping was either done online or locally in Ayrshire; with one exception. We can put him in East Lothian, about six months ago. He filled up his car in a petrol station in Dunbar. The day before, he bought his groceries in Tesco in Kilmarnock. The day after, he bought a takeaway pizza in Largs. But that one day he was on the other side of the country.'

'What was the date?' Haddock asked. As he spoke he opened a tablet computer.

'The twenty-second of August; a Saturday.'

The younger sergeant tapped the screen of his device a couple of times. As I looked at him a smile spread across his face. 'You cracker,' he murmured. 'That same day, Hector Mackail paid for lunch in a restaurant called the Rocks, in Dunbar. I checked with the owner yesterday; he matched the payment to the bill. It showed three covers.'

'Interesting,' Pye murmured, 'but he could have been there with Gloria and Hazel.'

'Sure,' I agreed, 'but that's not the way I'd bet. Mackail and Hodgson served together in Portsmouth for three years. In the last of those years, they overlapped with a sub-lieutenant called David Gates. Trust me on that,' I added. 'It's kosher.' It had taken Clyde Houseman half an hour to dig out their records.

'I believe that what they were doing was planning the theft of the *Princess Alison* from her secure boathouse in the Gareloch. It was handy for Gates,' I added. 'The Trident submarine base at Faslane is only a couple of miles up the road. He and Mackail stole the damn boat, I'm certain.'

'And Eden Higgins found out?' Haddock exclaimed. 'Is that what you reckon, boss?'

'Although I hate to say so, that's the way it's pointing,' I conceded. 'We know . . . that is Lottie and Dan know . . . that Jock Hodgson was tortured for information before he was killed. You two discovered that shortly afterwards, Hector Mackail died in a hit-and-run. David Gates, however, is untouchable, because of what he does. So instead, this week, his wife was attacked and his daughter was taken, only things went tragically wrong. I believe that the intention was to exchange wee Zena for the *Princess Alison*.'

'If she's still afloat,' Mann pointed out.

'Yes, exactly, and that's what we have to find out.'

'How?'

'That part of it is down to me,' I told her. 'After all, it's what I was hired to do.'

I hadn't worked my way through my agenda, but lunch arrived. It was well timed, giving my four companions the chance to absorb what they had learned about the others' investigation, and to consider the bigger picture.

It gave me breathing space also, to come to terms with a seemingly inevitable conclusion, one I had fought against: Eden Higgins, my client, my friend, my one time 'acting brother-in-law' as he had described himself at a gathering in the dying years of the last century, was a murderer.

He had been assaulted by Hector Mackail; a man enraged and embittered after being cheated out of his business. His boat, his pride and joy, named after his lost sister, had been stolen. Frustrated by an incompetent police investigation that had got precisely nowhere, salt had been rubbed into the wound by his insurance company's reluctance to settle his claim for the loss of his property.

Eden was a media hero; his PR people worked hard to maintain his image of a benevolent businessman. But nobody achieves what he had by being a soft touch. I knew that from my own experience, from the fact that he had employed private investigators to check me out when Alison and I had started getting serious, uncovering in the process a secret from my private past that I thought I'd buried beyond discovery.

If, as the evidence suggested, he had been offended by Mackail's reluctance to sell out to Destry Glazing, a Higgins Holdings subsidiary, and had used his power and his influence to ruin the man, and virtually steal his business, well, I shouldn't be too surprised.

And if, faced by the theft of five million quid's worth of property, he had displayed the same ruthlessness in pursuing it, if he'd had a blowlamp held to Jock Hodgson's foot until he screamed out the whole story in his secluded kitchen, signing Mackail's virtual death warrant in the process, well, that shouldn't astonish me either.

But if all that was the case, why had he brought me in, on the very day that the nasty, vicious Dean Francey had seized David Gates' daughter and hospitalised his wife?

That halted my analysis for a while, until I forced myself to take a mental step back and look at the situation objectively. When I did, an unpalatable possibility was clear.

Could it be that Eden had never believed that I would find the *Princess Alison*, or uncover the secrets of her theft? Was my role quite simple? Was he buying my reputation as an investigator, as he bought everything else, to force the insurance company to settle his claim?

If so the son of a bitch had underestimated me . . . and I wasn't having that.

As I finished my salad and looked around the table I realised that I'd been able to develop my thinking uninterrupted because everyone else had been ignoring me. Pye and Mann were deep in conversation, while Sauce Haddock was picking away at his namesake but absorbing everything the weathered sage that is Dan Provan had to say.

I sat back and allowed the gathering to bring itself back to order . . . or as close to that as is possible when Provan is involved. 'I was just telling the boy here,' he said, looking up at me, 'that the police service is going to hell in a handcart. We used tae know who our bosses were, and where we worked. Now we don't have a fuckin' clue. We're Glasgow, Lottie and me, and we get sent down tae Wemyss Bay.'

'You weren't sent,' I replied, 'you were called.'

He stared at me 'Who called us then?'

375

'Effectively, I did.'

'But you're history. How could you dae that?'

'Effectively,' I repeated. 'I still know who to call.'

'Hardly worth your while leavin', then,' Provan muttered.

I laughed. 'On the contrary, Bilbo. It's been very much worth my while.'

His eyes twinkled. 'I've always seen maself more of a Gandalf type,' he said, 'but it's true; you're lovin' this.'

'I'm loving watching how you can talk and eat at the same time,' I replied. 'I'll grant you there are things I miss. Times like these for an example. But I've been missing them since I became a deputy chief.'

'That's how you were crap at it.'

The ungrammatical grenade hung in the air for a few seconds, until I defused it by agreeing with him.

'That's exactly why,' I conceded. 'Just as your inability to master basic diplomacy while dancing on the edge of insubordination is how nobody's ever been tempted to promote you to inspector, even though you're probably the best detective in Glasgow. You've never aspired to being a wizard, Dan; you've always been happy to be a hobbit.'

'You know me so well,' he laughed. 'And I know you. You're a pure hunter. You cannae stop yourself.'

'I can,' I retorted, a little sharply, because he was getting to me, 'and I do. It's made easier because you are right about one thing. The police service is going to hell in a handcart, as I knew it would when I opposed unification, but even though I'm no longer part of it, that's something I will not allow.'

'How are you going tae stop it?' he challenged.

'Watch this space.'

I pushed my plate away, enjoying the silence as the waiter

cleared the table. He asked for our dessert orders. I pointed at Provan. 'He'll have Black Forest gateau,' I said. 'I could not bear to watch him picking sticky toffee pudding out of those teeth.'

He did, too, just to spite me, I'm sure, for everyone else declined the sweet course and went straight to coffee.

'Well,' I said once everyone had been served. 'What does everyone think of my analysis?'

Pye was the senior officer at the table; the others, even Provan, looked to him.

'I don't disagree with any of it, sir,' he said. 'I'm in no doubt that's how it happened. Eden Higgins as prime suspect? It can't be anyone else, can it?'

'No, it can't,' I concurred. 'But now the hard bit . . . proving it.' I paused, looking at Sammy and Sauce. 'You two, of course, you could walk away at this stage with brownie points. You've had three parts to your investigation and two of them are cleared up. You're in the plus column, even more so when you consider that a victim of your unsolved strand was the perpetrator in the first two.'

'Try telling that to the chief constable, boss,' Haddock chipped in.

'I will if I have to,' I promised him, 'but there are folk within the force who'll do that before me.'

'That's nice to know, sir,' Sammy murmured, 'but there's somebody you've forgotten: Anna Hojnowski, Anna Harmony, Singer, whatever you want to call her. I don't know why but I feel as if I knew her. There's no way I'm walking away from this without putting my hand on the collar of the person who shot her.'

I smiled at that; warrant card or not, I felt exactly the same way.

I turned to Lottie. 'You two, on the other hand, have a big, smelly unsolved on your hands. Jock Hodgson did one of two things; either he betrayed his employer or he did a pal a favour to right a perceived wrong. However you see it, what was done to him was obscene, and can't go unanswered.'

She nodded. 'Agreed, sir. From everything we know, the Edinburgh team and the two of us are looking for the same man. But where do we begin? Do we just walk into Eden Higgins' office and lift him?'

I sipped my coffee; it wasn't bad. 'You have cause to question him right now,' I suggested, 'but you cannot get this wrong, because he has too much influence. This whole story has an opening paragraph, and so far that is hearsay; it's a tale told twice, to different people, by the same person, Sauce's pal Macy Robinson. She's a journalist, so she'd be the first to tell you that for a story to be reliable you need two sources. The government might think it's okay to do without corroboration in criminal cases, but I don't. Somebody needs to talk to the person who makes the decisions within Destry, and verify that Eden knew how Mackail's business was shafted. Higgins Holdings benefited from it,' I said. 'But did he order it?'

'We'll do that,' Sammy Pye volunteered.

I nodded. 'Okay. Then there's Hodgson. Lottie, the images on the phone prove to my satisfaction that he was involved in the theft. He was an idiot to think that nobody would suspect him, unless he underestimated his boss. Maybe he believed that a simple denial would be enough. He might have been fired as engineer, but that would have been it. Sadly, he got that wrong, but . . .'

Mann put my question for me. 'Did Eden Higgins personally hold a naked flame to his foot?'

'Not only that,' I added. 'Was he physically capable of subduing Hodgson? Remember, he'd had his ankle smashed not long before that. I would suggest that while Sammy's looking at Destry, you divide the labour by arresting, isolating and questioning Walter Hurrell, Eden's driver, personal assistant, minder, whatever title you choose to give him.'

'If you say so, sir.'

'I do, and I say this too. Don't piss about with Hurrell; I know his background and he's dangerous. Get a warrant for his arrest from a sheriff; I'll help you draft the application. When you go for him, go mob handed. Maybe even use armed officers.'

'Are you saying he might have been Higgins' hit man?' Provan asked, licking the last remnant of his gateau from a corner of his mouth.

'I don't care for the term,' I said, 'but his track record makes him top pick for the job.' I paused. 'Now, back to the task of proving all this. We need to establish the link between Higgins and Dean Francey; those two are unlikely bedfellows, to say the least. Where could they have met?'

'Callum Sullivan.' All four of us looked at Haddock. 'Sullivan sold his company to Higgins Holdings for millions,' he continued, 'and stayed involved to complete the earn-out and maximise the price. We know that he had a great big party in his great big house in North Berwick, and we know that's where Dean Francey met Anna Harmony. But we don't know who else was at the party.'

'In that case, go and see Sullivan, Sauce,' I advised him . . . although it probably sounded like an order, 'and find out.'

There was nothing else to cover, other than the bill. I gave the waiter the universal signal, and dug out a credit card as he approached with the tab and a terminal in hand.

'How are ye going to do it?' Provan asked, as I keyed in my PIN.

'Do what?'

'Get back in. You're no different from me. You'll always have the itch and you'll always have to scratch it.'

I smiled at him, cheerfully, even though I knew he was right. 'There are other ways of soothing itches,' I said. 'Why would I want to get back in? As you said, the service is heading to hell in a handcart. Your problem is you're still on board.'

Fifty-Six

One of my cures for skin irritations called me that evening, on FaceTime. I hadn't expected to hear from Amanda Dennis in person, far less by video link, given that the head of MI5 tends to send messages rather than give them in person, but she and I go back a long way, and each of us knows things about the other that would send your average tabloid newspaper editor into a potentially fatal state of orgasmic delight.

'My chap Houseman passed on your inquiry, Bob,' she began without preamble. There was something about the way she said 'my chap' and the look in her eye as she said it that made me wonder, but I let it lie; I don't know her *that* well.

'Getting info out of defence intelligence is difficult at the best of times,' she continued, 'but when you're asking about one of their nuclear warriors . . . Jesus, you can hear the chains rattle as the drawbridge is hauled up.'

'Even though some of what I wanted to know is history?'

'Even though. The military works by a rule book. Its little brain can't cope without it and nobody has the authority to depart from it in any way. I had to go all the way to the head of their house to get an answer, and even then it had to be across the desk in his office.'

'With the recorder running, no doubt,' I suggested.

'Of course,' she laughed. 'We all have to protect ourselves. It's taken me years to get into this bloody chair. I'm not going to be forced out of it by some dispute over what I did or I didn't say.'

'How secure is this?' I asked.

'Secure enough,' she assured me. 'Even so, no names will be mentioned.'

'No need,' I said.

'No. The first part of the message is thus; on the dates you gave me, the officer in question was on shore leave. At the present time, he's operational, and not even the Prime Minister could speak to him.'

'How about the Queen?'

She grinned. 'Possibly, but only if her husband placed the call, him being the Lord High Admiral.' She paused, long enough for the smile to fade. 'This much I can tell you. The man is on a short cruise; there's a new piece of kit on his sub and they've taken it on a proving voyage. They're expected back at some point in the near future. Does that help you?'

I thought about it. 'Yes, it does,' I said. Then I really pushed my luck.

'You're joking,' she exclaimed when I told her what I wanted. Then she looked at me and saw that I wasn't.

'Can do?' I asked.

'Of course,' she replied. 'But bloody hell, Bob, this is going to cost you.'

'Name your price,' I said.

'I want you to agree to join my team. Not full-time of course, but on a case by case basis.'

We'd danced around the subject before but it was a very

serious request that she was making. I thought hard before I answered.

'Okay,' I told her when I was ready, 'as long as it doesn't involve me being a cowboy. I have a young family, and another on the way, and I really would like to see them all grow up.'

Fifty-Seven

'W hy do you need this?' Callum Sullivan asked. 'I'm a bit leery about passing people's names on to the police without them knowing.'

'It may be relevant to our investigation,' Sauce Haddock replied. 'That's all I can tell you just now.'

'Are you saying it might help you find who killed Anna?'

'It's one line of inquiry among many, but yes, that's possible.'

'Then it's yours, no problem. I'll look it out and get it to you. Email okay?'

'Absolutely. I'll text you my address. Thanks, Mr Sullivan.'

He ended the call, then tapped in his promised message and despatched it. 'Done,' he declared.

Pye grinned. 'Didn't you offer to go to North Berwick and pick it up personally?'

'Fuck off, sir,' the DS grunted. 'I forgot to ask you yesterday,' he continued, a few seconds later, 'since we were too busy talking about the boss; what did you think of our colleagues?'

'I liked them,' the DCI replied. 'Mann's formidable and Provan's a character.'

'It's all an act with him: the way he spoke to the big man, his whole rebel "Don't give a shit" attitude. There's a guy hiding behind that, and he's very, very clever.'

'You heard what Bob Skinner called him: "the best detective in the city" wasn't it? So why's he still a DS, that's the question.'

'I asked him,' Haddock said, 'straight out. He told me he was offered DI, when Mann was promoted, but he turned it down.'

'Why would he do that?'

'According to him it was so he could stay below the radar, but it was pretty clear to me, he did it for her. He worships the ground that large lady walks on. He loves her.'

Pye laughed. 'Romance in the ranks? That's a bit fanciful, mate. He's twenty years older than her.'

'Nonetheless. When you and Lottie were talking I asked him about her, whether she was married and such. He told me her husband's in jail. When he talked about him, his eyes were telling me that if the guy ever tries to come back, wee Dan'll kill him.'

'Indeed? Are you saying they're . . . ?'

'Hell no! That's the sadness of it. On the surface he acts like he's her uncle, but underneath . . .'

'Then I hope it stays that way. They're an effective CID team, obviously, but they'd probably make a lousy couple.' He unsnapped his seat belt as Haddock brought his car to a halt outside the building that was their destination.

The detectives stepped out, buttoning their coats against the bitter east wind as they surveyed their surroundings. The headquarters and factory of Destry PLC were located together in a long white building, by far the largest in an industrial estate in what once had been the New Town of Glenrothes, until it was stripped of that status by a Westminster government.

'One good thing about being part of ScotServe,' Pye remarked as they headed for the visitors' entrance, 'is that we don't have to tell our colleagues in Fife that we're coming on to their patch.'

'Yes,' Haddock agreed. 'Now name another.'

Double doors opened automatically, admitting them to a reception area, with a waiting area on the right and an enclosed booth on the left, where a young woman sat at a desk with a switchboard. She wore a headset and was speaking into its microphone as the newcomers approached. 'Just one moment, caller,' they heard her say, 'and I'll put you through.'

She flipped a switch, then rose. 'Yes, gentlemen?' She was tall, dressed in a black suit with a tight–fitting skirt that stopped just below the knee, and a man's white shirt underneath, the first two buttons undone to reveal a hint of cleavage. A badge on her lapel introduced her as Marcella Mega. The cut of her dark hair made Haddock think of Cheeky.

'We have an appointment with Mrs Stewart,' Pye began.

The receptionist glanced at a wall clock. 'Yes. You'll be her ten thirty. If I could see your credentials?' Her accent was not local; Edinburgh, private schooling, the DCI guessed.

The officers displayed their crested warrant cards; she leaned over the divider to inspect them.

'Thank you, detectives,' she said. 'If you'll take a seat; Mrs Stewart's running a little late.'

'No worries,' Pye replied. 'We'll stand, if you don't mind. We've been sitting all the way from Edinburgh. You worked here long, Ms Mega?' he asked, casually.

'Six months. I'm just completing the integration process.'

'What's that?'

'Hold on.' She stepped back to the board, flipped another switch, and announced their arrival to someone called Linda, then rejoined them. 'All new employees have to spend time in each department before we're finally assigned, regardless of our skills. I have a First in Chemical Engineering, but when I started here Mrs Stewart stuck a brush in my hand and had me sweeping the factory floor for a month.'

'Not in that suit, I'll bet,' Haddock remarked.

'Nor these shoes,' she laughed, raising a foot to display heels that accentuated her height.

'Is all your management located here?' Pye asked.

'Our executive management, yes; Mrs Stewart is the chief executive officer, as I imagine you know. She runs the place. We have a parent company, but that's based in Edinburgh.'

'Yes, we know that too. Do you see much of Mr Higgins here?'

'I've never seen him. Rory visits once a month, and once every three months Mrs Stewart and Mr Orchard, the production director, go to a board meeting in head office.'

'Rory?'

She looked at Haddock. 'Mr Higgins Junior.'

'He's informal, is he?' the DS asked, lightly.

'Not with everyone,' she replied. 'He and I have a little history, away from business. We've been on a couple of dates.'

A very small frown suggested that there might be no more to come.

'Didn't you like the movie?' Haddock ventured.

'It shows, does it?' she said. 'The first time, I did. Second time, I didn't like where he took me: a seedy little pole-dancing bar at the top of Leith Walk. We met the owner, Callum, a business friend of his, Rory said. He may have been, but they both spent a little too much time eyeing up one of the dancers. I went to the ladies, then left by the side door. We haven't spoken since.'

'Did you . . .' Pye began, but before he could ask whether there had been a third man present, a tall, lean, brooding guy, a door burst open and a stout middle-aged woman bustled into the reception area.

'Gentlemen,' she exclaimed, 'sorry to have kept you. I'm Linda Lee, Mrs Stewart's PA. She's ready for you now; follow me, please.'

She turned on her heel and headed in the direction from which she had come; following was their only option. She led them along a wide corridor. The far end was open, affording them a glimpse of a factory floor, filled with machinery and lengths of white material. The sharp sound of power saws assaulted their ears, until their escort opened a door on the right and ushered them into a small anteroom with another door beyond. It was open; another woman stood there, framed by it. She was the antithesis of her receptionist; she was clad in blue overalls and her white hair was wild.

She took a step towards them, extending a hand. 'Joan Stewart,' she announced, in an accent that was pure East Fife. 'CEO. Come into my sanctum; it's the only oasis of quiet we have in this bloody great shed.' She held the door open for them, standing aside as they entered. 'Coffee, gents?'

'No thanks,' Pye said, as the trio settled into chairs. 'We'll get straight to business if you don't mind.'

'Fair enough,' Mrs Stewart replied. 'I'm curious to know what that might be. You weren't very forthcoming with Linda when you made the appointment.'

'We want to talk to you about your company's acquisition of Mackail Extrusions.'

The woman underwent an instant attitude change; her open demeanour closed up tight. 'Destry didn't acquire Mackail. We bought its assets from the liquidator. There's a big difference.'

'What about its order book?' Haddock asked.

'We weren't interested in that. It didn't have many clients, other than ourselves, and those it did have were all our competitors. We bought a facility and brought it in-house, that's all.'

'Bought it cheap?'

'Market value plus five per cent.'

'Was it an auction?'

'No, we did a private deal.'

The DS pressed on. 'When you say "we", who do you mean? Did you handle it yourself?'

She shook her unkempt head. 'No. The negotiations were all done by our parent company. I wasn't party to them.'

Pye leaned forward slightly. 'Mrs Stewart,' he said, 'it's been suggested to us that Destry contrived to bring about the bankruptcy of Mackail Extrusions by withholding payment unreasonably for materials supplied.'

She bristled, visibly, almost comically, sitting bolt upright, her jaw jutting out as if she was ready for combat. 'Suggested by whom? Hector bloody Mackail? Who are you guys anyway?' she demanded. 'The Fraud Office? If you are, this conversation's over.'

'We're not, and it isn't. We're mainstream CID and we're investigating the circumstances surrounding the death of Hector Mackail.'

She blinked, once, twice, a third time. 'Hector's dead?' she gasped. 'I never knew. What happened? He didn't bloody top himself, did he?'

'No,' Haddock responded, 'somebody did that for him. Hit-and-run. It didn't make the national press, not at the time.'

'Well, I know nothing about it. I can assure you of that.'

'We're not suggesting that you do,' Pye assured her. 'All we want to do is establish the truth of stories we've been told, that Mr Mackail had a grievance against Destry and its parent company. It's a straight question, Mrs Stewart, in an unrecorded conversation. Did you starve him of funds or did you not?'

She took a breath, making her round cheeks even rounder, then let it out in a sigh. 'Look,' she said, 'Hector was naive. He turned out a good product but he was no businessman. He responded to the slump in the home improvement industry by jacking up his prices, not cutting them. He was his own worst enemy; he'd have gone bust anyway.'

'But you helped him?'

She nodded. 'The parent company told me to make him a decent offer for his business. I did but he turned it down. He got quite aggressive with me about it. When I reported back, I got the word to put the squeeze on his cash flow. It didn't take long after that till the bank called in his debt and he went under. That was no surprise,' she added, 'not with that bank.'

'Why not?' Haddock asked, curious.

'Because Eden Higgins has a twenty-nine per cent stake in it, held personally, not through the holding company. Some of the subsidiaries bank there.'

'I see,' Pye murmured, fighting off his surprise. 'What's the history of Destry?' he asked.

'My late husband and I founded the business twenty-five years ago,' she said. 'Initially we did replacement windows, but pretty soon we expanded into conservatories. James died from cancer in two thousand and three, but by that time the business was secure. He'd always majored on design and manufacture while I did everything else. The product range was established when he passed away, so it wasn't difficult for me to carry on.'

'When did you sell to Mr Higgins?'

'Two thousand and six. I recruited Justin Orchard after James died, to replace him, and by that time he was well established in the job. He had an idea for a new product range, free-standing modular glass garden buildings. I liked it, but it would have taken a lot of working capital to get it going, plus it would have been a gamble at a time when the economic storm clouds were just starting to show over the horizon. Around that time I met Eden Higgins at a Scottish CBI gathering. Do you know him?' she asked.

'No,' Haddock chuckled. 'We're just humble plods.'

'So was his sister, I believe,' she countered. 'That's why I asked. Anyway, we got talking. He had just started to diversify at the time, but he still thought like a furniture guy. Anything you could furnish, he was interested in it. A couple of weeks later he came to me and made me an offer for a controlling interest in the company, with an injection of new working capital. It was a great deal; I still have a one-third stake in a business that's gone from strength to strength under his management. I don't have any stake in Higgins Holdings, nobody else does, but I still draw salary, and dividend, from here.'

'His management,' Pye repeated. 'Is his style always as rough as it was with Mackail?'

'No,' Joan Stewart replied, firmly. 'That was unusual; it wasn't like Eden at all. Maybe that's why he didn't tell me in person; maybe he found it difficult, maybe he felt guilty.'

'Hold on,' Haddock intervened. 'Are you saying it wasn't Eden Higgins who told you to hold back payment from Mackail?'

'No, I'm not. Look,' she exclaimed, 'what he was telling me to do wasn't something you put on paper, or in an email, or even in a phone call. The message came from him, word of mouth, via his vicar on earth.'

'Who?' both detectives asked, simultaneously, in a duet.

'Sorry,' she laughed. 'That's what we call his right-hand man, Walter Hurrell. He gave me the instruction.'

Fifty-Eight

The morning after I'd made my promise to Amanda Dennis, I awoke from a confused dream. It was set at the beginning of the *Godfather* movie; I was the undertaker Bonasera and a grotesque male version of Amanda took the role of Don Corleone.

I'd given my friend a commitment that I hoped I wouldn't come to regret. When it became clear that I was heading for the exit door of the police service she had offered me, tentatively, a permanent role with the Security Service. I'd have been in charge of the Scottish outstation, installed as Clyde Houseman's boss. I turned her down, firmly, citing two reasons, the first being that in his shoes, I'd have resented me, the second, and by far the more significant, being that most of the work would have bored me rigid and that any that didn't might have involved an element of risk, the kind that I'd promised Sarah I'd avoid in my middle years.

She'd used the help that she was giving me with Gates to back me into a corner. I'd have done the same, but I'd been deadly serious in the proviso I'd attached to my acceptance.

Having put the daft dream out of my mind and having seen Sarah off to work, I had nothing to do. I had given my 'advice' to the four detectives; whether they took it or not, that it was up to them. With that time on my hands, I decided to devote the morning to administration.

Not that there was much of it to do. Along with her report, Carrie McDaniels had given me a detailed invoice; her terms specified 'Payment within seven days', but with the fate of the man Mackail and his company fresh in my mind, I decided to do better than that. I put the details of her bill into my purchase ledger, then set up a payment through my business bank account.

I had thought about playing a few holes of golf with anyone who might have been hanging around the club, but a note on the bank's website told me that it would take an hour before I could complete my cash transfer. That, and the fact that it was freezing outside, put exercise on the back burner.

That frustration, and the fact that it had to do with Carrie, triggered something that I'd forgotten completely: the memory stick that she'd given me with her report on the insurance claim for Rachel Higgins' stolen jewellery. Mentally, I'd filed it under 'Irrelevant', but with nothing else to do I retrieved it from the pocket where it had lain since it had been handed it to me, and plugged it into a USB port on my computer.

There wasn't much to it; as Carrie had said, the swag consisted of three items, a necklace, matching bracelet and a pair of earrings, diamonds set in platinum. Each had been photographed, at the insistence of the insurers, no doubt, and it was equally certain that these had been circulated after the theft to every jeweller in the land, and to all the auction houses.

Waste of time, all of it. There was no chance of any of it being offered for sale through any legitimate outlet. The stuff would have been sold on for one third of its insured value, tops, on the 'no questions asked' market, and would never be recovered.

Carrie had done a thorough job for her client; she had interviewed Rachel Higgins, the investigating police officers, and the management of Mackiltee Lodge, the boutique hotel where the theft had occurred. The story was consistent; the jewels had been put in the hotel safe overnight, and in the morning they were gone. No alarms had been triggered and the safe did not appear to have been forced.

In my time I had seen dozens of theft reports that were virtually identical; I had even compiled a few. In Carrie's, there was only one question I'd have asked that she hadn't. Or so it appeared; she might have covered the base and thought the answer not worth recording. All the same . . .

The phone number of the hotel was on the file. Out of nothing more than curiosity I dialled it.

My call was answered by one of those accents that had evolved through many generations of poshness. 'Mackiltee Lodge, Jane Mackiltee speaking. How can I help you?'

'Good morning,' I replied, in my finest Lanarkshire, 'my name is Skinner. I'm reviewing the insurance company report into a theft from your hotel a few months ago, of jewellery belonging to Mrs Rachel Higgins. It's nothing for you to worry about,' I added quickly. 'Just a belt and braces thing.'

'Will it lead to a reduction of the outrageous renewal quote we've just been given?'

'I can't promise anything,' I told her, truthfully. 'But you never know,' I added, vaguely.

'Ah well. What is it?'

'I just want to clarify one thing. Who put the valuables in the safe?'

'I did,' she said. 'I hope there's no implication . . .'

'Absolutely none,' I assured her, although there might have been. 'While you were doing it, did anyone else see you?'

'No.'

I was about to thank her and hang up, when I heard a slight hitch in her throat, an intake of hesitancy. 'Well,' she added, 'apart from the client, that is.'

'Mrs Higgins?'

'No, no, not her. Their security person, Mr, Mr . . . I can't remember his name off the top of my head, but it began with an H . . . not Higgins, he wasn't family, something else. He brought the items down, he showed them to me, and then he insisted on observing as I secured them. That's what happened.'

Was it indeed? I thought.

'No problem there, in that case,' I said. 'Thanks for your help.'

Fifty-Nine

It's all too easy for a cop engaged in a complex investigation to become obsessive; as soon as that happens his judgement is liable to be impaired.

I recognised the signs as I ended my call to Mackiltee Lodge. Walter Hurrell, not Rachel Higgins, took the stolen jewels to the safe and he watched the owner as she put them in there.

Yes, Bob, and that meant precisely what?

In all probably, it meant nothing. Hurrell was Eden's driver; of course he'd have taken them to the hotel, and been put up there, since it was remote. He was his minder, responsible for his personal security. It was natural that he should have taken the family valuables to the safe, and if he'd watched the owner as she put them in, he was only doing his job properly.

'Forget it,' I told myself, just as my email inbox pinged to let me know that I had a new arrival. I opened it and saw a message from Sauce Haddock, headed simply, 'For Info'.

There was no text, only an attachment. I clicked on it, and waited as the Word software booted up and a document appeared. The page was headed 'Callum O Sullivan', and the text below was a list of names, in alphabetical order; his party guests, for sure. I scrolled down from the top. Most of the names from A to G were unknown to me, apart from a European Tour golfer and a couple of football people, but one did stand out, even though it wasn't news to me. 'Francey, Dean', there because of his connection to Sullivan's nephew, Maxwell Harris.

It was when I got to 'H' that I sparked. I'd expected to see Anna Harmony, listed under her adopted name, but the entire Higgins family were there as well, Eden, Rachel and Rory. And so was Walter Hurrell.

Obsession edged towards paranoia: that name was coming up far too often. I was very keen to see him on video with Sammy Pye and Lottie Mann facing him across an interrogation room table. If I was a betting man, he would have been carrying my money in the 'Who shot Dino?' stakes, but the odds would have been miserably short.

I was still contemplating an imaginary call to Ladbrokes . . . other bookmakers are available . . . when the FaceTime icon started bouncing at the foot of my screen. I hit 'Accept' and waited for a few seconds, until my own onscreen face was replaced by that of Amanda Dennis. She had her back to her office window, and behind her I could see the grey pillars on the terrace outside.

'Quick one, Bob,' she said. 'Your man gets back tomorrow, six a.m. What do you want done with him?'

'I want him detained within the base,' I replied. 'They should say nothing about what's happened to his family. That'll be for the interrogating officers.'

'No.' Her face set in a frown. 'It'll be for you; only you can go in there.'

'Christ, Amanda,' I exclaimed, 'that'll cause a riot in ScotServe HQ. I'm breaking enough protocols as it is.'

'I don't give a stuff about ScotServe, or its increasingly

unpopular chief constable. That base is the most secure place in the United Kingdom and they won't have plods running all over it. You have standing within my service and it's on that basis that they'll let you in.'

'Okay,' I said, 'if that's the deal. In which case, I'll be keeping my visit strictly to myself, in the short term. Thanks for this, Amanda. Please tell them to expect me at midday.'

Sixty

'When I was a laddie,' Dan Provan said, 'I used to go fishin' with my grandpa, on the Clyde, where it runs through Cambuslang. There were hardly any fish there, and those that were wis only a few inches long, but every now and then we'd catch one . . . or he would. I can still remember them lying on the path, flappin' and gaspin' till he chucked them back in.' He smiled. 'That's how I feel now, like one o' them.'

'A fish out of water?'

'Exactly, Lottie. See where we were wi' Skinner yesterday, Newhouse? As far as I'm concerned that's the boundary of civilisation. Through here? Cannae get my breath.'

'I'll throw you back in the river when we're done here,' the DI promised, 'but first we've got Mr Hurrell to deal with.'

'Do Glasgow warrants count in Edinburgh?'

'Don't be daft. You know they do.' She looked at him, as they stood on the pavement. 'How do you think we should play this?' she asked, her higher rank deferring to his greater experience.

The sergeant glanced at the four large uniformed officers who stood behind her. 'Knock politely,' he replied. 'If that does nothin', one of these lads can knock a bit harder. The search warrant gives us right of entry.'

Research had established that the main home of Eden Higgins and his family was an entire house in Moray Place, restored by the businessman to its original eighteenth-century splendour. Its garden flat, which would have been part of the original servants' quarters, was occupied by Rory Higgins. Because access to the rear of the building was limited, all but one of the family cars were kept in a nearby lane. What had once been stables had become trendy mews conversions; Walter Hurrell lived in one, above a garage big enough to hold four vehicles.

The plan was to arrest him at home, when he returned from work in the evening, but the building had been kept under observation overnight and he had not been seen to leave. Because of the assessed risk, the cobbled lane had been sealed off at either end.

'You do the honours,' Mann said.

Provan stepped up to the green-painted door and rapped on the handle. They waited for a full minute then tried again, with the same lack or response.

'Enough?' Provan asked.

'Yes,' Mann replied. 'Let's go in.' She stood aside as one of the uniforms stepped forward with a red ram. One swing was all that was needed to open the door. The quartet, led by a sergeant, stepped inside and ran up the stairs, weapons drawn, with warning cries of, 'Armed police.'

Mann made to follow, but the DS held her back. 'No,' he said firmly. 'This is their job. We wait till it's clear. I once saw a young DC get shot by going in too early.'

As he spoke, the leader of the armed squad reappeared, at the top of the stairway. 'You can come up now,' he called to them. 'He's in . . . but then again, he's not.'

Provan led the way. 'In there,' the other sergeant said, pointing towards an open door.

Walter Hurrell was sitting up in bed, naked, leaning back against the headboard, with a duvet bunched at his waist, and a gun lying in his lap. He was staring at the doorway, with the same expression that had registered in his eyes in the instant before he was shot, neatly, just above his right eye.

Sixty-One

'Don't take this personally, Detective Inspector,' DCC Mario McGuire murmured, solemnly, as they stood on the wide stone steps. 'This isn't me elbowing my way into your investigation; it's me supporting you.'

'I know that, sir,' Lottie Mann replied. 'If you hadn't said you were coming I'd have asked for you, or someone else senior who knows Edinburgh. I'm a Weegie cop; people like this are well above my pay grade.'

She looked up at the towering grey terraced mansion. 'In Glasgow we wouldn't call this a house; we'd call it a hotel.'

The black-painted front door swung open. A man stood, holding its handle, surveying them as if he was deciding whether to send them to the tradesman's entrance. He was slim, age mid-fifties, Mann guessed, and perfectly groomed. He wore what McGuire recognised as the unofficial uniform of Her Majesty's Counsel, black jacket, pinstripe trousers and a blue and white striped shirt.

'Officers,' he said. 'Mr Higgins is ready for you. He is in the ballroom; if you'll come this way.'

'Are you Mr Higgins' lawyer?' McGuire asked as they climbed a wide flight of stairs, lit from a cupola above.

403

'No, sir,' the man replied without a flicker of a smile. 'I am Robotham, the housekeeper.' From his right, the deputy chief heard a snorting sound that might have been a suppressed laugh. 'This residence,' he continued, 'takes considerable management, as you can imagine. Mr Higgins regards it as a national monument, because of its considerable history. In the nineteenth century it was the residence of two lords president of the Court of Session. Later, like many houses in Moray Place, it was put to commercial use, finally as the offices of an accountancy firm, before Mr Higgins rescued it and restored it to its original state.'

The DCC wondered whether that had included the small security camera that had observed their arrival, but decided not to ask.

The ballroom was on the first floor; it was huge, accessed by eight-foot-high double doors. Mr Robotham opened the one on the right and held it for them. 'The police officers,' he announced.

The space was huge; the room covered almost the full width of the house. The far wall was mostly windows, and there was a wide fireplace at either end with marble mantelpieces and mirrors above. There was a Persian rug on the floor; looking at it the DI suspected that its floor space was the equivalent of her entire house, and more.

For a brief moment, she thought they were alone, that a trick had been played, until she realised that McGuire was looking to his right, where two high-backed chairs were set in front of the hearth, in which a log fire burned. A small middle-aged man stood beside one of them, looking at them. Beyond him, with an elbow crooked against a corner of the mantelshelf, there was a taller figure, someone both officers knew well.

'Welcome,' Eden Higgins said, moving to greet them as they approached. 'I hope you don't mind me asking Mr Skinner to join us. I'm alone here; my wife and son have flown to Monaco for the weekend in the company jet. As soon as I heard what had happened, I was shocked, I felt the need of a friend, so I called him and asked him to come.'

Skinner glared at his back. 'But you didn't tell me why,' he exclaimed. 'I have no locus here. I'm not a lawyer, I'm nothing more than a private citizen.' His eyes moved to the new arrivals. 'I've only just arrived myself,' he told them, 'and heard about Hurrell.' He moved away from the fireplace. 'I'm out of here, Eden.'

'Bob,' Higgins protested, 'I asked you here as a friend, nothing else. I was appalled when I heard about poor Walter. He was my right-hand man. Other than my family, I had nobody closer. I just can't believe that he'd kill himself.'

To McGuire, the man's distress seemed genuine. 'It's all right, Mr Higgins, we have no objection to the chief,' he smiled as he realised that his tongue had slipped, '. . . to Mr Skinner being here. Bob, stay, please. This isn't a formal interview; it's not a problem.'

Skinner looked at Lottie Mann. 'Is that okay with you too, Inspector? I take it that you found Mr Hurrell?'

'It is, and I did,' she agreed, as the quartet moved back towards the fire.

'Where's your evil twin?' he asked.

She smiled, briefly. 'Dan's still at the scene,' she replied, 'supervising the search.'

'You're sure that it was suicide?'

Mann nodded. 'It seems nailed on. He was sat up in bed, with an empty bottle of red and a glass on the table beside him.

There was one shot just above the right eyebrow, with powder burns around the entry wound.'

'Was there an exit wound?'

'Yes. The bullet was embedded in the headboard. It's been sent for comparison.'

'Did they do a gunshot residue test on him?'

'That was being done when I left,' Mann said. 'Given the proximity of the shot, there'll be particles all over the bed, but if there's a concentration on his hand and forearm, that'll prove he shot himself.'

'Weapon?'

'The CSIs said it's a Smith and Wesson Bodyguard automatic, point three eight calibre. A lethal little bastard.'

Skinner nodded. 'Yes it is,' he agreed. 'I know 'cos I've been shot by one of them,' he added, deadpan.

'Why?' Eden Higgins exclaimed. 'Why would Walter shoot himself? And where would he get a gun, for God's sake?'

'He was ex-military,' McGuire pointed out. 'That wouldn't be a problem to him. As for the why . . .' He paused. 'Sit down, please, Mr Higgins.'

The billionaire, still looking slightly dazed, nodded and sank into one of the armchairs. 'I just don't get it,' he murmured.

'When DI Mann found Mr Hurrell's body,' the DCC continued, 'she and her colleagues were there to arrest him for questioning in connection with the murders of three people. One of them was Jock Hodgson, who helped Hurrell crew the *Princess Alison*, your missing boat.'

'Why?' Higgins vocabulary seemed to have been reduced to a single word.

'Jock helped Hector Mackail steal the *Princess*,' Skinner said, bluntly, 'he and another man. It looks certain that Walter Hurrell killed the two of them, in retribution. What my friends are getting round to asking you, Eden, is quite simple. Did you know, and was he acting on your orders?'

The man stared up at him; for all his influence and all his wealth, he seemed very small and vulnerable.

'No,' he protested, weakly at first. 'No!' he repeated, more loudly. 'No!' he shouted, grasping the arms of his chair and pushing himself to his feet. 'No, I did not!' He glared at Skinner. 'Bob, get your damn friends out of here. If they want to speak to me again, they can contact my solicitors. As for you and I,' he added, with an icy edge to his tone, 'our business is done too. Send me an invoice for your services.'

Sixty-Two

$\mathbf{M}$y words to God's ear, I didn't want to be there. I'd had enough, for that time, of Eden Higgins and the saga of his bloody boat. Plus I had other priorities; chief among them was a dinner reservation for two at La Potinière in Gullane. Sarah and I have a few anniversaries and that night was one of them.

But she was busy too, performing a short-notice autopsy on the late Walter Hurrell, so, when Mario McGuire asked me if I'd sit in on a case conference he'd called in the old Fettes building for late afternoon, I had no legitimate grounds for refusal.

'Okay,' I told him, 'but Andy's going to shit himself when I send him a bill for my time.'

The big guy knows me well enough not to take me seriously. 'Bugger off,' he chuckled into the phone, 'you offered your help, remember. Come on, Bob, you know you can't step back now. '

'Maybe I should. I'm a witness in the Zena abduction . . .'

'Which will never come to trial,' Mario interrupted to point out.

'Beyond that,' I continued, 'I'm a witness in the Hodgson killing, and to cap it all, I'm involved through my work for my former client. Seriously, when your chief constable finds out I attended your meeting, the stuff I mentioned earlier really will interface with the ventilator.'

'He knows already. I told him; told him about you introducing west to east at the Newhouse as well.'

'How did he react?'

My friend shrugged. 'As we've come to expect. He threw a monumental hissy fit, and asked me what the hell I thought I was doing. I said that I was using all available resources to trace and apprehend a multiple murderer and that he could moan about it if it doesn't work, but not before. I didn't bother to tell him that we've cracked it already. I think you could say,' he added, 'that he and I are not speaking.'

If his confrontation with his boss was preying on Mario's mind, he didn't let it show as we gathered round the table in the small conference room at the end of what had been the command corridor of the force in which I spent all but the last few months of my career.

I sat beside him, but deliberately I drew my chair back a little, as if to make it clear that I was only an observer.

Each of us had been given a folder. It had been compiled by Haddock and Provan, under my unofficial supervision, and contained a comprehensive review of the spider's web that the case had become. Mario tapped his. 'Take us through it, DCI Pye,' he said.

The timeline began with the collapse of Mackail Extrusions, and Higgins Holdings' purchase of the wreckage.

It started to move with Hector Mackail's reported visit to Eden's office and the assault which had left my client with a fractured ankle, treated, as young DC Wright had discovered, at a private hospital near Edinburgh Zoo.

A few weeks later, Jock Hodgson visited Dunbar, where, it was believed, he had lunched with Mackail, and another naval colleague, David Gates.

A further week elapsed and the *Princess Alison* was stolen, with a two-month abortive police investigation ensuing. A swift internal inquiry by DCI Sandra Bulloch had established that its shoddy incompetence had been covered up, by the outgoing Assistant Chief Constable Bridget 'Bridie' Gorman, but that was not part of the folder.

The day after the police search was declared closed, Jock Hodgson's home was burgled. The crime was reported, but it fell into the 'probably no chance' category, and wasn't prioritised by the local CID division.

The same weekend Eden and Rachel attended a business symposium in Mackiltee Lodge, where her jewels were stolen from the safe, having been put there under the supervision of Walter Hurrell.

A few days later, the Higgins family and Hurrell attended Callum Sullivan's celebration in North Berwick, where they crossed paths with Dean Francey.

Five days after that, Jock Hodgson was tortured and murdered in his home.

Two weeks and three days later, Hector Mackail was knocked down and killed by Dean Francey, driving his father's van.

Six weeks on, Grete Regal was attacked and her daughter Zena abducted, by Dean Francey, only for the idiot to screw up by colliding with me in the Fort Kinnaird car park.

Hours later he was silenced, along with the unfortunate Anna Harmony, who should have stuck to pole-dancing.

Two days later, Hodgson's body was discovered.

Finally the trail led to Walter Hurrell; but not before he shot himself. The gunshot residue test had proved conclusively that he had fired the pistol found on the bed.

'Let's not kid ourselves here,' I said, after Sammy had finished. 'Despite Eden Higgins' protests, we're all asking ourselves, me included, whether Hurrell was acting alone, or on his orders.'

I paused; five people were looking at me. 'The answer?' I continued. 'Truthfully, I don't know. He might have; he did start the ball rolling by bankrupting Mackail, because he refused to be bought out.

'But it doesn't matter a damn, as all of you must realise. Suppose Eden was behind it all, you will never prove it. This gathering is about finalising a report to the Crown Office, end of story.'

'What's this jewel theft doing in the timeline, Bob?' Mario asked.

'Maybe nothing,' I replied. 'But . . . Francey was paid five grand, probably to kill Mackail, and he'd have been getting more for snatching the child. That wasn't going to be done by bank transfer. It's possible that Hurrell opened that hotel safe during the night and took the jewels . . . pretty easy since he'd seen the combination . . . then flogged them to raise some black cash, knowing that the loss to Rachel would actually be a hit on the Edinburgh Co-operative insurance company.'

'Makes sense,' he admitted. 'But here's another question. Why would Higgins hire you to find his boat if he knew that Hurrell was in the process of killing off the people who stole it?'

'He didn't hire me to do that, not really,' I told him. 'He hired me to review the police investigation and to cover any bases that Inspector McGarry hadn't, so that he could compel his marine insurer to settle for the full amount of the loss. And suppose he did know, when he and I met he had no idea that

Zena Gates had been found dead or that you were on to Dean Francey and his girlfriend.'

I looked beyond Mario, at Provan. 'What do you think, Dan?' I asked.

The sage frowned. 'Ask me again when they've compared that bullet wi' the others.'

I nodded. 'It'll match,' I said.

Lottie Mann spoke up. 'Come on, Mr Skinner, what do you really believe? I can't take "It doesn't matter", not from you. Did Higgins order everything, or was Hurrell acting on his own, without any instruction?'

'How often do I have to say it?' I retorted. 'There's no evidence to implicate anyone but Hurrell. That's what I believe: it's what I know.'

'Then it's done,' she murmured, 'because we can tie him to everything, but nobody else. In his flat, we found Hodgson's laptop, and a couple of silver cups that were on the stolen property list from the Wemyss Bay break-in. We also found seventy grand in cash, old notes. DCI Pye says they're similar to the money he found in Francey's place.'

Haddock leaned forward. 'Now that we know what we're looking for,' he volunteered, 'we've been able to match a couple of partial prints on Dino's stash to Hurrell.'

'There's something else,' I confessed. 'It's not in the folder because my source can't be named, but it's a fact, nonetheless. Hurrell was kicked out of the Special Boat Service for being trigger-happy.'

'That cracks it,' Mario declared. 'He planned it, he funded it and he paid for it. I'm calling it a result.' He turned in his chair and looked me in the eye. 'Are we agreed on that?'

I sighed as I picked up my folder and opened it. In fact that outcome was deeply unsatisfactory to me: Walter Hurrell had been other ranks, not an officer. He obeyed orders; he didn't give them.

I flipped through the pages, letting each one fall on the one before, until notes gave way to photographs and they began to turn over less smoothly. Finally, they stopped, at a print I hadn't seen before, and yet one that was strangely familiar.

'Fuck!' I whispered.

Then I slammed the folder back on the conference table.

'No, Mario,' I said, 'we're not.' I pointed at the four detectives. 'You lot,' I ordered forgetting my civilian status, 'get back to Hurrell's place, get down on your hands and knees and start looking.'

'Looking for what?' Haddock exclaimed.

'Another bullet hole,' I told him. 'I'd join you,' I added, 'but I'm taking my other half to dinner.'

Sixty-Three

No, I hadn't said anything about Gates being back from his mission. At that moment it wasn't relevant, and there was a further possibility holding me back; if I'd told Mario that the Ministry of Defence had banned ScotServe from its premises, it might have triggered a pissing contest that would have got in the way of progress.

Sarah and I made it to La Potinière. The Hurrell post-mortem had been uncomplicated, so routine that she even had time to write up her report. She'd printed a copy for me, but absolutely forbade me from reading it over the dinner table.

Next morning, I had Saturday breakfast with the family, light, to preserve the glow of a superb meal the night before, read the online papers, and then headed west. For company I chose an album by John Legend, because it matched my mood; contemplative.

I had switched off my phone the night before, and I left it that way. I didn't want to be disturbed by feedback from the search of Hurrell's flat . . . not least because I knew what they'd have found there. I didn't want to be interrupted by a call from Sir Andrew Martin, who had left a testy message with Trish while Sarah and I were at the restaurant, asking, nay, demanding, that

I phone him. I had a serious day ahead of me and I didn't want to be diverted by anything, friend or foe.

As I drove, I found myself thinking about fatherhood. I'd left home feeling guilty about missing any part of a termtime weekend with my children, but what I was going to do could not be put off. I was going to see a father, and I was going to give him the worst news he'd ever had. I couldn't imagine myself in his shoes.

Being a parent is maybe the only thing in my life that I believe I've done well. When I turned fifty, Alex gave me a 'World's best Dad' mug, among my presents. Inside it was a handwritten note that said simply, 'I really mean that, Love A.'

I've never raised my voice to any of my children, far less raised a hand, because I've never had to. Since I've never had to, logic suggests someone must have been doing something right. With Alex, there was only me for most of the time.

Looking back on my life, the years I spent bringing her up, as a single parent, were huge. Sometimes it wasn't easy . . . the first task I ever gave Mario McGuire as a young PC was looking after her, when I'd had no choice but to take her to a crime scene . . . but I believe that giving her a solid platform on which to build her success has been my greatest achievement, so far. I'm determined to match it with all the others, even Ignacio, although I'm coming very late to the game with him. As for Sarah's bombshell . . . a name she will carry until she puts in an appearance . . . I will be over seventy by the time she's ready for her maiden solo flight.

David Gates and Grete Regal weren't going to have the pleasure of those years, with their little Zena. They were going to have to live with her death, if they could.

John Legend had become Mary Coughlan by the time I

cleared the village named Rhu and started heading up the Gareloch. I was close to Her Majesty's Naval Base Clyde, a lumpy title universally changed to 'Faslane' in popular usage, but there was one call I wanted to make on the way.

I'd only seen photographs of Eden's boathouse, but it was on my way, surprisingly close to the base, in fact, and so I had to take the opportunity to see it up close. Thanks to Google Earth, I knew exactly where it was, only a few yards off the main road that ran along the loch side.

It was big, no doubt about that. A private black-topped road ran from the gated entrance down to a sliding double door, the only landward entry point. It was set in the west side, secured by a shiny new padlock, a replacement, no doubt, for the one they'd sheared off with a bolt cutter. Dead leaves were piled up against it, a sign that it hadn't been opened for a while.

Having seen all I wanted, I drove on; a couple of miles down the road, I reached the roundabout at the north gate, the main entrance, where I was expected. The fences were topped with rolls of razor wire, sure, but I'd seen the same at many other secure establishments that I've visited during my career. There was no sign that read, 'Home of your very own nuclear deterrent', nothing to indicate that the place was different, and yet it was, even to me.

It may have been its incongruity in its beautiful location, or it may simply have had an aura of evil about it. Whatever, it gave me the creeps. With a sudden flash of insight, I knew that if my life had taken another course and given me the power of a prime minister rather than that of a mere chief constable, HM Naval Base Clyde would not exist.

Naturally, given what they were guarding, the MoD police at both gates, inner and outer, were armed. They had been told to expect me; the only credential that I had to present was my driving licence, that got me through each point, although my car was inspected at the second stage and I was given a pat-down search.

Once that was done, the officers at the second gate gave me clear directions to a building at the southern end of the massive base; they called it HMS *Neptune*. The people there weren't armed, but they were still pretty straight edged. I was greeted by a petty officer and escorted to a room with a view of the loch, where a uniformed man was waiting. He was so sharp he looked as if he could have cut steel.

'I'm Tim Boyne,' he said. 'Captain Boyne, Lieutenant Gates's CO. I'm also his friend, and I'm concerned for him. I was asked to keep him on base without explanation, and I've done that. I gather you have some sort of connection with the Security Service, Mr Skinner. Perhaps you have the authority to tell me what this is all about.'

'I have a very loose connection with MI5,' I advised him. 'It was the only way I could get in here, to see Lieutenant Gates privately. An easy alternative would have been his arrest as soon as he left this place, but there are circumstances that make that undesirable.'

'Arrest David?' Boyne exclaimed. 'Why?'

'This man's your friend,' I countered. 'Do you want to keep him in a career?'

'Of course, but . . .'

'So do I,' I said. That was true; it was the real reason, beyond Gates's personal security, why I'd had him held before he stepped, officially, onshore. I knew what he'd done, and I knew why he'd done it. I knew also what had been done to him, and I reckoned that was punishment enough.

417

'I need to have a private meeting with Lieutenant Gates,' I continued. 'We're going to discuss certain matters, and then I'm going to have to give him some very bad news. I don't want our conversation to be eavesdropped, not even by you, Captain, and I sure as hell don't want it recorded. Are we clear on that?'

The submariner nodded. 'We are. Am I ever going to know what this is about?'

'Only the bad part, I'm afraid,' I replied. 'I'd guess he might need to share that with you when we're done.'

'Then let's get on with it. I'll fetch David and leave you together. There are no hidden microphones in this room, I promise.'

He left, and didn't return; instead, when the door reopened, David Gates stepped into the room, unaccompanied. I knew it was him; there had been a passport image in the investigation folder. Dark, lean, but shorter than I expected; he couldn't have been more than five feet six.

'Mr Skinner?' he began, tentatively. It occurred to me that he was still uncertain how to play the game, back foot or front, cautiously or assertively. In his shoes, held on the base overnight without reason being offered, I'd have taken the latter approach.

I nodded, ushering him to a couple of seats beside the window.

'What do I call you?' he asked. 'Is it plain Mister, Chief Constable, or what?' He'd recognised me too; damn that media profile.

'Anything you like,' I said. 'Call me Ishmael.'

He smiled. 'I'm a submariner, not a whaler. But I did love *Moby Dick*. What's this about, Mr Skinner?"

'Did you enjoy your lunch?' I asked.

His face screwed up in bewilderment. 'What lunch?'

'Your lunch in the Rocks, in Dunbar, with Jock Hodgson and Hector Mackail.'

'Fuck!' he gasped. 'You really are a spook.'

'No I'm not,' I assured him. 'I'm not even a cop any longer. I know about your lunch because of some good work by real police officers, and I know this through my own instincts and experience. You and Mackail stole the *Princess Alison*, Eden Higgins' five-million-pound motor cruiser, from its boathouse just along the road. You did it out of revenge, to get even for your pal Hector being bilked out of his business by Higgins Holdings, and maybe for your wife's indirect loss for the same reason.'

He tried for an impassive expression as he stared at me, but fell well short.

'We're not going to bother with ritual denials, Lieutenant, are we?' I murmured. 'No, there would be no point, because I know and you know it's true.'

'I think I need a lawyer,' Gates said.

'No you don't,' I told him, 'because, believe it or not, I'm on your side.'

He switched back to bewildered mode. 'Why?'

'Natural justice,' I replied, 'because this is where we get to the bad part. Your friends are dead. You stole the wrong fucking boat, David.'

'What? How? What are you saying?'

I explained exactly what I was saying,. chapter and verse; that the truth had been burned out of Hodgson, then he'd been shot, his killing followed by the casual, non-accidental death of Hector Mackail.

'If you hadn't been at sea, you might be dead too,' I said. 'Unfortunately, once you've heard the rest of the story, you're going to wish that you were.'

I gave him a minute to gather himself, and then I told him what had happened to his partner and daughter, and who had done it. When I'd finished, he sat there, looking at me as if I was mad. 'I'm sorry,' I said, 'terribly, terribly sorry. I hate being the man to give you this news, but I know the whole story, and I thought it was important that you heard it in context.'

Then he started to cry; I wanted to join him, but instead I left him alone with his grief. Captain Boyne was waiting in the corridor outside. I told him what had happened to Zena and Grete, then stayed where I was while he went in to comfort his friend.

After ten minutes, he reappeared. 'David wants to talk to you,' he said. 'I'll fix up coffee for us, and a brandy for him.'

I went back into the room. Gates was red eyed, but composed. 'The guy who did it,' he murmured. 'You said he's dead?'

'Yes. The belief is that Zena's death wasn't meant to happen, and that the person who paid Francey to kidnap her silenced him after he screwed up.'

Gates' eyes were icy. 'Just as well. It saves me the trouble.'

'I can't argue with that,' I told him. 'The girl, though, Anna; I'd like to think that she didn't understand everything that was going on.'

'I don't care,' he retorted. 'They can all fucking die. You said that Higgins' man paid for it, and for Hector to be killed.'

'That's how it looks; and he's dead too.'

'And Higgins?'

'There's no proof and no suggestion that he ever knew.'

'Do you believe that?'

'I believe in proof,' I replied. 'That's all I'll say.'

'Then I'll find out for myself.'

I shook my head. 'No, you won't. Your wife is going to

recover, and you're going to take care of her, not go crashing off on a vigilante mission. Leave that stuff to people who're good at it.'

'That'll be difficult,' he snarled.

'But you'll manage.' I paused for a second. 'Now tell me,' I continued. 'Where's the *Princess Alison*. I have a personal interest in her that you wouldn't understand.'

'They haven't found her?'

'No. And every marina in Britain and Ireland capable of holding her has been checked.'

'You'd been looking in the wrong place,' Gates retorted, with a twisted, humourless smile.

And then he told me where she was.

'I need to see Grete,' he said, as I was still digesting the simple mistake we'd all made.

'You will,' I promised, 'this afternoon. I will take you straight to the hospital. But after that,' I added, 'you and I are going on a trip. Go and get your gear.'

He left to do as I'd told him. Once the door had closed on him I dug out my phone and switched it on. As soon as I had a signal, I called Mario.

'Bob,' he exclaimed. 'Where the hell are you? I've been trying to call you all day. I asked Sarah where you were but she said she didn't know either.'

'I didn't tell her,' I laughed. 'If you're that fussed you can have my phone triangulated and then you'll understand why. Where's the fire anyway?'

'Under the chief constable,' Mario retorted. 'He's had Eden Higgins' lawyer making all sorts of threats. He even had a call from the First Minister. You do know, don't you, that Eden's a major backer of the SNP?'

'I didn't,' I said, 'but I don't give a bugger either. What's happening in the grown-ups' world?'

'You were right,' he replied. 'The CSIs found another bullet in Hurrell's place. But so what? He could have tested the gun. If you're going to blow your brains out you want to make sure you do it right.'

'How many bullets were missing from the magazine?' I asked.

'Only the one,' he admitted.

'So you're saying that Hurrell fired a test round and then reloaded? Why? Was he planning to shoot himself in the head seven times?'

'Come on,' Mario protested. 'He could have fired the test any time.'

'He could,' I agreed, 'but that's not what happened. Fuck me,' I sighed. 'You really are missing me. Tell Sammy and Lottie to get the scientific team back in there, with Dorward in charge so it's done right. This is what they're looking for: there and somewhere else too.' I spelled out my thinking for him.

'You serious?' he asked when I'd told him.

'Never more so,' I assured him. 'Now, in return for the large favour I've just done ScotServe, I want one from you in return.'

'What's that?'

'I need to borrow your helicopter.'

Sixty-Four

High noon on Wednesday and the gang were all there.

Where? Gathered on the roadway that led down to Eden Higgins' boathouse, all of them there on my summons.

Eden had been stroppy when I'd visited him four hours earlier in Moray Place, to advise him that his presence would be required, along with that of his wife and son.

'I hate unfinished business,' I told him. 'In fact I don't allow it.'

'I thought I made it clear,' he snapped, 'that your input was no longer needed.'

'I'm not a tap you can switch on and off,' I barked back at him. 'Trust me, Eden,' I added, 'if Alison was still alive, she'd be standing beside me at this moment, telling you to be there.'

A slap across the chops wouldn't have brought him into line any more quickly. 'What's it about?' he asked, his usual quiet demeanour restored.

'Patience, friend,' I replied. 'You'll find out.'

'I don't like grandstanding, Bob.'

I smiled. 'Me neither as a rule, but sometimes . . .'

Rachel Higgins was furious as she stood beside the Bentley;

she looked good though, in a fur jacket and hat, her designer jeans tucked into calf-length boots.

Rory Higgins was curious as he locked the car; a light smile played with the corners of his mouth. All the same, his expression suggested that what was coming had better be good or his mood could change very quickly.

Eden was reserved; his outburst that morning had been unusual in a man who was not given to letting his emotions show on the outside.

Rory had driven his parents from Edinburgh. I suspect that it had been something of a treat for him. His father had offered me a seat when finally he'd agreed to come, but I told him I preferred to make my own way.

'Come on then, Bob,' he said, in a 'humouring him' tone of voice as we stood waiting. 'Get on with your Poirot moment.'

I held up a hand. 'Not yet.' I looked back along the road, towards Rhu. 'But soon,' I added, as I saw three cars approach in convoy fashion. The lead vehicle had blue lights on top.

They came to a halt at the entrance gateway and five others stepped out, joining us in the unseasonably warm sunshine: Mario McGuire, in plain clothes, and his four lieutenants, Pye and Haddock, Mann and Provan. Only the DCC knew all of the story; the others were in for something of a surprise.

'What the hell?' Eden exclaimed as they walked towards us, looking vaguely like the cast of *Reservoir Dogs*.

'You called it my Poirot moment, chum,' I said, 'and you were right. Since I seem to have become a consulting detective, I thought I'd wrap this up in the grand manner.' I dug into my trouser pocket and produced a key that Mario had given me the day before. 'This was found in Hurrell's flat,' I announced as I moved towards the boathouse door. 'It fits an Abus padlock, which this is. Let's hope it works on this one or I'm going to look a right twat.'

It did. I slid the newly freed doors apart, letting the others see what was inside. Back, secure in her mooring, was the *Princess Alison*, all seventy-five feet of her.

'My God,' Rory laughed. 'How big a hat did it take for this bloody rabbit?'

Rachel stared into the boathouse, eyes wide.

Eden smiled. He took a step towards me, extending his hand. 'I'm sorry, Bob,' he began. 'I never thought for one moment . . .'

'I know you didn't, so you'll allow me the grandstanding.' My own hand stayed by my side.

He nodded. 'Absolutely. Where did you find her?'

I walked into the great shed, and threw a switch beside the door, turning on the strip lighting, as the others followed. 'Orkney,' I replied. 'The last thing anyone thought, me included, was that she'd have been taken north, but she was. She's been moored in a marina since the day after she was taken, renamed, as you'll see from the boards that were covering her original markings. They called her MV *Revenge*. Appropriate, because that's what it was.'

'How did you get her back?' Rory asked.

I shrugged my shoulders. 'I drove her back,' I replied. 'Well, to be honest, the other guy did most of the driving.'

'What other guy?'

'One of the two who borrowed her in the first place.'

'Who stole her, you mean,' Eden murmured.

'No,' I replied, 'I mean it. They borrowed her; that's what it's going to say on the completed police file, and on the report to your insurers.'

He frowned. 'I'm not getting this.'

'You will,' I assured him. 'Here,' I exclaimed, 'do you fancy testing her out, just to satisfy yourself that she's okay? My friends here have been working their buns off dealing with the aftermath of her disappearance. They deserve a wee bonus.'

'I suppose I owe you that much,' he conceded.

That much, and my fee for finding the thing, I thought.

'Excellent.' I jumped on board. 'Join me, everyone.'

'Really!' Rachel complained to her husband. 'Do we have to?'

'Just a short trip,' he said, 'a run out into the Gareloch and back.'

She scowled. 'You all go, then. I'll stay here.'

'Aw come on, Rachel,' I called from the control deck, 'don't be a wuss! The fridge is rebooted and the champagne's cold.'

She threw me an icy look, but mounted the short gangplank and came on board. Everyone else followed, with varying degrees of enthusiasm; Dan Provan and Sammy Pye were positively reluctant.

I went through the start-up procedure as David Gates had shown me, then pressed the remote that raised the sea gate. Having appointed myself captain, I told Rory to cast off.

Gates had reversed her in when we had returned from our two-day journey down the west coast of Scotland, so leaving the dock was easy. I edged her away from the shore, very slowly, then opened the throttle a little, steering her between the buoys and out into the sea channel, wondering idly what I'd do if a Trident sub surfaced suddenly beneath us.

'Are you a sailor, Sammy?' I heard Sauce Haddock ask. 'You must be, since you're so fond of North Berwick. How about you, Dan?'

I glanced round at the wee DS, and thought I detected a faint green pallor in his complexion. I couldn't hear Pye's reply, but I can lip-read 'Fuck off' well enough.

I didn't go much further, only a few hundred yards, until we were clear of any other Saturday-morning sailors. When I was satisfied it was safe, I cut the engines and pressed a button to drop the anchor, then waited until we were solidly moored.

'We don't want to sit here, Bob,' Eden warned. 'It'll get cold pretty quickly.'

'I know,' I said, 'but we need to talk. We parted on bad terms last week, and that needs to be sorted, if only to get Sir Andrew Martin off DCC McGuire's back. Let's go down one.'

Rachel had taken my unsubtle hint about the champagne. On the lower deck a tray waited for us with nine blue plastic flutes, each half filled. She distributed them without a word or a smile.

'Cheer up, Mum,' Rory pleaded. 'This is a celebration, of sorts.'

I contradicted him. 'Oh no, it isn't. Your family has this boat back, but at some price. Isn't that right, Eden?'

He nodded. 'Yes. But I repeat, I knew nothing about any of it.'

'I know,' I said. 'Finally I'm satisfied that Walter Hurrell wasn't operating under your orders.'

'Walter wasn't what?' Rory exclaimed.

I let his question lie; instead I put one to him. 'Do you remember Callum Sullivan's party?'

'His divorce celebration? Of course; only too well, but how did you know about it?'

'Through DCI Pye and DS Haddock,' I told him. 'They had

427

it from Sullivan. You remember it because there was a bit of a stooshie, and you were in the middle of it.'

His face reddened. 'Don't remind me.'

But I did. 'You'd had a few, and you came on to a girl. I'm guessing this part, but I'm pretty sure I'm right. Her name was Anna . . .'

'I'll take your word for it,' he interrupted. 'I never found out.'

'No, I don't suppose you did,' I conceded. 'But you recognised her, for you'd seen her before, dancing on the bar in tassels and a G-string in Sullivan's bar, Lacey's. It was the night your girlfriend, Marcella, walked out on you, as she told Pye and Haddock. When you saw her again at the party, drink taken, you probably imagined she'd be amenable, given her line of work, so you came on to her . . . way too strong, as it happened. She protested, and you were, not to put too fine a point on it, filled in by another guest.'

Rory winced as he nodded. 'I thought I could handle myself, but that lad was a fucking psycho.'

'He was indeed,' I agreed. 'Did Walter Hurrell see this happen?'

'Yes, he did. I had a beef with him afterwards; I wanted to know why he didn't pitch in. He said that he didn't want an all-out brawl to develop. He promised me that he'd deal with the guy privately later on.'

'He dealt with him, all right,' I said. 'He recruited him; first of all he paid him five grand to kill Hector Mackail. After he'd done that, he gave him another job, to abduct the child of the other man who, quote, borrowed, unquote, the *Princess Alison*. The police believe the child was going to be used as leverage to force her father to say what had happened to the boat. It went wrong; Zena died.'

As I was speaking, I was watching Rory like a hawk, never taking my eyes off him, studying his every reaction. At that stage I had only one uncertainty left: did he know anything, anything at all?

His expression as I broke that news gave me my answer; it was pure astonishment, adulterated only with horror, and it was sincere. Sincerity is the hardest thing in the world to fake, and Rory isn't that gifted.

'That was him?' he gasped. 'The lad I had the battle with? Francey, the fellow who was found shot?'

'That was him,' I confirmed. 'And the woman found dead and burned with him, that was Anna, the dancer you and he fought over. The bullets that killed them, Rory, came from the same gun that was found beside Hurrell's body, when DI Mann and DS Provan over there went to arrest him.'

He looked across at the two cops. 'Established,' Mann said, 'beyond any doubt. Them, and the bullet that finished off Jock Hodgson, they all came from that gun.'

He gazed at his father. 'Dad, did the police tell you all this?'

'Yes,' Eden whispered. 'They confirmed it on Saturday.'

'I've been back since Monday, and you haven't said a word to me?'

'That's because he was afraid you were behind it,' Mario McGuire's strong voice seemed to startle father and son, 'scared that Hurrell was acting on your orders. Isn't it, Mr Higgins?'

'I'm sorry, Rory,' Eden admitted. 'I knew I hadn't done it; the alternative terrified me.'

'You thought I was a killer?'

'I was afraid you might be.'

Rory whistled. 'What a fucking tragedy that would have been,' he said, bitterly. 'What an effect it would have had on the business. That's what you were really afraid of, Dad.'

'No!'

'Come on, we both know it's true. Higgins Holdings is the child you love most of all. I'm just an employee.'

'Nonsense!' Eden protested. 'That's not true.'

His son laughed. 'Dad, I'm a message boy. Every one of the general managers of the subsidiaries is paid more than I am.'

'Come on, that's part of the learning process. You know that.'

'What? Like Marcella over in Destry; a first-class honours graduate sweeping the floor and working the switchboard?'

'Hah!' his father retorted. 'Listen to the poor downtrodden boy who's just come back from a weekend in Monaco.'

'This boy's a qualified pilot,' Rory shouted back at him, 'which means you only need to employ one other person on the flight deck.' I was about to intervene, but he was in full cry, so I let the family bitterness come out. 'You know what really got to me, Dad? When Mackail, the poor fool you stitched up, knocked you down that flight of stairs in the office, it wasn't me you shouted to for help. It was Walter.'

Eden turned to me. 'Do you hear this, Bob?' he sighed. 'Help me here.'

'I wish I could,' I said. 'But you know what? I'm standing here and I'm thinking about your sister, God bless and keep her.

'I'm remembering the time she told me that you wanted her to leave the police and join Dene Furnishing. "As what?" I asked her. "Personnel director? Sales director?" No, she told me, you wanted her to be head of security, and you were going to pay her two whole grand more than she was getting in the police. She was a sergeant at the time, about to be promoted to inspector, which made your offer worthless, even in financial terms.'

It was my turn to sigh. 'Eden, you have your business empire and you have your executive toys, like this one, although it has to work for its keep as well, and I'm sure it'll be tax-deductible in some way. But you're a cold little man, with no real insight into the feelings of those closest to you. Honest to God, I'm amazed that people love you, but they do.'

'I want his name,' he snapped.

'Whose?'

'The name of the other man who stole my boat.'

'No,' I laughed. 'You're not having it. I told you, he borrowed it.'

'He stole it!'

'Look, just shut up!' I shouted, forgetting for a moment that I wasn't there to lose my temper. 'Do you know what that man is doing now? He's with his wife, in Edinburgh Royal, where she's recovering from the fractured skull that Francey gave her. When she's fit enough, their first priority will be to bury their dead child. You will forget about him.'

'He should be prosecuted,' Eden muttered.

'Not going to happen,' I told him, back in control of myself. 'The Lord Advocate will never allow it, and your friend the First Minister won't either. Leaving aside the fact that there's precious little evidence against him, other than his own confession, which isn't recorded anywhere, he's protected. Don't go after him, Eden. I'd a tough enough job stopping him from going after you.' I raised my plastic flute to my lips and sipped some flat champagne. 'Cheers, by the way.'

He scowled at me. 'So that's it? I get my boat back and nothing else. Walter's death is suicide and the whole case is closed?

'I wish it was,' I said.

'What more is there?' he protested.

'Walter Hurrell didn't kill himself.'

'What?' He looked at Mario, then Mann. 'But you said he did.'

'Oh, he fired that gun all right,' Lottie replied. 'But he was well dead when he did. When we took another look at the flat, we found another bullet, on the right side of the bed, wedged between the floor and a skirting board. Whoever shot him wiped the pistol clean, put it in his hand, fired again, and then put another bullet in the magazine. Only Hurrell's prints were on the weapon and it appeared that it had only been fired once.'

'Whoever shot him,' Eden repeated. 'It could have been anyone.'

'But it wasn't,' I said. 'My other half is a pathologist. She did Hurrell's autopsy, and she is meticulous. One of the things that she checks for as a matter of routine is sexual activity; when she did that with Hurrell she noticed something unusual. There were traces of soap in his pubic hair. She gave it a good comb through and she found something else; it wasn't all his. There were a few hairs in there that had become detached from another person . . . female, in case anyone's wondering.'

I looked around, steadying myself with a hand as the boat rocked on a sudden swell. 'A further detailed search found matching hairs to those, attached to a large blue towel in the bathroom. The hypothesis is this. Hurrell's partner washed his genitalia after he was dead, in an attempt to remove all traces of herself and then washed herself, possibly took a shower.' I paused. 'Now why would she do that?' I asked.

'Why?' Rory repeated.

'Possibly because she had to be somewhere in a hurry,' I

replied. 'What time did you take off from Edinburgh last Thursday night? '

'Nine o'clock. It was supposed to be eight, but we were held back because Mum was . . .' He stopped, abruptly. 'Hold on a minute. What are you suggesting?'

'Yes,' Eden exclaimed, 'be very careful here , Bob.'

'I'm being as careful as I can, but this is a fact. There's a CCTV camera at the end of Moray Mews. It covers the front entrance of every property there. Walter Hurrell died around seven on Thursday evening. The street camera shows nobody entering or leaving his flat at all on that day, yet somebody left there.'

'Then it must have been by the back entrance,' he declared.

'Agreed,' Sammy Pye said. 'Your house has a back door as well, doesn't it, sir, through the garden flat where Rory lives? And you have a security system, professionally installed, professionally maintained, with central video monitoring of cameras throughout the house, and also at each entrance.'

Eden nodded. 'That's correct.'

'Yesterday morning,' Pye continued, 'under the terms of a warrant granted to us in private by the Sheriff Court, we took possession of the full day's recordings for last Thursday. They show Mrs Higgins leaving through her son's flat at a quarter to six and returning by the same route at ten past seven. Ten minutes later they show her leaving by taxi. We have the cab number, and we've spoken to the driver. He confirmed that he took her to the airport. He said she seemed agitated, and told him to get a move on. Not a good idea,' he added. 'He made a point of catching every red light along the Queensferry Road.'

'Do we need to prove it by DNA comparison?' I asked. 'It'll be done easily and it'll be conclusive.'

'No,' Rachel whispered, as everyone on board stared at her with the same intensity, even Dan Provan, whose last surprise had probably come fifty-something years earlier when a midwife picked him up by the feet and slapped him on the arse.

'Silly man, he'd gone too far.'

'Did he want more money?' I asked. 'Was the jewel money not enough?'

She looked at me, right eyebrow raised. 'Did he ever want more!' she snorted.

'Rachel!' Eden shouted, rushing across to stand between us as if he could protect her. 'Shut the fuck up! Don't say any more.'

'It's too late for that,' she chuckled, 'way too late. What he wanted, Bob, was for me to leave Eden and go off with him. He knew that half of all this is mine, and he was greedy.' She patted her husband on the shoulder. 'My husband may be a boring, neglectful little man, and I may have sought other options from time to time, but I'd never leave him.'

I nodded. 'How long were you and Hurrell . . .'

'A few months. It was my initiative. He was guilty and fearful for his job after the first time, but he was in my pocket by then.'

'Was it also your initiative for him to kill Mackail?' Mario asked.

'Damn right it was,' she retorted. 'I was there when he assaulted Eden. I'd have called the police, but Eden wouldn't hear of it. Pity about that; in hindsight I can see that if I had done, he'd have been arrested and none of the rest would have happened.'

She had a point; that hadn't occurred to me.

'When we found out from Hodgson that he'd stolen the boat, well, that was it.' She looked at me again. 'Walter went too far there,' she said. 'I was appalled when I heard what he'd done, but again, it was too late.'

'So you told Hurrell to kill Mackail,' I challenged.

'I told him to scare him as badly as possible.' I didn't believe that, but I led her on. 'Again, Walter went too far.'

'And the child?'

'You were right. She was to be held until her father told us where our boat was.' She glanced at Eden, who had slumped on to a bench seat beside her. 'His name is Gates, by the way,' she told him, 'but Bob's right. He drives a missile submarine, and that, I imagine, makes him pretty much inviolable.'

'And Francey?'

'Walter did that, of course; he decided the man was a risk, and shut it off. There, I wasn't too angry when I heard. The lout assaulted my son, after all.'

'His girl didn't, though.'

Rachel shrugged.

'When did you decide that Walter was a risk himself?' I asked.

'Who says I did?' she shot back. 'You have no sight of me entering or leaving his place last Thursday, only my going and coming from Moray Place. As for my . . . my traces, as it were, I was a regular caller, so you can't pin them to that night. The extra gunshot he could have fired himself any time, and if he washed his cock regularly, so what?'

Her self-confidence restored her husband. 'You're right, Rachel,' he said as he stood. 'Silence from now on and let's fight this thing.'

I nodded. 'You do that, Eden. But please don't hire my Alex for the defence. I wouldn't want her to go down in flames this early in her career at the bar.'

'Don't you have confidence in her?' Rachel asked.

'Oh yes,' I laughed, 'make no mistake about that. If you want to brief her to enter your guilty plea, that'll be fine by me: because you are done, by two things.

'One is that ring you're wearing on your right hand, that nice emerald and diamond piece that I noticed last Monday. I've seen it since then, in a photograph attached to the list of property that Jock Hodgson reported stolen from his house, along with his laptop.

'Two, and even more damning, on the day of that burglary, and three days later when the poor bugger was tortured and killed, Walter Hurrell was in the Spire private hospital having a hernia operation. I know this because it was on the medical records made available to my dear lady when she did his post-mortem.'

I watched her confidence evaporate, like a piece of ice in the California sun. It seemed to flow out of her.

'You didn't only leave hair samples on Hurrell,' I continued. 'You left some prime specimens on the floor around the chair where you tied Hodgson up. They've been matched already. Doing that wouldn't have been a problem for you, by the way. You're a strong woman, and he wasn't the fittest bloke, plus you had a gun. Isn't all of that right, Lottie?'

'Yes indeed, sir,' Mann called out. 'We also found a butane blowlamp tossed away in the garage. There was a bar code on it that told us it was sold in B&Q Hermiston Gate, Edinburgh, just after nine on the day Hodgson died. And that in turn led us to the buyer. A classic mistake of the amateur criminal, sir.'

'I know the one you mean,' I said. 'You should never pay by card, Rachel, always cash.'

I looked at Eden and then at Rory. 'I'm sorry, guys, she did it, and more. At this moment DCC McGuire has people searching every CCTV tape from last Monday evening, trying to find Rachel's car on the way to and from the Flotterstone Inn to the meeting I believe she had Hurrell set up for her. And they'll find it. Your security tapes show her leaving Moray Place on that evening, and getting home just in time for her birthday party.

'Sammy, Lottie,' I said to the two senior detectives, 'you should make the arrest together. That way you'll both get brownie points with the chief constable.'

Sixty-Five

Eden's insurers were as good as their word, almost. They met the full cost of my investigation, but they claimed that they had only ever offered two per cent of the insured value, not the ten he had mentioned. Still, a hundred grand wasn't to be sneezed at. I thought about buying a smallish boat with the cash, but not for long. Instead I put two-thirds into a trust fund for Ignacio, Mark, James Andrew, Seonaid and Sarah's bombshell, and donated the rest to children's charities.

Mario's search team did find video of Rachel's car heading to and from the Flotterstone Inn, but there was no clear image of her at the wheel. She ran out of luck, however, in Wemyss Bay, when Jock Hodgson's nosy neighbour, who never let anything pass her by, told Dan Provan that she had seen her heading towards his house on the day of his murder.

That was enough for the Crown Office to charge her with the torture killing. She pleaded guilty and was sentenced to life with a minimum tariff of eighteen years. The murders of Mackail, Dean Francey and Anna Harmony remain unsolved, officially, the files still open should evidence turn up in the future, but it won't.

When the case was heard, the Lord Advocate, who appeared

for the Crown, went out of his way to praise Sammy Pye and Lottie Mann, Sauce Haddock and Dan Provan.

By the time Rachel appeared in the High Court, Eden had been in Monaco for three months; he won't be back. Rory is running Higgins Holdings, and has poached Marcella Mega from Destry as his executive assistant.

The First Minister did indeed offer me the chair of the Scottish Police Authority. Rather than tell him where to stick it, as I'd let Mario believe, I told him who to stick in it. He accepted that advice and appointed Sir James Proud, my predecessor as chief in Edinburgh and one of my two career mentors.

Jimmy will have a new chief constable to call to account. Sir Andrew Martin, my former best friend, was accused by a tabloid newspaper of nepotism in promoting his ex-wife so that he could be closer to his children. The source was never revealed, but if he was a wizened would-be wizard, I wouldn't be astonished.

The charge against Andy was an insult to Karen, and her solicitor won a very quick apology, but the mud stuck to him, and he felt compelled to resign. Or did he realise that he was in over his head and take the easy way out?

I don't know and I don't care, but I am very happy that he was replaced by his senior deputy, Margaret Rose Steele, who should probably have had the job in the first place. I still hate the very notion of a single Scottish police service, but at least now it's in safe hands, far safer than Andy's or mine.

I'm still waiting for Amanda Dennis to call me and hold me to that promise I was forced to make. I know she will, at some point, but I'm in no hurry. I'm perfectly happy working part-time for InterMedia, and basking in the glow of impending fatherhood, yet again. Sarah's bombshell will drop around the same time that Ignacio is released from prison. That will be interesting to say the least.

And Bob Skinner, consulting detective? What about him?

He's open to offers, on condition that they're interesting and challenging. Speaking of which, I've just had a message from my grown-up daughter, the fledgling solicitor advocate at the Scottish Criminal Bar, to say that she needs to speak to me urgently, 'about a problem that's come up'.

I wonder what that could be.

Discover the highly acclaimed Bob Skinner series by

Quintin Jardine

Find out more about Edinburgh's toughest cop at www.quintinjardine.com

Skinner's Rules	Stay of Execution
Skinner's Festival	Lethal Intent
Skinner's Trail	Dead and Buried
Skinner's Round	Death's Door
Skinner's Ordeal	Aftershock
Skinner's Mission	Fatal Last Words
Skinner's Ghosts	A Rush of Blood
Murmuring the Judges	Grievous Angel
Gallery Whispers	Funeral Note
Thursday Legends	Pray for the Dying
Autographs in the Rain	Hour of Darkness
Head Shot	Last Resort
Fallen Gods	

headline

THRILLINGLY GOOD BOOKS FROM CRIMINALLY GOOD WRITERS

CRIME FILES BRINGS YOU THE LATEST RELEASES FROM TOP CRIME AND THRILLER AUTHORS.

SIGN UP ONLINE FOR OUR MONTHLY NEWSLETTER AND BE THE FIRST TO KNOW ABOUT OUR COMPETITIONS, NEW BOOKS AND MORE.